"*VIOLATION* HAS SUCH PRIMAL POWER THAT THE STORY EVENTUALLY SWALLOWS YOU UP.
Not an easy accomplishment for most authors, but North is unlike most suspense writers."
—*Chicago Tribune*

"Mines the deepest human emotions... grabs us by the heart and doesn't let go."
—*Redbook*

"Filled with a shocking level of suspense... brilliant, thought-provoking, and poignant."
—*Midwest Book Review*

"Fresh and exciting...unflinchingly realistic."
—*Booklist*

Praise for the bestselling books of Darian North

Violation

"Once again, North creates suspense fiction out of hurt people caught in untenable situations, this time netting her best score yet." —*Kirkus Reviews*

"Intriguing . . . effective. . . . North creates a legitimately frightening villain . . . hard to stop reading." —*Sunday World Herald* (Omaha, NE)

Thief of Souls

"*Thief of Souls* is strong stuff. A genuinely frightening tale . . . gathers such momentum that it becomes hard to put down and even more difficult to get out of one's mind." —*Chicago Tribune*

"[North] tosses her protagonist into one situation after another, each more terrifying—emotionally as well as physically—than the last. . . . No reader will be able to resist rooting for him as he fights for his wife, his daughter, and ultimately his own soul." —*Minneapolis Star Tribune*

"Takes the reader into the darkest recesses of the human heart and mind . . . a work of mind-possessing suspense and psychological terror . . . thoroughly researched, its characters are totally credible and fully developed. . . . A must read." —*Tulsa World*

continued on next page . . .

"Convincing. . . . Taut suspense, good dialogue, and believable psychological insight mark this thriller." —*Library Journal*

"North is heartrendingly precise." —*Kirkus Reviews*

"Boy is this powerful stuff! I was enthralled." —*Poisoned Pen*

"Frightening . . . immerses the reader in the dangerous yet fascinating world of cults." —*Knoxville News-Sentinel*

Bone Deep

"A terrific read . . . a gripper!" —*Washington Times*

"Explosive suspense . . . impressive and believable!" —*Tulsa World*

"Rousing. . . . An unusually entertaining novel." —*St. Louis Post-Dispatch*

"Startling. . . . A taut, compelling, fast-paced thriller. . . . Sure to be a hit with fans of Patricia Cornwell." —*Library Journal*

"Relentless suspense . . . top-notch." —*Booklist*

"Appealing and convincing." —*Publishers Weekly*

"North pulls out all the stops." —*Kirkus Reviews*

"Fascinating." —*Orlando Sentinel*

Criminal Seduction

"Transcends the usual suspense thriller. This is a skillfully, beautifully written novel, a riveting tale of power, love, and death; unpredictable up to the page-turning finale." —Nelson DeMille

"Unique, unusual, complexly involving . . . a strong, intricate story . . . incredibly gripping, multidimensional, exciting." —J. F. Freedman

"A thriller that attacks the heart, the mind, the gut. Takes us to the very epicenter of many lives in violent flux—characters wonderfully delineated. This book *cooks*." —James Ellroy

"The mysteries unravel at exactly the right pace." —*Chicago Tribune*

"Complete with eccentric characters, a strong narrative, and a stunning conclusion, this novel has it all. Should make the best-seller lists." —*Tulsa World*

"The characters are well drawn and interesting, the plot is twisted and supple." —*Booklist*

"Highly entertaining . . . engrossing, inventive, and totally captivating, with riveting courtroom scenes and dialogue. . . . Compulsively readable. . . . Highly recommended." —*Library Journal*

"Compelling." —*Publishers Weekly*

VIOLATION

Darian North

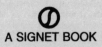

A SIGNET BOOK

SIGNET
Published by New American Library, a division of
Penguin Putnam Inc., 375 Hudson Street,
New York, New York 10014, U.S.A.
Penguin Books Ltd, 27 Wrights Lane,
London W8 5TZ, England
Penguin Books Australia Ltd, Ringwood,
Victoria, Australia
Penguin Books Canada Ltd, 10 Alcorn Avenue,
Toronto, Ontario, Canada M4V 3B2
Penguin Books (N.Z.) Ltd, 182–190 Wairau Road,
Auckland 10, New Zealand

Penguin Books Ltd, Registered Offices:
Harmondsworth, Middlesex, England

Published by Signet, an imprint of New American Library, a division
of Penguin Putnam Inc. Previously published in a Dutton edition.

First Signet Printing, October 1999
10 9 8 7 6 5 4 3 2 1

REGISTERED TRADEMARK—MARCA REGISTRADA

Printed in the United States of America

PUBLISHER'S NOTE
This is a work of fiction. Names, characters, places, and incidents either
are the product of the author's imagination or are used fictitiously,
and any resemblance to actual persons, living or dead, events, or locales
is entirely coincidental.

BOOKS ARE AVAILABLE AT QUANTITY DISCOUNTS WHEN USED TO PROMOTE
PRODUCTS OR SERVICES. FOR INFORMATION PLEASE WRITE TO PREMIUM MAR-
KETING DIVISION, PENGUIN PUTNAM INC., 375 HUDSON STREET, NEW YORK, NEW
YORK 10014.

To
my father,
Darwin Gidel,
who taught so much by example
and to
Judy Wall

We have to distrust each other. It's our only defense against betrayal.
                                    —Tennessee Williams

No passion so effectually robs the mind of all its powers of acting and reasoning as fear.
                                    —Edmund Burke

THE PAST

I

She fought him, pleading and screaming when her mouth was uncovered, scratching when she could and even biting. Terror had stripped away seventeen years of music lessons and manners, scoured away the cultured layers of female behavior, and seared away eons of human civilization, paring her down to one basic need—survival. But the pain eclipsed even that. It howled in her head, banging and clawing at her skull from the inside so that instinct failed, reducing the primitive signals in her brain to neural electrical storms.

Now and then a wisp of thought drifted in.

Is it over? Is he gone?

But the thoughts were almost without meaning because her brain could neither analyze nor record them.

Am I dying?

Consciousness slipped. Then she was aware of movement and fresh explosions of pain as she was carried outside and laid on the ground. Her cheek brushed remnants of bone and fur where feral dogs had torn apart a rabbit some weeks earlier. She smelled soil, grass and dry weeds, the faint musk of decay. Her eyes were open to the moonless sky, and the penetrating darkness made her shiver. Pinpricks of light stared down at her. The earth soaked up her blood. And her last flash of reason was a dawning of recognition, an acceptance. She was alone. Like the rabbit.

THE PRESENT

2

Spring. Finally. A day to banish the chill of a long snowy winter and rainy April, sky a crystalline blue, sun coaxing everything to life and penetrating muscle and bone so that he too was touched with renewal, transformed into someone less morose and more energetic than the thirty-seven-year-old wreck of an ex-cop that he was. He had been inspired to run sprints or do bench presses but, having access to neither track nor weights, he had settled for backyard destruction. His object was a large dead thing. His weapon was an ax. And to accompany the effort he had carried out the portable CD player loaded with his favorite recordings of Tchaikovsky's Fourth and Fifth Symphonies.

He chopped. The sun and the music fueled him. He was a powerful, blissfully mindless machine. Rhythmic, strong, and smooth. After a while his muscles began to burn and a dull ache marked the path of the bullet through his back. It was good. Very, very good. One of the best days he'd had in a long time.

But such a thought begged to be doused in cold water so he was not surprised when the doorbell sounded faintly over the music. His swing faltered and the fine mood was broken. The bell rang again. Ignoring it, he tried to recapture his chopping rhythm. There were no drop-in acquaintances in this life he'd made and he was not in the market for magazines, cookies, or religion. Packages could be left on the porch; Eureka was still a place where things could be left on porches. So let them ring, whoever they were, and then let them go away.

Some minutes passed and he thought he had escaped.

"Jack! Are you back there?"

Something between a groan and a growl rumbled in his throat. Just what he needed. A surprise visit from the remora.

The boy appeared at the corner of the house, apparently having wrestled his way through the collapsing side gate. Newly thirteen, he was awkward and uncertain, bearing a defensive mantle. Everything about him—ragged clothes, lank sandy hair, slouched shoulders—was designed to convey an attitude of disregard. He was a poster boy for I DON'T GIVE A SHIT, yet his eyes said just the opposite. And those damn eyes always got to Jack.

Scanning the yard, the boy came up with a toneless "Wow." It was not complimentary.

Annoyed, both by the disturbance and by the fact that the kid had obviously decided he could waltz

4

in uninvited, Jack lowered the ax blade, turned down the music, and put on a serious scowl. "You aren't cutting school, are you?"

"Early dismissal today," the boy answered, toeing the earth with his worn athletic shoe.

"Don't they have a bus on early dismissal days?"

The boy shrugged. "I didn't get on it."

Damn, the kid was irritating. Jack mopped his forehead with his shirtsleeve, catching a whiff of the scotch that had put him to sleep the night before. What did the boy want from him, anyway? Did he think he could blow off the bus and then con a ride?

"How are you getting home?"

Again the shrug, this time indicating that getting home was not a concern. The kid had a million shrugs with subtle meanings, but all were rooted in indifference. A giant all-encompassing indifference. He was the king of indifference. Well, two could play that game. Jack hefted the ax and attacked the gnarled base of the monster again.

After a long wordless stretch the boy finally said, "That was a really old rhododendron."

A rhododendron. It was just like David to know that. The boy was a walking encyclopedia on the natural and scientific, though he seldom chose to reveal that side of himself.

"Did you kill it?" the boy asked.

"No. Why would I kill it?"

Another infuriating shrug.

Jack chopped. He continued to hack at the dead

monster until his arm muscles cried for relief and each swing was forced out of sheer willpower. As long as the boy was there watching he could not allow himself to quit.

"When you were a policeman, did you learn a lot about lying?" the boy asked suddenly.

Jack let his swing fall flat and the ax head thunked into the ground. He was so relieved at the excuse to stop that he was not irritated by the question, but he frowned anyway, just for the sake of appearance.

The boy hunched into himself and looked down so that his hair fell forward and obscured half his face. "I mean, did you have to know why people lied and what the lies meant?"

What the hell was this about?

"That was part of the job," Jack answered carefully. "Sure. Recognizing lies . . . deciphering lies . . . outsmarting liars. A detective needs a Ph.D. in BS." And, he added to himself, a detective needs to be the best liar of all.

The boy nodded as though this confirmed what he had already believed, and Jack saw that he was struggling. There was something big on David's mind, some major problem just beneath those shrugs, and he was dangerously close to dumping the problem right there in Jack's backyard. Great. He'd had to put up with the kid tagging after him when he was doing the landlord-handyman routine and he had even put up with having the kid "help" on weekend projects but he was not going to let a drop-in-anytime habit develop and he sure as hell wasn't about to start playing child psychologist.

He squinted up at the sky as though he could read the time there. "I need to get this finished," he said. "Don't you have homework or something?"

He might as well have said, *What's the trouble, son?* the way the boy looked up at him, brow furrowed in determination and facial muscles fighting against a display of emotion.

"Why would someone lie about everything in their past—where they're from and where they went to school and even who they were married to and everything?"

Jack sighed and considered the question, apprehensive about where it was leading. "The person could be hiding. Or they could be ashamed. Or they could be evil scum." He mopped his forehead again. "A lot depends on who's doing the lying."

In a voice so low that it barely carried, the boy said, "It's my mother."

Christ. Didn't they have school counselors for this kind of thing? Jack leaned the ax against the pile of amputated limbs.

"What makes you think she's been lying?"

Another shrug.

Jack's own mother had been far too sensual and flamboyant for him when he was young. During adolescence he had become fervently convinced that he was adopted and had spent nearly a year trying to persuade his brother and the twins to join in his suspicions. And this kid certainly had reasons for maternally inspired denial because Thea Auben was a genuine pain in the neck and even loonier than most women.

"You know, David, detectives working a case can get a feeling—a gut instinct—and it can really grab hold of them, but that doesn't necessarily mean it's right. Sometimes it can be dead wrong."

"This isn't like that," the boy insisted. "I mean I have had"—shrug—"feelings and questions. Stuff I wondered about and couldn't understand. But this is all true stuff."

"Factual, you mean? Based on concrete evidence?"

A nod.

Jack frowned, clicked off the music, and started toward the house. Halfway across the yard he glanced back. "You coming?"

They went through the back door into the mudroom. While Jack washed, the boy studied the rack of fishing equipment along the far wall.

"Interested in fishing?" Jack asked, glancing over his shoulder as he toweled off his arms.

The boy's answering shrug sent Jack's irritation level to a peak. "You like fishing or not?" he snapped.

"Never tried it," the boy admitted grudgingly.

Jesus. No wonder the kid was a mess. Here he was living in the heart of redwood country right on Humboldt Bay with cold clear-running streams on one side and an ocean on the other, and he'd never been fishing. What a crime. Jack was taken back in time to his own childhood, learning to fish under the watchful eye of his father. When had his father presented him with his first scaled-down rod and reel? Before or after the pony? He couldn't recall. This boy had never had such opportunities. His father had died before he was born, and there were no uncles or grandfathers taking up the slack.

"I suppose you haven't had lunch."

"I'm not hungry."

"Me either, but it's past lunchtime and we're going to eat."

He moved through the kitchen and the boy's eyes followed him. That was where the hunger was—not in the belly but in the eyes. If he could only avoid those eyes.

"You planning to give me a hand here, or just watch?"

"What do you want me to do?"

"Get glasses. Find something you want to drink. Pour me tea out of that pitcher in the refrigerator. And be careful. Don't move any cards."

The boy stared down at the lines of cards and the pages of tallied scores on the kitchen table.

"That's solitaire, isn't it? My mom plays solitaire on the computer."

"Solitaire on the computer?" Jack shook his head at the thought, thinking about the feel of the cards, the slickness beneath his fingertips, the snap of a new deck. None of those satisfactions would exist on a computer. "What does it do," he asked, "show each hand like a picture?"

"Yeah. It's just up there. You click and it's instant."

"But you miss laying out the hand, creating the pattern, seeing the numbers and the connections as they fall. . . ."

The kid looked at him as though he'd suddenly started talking about receiving alien radio waves through his teeth.

"Here." He handed the boy a paper plate barely supporting a hot microwaved burrito.

They ate standing at the kitchen counter. Jack hoped there would be no further discussion of lies or mothers, and there wasn't. The boy focused on his food in complete silence, eyes downcast and shoulders hunched. Which was fine because Jack had had enough adolescent angst or whatever it was. He consumed his burrito without tasting it, then watched as the boy took one slow resigned bite after another.

"All right. What evidence do you have?"

The boy exhaled as though he'd been holding his breath. "There's no record of my mother being born where she says she was. There's no record of her going to school where she says she did. She doesn't exist in any databases. And there are no birth or death records for my father, either. Or a record of their marriage."

Jack was momentarily taken aback. "How did you come up with all this?"

Another shrug. "Research. I got a book called *The Computer Detective*. It's pretty easy."

"Does your mother know what you've been doing?"

"No."

"You've come up with all negatives. You have an absence of evidence rather than evidence."

"So?"

"You have no proof of anything. All you know is that you can't find the data. That usually indicates a problem with the investigative techniques. And from what I understand about computers, one tiny glitch, even a misspelling, can throw everything off."

"Yeah," the boy agreed reluctantly.

"You could ask your mother why you can't find the information."

"No!"

Jack studied the kid's face, wondering whether the note of panic was the result of secrets kept or pride threatened. "What got you started on this anyway?"

"I . . ." Red crept into the boy's cheeks and he immediately lowered his eyes. "I was talking to a friend and he got me thinking." He shrugged. "I was already bothered by stuff. I mean my mom never wants to answer my questions and she's always changing the subject or trying to distract me. And when I think back to stories my grandma told me— they don't make sense."

"Like what?"

"Just stuff she said when she was in the hospital."

"Your grandmother could have been mixed up. Sick people get confused."

"Yeah, but there were lots of other things . . . little things. And why don't we have more pictures from before I was born? Why don't we have pictures of my dad. We have one old beat-up picture of him in this group of guys where you can barely see his face."

"Again, that's an absence of evidence. It doesn't prove anything."

"Maybe. But it's weird."

"Not necessarily. Things get lost during moves or destroyed in fires and floods. Then again, some people are savers and some aren't. You won't find much memorabilia in my house, but that doesn't mean I'm lying about my past."

"You don't lie, you just won't talk about it."

Jack threw his plate in the trash, ignoring the remark. "I think you're jumping to conclusions." He held up a hand, ticking off points on his fingers as he went through them. "You could have a problem in your computer search methods. Your grandmother could have been confused and disoriented when she was sick. Keepsakes could have been lost or destroyed. And . . . if you look at it from your mother's point of view . . . could be she's trying to avoid the past because she doesn't like to be reminded of your father's death."

The boy responded with a one-shouldered skeptical shrug.

"Let's face it," Jack said, attempting to lighten the conversation. "All adults are a little weird."

"My mother's majorly weird."

Jack got out the pitcher of cold tea for a refill, thinking of Thea. From what he knew of the woman he wouldn't have declared her weird, but she was definitely unique. Somehow she managed to be both a control freak and a free spirit, a woman with alphabetized books and perfectly arranged canned goods who had turned her back on conventional society and made her own rules. Thea Auben was a puzzle. And he had to admit that he had sensed something beneath all that organized efficiency and shy reserve, something elusive, something that had pricked at his cop's intuition as well as his male instincts. Could there be a dark secret surrounding David's paternity? Could the boy be prying open a real can of worms?

It occurred to him that he should probably give Thea some warning as to her son's state of mind, but he couldn't imagine having such a conversation with her. She had always been distant and aloof, definitely beating him in the eccentric recluse game. He knew her only through the comments her son made and from observing the way she lived in his house. In truth he barely knew her at all. It almost seemed he'd had a clearer understanding of her on the day they met.

"Hi. I'm Thea Auben and this is my son David. The real estate agent said yours was the only available rental in the area that might be close to what we're looking for."

"What are you looking for?" he'd asked, silently curs-ing the real estate woman because the last thing he wanted was to rent to a helpless, needy single mother. He could just imagine her calling him out to change lightbulbs and empty mousetraps, or engaging him in long late night discussions because she had no one else to talk to.

"We want a good solid house that's away from town but not so isolated that it's a problem for David to get to school," the woman said. "We want to be as close as possible to the forest."

"Are you sure you want to be out so far? There are places for rent in town. Close to everything. Your son could walk to school."

"No," she said emphatically. "We want to be out."

"Are you new to Eureka?"

"Yes. From Sacramento. But we've always wanted to live near the redwoods, haven't we, David."

The boy nodded. His eyes were as measuring and cau-tious as a veteran homicide detective's.

"I'm fairly new here myself," Jack admitted. "My uncle and aunt were longtime residents. The house I'm renting out was theirs." As he spoke he studied her with a cop's eye.

White female. Average height and build, with the kind of face that gave witnesses trouble because there was nothing irregular about it, no one feature that demanded notice. Hazel eyes. Brownish chin-length hair that was clean and shiny but otherwise left to go its own way. Clear skin with a slightly tanned appearance; maybe her natural complexion? Basic jeans and T-shirt. No major cosmetics use. Probably late twenties to early thirties, though there was a quality she had—a shy reticence, a wary self-consciousness, a nonspecific anger—that made her seem younger. All told she was nice-looking, but in a quiet way. Not the sort of woman he'd always been attracted to. Definitely not the sort of woman that frequented the cop bars or the flashy hangouts he had favored in L.A. Yet, there was something compelling about her, something that stirred his protective impulses.

"We just lost my mother," she said, clearing her throat against a still raw grief. "And we've come here to make a new start."

"To stay," the boy said with a determination that spoke of previous disappointments.

A young woman on her own with a kid. Jesus. He hadn't wanted to be a landlord at all, had fallen into it because he didn't want to live in the house himself and property sales were way down. But when he decided to follow the real estate agent's advice and take on renters for a while he had imagined a solid family moving in, with lots of household experience and a dad who was capable of repairs and maintenance.

"I don't know how much the realtor told you, but the house is on the Avenue of the Giants and it actually sits behind a shop . . . one of those places that was built to sell souvenirs to tourists."

She bit the corner of her lip and cast a doubtful frown at her son.

"I've got the shop leased to two women who've started

a sort of artists' cooperative, trying to sell area art along with the souvenir junk, and I've got to warn you, the shop will be noisy and crowded during the summer. Avenue of the Giants has actual traffic jams during high tourist season."

"But the house is behind the shop, right?" the boy asked. "People wouldn't be coming to the house first or anything. . . . I mean, the real estate lady said that from the road you wouldn't even know there was a house back there."

"Right," Jack admitted. "But that means there are no neighbors to watch out for you. There's nobody close by to lend a hand. And in the winter when the shop is closed you're pretty isolated back there."

He waited while the mother and son exchanged nervous glances.

"The school bus can always get through on the highway though, right?" the boy asked.

"Probably," Jack said. Why should it be his problem that these two needed a place to live? Let someone else take on the responsibility. "I should also warn you that the two women who run the shop are . . . well, they've got an alternative lifestyle. And their friends—all the artists who'll be bringing art and hanging around the shop— they're a doped-up freaked-out bunch. It could get a little wild. I don't know if that bothers you."

"Why would that bother us?" she asked as though angry at the idea of anyone being bothered by it.

Damn. Wasn't there anything he could say to scare her off? "You'll have to have plenty of that attitude if you're *going to stay out there by yourself. Humboldt County is a real magnet for alternatives—witches, ganja growers, mountain-man wanna-bes who live out in the trees without electricity or plumbing, ecology radicals who would kill a person to save a tree and timber executives who want to kill the ecologists and clear-cut the world."*

"And ex-policemen," the boy put in, eyeing Jack for a reaction.

Jack vowed to throttle the motormouthed real estate agent next time he saw her.

"My point was that you'd probably feel a lot safer being in town," Jack said, ignoring the boy's comment.

"But I thought this was a safe place." Her sudden alarm told him that at last he'd struck a chord.

"Oh, let me tell you . . ." Jack said, winding up to exaggerate the crime rate and the incidence of serial killers drifting through, to give a few lurid accounts of territorial bloodshed among the marijuana growers, and to elaborate on the danger to innocent hikers who lost the trail and strayed into forbidden fields, but he made the mistake of meeting the boy's eyes for a moment and his entire windup evaporated. "It is pretty safe for the average person," he conceded. "I guess the wackos balance each other out."

The woman and boy exchanged a wordless communication, then she asked, "Can we see the house now?"

"It's a twenty-to-thirty-minute drive from here. Are you sure you're interested?"

"There was nothing else," she said wearily.

He hesitated. "Okay. You can either leave your car here and ride in mine or follow me."

"We'll follow," she said quickly.

He started toward his car, then turned back. *"Winter is different here than in Sacramento."*

"We know. We researched it."

"We research everything," the boy added.

Jack sighed. He glanced at their car. It was in rough shape and he suspected that everything they owned was packed into the trailer.

"Did the realtor tell you the rent?"

"Yes. It's in our price range."

They looked so tired and vulnerable, yet they weren't pitiful at all. The woman had dignity. He'd always been a sucker for dignity.

"Well . . . the rent's negotiable," he told her, though lowering it would erase his slim profit margin.

"If we like it we won't argue with you about the price," she said. *"I'm sure it's fair."*

"The realtor has it listed a little higher than what I was asking."

That had been the previous June. A little less than a year ago. After they moved in he'd kicked himself for the momentary bout of insanity that caused him to rent to a single mother and lower the rent as well, but she had turned out to be the perfect tenant. She asked for almost nothing and had even tried to discourage him from the maintenance and repairs he'd felt compelled to do, preferring to live with problems rather than have him intrude on her privacy. The woman had proven herself to be stubbornly and relentlessly self-sufficient. Self-contained. The phrase popped into his mind with amusing irony. It referred to the expensive camper units that some tourists vacationed in. Self-contained units. Meaning they had their own batteries and generators and water supplies and whatever. That was Thea. She needed no outside help, no outside energy, for her closed little world to function. And he had to admit a certain admiration for her. She had achieved what he aspired to.

In fact, when he considered his own situation—with property owned so that he was guaranteed freedom of habitat; with money coming in through disability, pension, and trust payments so that he never had to work or expose himself to a workplace community; and with no dependents or pets at all—he should have had the recluse's advantage. Yet he had blown it. After only a few months of living alone in his uncle's isolated house, he'd rushed to the realty office and bought a home on the edge of Eureka with neighbors in sight. And what had he been doing with his no-colleagues, no-forced-fellowship, no-dependents time? Mornings he usually went to the doughnut shop and afternoons to the coffee shop, sitting alone, but still within a circle of humanity, acknowledging people who nodded to him, occasionally allowing himself to be drawn into conversation. Nights were even worse. He parked in front of the television or found his way to one of the area's dank bars to sit silently amongst other pathetic male patrons in the smoky darkness and hit on women he'd never look twice at under a forty-watt bulb. Some recluse he was.

Thea on the other hand had managed to erect an invisible barrier around herself even though she worked, had to rent her home, and was responsible for a child. She ran some kind of computerized service out of her living room, bypassing the whole workplace scene, and according to David, she conducted the business so that there was never any face-to-face contact with her clients. And she sure wasn't a regular at any of the local hangouts. From what he had seen and heard she spoke only when spoken to by shopkeepers, bank tellers, and other unavoidable members of the community, causing some people to think her shy and others to label her as antisocial.

According to David she hadn't made one friend in the area and he was not aware of her having friends in their last town either. Whenever she drove to Eureka, whether it was for groceries or to see a movie, she arranged it to include her son. Her entire life seemed to revolve around the boy. But this was where her carefully fortified, perfect little existence faltered. Though she was a concerned and involved parent, there was something wrong. Something off. She was so centered on her son that she couldn't allow the kid room to breathe or grow. She couldn't see that David was all mixed up and speeding toward an emotional train wreck.

"I don't think your mother would intentionally lie to you about the past," he said, lying to the boy.

The kid appeared to struggle with his thoughts a moment. "What if my father didn't die? What if he's alive and she's been hiding me from him? I see stuff like that in the news sometimes where parents hide kids from each other."

"That's pretty hard to believe."

"Okay then, you try," the boy challenged. "Just try to get her to tell you things about the past and about my father. Make her tell you his exact name and where he was born and died. And then call up some of your cop friends and ask them to check."

"Hey, I'm not in on this! I'm not suspicious of your mother and I'm not grilling her. Neither should you. Instead of acting like an adolescent jerk and coming up with all this bullshit you should be helping her, making life easier for her, showing some gratitude for all she's done to take care of you."

The boy reacted as though he'd been slapped and his eyes brimmed dangerously with moisture.

"You just want me to go away and leave you out of it! You don't care what's wrong or what's true as long as it doesn't bother you! You don't care what happens to anybody!"

With that the boy spun and slammed out the door. Jack stood for a moment, staring down at the careful rows of his ongoing solitaire game. Fine. Now he was rid of the kid and he could get back to work. He dumped the half-eaten burrito in the trash and headed back out to the yard. Back to digging out the monster rhododendron. He picked up his ax, stared at the mangled base of the plant, sighed, threw the ax down, and went into the house for his car keys.

"Damn, damn, damn," he muttered as he started his battered green Bronco.

The kid was a fast walker. He had made it almost to the highway by the time Jack pulled up alongside him and leaned his head out the window to say, "Come on . . . get in."

The boy continued walking as though Jack were not there.

"Come on. I need to go out to the place anyway. I have something to talk to your mother about."

With a wounded yet measuring look the boy turned and glared. Curiosity won out over pride, though. "What are you going to talk to her about?"

"House business."

"Promise you won't tell her . . . you know . . . all the stuff about my father. I mean, you could try to find out things from her but just leave me out of it."

Grudgingly Jack agreed. "But it's only for now," he added. "It's not blanket immunity."

With a sheepish grin the boy opened the passenger door and climbed in.

3

Althea Auben was busy at her computer, finishing a major work project. The final polishing took up the morning and then after lunch she was absorbed by the mechanics of transmitting the report that had consumed three weeks of her time. When she was through she suddenly realized that her son was not home yet and that he should have been because it was an early dismissal day.

"David?" she called, walking through the house, thinking that he might still be angry at her and if so could have come in quietly and avoided saying hello.

He was not there, though. His book bag was not there. The kitchen door had not been opened and left unlocked as it always was when he came home.

She checked outside, even walking around to the front of the shop, though it was closed on weekdays until the start of tourist season. No David. She hurried back into the house to use the phone. Calls to the school office and to his friends revealed that the bus had made the usual run but no one knew whether David had ridden it. No one knew where he was. This had never happened before.

Thea Auben had fought many demons in her efforts to be a good mother to her son. Humboldt County was for her a last stand or a new start, depending on perspective, and she had built a safe and happy life there, a life that ran with the precision of a finely balanced metronome. Everything had a place and a schedule. Each day was exactly as it should be. She had control, both external and internal, and all was right with her world. Except that her son was not home on time. To any other mother of an adolescent this might have caused only minor annoyance, but to Thea it was a severe and threatening jolt.

She paced back and forth in the front yard, rubbing her palms against the faded denim of her jeans, plucking at the hem of her oversized cotton sweater. Periodically she raised her arm to check the watch face of the sterling-silver dragonfly cuff that circled her wrist. The art deco watch had been her birthday gift to herself and was still new enough that she usually felt a conscious pleasure from reading the time. She had bought the watch to celebrate her success, to reward herself not only for surviving to thirty but for discovering the tough angry resilience that had lifted her out of pathos. Now the watch seemed a warning. Had she grown too complacent? Too happy? Had she flown too high? Was she about to be punished?

A faint breeze played in the crowns of the redwoods that towered behind the house, and the air was so pure and spring-warmed that it was a joy simply to breathe. Humboldt was everything she had hoped it would be. And then there was the house itself, her beloved house, made entirely of heartwood in the style of a fairy-tale cottage, as solid and comforting as a bedtime story. A perfect place and a perfect house.

Too perfect. She should have realized that it was all too perfect.

Twisting strands of her hair around her finger tightly, she made more circuits in the grass. "Where are you, David?" she whispered under her breath. "Please, please come home."

But then maybe it wasn't time for punishment yet. Maybe this was just a warning. Or a test. Her first test as the parent of a teenager? David had turned that dreaded corner two months before and she had known as she watched him blow out the thirteenth candle that he was already changing. Taking on a fragile but immutable form. Her malleable child had begun to harden, like clay exposed to air. And with these changes her sunny, sweet-natured son had been infected by a general and all-encompassing anger. It was always there, like the background pulse of a percussionist playing pianissimo, a subtle underscoring of every mood and expression.

The longer she considered this, the more probable it became. She was being tested. He was retaliating for their scene the previous night. *I'm not ready*, she thought. *I do not know how to handle a teenager.*

She'd found an English paper with a big red D slashed across the top and she had asked for an explanation. Math and science had always come easily to him but English and history were a struggle that she had always had to nudge him along in. Expecting the customary contrition or excuses, she had been taken aback by his sullen and vaguely sarcastic response, and she had snapped at him, waving the composition for emphasis.

"This is laziness, David!"

"Stop nagging at me! You're always nagging at me!"

"You don't want nagging? How about action then? How about I block your on-line access if you don't try harder in English! Would you like that better than nagging?"

"All you do is yell at me and try to make me miserable!" he had shouted, his face twisted with the agony of holding in tears.

"David . . ."

Then he was gone, stomping down the hall to shut himself in his room and leaving her at a loss because she knew she should demand that he come back out and she knew she should lecture him about how rude and unacceptable it was for him to stomp away when she was not finished speaking, but somehow he had left her feeling guilty. Feeling that she should apologize to him and bake him brownies. How did children do that so well? Instilling guilt seemed to be an inborn skill, and now she wondered if his not coming home on the bus was the emergence of something even worse. The "I'll show her" instinct. Guilt wasn't enough anymore. He was going to punish her, too.

Damn. If she could just rise out of herself like those people did during near-death experiences, if she could just look down from some lofty distance, this would all be very funny. So many clichés and so much absurdity.

Look at that grown woman getting her strings pulled by a thirteen-year-old. Look at that neurotic caricature of an overprotective mother, falling apart the first time her adolescent son is late. Look at all the pacing and hair twisting. Next thing she'll be wringing her hands like Lady Macbeth.

She crossed her arms, holding them tightly to her chest to prevent any more twisting or wringing, and sat down on the edge of the garden bench. She was still. She had complete control. She was not falling apart. Besides, pacing was a perfectly normal activity. She had always paced so it wasn't a symptom of anything. It was just a personality trait. As if to offer proof, her memory served up a vision of her pacing before the Juilliard audition, making elliptical circuits of the room.

"Sit," her mother had ordered. "You're wearing yourself out!"

"Please, stop nagging me! You're always nagging me!"

Oh, God . . . had she said that?

She jumped from the bench and resumed pacing.

"Where are you, David?" she demanded, rocked by a sudden blast of fury.

How dare he pull this stunt! If he thought he could get away with this kind of thing he was in for a big surprise. But then the chill wind of panic rose to whip away the anger. Should she call the hospital? The police? Should she call the principal of the school at his home? Should she get in her car and drive into town to search?

Alone? You're going to drive to town alone?

Just calm down, she cautioned herself silently. David might call. She had to stay home in case he called for help.

Right. That was a good excuse not to drive off alone.

She went back into her house and stood in the kitchen. The afternoon sun was beaming through the window grilles, filling the room with stripes of light and shadow. She stared at the telephone, willing it to ring. When it did not she picked it up and dialed the police station.

"Officer Count," a man answered, and she explained that her thirteen-year-old son was late coming home from school. Officer Count asked her a few questions, told her not to apologize for bothering him, told her he had kids and he knew how they caused worry. "But," he stressed, "this isn't a little guy, and he's not all that late."

"I shouldn't have called," she said, feeling foolish.

"No. That's what we're here for." He chuckled. "I gotta tell you though . . . the weather being as nice as it is . . . I'd be more worried about him if he went straight home and turned on the television. Kids are *supposed* to be out on days like today."

"But he's never done this before." She hated admitting that she had lost control of her son and she hated the way the policeman was verbally patting her on the head and she hated the helplessness that was creeping into her voice.

"Hey, this is his first beautiful spring day as a thirteen-year-old. Know what I mean?"

"Yes. All right."

"Call me back anytime you want, but I'm betting he'll come home soon. And remember, Eureka may have its share of property crimes, but statistically speaking it's a safe place."

She slammed the receiver down. *How dare he speak of statistics!* Statistics didn't mean anything to those victims who fell into the wrong end of the percentages, however small they were. *The guy is a cop and he's rattling about statistics?* He should know that bad things happened and that they happened despite statistics and illusions of safety. That essential truth was the ruling center of her adult life.

Then again, Officer Count was probably right.

She walked down the windowless hallway and

into another pattern of light and shadow from the afternoon sun pouring through the ornate iron grilles over the living room windows. Absently she crossed to the shelves holding her rows of small terrariums. At first glance they appeared to hold only dead twigs and branches but inside were pulsating cocoons, creatures suspended between crawling and flying. She did an automatic scan for signs of emergence, then turned to her computer, where cartoon butterflies fluttered stiffly across the screen courtesy of a screen saver sent by an on-line friend. Three butterflies. Two butterflies. Five. And then the pattern repeated. Three, two, five. Like the notes in a musical phrase.

This was her place of work—the home of Independent Research Incorporated, her freelance business. Using on-line information services, electronic libraries, book dealers, and the web, she transformed herself into a skilled hunter tracking down facts and figures, a clever gatherer assembling information and references. She communicated with her clients only by e-mail, telephone, or letter, never face-to-face, and so she was able to present herself as competent, confident, and capable. They never saw the real Thea. In this room, behind her screen of electronic wizardry, she was just like the man pulling the levers behind Oz, conjuring a strong and dazzling facade, a false shell of poise and wisdom. Here, in this room, fingers flying over the keys, she was a different person—the person she should have been or perhaps would have been. The real person. And the magic extended beyond work to on-line friends. Through the computer she had a life beyond motherhood.

The back door opened. Heart thudding, she rushed to the kitchen and there he was—her child, her vulnerable little boy in the overgrown scarecrow disguise.

"Where have you been!" She had a fierce urge to both shake him and hug him, but did neither.

"I had to talk to Jack," he said, shrugging as though the circumstances were beyond his control. "Sorry. I was gonna call but . . ."

"Jack? You scared me to death so you could talk to Jack? How dare that man think that he can—"

"Mom! It wasn't his fault. It was my idea. And I said I was sorry. . . . Okay?"

His eyes met hers, belligerent and unapologetic, completely unresponsive to either her anger or her anguish. He was casting aside her authority like outgrown clothes and, looking into his eyes, she could already see him leaving. She could see him grown and gone. See herself alone. And for the briefest of instants she saw something else . . . someone else— the shadow of a stranger. She sank into one of the kitchen chairs, hugging herself against a chill that had nothing to do with the air temperature.

Struggling to regain composure, she assured herself that this was simply a phase. She remembered her mother saying, "*Just wait till you're the parent of a teenager. That will be your punishment for everything you ever did to me.''* That had to be a universal truth, uttered in every language across the generations.

She attempted a rueful smile and said, "So I guess this is the start of the terrible teens, huh?" though she knew that their troubles went much deeper than that.

"I guess," he agreed, almost relaxing into a grin. Then his expression changed and he was the adversary again. "Jack's here—outside looking at a faucet." He hesitated. "I thought maybe we could invite him to dinner since he brought me home and everything."

"No dinner company. House rule. Always been that way. Always will be."

"Why?"

"Because . . . I'm the mother and I say so."

"It's a stupid rule! Kids in my school are always eating at each other's houses. Other people have company for dinner all the time. And Jack won't care what he eats."

Other kids are always eating at each other's houses. . . . Suddenly she recalled dinners at her best friend Rosalie's house, sitting at the table without saying a word. Rosalie's mother jumped up and down to fill glasses, and her father criticized the food and teased about Thea not having a tongue, and her brother kicked them under the table as he noisily shoveled food into his mouth. Those dinner occasions were the only times she shared a meal with a full-fledged family. Was that what David wanted? Enough people at the table to equal a family?

"So it's the 'other people' defense," she said, trying for humor.

"You say that like it's a joke but it's not a joke because we live like freaks!" He turned away from her as though he might run from the room, but then he turned back with an expression that was earnest and pleading. "You said it would be different after we moved here, Mom."

"And it is, isn't it? I've given you more freedom."

"Freedom . . . yeah, right. You stopped holding my hand when I cross streets."

"I'm responsible for your safety, David. That's part of my job as your mother."

His jaw muscles showed a tight ridge as he glared at the floor.

"I've been taking you places, haven't I? Movies . . . the park . . . old town in Eureka. We've been having fun together, right?"

"As long as we go to places that you pick and as long as we're home by dark," he said accusingly. "And you still won't go out by yourself."

"I've been to school functions."

"Not the big ones in the auditorium, and not at night."

"I'm working toward doing more."

"Not fast enough! Nothing is changing fast enough! You've got to go to a doctor or something, Mom. My teacher told us about people with agoraphobia and they sound sort of like you. Maybe you've got a sickness that could be cured, you know?"

In a fraction of a second she went through hurt, anger, sympathy, and then into caution, because she sensed that pushing him too hard now, issuing ultimatums that she could not enforce, would do further damage to her fraying authority.

"I have no fear of the marketplace, David. In fact, I think big grocery stores are pretty pleasant. So stop overdramatizing the situation. I'm shy. People make me nervous. Strangers give me the jitters. And I am very cautious. . . . You've seen the crime stories in the news."

"Oh man! This is *Eureka*, Mom."

"Bad things can happen anywhere. You think only nice law-abiding citizens are traveling through here on the highways? You think postal workers and electricians and high school students in perfectly quiet little towns don't snap sometimes and pull out their automatic rifles? You think that ordinary people . . . seemingly normal people . . . don't have evil in them?"

"Talk about overdramatizing! Listen to you. Next thing you'll be talking about the devil." He took a deep breath and blew it out through clenched teeth. "Jeez . . . I want to have friends over and you blow it up into this big deal. . . ."

"Maybe I have been too strict about the no-company rule, but remember—I work at home. This house is my office and offices don't generally have company trooping through them."

He did a half eye roll. "That's just an excuse. We live like . . . like this is a fort and we're in enemy territory."

"All right. We can invite one of your friends to dinner over the weekend. Tommy or Reg . . . More than dinner if you want. A sleepover. I'll take you to the video store for some tapes, and we'll buy junk food. It'll be like a party."

He exhaled heavily, shaking his head, "That's not what I'm talking about, Mom. I don't want some stupid party. I just want people to be able to come here. I want . . ." He looked around as though searching for words. "I want us to be normal."

Translation: He wanted *her* to be normal. Well, she couldn't really fault him for that. Although kids might want to be wild or crazy or offbeat themselves, they wanted parents who were dull and predictable and made from the same mold as everyone else's parents. But at least the argument was more familiar territory.

"Gee, is there a manual for normalcy?"

"Not funny, Mom."

This was all happening so quickly. Her own son was threatening her safe well-ordered existence. The one person she would have done anything for was asking for something she couldn't do. Or could she? She drummed her fingers lightly on the table and stared out the window. How much farther could she go? She turned to meet David's eyes. They were a clear fair-weather blue, even when his face was stormy.

"I will try to be more relaxed about company in the house," she said, "if you'll try to have a better attitude."

He peered at her as though scrutinizing her intentions.

"What about Jack?"

"Being more relaxed does not include having Jack to dinner."

"Why?" There was no childish whininess in the question. He had the steely calm of a determined adult, a steely calm that was both infuriating and impressive. It would be an admirable adult trait. Someday.

"It's . . ." She was undone by his calm and by having to justify herself to him, and she was stricken by guilt because she had not fully realized how much he was suffering from the solitary life she led.

"Well . . . you know . . ." She was close to pleading now, but she tried to hold her ground. "A dinner invitation implies that . . . that we want to be more friendly with Jack than we are."

"Oh? I've got news for you—I do want that! And you would too if you'd just get to know him better."

"He's our landlord, David, not a friend or relative."

"I wish he was my uncle or something. I wish he was my father! But it wouldn't matter who he was, would it? You hate everybody. You wish everybody in the world was dead."

"David!" She stood to face him.

"It's true! And if Jack can't stay to dinner then I don't want to eat here either."

She blinked, stunned, while her son stared back at her in obstinate silence. Then she sank back into the chair, feeling desolate and unnerved.

"The man probably doesn't even want to eat here," she said bleakly.

Her son studied her face for a moment, questioning whether the statement had been a capitulation. Then his entire face lit and he moved behind her chair to rest his hands on her shoulders, offering comfort as though their roles had completely reversed. "I'll convince him. And it will be okay. You'll see. This will be good practice for you."

Tears welled in her eyes and she quickly brushed them away. Her son. Oh God. Her little boy. He was everything. Without him she would have been sucked into the black hole. As long as she still had him anything was possible. But why was David so interested in Jack? What did he need from Jack that she wasn't giving him?

You're jealous of Jack.

Yes. All right. She was jealous of David's adoration of Jack. And she was threatened by it. But was her son captivated by Jack in particular or was the man just a familiar and convenient object for some special male bonding need that David had developed? And how much of it was related to David's growing interest in a father figure? She'd never had a father around herself and she knew that many children grew up in fatherless homes. It wasn't that uncommon. So maybe it was the unknown that obsessed David—the fact that his father was a ghost floating behind layers and layers of obfuscation. In that case she ought to be thankful for Jack and see David's worship of the man as a blessing. Maybe a relationship with Jack would divert David from further paternal questions.

"I guess I'll survive," she said.

He gave her shoulders a quick squeeze. "Wow. Okay. Let's see . . . We don't have any beer. He likes beer, but he also likes tea."

"I suppose tea is in my repertoire," she said, rising and reaching for the teakettle beside the stove.

"But that would be hot and I've only seen him drink cold tea."

"So, we'll put ice in it."

When the knock came, they stopped and looked at each other.

"Come in!" David called.

Jack Verrity stepped through the door looking as rumpled and worn as always. On first glance he could have been mistaken for a homeless person, but it was all surface. Beneath the mess he had an unslouched, almost elegant bearing and mannerisms that were economical and steady. His eyes could be disconcertingly probing and intelligent and, whenever he loosened up to the point of using more than four words, he sounded educated.

"I need to wash," he said brusquely, displaying mud-smeared hands.

She motioned toward the hall. "You know where the bathroom is."

Jack went down the hall and they shifted into high speed, she putting the kettle on and getting out tea bags, David dumping ice into a pitcher and then standing on a chair to reach the good glasses that they seldom used because she still thought of them as her mother's.

This won't be so bad.

Yes it will.

You know the man. It's not like he's a stranger.

Ha, since when does that matter?

David will be here the whole time.

You could still lose it.

When Jack stepped back into the room he looked at the three glasses of iced tea on the kitchen table with a stutter of confusion that quickly darkened into a scowl.

"What's this?" he asked, more a demand than a question.

"It's tea just the way you like it," David said. "Come and sit down. You said you needed to talk to my mom, right?"

What a grouch he was. She could not understand why David found him so appealing. But then, if David was hungry for a man's company there weren't many cheerful candidates to choose from. Most of the men she came in contact with were grumpy or intimidating or generally threatening—as though they had a fuse burning inside that could trigger an explosion any minute. Sometimes it seemed that the only males who smiled at her were the ones trying to sell something, and even that wasn't a certainty because old Tom who ran the nearest gas station always glowered through the process of filling her tank and taking her money.

There had been times when she thought that she was at fault. That she gave off some mutant pheromone that aggravated the opposite sex. But these thoughts only surfaced in the blaming-herself-for-everything periods and she tried not to fall into those anymore. She kept the blame at bay with her own form of anger—a quiet but steady little ember that sometimes got lost or buried, but was always alive. She had to keep it alive because it was the fuel for all the strength and determination she'd managed. And she fed that glowing bit of anger constantly with books and articles on violence, with childhood memories that could be reinterpreted. Like memories of Rosalie's father—a church elder and Little League coach who, in the privacy of his home, shouted obscenities at his cowering family or threw plates of food against the wall or punched out the window screens. Like memories of a neighbor who sulked and scowled and withdrew, a different expression of hostility but just as effective because his wife and children and indeed all the neighborhood kids had always tiptoed around him in fearful silence.

She was not to blame. Men were to blame. The culture that fostered and permitted so much male malice and bad behavior was to blame. She clung to that. She fanned her quiet anger with that. Male equaled *malus* equaled bad. Why? That question was one she thought about often but never managed to answer. All she knew for certain was the truth of it.

Or was she exaggerating everything to justify her own fears? Was she trying to validate what she couldn't change about herself and rationalize her feelings? Was there a whole world of happy families and wonderful men existing somewhere out there beyond her awareness?

She stood near the sink and watched David coaxing Jack to the table. Like an animal tamer maneuvering a tiger. That simile amused her so much that she had to bite the inside of her lip to keep from smiling. Males were supposedly programmed to be aggressive, uncooperative, and antisocial. Females and dependent offspring were supposedly the major civilizing influence. Could it be that men resented women and children for their roles as tamers? Maybe all that simmering anger arose as a result of their having to fit into modern civilization, and since they couldn't lash out at civilization itself, they aimed at the bearers of civilization.

Whether this was justification or not, she hadn't imagined all those crime statistics and horrible news stories in which the perpetrators were almost always men. And she certainly hadn't imagined her own experience.

But where did her son fit into this? Her son who would be a man one day.

No. Too disturbing. Can't think about that now.

Only in the perfect worlds of books and televison had she known men with unfailingly gentle attitudes toward women and children. And of course, those men were all fictional.

She watched Jack turn one of her kitchen chairs and sit half sideways as though declaring himself only half committed to being there. To her he was almost as exotic and fearsome as a performing tiger. To her, humanity consisted of women and the young. Men were The Other. Barely domesticated, wild, and untrustworthy creatures. Dangerous creatures. She had had neither a male friend nor lover since reaching adulthood, unless she counted her chat-room buddies on-line . . . but she didn't think of cyberfriends as either male or female. Despite the fact that the pseudonyms could be gender-specific, she thought of the disembodied communicants on the Internet as akin to that staple of old horror and sci-fi movies—live brains floating in jars. Possessed of their essential human qualities but without any of the messiness of the physical or any of the potential for destruction.

But hadn't *she* always felt a bit like a floating brain, disconnected from the world and from her own body? Since her recovery anyway. So that probably meant she was a little bit crazy and her perceptions of men and everything else in life were skewed. Or maybe it heightened reality. Maybe a touch of neural damage was enlightening.

A silence fell in the room and she realized that both David and Jack were looking at her, expecting something from her. She had been so detached from their interaction that she hadn't heard whatever question or suggestion was posed.

"Mom . . . ," her son said in his warning voice. If Jack hadn't been there the full phrase would have been "Mom, you're spacing out again."

"Sorry," she said.

Jack continued to look at her, interest kindling in his eyes and deepening into an intense laser beam of a stare.

Quickly she turned to wash a dish in the sink. Jack was too big for the room. He took up all the space and used all the air so she couldn't get enough to breathe. What if she'd made him mad by not listening?

"Don't do that now, Mom," David insisted. "Come sit down."

She carried the kitchen towel with her, clenching it tightly in both hands. As she sat down across from Jack he shifted his chair so that he was closer to the table. Was that a threat? Her palms felt clammy and a tight flutter started beneath her ribs. David seemed oblivious.

Jack lifted his glass. "This is good tea."

David, who had never been interested in iced tea, took a drink as though savoring a fine wine, then announced, "I've got a lot of stuff to do in my room," and headed for the door with the glass in his hand.

She opened her mouth to say *Stay here!* but before she could speak David turned back with "Oh . . . Did you ask him, Mom?"

She looked from her son to Jack.

"We wanted you to stay for dinner," David said. "Could you? Please?"

Jack appeared vaguely flustered. "Dinner? I don't know . . . I—"

"It's not a big deal," David insisted, though it clearly was. "You fed me lunch and you brought me home." He shrugged.

Hearing this made her angry again. He had lunch with Jack while she was pacing the floor, worried sick? She glared at her son but it went unnoticed. The boy was blind to everything but Jack.

"Okay," Jack agreed. "If you're sure . . ."

A wide grin broke on David's face. She couldn't remember the last time she had seen him so vividly happy.

"Yeah, well, like I said—I've got stuff to do in my room."

"I'm going to need your help soon," she said to his back. He gave a noncommittal wave without looking back, then disappeared into the hallway, leaving her alone in the airless kitchen with the too-big man.

She drew a deep breath and looked at Jack. "Didn't you think I'd be worried?" she asked. "You could have at least made him phone me so I'd know where he was."

Jack appeared puzzled for a moment, then shook his head. "I just assumed he had already talked to you." He shook his head again. "You can't let him get away with that."

"I know," she snapped. "He is my son. I've taken care of him just fine for years." She twisted the towel on her lap under the table. Her heart was galloping behind her ribs. The kitchen walls were inching inward, shrinking the room around her.

Go ahead, Thea . . . have a breakdown. Get really demented. That will make him think twice about staying for dinner.

"It's nice outside," she said, standing abruptly. "Why are we in here?"

Jack followed the woman outside to sit in the garden chairs. She seemed nervous and distracted, but then she usually seemed that way to him. Today she was also cranky and irritable. Ordinarily she made an excuse and disappeared, which was fine with him, but this time David had trapped them into sharing each other's company. Maybe she was angry about that.

"These are great chairs," Jack said. "Handmade cedar?"

She nodded.

"Get them around here?"

"What?"

"The chairs?"

"I ordered them from an on-line company. They were just delivered a few days ago."

"On-line? You mean . . . with the computer? You buy things with the computer?"

She attempted an edgy smile. "You can find anything on-line. Without ever leaving your house."

"Anything?" he challenged.

"Anything," she repeated. "News, books, games . . . friends."

He did not bother to conceal his skepticism. "Friends on the computer?"

"Yes. Good friends. People you can rely on."

"And you only know them through the computer? You never see them? You never make any kind of physical contact?"

"That's not important," she said defensively.

"But you've never met these people. They could be lying about who they are and what they think."

"Those risks aren't limited to cyberspace. People lie when they're face-to-face, too."

"Okay," he admitted. "But when you're physically with someone you have chemistry and intuition and all your instincts working. Whereas communicating electronically leaves you in a vacuum. You have no idea how these people relate to their environment or how they respond to others, and you can't touch or smell them, or hear the subtle variations in their voice or see that whole range of body language and expression that we base our judgments on."

She leaned forward slightly, giving in to the pull of the conversation. "It hasn't been a problem for me. What about people who become friends as pen pals? What about that woman who wrote an entire memoir about her correspondence with an English book dealer she'd never met? They became very close but it was all through words on paper."

"Not in a total vacuum, though," Jack insisted. "The woman knew for a fact that the man was a noted book dealer and she also wrote occasionally to his staff so she knew of him from others. As for him, I think I read that he was aware of her occupation and was acquainted with people who actually knew her."

Thea appeared surprised.

"Shocked?" he asked, amused but not at all offended. It felt good to tease her a little and to use his wit for a change. "Is it the fact that I'm capable of thought or that I can speak in whole sentences?"

She lowered her eyes to study the butterflies in the faded print of her dish towel.

"All right, I confess," he said, teasing her a little just for the hell of it. "I secretly subscribe to the *L.A. Times* and that's where I read about the memoir. Like Will, I only know what I read in the papers."

With her head still down, she looked up at him through thick lashes and shot back with, "That may have been fine for Will but today's average newspaper is written at a fourteen-year-old's level so that doesn't say much for what you know, does it?"

All right . . . the woman had a little something to her after all. But then he'd always known that. He just hadn't been interested in what it was. Now, because of the kid . . . Damn! What the hell was he doing? He did not want to get involved in whatever mess David was stirring up.

"Not the *L.A. Times,*" he countered. "The level there is at least fifteen. Or it was until the advertising department took over the newsroom."

A genuine smile lit her face, revealing crescent dimples and a slightly crooked front tooth; then self-consciousness returned and she retreated to staring at the faded butterflies.

"Seriously," he said, "don't you think there's an inherent danger in these cyber-relationships? In opening yourself to people who are so completely disconnected and hidden from you?"

She lifted her chin and narrowed her eyes, annoyed either by the line of thought or with him for pursuing it. "How can there be danger when you're never physically exposed to the other person? If I meet someone in the flesh, something really bad could happen to me. If I meet someone on-line, I'm completely protected."

"How about all the perverts and pedophiles they've been catching on-line?"

"I'd know if I was talking to someone like that."

"That's exactly what Ted Bundy's victims believed and he was right there looking them in the eye."

The narrowed eyes turned into a full-fledged glare. "Are you trying to ruin my computer fun?"

He held up his hands. "Hell no. I'd never come between a hacker and her electronic pals."

She looked toward the house, probably wishing the boy would appear.

"So educate me . . . ," he said. "Here I am discussing all this as though I know something about it, when all I've ever done with a computer is the sort of thing where you peck at the keys, follow the instructions, and hope for the best. I don't really have a clue as to how on-line or the web or any of that works."

"It's simple." She paused in thought a moment, probably trying to figure out a way to explain this simple thing to him.

"It's a whole world," she said. "An alternate world of places and people. You enter it electronically and then you can go anywhere, either by typing in an exact address or by exploring and doing searches. In just minutes you can go to a store in Chicago or a library in Sweden or a high school in Moose Jaw, Saskatchewan. It's all out there. Right at your fingertips."

"So . . . you write letters back and forth?"

"You can. But it's so much more. There are information databases. There are web sites dedicated to informing, selling, persuading . . . whatever. . . . For instance, public television has a site with transcripts of shows. And then there's electronic mail—e-mail—which is pretty much an instant method of letter writing. And bulletin boards where you can post notices and messages, and you can read other people's postings, and you can reply to each other's postings. And then there are chat rooms with live interaction . . . dialogues that happen in real time. Just like I'm talking to you now. I say something, then you say something. The only difference is that it's typed."

"Chat rooms, huh?"

"Thousands of them that you can click into. Big ones with thirty people trying to talk at once. Or smaller ones with themes—divorce or philosophy or flower arranging . . . whatever. Or little out-of-the-way places that feel like a neighborhood coffee shop where the same people have been meeting for a long time. I go to a place like that at night when I can't sleep." She ducked her head so that her hair fell forward around her face. "And then there are private rooms for people who don't want an open chat."

"Let me see if I've got this right." He laced his fingers on top of his head, leaned back, and grinned. "When you can't sleep, you go to a coffee shop on your computer and meet friends?"

She twisted the towel into a tight knot in her lap.

"David likes it, too," she said, defensive again. "I got him his computer for school research, but he's on it every evening, using my account to cruise and talk."

Suddenly nothing was amusing anymore and the great weariness that had started in Los Angeles and traveled with him to Eureka rolled back over him like high tide settling into a rock pool. In the distance a hawk dipped and soared above the tree line. He focused on it without pleasure or interest.

"I know you make your living with a computer," he said. "And I know the technology has uses. But I'm not so convinced that it's a good thing. People were already getting too far removed from nature and from each other. This computer stuff makes it all worse."

Which probably sounded like a strange opinion from a man who had removed himself from his previous life and was attempting a hermitlike existence in a town where he had no family or history. But if she noted the contradiction she didn't comment. Maybe she was, like him, too tired to care.

They sat in uncomfortable silence for several minutes.

"There's something I've been thinking about," he said finally. "I was going to wait before I said anything. . . ."

"What?" she asked sharply.

"I'm ready to sell this place."

She stared at him, stunned and stricken.

"I hate being a landlord. Hell, I can barely keep up with my own house."

"But you don't have anything else to do."

That one rankled, but—she was right. "Be that as it may, I still hate being a landlord. Don't look so horrified—I'd like to see what we can work out. If you're paying rent you may as well be making mortgage payments."

"I can't buy," she said, swallowing hard and turning to look at the house as if she were already losing it.

"Don't worry. I'm going to figure out something. Even if you don't have a down payment, there's got to be a way if I'm willing to finance you."

"No."

"Why?"

She was beginning to look like a perp who'd been asked to go to headquarters.

"A lot of reasons."

Her tone said that it was none of his business. That made him want to dig all the deeper.

"Is it legal trouble?"

Suddenly she had a panicky wild-eyed look that told him he was getting warmer, and all the little bits and pieces came together for him in a guess. "You're hiding, aren't you? Running from someone or something."

She stood abruptly, knocking over the little table between them and tumbling their iced tea to the ground.

"My mother's glasses!"

He scooped both glasses off the ground and held them up. "They're okay. Look." Somehow the ground was soft enough or the angle of the fall gentle enough that they had survived intact. He righted the table and set the glasses back on it.

"What is it, Thea? Unpaid bills? A stalker? Witness protection? What are we talking about here? If I knew, I could help."

"No!"

"I've still got contacts . . . cops, journalists . . . people I can ask things, people who know how to—"

"What! Are you threatening to investigate me?"

"That's not what I meant."

"You want to pry into my life and take my son away!"

The fear of losing her son cued him. That was the core of it. Was it a custody battle?

"Thea . . . Is it David's father? Are you hiding from him?"

She took a step back and put her hands up as though warding off attack. "Get away from me! Leave us alone! Leave David alone!"

"Leave . . . David . . . alone?" He repeated the words in rueful disbelief, suddenly furious at her and her pest of a son. Mostly furious at himself. This was not his business. He was no longer a peacekeeper or an agent of the law. He was no longer concerned with the world or the people who lived on it. The

world was a cesspool and most of its inhabitants
were scum. He needed no further proof of that.

"You'd better tell the kid to leave *me* alone. Tell
him not to pop up at my house uninvited. Tell him
to stop breaking things out here just so he can call
me out to fix them!"

She ran.

"Wait!" he called, lunging after her.

But she bolted into the house and slammed the
door in his face.

Thea threw the dead bolts on the door, slammed
the solid wooden shutters into place over the barred
windows, and leaned against the kitchen wall gasping for breath and shaking.

Then the pounding began.

"Thea! Please let me talk to you."

The pounding went through her skin and into her
head. She covered her ears, cupping her palms to
block out the pounding with air pressure, but that
brought instead the rushing sounds of the sea. She
jerked her hands down.

Here we go. The roller coaster to hell.

Images assaulted her. Water lapping against the
shore. Eyes behind dark glass. Running through the
night. Total darkness and terror. Not fear, because
the intellect still functioned during fear; this was pure
primal terror. She would shriek and snarl and bite if
the hand weren't so tight over her mouth. She would
kick and claw if her limbs weren't pinioned.

No! It's not happening, you idiot. Nothing is happening! You're safe in your house.

"Thea! Thea, please open up!"

Back pressed to the wall, she faced the bolted door that stood between her kitchen and the rest of the world. But there was no escape. She was trapped in the nightmare now and there was nothing to do but count her way out to her safe place—though she thought she'd grown beyond that. She thought she'd cast aside that stupid crutch.

"Just talk to me!" Jack shouted.

She closed her eyes and counted. All the way to safety. To the safest place in the world.

When the pounding and shouting finally stopped, she opened her eyes and there was her son, standing in the hall doorway staring at her with a wild, scornful anger.

"I guess Jack's not staying for dinner, huh?" The bitterness in his voice was scathing.

She lifted an unsteady hand to her forehead. Her son. She had to pull herself together for him.

"You're going to make him stand out there and beg? You won't even talk to him?"

"I'll talk to him later," she said in a voice barely above a whisper.

His face hardened and red crept up his neck and into his cheeks. "Is this how you treated my father? Is this why we're alone?"

She was stunned. Through the years of curiosity, through the past months of intense wistful paternity questions, he had never been accusatory or attacked her. He had always dealt gingerly with the issue.

She looked toward the solid wood door. Because of the shutters she couldn't see out, but she thought that Jack had given up and was walking to his car. It occurred to her that he could have opened the door with his key. He could have forced his way in if he'd chosen to.

"You can still go after him," David said, voice laden with emotion.

She shook her head no. His mouth quivered and tears welled in his eyes.

"Oh David . . ." She reached for him, but he batted her hand away.

"You think I don't know things?" His face contorted. "You think I just accept how weird we live and how crazy you act around people? You think I don't realize that we've been hiding? You think I still believe everything the way I did when I was little and you and Grandma told me all your bullshit stories about my father dying. Well, I'm too big for stories now. I want the truth. I want to know why there's only one picture with my father in it. One stupid picture that barely shows his face. And I want to know where my birth certificate is. And . . . Shit!"

He looked up at the ceiling and raised clenched fists in the air as though cursing God. "Where's our past before California? Where did we really come from? Where was I born? Who are our relatives?"

"I've told you—"

"You've lied to me! I know it! So just stop! Don't open your mouth if it's going to be another lie!"

An involuntary sob started in her chest and she pressed her fingers to her lips to hold it in. Or was it to hold in the lies? The lies that kept them safe. The lies that protected them.

"I think I have a father somewhere."

Frantically she shook her head. "No, David. No."

"I think I have a father who's alive and who doesn't know where I am."

"No!"

"I think you stole me from him when I was a baby!"

"No. I swear to you, that's not true!"

"What *is* true, then? Are you finally going to tell me?"

Silence stretched between them.

"Are you?"

"I can't."

"Then I'll find out for myself!"

He whirled and ran down the hall. The whole house shuddered at the slamming of his bedroom door.

"Oh God, oh God . . ."

And suddenly she was not alone in the room. IT had found her. She covered her head with her arms and slid down to sit against the wall. Deep breaths. In out, in out. That's what they taught her. Control it. Beat it.

This is my home. I am safe. My son is safe. The doors

*are bolted and the windows are secured and we are safe.
And I can count to my special place again. I can take
myself there until the monster is gone.*

But no amount of counting could dispel this monster because it wasn't a flashback or a phobic reaction or a product of her overactive imagination. It was fact. It was truth. Out of the cage with claws and fangs as sharp as ever. The monstrous truth that she'd locked away so deeply, prying open the brittle box of her soul to shut it inside, then pushing the thing down and burying it, smoothing it over, covering it with time and pretense until she hadn't been just denying it—she had banished it. She had erased it from existence. The truth . . . that her beloved son had been conceived in rape . . . that in her child lived her destroyer. Her brutalizer. Her murderer.

4

Dear Orion,

My mom is so crazy! I hate her! She is totally flipped out and I'm sick of it. Totally, totally fed up! And it wasn't even over the Dad issue this time either. All I wanted was for Jack to eat dinner with us and you'd think I asked for a serial killer to spend the night. She is such a psycho! It's funny how when I was young I never noticed. I guess I just didn't know any better and I was kind of a shy nerdy type myself without any friends or sports or anything. Everybody probably thought I was as crazy as my mother! But now it's different. Now I know what's normal and what's not, and SHE IS NOT! I mean, what is her problem? If she thinks I'm going to live like her and be like her the rest of my life then she's got a big surprise coming.

There's no new Dad information since my last e-mail. She's still lying about everything and pretending like she doesn't know what I'm talking about. Sometimes I wonder if she's even really my

mom. I mean, what if she's some loony from an asy-
lum who escaped and kidnapped me? But I guess
that would mean my grandma was a loony too and
she wasn't. If my grandma was still with us things
would be a lot better.

You're the only person who listens and cares and
takes me seriously. Reg and Tommy are fun to
fool around with but they go into real butthead acts
when serious stuff comes up. They're like . . .
duh . . . and then they start laughing about some
booger joke or something. And you were right
about not counting on Jack. I kind of brought up
the subject without telling him too much and he
was totally NOT interested. Like I was some kind of
idiot for even having questions. Don't worry—I
didn't tell him too much and I never mentioned anything about you or all the help you've been giving
me, so even if he does rat me out to my mom there's
no real damage he can do. You're the only real
friend I've got. You've never made fun of me for
thinking the whole Dad Thing is screwed up and
my mom is jerking me around. And I can't believe
how much you've helped me. I never would have
figured out all the web sites and stuff without you.
I sure never would have known about the death
certificate stuff because there's nothing about that in
this dumb Internet detective book I bought. And
I don't think I would have ever figured out how to
trace the part of the country where my mom
was from.

VIOLATION

You're the only humanoid on earth that I am totally connected with. I hope you're home and get
this and write back fast. I am going berserk here and
don't know what to do. Maybe I should go for a
hike out into the forest for a few days. That would
give my mom something real to freak about and
maybe she'd wake up!

Your friend, Astroman (David)

Dear David,
I just turned on my machine and got your E.
Checked with the system but you're not signed
on anymore. Hope you haven't already hiked off into
the trees. I'll stay on so if you write back I'll be
here for you.
Sounds like you had a major implode there with
your mom. No surprise though, right? Didn't you
say last week that you could see it coming? The
question is now, what are you going to do?
You're right to think that the next move is yours and
it needs to be a major statement. The forest plan
might very well teach her a lesson, but what would
it do to further your own goals? Nothing. You
have to come up with a strategy that will advance
your cause WHILE she's learning her lesson.
Maybe it's time to take charge of finding the answers
you want. Remember, no one else is going to
solve your problems. If you want changes in your
life you have to make them yourself. Even someone who loves you like your mom does is not going

to straighten out your life for you. YOUR life is
YOUR job. And it sounds like the time has come for
you to assume control of that job.

Hang in there, Orion

P.S. Remember: Don't save any of our communications. Delete everything. They could be used
against us.

Dear O,
  I had to do my homework, but was I ever glad to
sign back on and see your mail. You are totally
right. It's time for me to find real answers. If she has
her way she'll have me going crazy and never
learning the truth so I have to take control of my
own life now. I saw an ad on television for some
detective agency that finds people. Their offices are
in San Francisco. I have money saved and I could hire
them to find out about my dad. I could even take
the bus to SF to talk to them.

D

Dear D,
  Hey there buddy :) Now you're talking! A detective
agency is very expensive though and you have to
be careful because I've heard that some of them (particularly the kind that put ads on television) are
out to cheat you and they don't even have any legit
detectives on staff. What's wrong with your own
detective skills anyway? I think you've been doing a

terrific job so far. Your money would go a lot further if you did the legwork and used your bucks for travel and expenses. You can surely do everything that one of those bargain detective outfits can do.

Let's get out of this mail and get into a chat room. Meet me at the usual place, ok?

O

Orion: *I'm here.*

Astroman: *Hi. Do you really think I could do major detective stuff?*

Orion: *Absolutely! You're thirteen and in lots of cultures that's considered a man. You know, David, it took a lot of courage for you to get as far as you have in the questioning process and there's no doubt in my mind that you have what it takes to turn this into a real quest. Your mother will be upset but eventually she'll come to respect you for the decision. What greater quest can there be for a man than to search for his true father?*

Astroman: *But how would I start?*

Orion: *Think about it. You've learned that your mom lived on the East Coast, right? Probably the New York/New Jersey area. There's your start.*

Astroman: *Sure! What am I gonna do? Beam myself there?*

Orion: *You were going to ride a bus to San Francisco, remember?*

Astroman: *You think I can take a bus all the way across the country?*

Orion: *You can go anywhere on the bus. You just
have to make a lot of changes to different buses
and it takes a long time. Up to a week for cross-
country.*

Astroman: *A week on the bus?*

Orion: *Depends on how you do It. How many
nights you have to sleep in bus stations waiting
for connections and all that. It's not cheap either
when you figure that you have all those meals on
the road plus the bus ticket.*

Astroman: *That sounds shitty.*

Orion: *You're right. Much better to fly. When you
add in meals and incidentals the price is close to the
same and you don't have all the hassles or the
wasted time.*

Astroman: *But there's no airport in Eureka.*

Orion: *So you take the bus to San Francisco like
you planned. When you arrive at the bus station
there transfer to another bus that will take you out
to the airport.*

Astroman: *Think they'll let a kid buy a plane ticket
by himself?*

Orion: *Good point. You're always a step ahead of
me. I could probably set a ticket up for you from
my end.*

Astroman: *You'd do that for me?*

Orion: *What are good friends for?*

Astroman: *How will I give you the money to pay
you back?*

Orion: *You can just hand it to me.*

Astroman: *What do you mean?*

Orion: :) *Come on buddy! Remember that map I e-mailed you to download? Remember where I live?*

Astroman: *Yeah.*

Orion: *You're not going to come out to this part of the world and pay to stay in dumpy hotels or sleep on park benches when you could bunk with me and use my place as your headquarters—are you? I'd be pretty insulted.*

Astroman: *Wow! Are you sure?*

Orion: *Of course I'm sure.*

Astroman: *Wow. That is so cool. What'll I tell my mom?*

Orion: *Nothing. If she even gets a hint of your plans she'll truly flip out, lock you up and probably call the police.*

Astroman: *But I have to at least leave her a note so she won't think I'm kidnapped or something.*

Orion: *It's too big a risk. It'll take you half a day of bus riding to make it to SF and get on a plane. If you left a note and she found it too soon she might call the police and catch you at the SF airport. Just leave. No notes. Soon as you get to my place you can e-mail her to let her know you're okay.*

Astroman: *Wow. This is pretty awesome. You know though. . . . I'm wondering. . . . There's only a month or so until eighth grade graduation. Maybe I should wait for summer vacation before I do this.*

Orion: *It's up to you. But one of your objects was to teach your mom a lesson so that she'll learn to treat you differently. If you let this whole blowup pass by without taking decisive action you won't have taught her anything and she'll probably think she's won and things might get even worse for you. Your grades are passable aren't they? If you're away for a little while your school will still let you graduate.*

Astroman: *Yeah. I guess so.*

Orion: *It's a go then! Countdown to launch. I'm going to sign off for about thirty minutes and see what I can do about a plane ticket for you. I'll try to make arrangements so that you can pick it up at the ticket counter in SF when you check in for the flight. While I'm at it I'll check the bus schedule from Eureka to SF. Most likely it'll work out so that you go into Eureka in the morning just like you're going to school (pack only what you can carry in your book bag so your mom doesn't get suspicious). Then instead of going to class head straight to the bus station. Does your school call your house if you're absent?*

Astroman: *No. That's only for the little kids.*

Orion: *Good. What time do you usually get home from school in the afternoon?*

Astroman: *Around 3:30, 3:45.*

Orion: *Great. So you'll have the whole day before anyone really starts looking for you.*

Astroman: *What day do you think we'll do it?*

VIOLATION

Orion: *Tomorrow if I can get the ticket.*

Astroman: *Tomorrow?*

Orion: *Damn right, David. I am here for you and I'm going to do whatever it takes to make sure that NOTHING stands in the way of you reaching your goals. Meet me back here in thirty minutes. And remember—not a word to anyone.*

5

Patience. He had infinite patience, a great virtue for a hunter, and Orion was after all the star-crossed hunter who stalked the night skies. He would have preferred using Apollo and had even tried the screen name briefly to test the response, but then had switched to the constellation theme as a lure for David. Now he saw that the image was perfect. Orion . . . ancient and revered hunter. He studied his face in the small oval mirror beside his computer monitor. A narrow smile twisted his mouth upward. The smile of the victor . . . the conqueror . . . the winner. What a beautiful expression. What an exquisitely sweet moment. A phantom frisson began in the arches of his feet and traveled up until it charged his entire body and he closed his eyes, reveling in the power—the power of the hunter closing in on his prey.

He rested his hand on the telephone. Everything was in place, waiting, honed into a finely tuned mechanism that required only one phone call to activate. One call and there would be tickets at counters for the boy so that he could travel freely on a bus, then a commuter plane, then a nonstop commercial flight—all under the false name that matched the identification card and birth certificate that had been sent weeks ago in an envelope with the return address of a nonexistent astronomy association. *"These might come in handy, David. Real detectives always use assumed identities. Hide them well until you need them. Your friend, O."*

So much work and planning and research had gone toward the anticipation of this moment. It was no small task to transport an adolescent thousands of miles without leaving a trail. He had considered the possibility of driving out to pick up the boy himself, but that was too time-consuming, too unwieldy, and it allowed too many opportunities for a change of heart. This was best. Once the boy was started, the ticketed anonymous travel would create a momentum that carried him forward.

Only one call and it would all be set in motion. He lifted the receiver of his corded landline telephone, punched in the caller ID block and then the number. As he listened to the clicking of connections and the ring at the other end he smiled into the mirror again. So much delicate coaxing and leading, so much playing of the line, and now, finally, the boy was at the edge of the trap, reaching for the bait, ready to take that final and irrevocable step.

6

Thea looked at her bedside clock. Two a.m. She had been trying to sleep for several hours, lying quietly in her soft bed in her softly lit room, but she could not quiet her anxieties. She had tried so hard to carry on her mother's legacy—to give her child a good life and shield him completely from the past—but now it felt as though everything was being tainted by the truth she could never give him.

Her entire adult life was a construct of lies, as ill-conceived and flimsily connected as a child's building project, and now, with a few well-aimed hits from a determined teenager, it was teetering on collapse. But what could she do? What should she do? How could she tell her son that he'd been conceived in the ugliest, most hateful manner imaginable? That his biological father had been a complete stranger who raped her and then tried to kill her. How could she explain that the lies had been engineered by her own mother in a desperate and heroic effort to remove them completely from the reach of that monster who would one day be released from prison, to spare them the judgments of those who would always see her and her misbegotten child as stigmatized, and to insure that no one questioned where David belonged or who should be responsible for him?

"You never can tell with all those civil service workers and social agencies, Thea. If they knew the truth they might declare you an unfit mother . . . damaged in the head, you know . . . and me . . . well, I won't last forever so they'd want to give David to someone younger. And what with all those fathers' rights things going on . . . Rusket might be able to sue for custody from prison. Don't you know some shyster attorney looking for a case to get him in front of the television cameras would love it? I'm telling you, Thea—we have to keep hiding and never let anyone back on the Island know David exists. Before you even knew what was happening I gave this trouble to God and he cleansed me. What I've done isn't a sin. These lies are blessed."

The lies had been spun out of love. To keep them safe. To give David a normal life. But she could never explain that to him. And therefore she could never give him the one thing he hungered for—the truth about his father.

What could she do? Would it be enough for him if she could fulfill his other wishes? If she could somehow force herself to be closer to his concept of normal? If she could facilitate and encourage his fledgling relationship with Jack? Would that be enough to defuse the ticking paternity bomb?

Stop thinking about it or you'll never get to sleep!

She thought about getting up to play solitaire on the computer a while, but she had been struggling to keep more regular hours, partly because it made household routines easier, and partly because she was striving to appear more "normal" in her son's eyes. She could play for just a little while, though, without staying up all night. Just long enough to calm herself. Solitaire on the computer was a drug for her—easily taken and only mildly addictive. The changing patterns and simple demands of the game blocked out all other thoughts and allowed her complete escape. There was no regret or agitation, no sadness or anger, no wistful yearning, no loneliness consuming her—just red, black . . . black, red . . . counting down, counting up, with the cards appearing in never-ending variations so there was always a satisfying element of unpredictability.

The women on television programs never played solitaire. They were too busy with people—husbands or friendly ex-husbands, boyfriends . . . or at least a handyman hanging around. They had friends who they shopped with and lunched with and talked with for hours on the phone. They had people at work who were almost like family. That was the "normal" her son longed for.

But what about the mothers of David's friends? They weren't television-normal. She had spoken to them briefly on occasion and they seemed okay, but David had mentioned things that hinted of ugly divorces and custody battles, and during the class meeting in October when she and a number of other parents had crammed into student desks at ten a.m. to listen to the teachers' goals for the year, Tommy's mother had been drunk. Not falling-down drunk, but conspicuously anesthetized. So it wasn't as if life was television-perfect at his friends' houses either.

Stop thinking!

She got out of bed, pulled on the long zippered sweatshirt she used as a robe, and padded down the well-lit hallway to listen at David's door. Silence. She eased the door open. His was the only room in the house without a nightlight. It was completely dark. Glowing planets and stars winked at her from the accurate night sky he had so carefully assembled on his ceiling, and beneath the dreamed-of heavens her little boy slept. No longer little. In the spill of light from the hall she could see the innocent, unguarded face and the gangly arms and legs sticking out from under the tangled covers, and she felt a rush of love so intense that it brought tears to her eyes. She wanted to protect him, needed to protect him. The instinct was as fierce as ever, yet he was pulling away, resisting and resenting all her efforts.

He seemed so vulnerable to her with the weight of the darkness pressing around him. She wanted to tiptoe in and switch on the desk lamp that she had always kept burning for him when he was younger, but that would infuriate him. He insisted on sleeping in the dark now. And he insisted that she stay out of his room.

She looked around his private space. Though his monitor was off, a tiny green light in the tower indicated that the computer itself was on. Earlier she had listened at his door, agonizing over whether she should try talking to him, and she'd heard the click of his fingers on the keyboard. There were no big reports or projects due so she knew he'd been on-line in a chat room, probably telling techno buddies what a terrible mother he had and what a deprived life he led. Or maybe telling the whole damn wired world of adolescents that he suspected his mother was lying to him about his father. Hearing the staccato of the keyboard so far past his bedtime had rekindled her anger and she had been perversely tempted to throw open the door and shout, "You're right! I've been lying! And I'm going to keep on lying so get used to it!" She probably should have at least banged on the door and ordered him to bed, but she had turned away without a word because she couldn't stand the thought of doing battle again when she was still stinging from their last round.

She could go in now and unplug his computer. She could unhook the monitor or the tower and carry it to the closet in her bedroom. That would send a message. But then, sneaking in while he slept might be construed as an act of cowardice—which it would be—and the guerrilla action would probably take their war to a level that she was not armed for yet. Better to let it rest. When he got home from school tomorrow . . . today, actually . . . she would attempt a discussion. They would both be calmer then. And she would let him have his friends over, and she would put things back together for him with Jack, and she would find a way to stay in the house and everything would be fine. Everything would be fine.

Gently she pulled his door shut and returned to her bed, ready to try sleep again. This time she lit the collection of scented votive candles on the dresser and turned out the lamps, telling herself that the candles would be soothing and would help her relax, not allowing herself to consider other reasons for them.

She slipped back into bed. It was an antique cherry four-poster, big so she could spread out, and she had ordered the most beautiful matching sheets and piles of pillows and a hand-stitched antique quilt in a tree-of-life pattern. It was a bed fit to be shown in a magazine. A bed that she'd thought would ease away all her cares and transport her into sleep every night. All it did, though, was give her something nice to roll around in during the insomnia.

The lighted dial of the clock read two-thirty. On bad nights the hours from two in the morning till sunrise were always the worst. She knew that the body had a natural schedule when different functions were either low or high. This then had to be the low point for rational thought and the high point for dream-thinking—that swift and formless passage of emotions that seized the brain like a fever, bringing fear, anxiety, and regret. Sometimes bringing stark terror or manic planning for the future. Sometimes bringing fantasy and sweet amorphous desires.

She tried to elude the dream-thinking and to summon sleep with memory games—how many major California highways had she traveled on and how many bushes were there in the yard of their Sacramento home, and how many towns could she remember from Nassau County, Long Island? When that didn't work she released herself to the golden light of the candles. Flickering, dancing light. And she closed her eyes and imagined dancing . . . very slow, with a long silky dress swaying against her legs. Dancing with a man. Someone from a movie. Someone gentle and perfect who was whispering how much he loved her. His hand at the small of her back. Her head on his shoulder. Slow . . . very slow. Liquid warmth spreading through her like candlelight. Like her blood was alight. But her dance partner slipped away and she was alone. As usual.

She stretched out her arms and studied her hands in the flickering candlelight. They were so much smaller than men's hands. Than Jack's for instance. She had noticed his hands as he sat there in her cedar chair. Long hands with squared nails. Very quiet hands that rested on the chair arm, seldom gesturing as he spoke. Did men look at women's hands? Probably not. From what she had seen they were too busy staring at breasts and legs to ever notice a woman's hands. She traced her fingers over her face, her ear-lobes, and down her neck, noting the smoothness and the contours as though examining a stranger's body.

Her hands continued moving down, over her collarbones and to the firm swelling of her breasts. She felt her nipples harden beneath the cotton gown. She slid her hands over her flat belly, feeling the pulse beat there. This body was a foreign thing to her, completely separate from her mind and from her identity. It was an annoyance, requiring attention and care, sometimes rebelling with illness or disturbing her with insistent demands. Aching with vague and elusive desires. Like now. Sighing, she flipped onto her stomach, resenting everything that defined her physically as female. She felt imprisoned by her body, enslaved and tormented. If only she could shut off the restless heat, the unnamed yearnings. If only the whole world could be like her interactions on the computer—minds meeting minds; emotions in their purest forms.

She drifted, staring into the hypnotic candle flames, until finally her eyes closed.

Darkness. Moonless, starless, thick and shifting darkness. Pressing in on her. Suffocating her. Sick. Oh, God I'm sorry. Darkness that becomes a hand. Hands. Arms. The monster drags her across the ground toward a house.

No air. Lungs shrieking for air. Vision slipping. This is it. I'm dying. But then another monster rises to fight him. Clawing, screaming, biting. A monster from inside her.

"Fucking bitch!"

He punches her in the stomach and she drops, gasping and retching. He kicks her back and head. "Stupid cunt!" Then he turns away. Leaving? Muttering as he looks for something on the ground. "Fucking spoiled brats. Fucking idiots."

He's looking for the rock. The rock to smash her head. And this time she knows what he is going to do to her and she could get up and run, but she's paralyzed. And suddenly there are eyes staring down. Rosalie. Her mother. Rosalie's brother and parents. Her flute teacher. The admissions adviser from Juilliard.

"You lied, Althea. You broke God's rules and forgot your place. You have to be punished."

"I'm sorry! Please . . ."

But the words are trapped inside her because she's possessed by the monster, paralyzed by the fear, and the eyes vanish because he's back to claim her, looming over her, blocking out the sky with his rage, becoming the sky, pale moon face, lips pulled back from glinting star teeth, upraised hand holding the rock . . . rock of sleep . . . rock of death.

She bolted upright in bed, sweating and shaking. That was it. No more. She turned on every lamp in the room, blew out the guttering candles, zipped into the sweatshirt robe, and padded barefoot to the bathroom, where the shower stall light was on. There she splashed cold water on her face and brushed her chin-length hair, avoiding the mirror as she always did.

VIOLATION

She made a cup of almond tea and carried it to the living room, where she sat down at her computer. Absently she watched the butterflies flap across the screen. She was current with her work but there were inquiries from prospective clients that she could answer. Or she could double-check the articles she'd proofread for the upcoming SOS newsletter, a monthly task she donated to the Save Our Sequoias group. It was an organization she'd learned about and aided before she moved to Humboldt County—a smaller, rawer, more strident version of the legendary Save-the-Redwoods League. Headquarters for SOS was in Washington, D.C., to gain access to the politicians whose decisions spelled life or death for the forest. She had never met any of the people on the board. She had never been to any of the rallies they had staged around the country. She had not even gone out to the big Cut-Less Demonstration they had sponsored to call attention to the endangered Headwaters Forest, and that had been held less than an hour's drive from her house. Practically in her backyard!

It was disgusting. David was right to be furious at her, because she was furious with herself. Headwaters Forest, for God's sake! The last existing stand of old-growth redwoods in private hands. And she'd planned to go, planned to take her son and join the hundreds of people coming from all over the country to declare that Headwaters shouldn't be cut down, that irreplaceable two-thousand-year-old trees are a treasure that belongs to the nation and to future generations, not to one man with dollar signs in his eyes. She had risen with the sun and packed lunches and awakened David, and even gotten to the point of putting on her coat. And then she had frozen. She had thought of all those strangers . . . standing amidst all those unknown people . . . exposing herself to all those eyes and being jostled, being scrutinized and possibly spoken to, being . . . what? . . . approached, singled out, marked, followed? . . . by so many men. All those men. And she could not go.

And so she had stayed home, walking for hours on the treadmill that faced the living room window looking out into a redwood grove. Hating herself. Hating the fear that lived within her—as silent and relentless as a cancer. Hating the weakness that allowed the fear to rule. Fear that was stronger than passion or commitment. Fear that had become the monster.

She buried her face in her hands. No wonder her son despised her and wanted another parent—a more solid, more reliable parent. Like the invented ghost father. Like Jack. A wave of the bleakest gray washed over her.

Cut that out! No depression allowed. Who ever said parenting would be easy? It was hard for everyone, not just her.

She straightened, drew a deep breath, and clicked her computer to life. With practiced motions she moved the cursor to connect to her service provider.

"Time to go out," she said. Time to shed her troubles and go out. That was the way she thought of it: going out. Just as if her friend Rosalie was honking the horn outside and she'd grabbed her jacket and called to her mother, "I'm going out for a while."

One shift of the cursor, two clicks of the mouse button, and she was going out. She straightened her shoulders, tucked one side of her hair behind her ear, and waited, feeling the lightness and anticipation of striking out to meet friends. The logo winked at her, then the initiating modem message flashed. Who would be out tonight? Would *he* be there? No . . . she couldn't allow herself to get her hopes up. He might never be there again. But some of her circle was certain to be out and they would be happy to see her.

As soon as the server's welcome screen appeared she hit the button for the chat rooms and then scrolled to the Night Owls. Night Owls—6. Six people were in the room. She clicked into it and a large open rectangle filled her screen. The movement of typed lines told her there was a lively ongoing conversation. Quickly she read the list at top right to see who was in the room. Her own screen name, Butterfly, had appeared at the top. *He* was not listed. But then she hadn't really expected him to be. She hadn't heard from him or seen his name in nearly two months.

Hi everyone, she typed, smiling to herself as she read six enthusiastic responses. Here there was no fear, no anxiety, no darkness. The men were not threatening. The women were not condemning. Here there was safety and friendship. And so she passed the nightmare hours in good company, never imagining that her next nightmare would strike in daylight.

7

Jack rose the next morning with a sour taste in his mouth and a fog in his brain from a night of scotch and solitaire, a night spent with one ear cocked toward the phone. He had expected Thea to call and apologize. She hadn't.

Thea. Just thinking her name aggravated him. Why should he care if she called or if he ever spoke to her again? He had only been nice to her for the boy's sake. What the hell was wrong with the neurotic little witch anyway . . . freaking out like he was Jack the Ripper instead of Jack the landlord. Couldn't she see that he was trying to help? Couldn't she see how much her kid needed him? Fine. If she wanted him to leave the boy alone, then he would.

He wasn't in the market for friends. And if he was he wouldn't have wanted a screwed-up thirteen-year-old. Or a screwed-up female. Or any kind of female. Women were trouble. Big trouble. Just like money and power. Women, money, and power—that was the evil three that kept every police department in the world busy. Oh, sure it was probably fairer to say sex or passion, or gender-directed rage rather than women, but from his perspective "women" said it all. Women were either unrealistic or duplicitous or both. They were faithless friends and unfaithful lovers . . . the cause of endless grief and limitless anger. The last thing he wanted or needed was a woman complicating his life.

To work off his agitation he put Mahler and the rawest Mussorgsky in his CD player and began ripping the old linoleum from the kitchen floor. He knew full well that he would probably not get around to replacing it. Both house and yard testified to the fact that the destructive part of renovation was therapeutic for him but the rebuilding was not.

The brittle linoleum came up easily. When there was no more to remove he sat back on his haunches and considered other projects. But then the irritation struck anew because he realized he was still hanging around the house, listening for her call. He shoveled the shards of old flooring into garbage bags, did a haphazard turn with a broom, then pulled on sweats that he'd hacked into shorts, turned on his answering machine, and struck out. After a stop at the coffee shop for a sack lunch he drove to Rockefeller Forest and parked the Bronco in the small turnout along the road.

Humboldt County in northern California was a last stand for most of the surviving old-growth coastal redwoods, Sequoia sempervirens, a species that has existed on earth for a hundred and eighty million years. Within the relatively brief history of the state of California the sequoias had been nearly wiped out. Indiscriminate clear-cutting, development, and pollution had decimated the forests. In the span of his own thirty-seven years, with each visit to his uncle, with each fishing or camping trip, he had witnessed the creeping destruction. Not just of the trees but of the entire ecosystem that the trees anchored. Still, it was all of a piece . . . this destruction. Humanity might be a noble concept but, given the chance, people—whether individuals or groups—tended to be greedy, grasping, self-absorbed monsters, conscienceless and corrupt, completely amoral. And shamelessly hypocritical.

Eureka was a microcosmic display of it all. The town was in a heavenly spot between the redwoods and the blue Pacific, right on Humboldt Bay. But heaven hadn't been maintained. Fish populations were declining around the bay. Native salmon stocks had been devastated. Rivers and streams were fouled with silt washing down from clear-cut areas that no longer had trees to hold the topsoil. Watersheds were ruined. Animals were disappearing. Acid rain was falling. And the UV rays beaming down through the depleted ozone layer were going to burn it all up anyway and fry everyone's eyeballs so that any survivors would end up burrowing into tunnels and living like blind mole rats. But all people did was complain and moan, shifting the blame and fretting over practices elsewhere. Those damn big cities were ruining the air. Those damn Easterners were producing too much landfill garbage. Those damn foreign trawlers were overfishing the oceans. Those damn foreign industries were spewing pollutants. Those damn foreigners were clear-cutting rain forest down in South America.

Didn't anybody get it?

Deep breaths, he ordered himself. *You moved to Humboldt to leave Los Angeles and those agonies behind. Don't take on a whole new war. The town isn't really your town. The woman isn't your problem. The boy isn't your child. All you have to do on any given day is eat and sleep, amuse yourself a little, take care of your needs . . . that's it. These are not your battles. You have no responsibility for anyone or to anyone.*

He concentrated on the deep breaths until he'd turned down the internal rant, then he struck out into Rockefeller. Ten minutes on the familiar trails melted away his agitation. The forest had always had that effect on him, like a mental and emotional scrubdown. He relaxed, inhaling the newly minted air straight from nature's lungs and soaking in the quiet magnificence of this older, gentler world. It was an ancient forest by human standards, and when he was deep into the heart of it he was quickly awed by the mighty timelessness there. The trees were heroic to him, valiant sentinels, struggling against massive odds to pump out fresh oxygen and hold the soil.

But nothing was as he wished it to be. He had not

managed to become the self-sufficient mountain man as he'd intended. The forest wasn't mighty and timeless at all—it was fragile and probably doomed. And Humboldt wasn't the haven he'd thought it would be. The town was beleaguered in many ways, full of millworkers who no longer had mills to work in and fishermen who couldn't catch enough fish to support their families. The area had become a center for society's dregs—spiritualists and motorcycle gang members, environmental radicals and teen runaways, the retired and the retiring, the idealists and the idealless, misfits, nonconformists, and burnouts of every stripe. Topping it all off, Humboldt had become a sensimilla-growing region, attracting everyone from aged hippies cultivating a personal supply to ruthless commercial growers who patrolled their crops with high-powered rifles—necessitating posted cautions not to stray from marked hiking trails.

Humboldt was not what he'd thought it would be and he saw now that he'd been attracted by a Humboldt that existed only in his imagination and in his childhood memories of blissful family vacations. What the other newcomers were attracted by he didn't know. But there was something, some magnetic quality, that caused the walking wounded to drag themselves north to redwood country. Maybe they too had suffered from a romanticized image of the area or maybe they saw it as the place to make a last stand, to take root and fight for survival along with the trees.

He had wondered before why Thea came, and now he thought he had the answer. She had come because Humboldt was a good place to hide. It was just a hunch on his part because he had no solid evidence, but the hunch felt solid. David had definitely stumbled onto something with his suspicions. Maybe the boy had the details mixed up, but he was damn sure reeling in a line that had a fish at the end. Thea was hiding from something or someone, and she was terrified.

If she had just let him help . . .

Damn! She had to be one of the most exasperating females he'd ever met. And that said a lot. Exasperating female was probably redundant though. Like unknown stranger or baffling enigma.

Thea . . . Thea . . . Thea.

How did he get back to thinking about her again? *Walk, breathe, concentrate on the forest. Think about how old the trees are. Older than engines or electricity. Older than most modern civilizations. Think about the path, cushioned with spongy redwood fur and needles from eons of windfall, probably the same path used by animals that were extinct now and generations of people who'd never seen a European face.*

Wandering thoughts were never good because they always wandered in the wrong directions. Focus. That was it. He had to focus. Rockefeller Forest was his favorite place in the world. He was lucky to be there. He was lucky it still existed. In addition to the sheer weight of time that reduced all human concerns to insignificance, he liked the grand scale of it all. Though he was a fairly big man he always felt he'd stepped into a giant's world. First there were the trees, towering over everything at two hundred, three hundred, some reaching nearly to four hundred feet high. Then there was the undergrowth. The paths were crowded with sorrel, a plant that had always looked to him like clover on steroids. Here the sorrel was lush and enormous, growing as high as his chest in places, making shamrocks for giants rather than leprechauns. And then there were the ferns. Chain Fern and maidenhair and wood fern and licorice and bracken and more that he couldn't remember. Canyons of ferns. Valleys of ferns. Hanging cascades of ferns that looked like green waterfalls. Huge clusters of graceful fronds that seemed to spring from everywhere, from cracks in rocks and atop fallen trees . . . ferns growing so large that a Volkswagen bug could have been hidden by one plant. Well, maybe two plants.

He boosted himself up onto the smooth surface of a stump that was as big as the White House dining table and, with legs dangling over the edge, ate his lunch. Then he lay back with his hands laced behind his head, staring up into the swaying tops of the trees, listening to the faint creaks and sighs. His eyes grew heavy and closed.

Later, he woke from a disturbing dream featuring his ex-wife. He'd been calling her name, "Eliane! Eliane!" chasing her with blood soaking through his shirt and covering his hands. A stupid dream. Pointless. He scrubbed roughly at his face and shook the dream from his head. Then he packed up every scrap he'd carried in, shouldered his day pack, and jumped down to the spongy ground.

He started out walking, and then, without any conscious effort, his stride broke into a jog. Running used to be a religion for him, but he hadn't done it much in the last few years. At first he'd told himself it was because the motion made his injured back ache, but then the wound healed and he'd accepted that he didn't have the desire to run any longer. Now he needed the speed. His legs moved and his heart pumped and he felt fast. Fast enough to outrun every emotion and reach a place where there was calm and peace. Where there were no bad memories, no aggravations from the present, and no guns waiting in the closet.

But suddenly it struck him—he had not imagined himself eating his gun for a while. Quite a while. He slowed to a walk as the realization overtook him. Strange. He had believed he would never heal. He had moved through a thick gray fog, his days running into each other, bleak and indistinguishable. But somehow, so gradually that he hadn't even noticed, the fog had dissipated. The grayness had given way to occasions of genuine light. He was better. And whether he liked it or not, whether he thought it was insane or not . . . he cared again. He cared about his backyard and about the redwoods and about humanity losing itself in technology. Most of all he cared about David. David and his screwed-up mother.

How had this happened?

He rolled the question around in his mind until he was back to a morning seven or eight months ago. He had dragged himself out at the insistence of his shop tenants. Wearing the same clothes he'd had on when he passed out on the couch the night before, he had driven out to repair a broken board on the shop porch. The boy had been roaming around the yard. While Jack worked, the kid edged closer and closer until he was up on the porch and rummaging through the tools.

"Get out of there!"

"I'm not hurting anything."

"That's not the point. Stay out of my tools and quit bugging me."

The boy watched his patching efforts a moment. "You're not a very good carpenter."

"And I suppose you are?"

"I never tried it, but I like building models."

"Why don't you go build one now."

Instead of leaving, the boy hunkered over the tools again. "What are all these different kinds of hammers for?"

"Hell if I know. I bought the toolbox at a garage sale."

"Wow. With everything inside?"

"Just as you see it."

"Must be fun experimenting with all this stuff."

He hadn't bothered to reply. Nothing was fun. Tools

were tools. And he hated being asked to fix things that he had no idea how to fix. He hated it that he had ended up a landlord and that he was obligated to fix things he didn't give a damn about. He turned so his back was to the kid, ignoring him in the hope that he would go away.

Instead of a retreat he heard a series of clanks and thumps.

"What are you doing!" he'd demanded, swinging around to glare at the boy.

"I'm putting everything in the right compartments. It was all messed up."

"Stop it. I don't want your help."

The kid didn't back down. He didn't sulk or pout. His gaze was direct, measuring and sharp.

And something happened. That defensive posture, those clear ingenuous eyes that expected nothing but hoped for everything, those eager hands setting right what was perceived as wrong—all of it settled into Jack, silent and invisible as the ultrasound treatments that had broken his scar tissue adhesions after surgery.

"Okay, if you're so interested in my tools you can load them in my car for me."

"You're leaving already?"

"I'm finished. I'm going home."

"Are you going to do any work at your house?"

"Maybe."

"That's such an old house. There's a lot you should do to it."

"What are you, a junior member of the preservation society?"

The boy shrugged. "I was just thinking . . . if you were going to do stuff . . . I could help. You know . . . hold things and whatever. Carpenters usually have helpers."

"Even bad carpenters?"

The kid grinned. "Especially bad carpenters."

"Your mom might not approve. You could get hurt."

"I'm not a baby."

And that had been the beginning of his connection to the boy, a connection that now led to other scenes in his memory—the day David had finagled an invitation to help with Jack's ongoing bathroom renovation. They had been struggling with pipes and wrenches and he'd made a sarcastic remark about their noisy efforts sounding like a John Cage piece, and David hadn't known who John Cage was, hadn't known anything about music history at all.

"Don't they have music class in school anymore?" he had asked.

The boy shrugged.

And suddenly music had seemed important again. Music to share. He had been seized by a lust for music that was so powerful he had dropped everything and taken the boy with him to buy a stereo system for the house and a portable CD player/radio that could go anywhere. Music. When he'd dismantled what was left of the home he'd shared with Eliane and turned his back on Los Angeles, he had also abandoned his lifelong affair with music. He had cut himself off from all things musical, shedding that part of himself just as he had shed all the other components of his identity. He had dismissed it, raging silently against it as a lie and a narcotic and a tawdry emotional stimulant, as he disposed of his carefully chosen state-of-the-art equipment and the music collection he had spent so many years accumulating. When he settled in Eureka he had been free of all encumbrances, and entirely music-free. Even the presets in his car had stayed at news and talk stations.

All that had been swept away in one moment with David, hunched over a leaking pipe, dirty and sweating and frustrated. In that one moment of concern for what David had missed he had become acutely aware of what he himself was missing. Since then he had managed to infect the boy with a mild case of musical appreciation. Lamenting his own lack of musical talent, he had even looked into lessons for the boy, brass or sax or strings . . . whatever. But David had not been very motivated to play, insisting that his mother wasn't musical and so he didn't have the right genes for it. The boy's head was in the stars, literally, and his mother encouraged the science over music. If anything she seemed to resent Jack's efforts. Whether that was from a disdain for music or a disapproval of Jack, he couldn't say.

Maybe she was afraid because she could share the computers and the science and math with her son, but if he got into music she would be lost. Jack thought of himself as trying to give the kid a gift, a lifelong pleasure, but maybe she thought Jack was trying to steal David away through music. Then again, maybe she was just being a bitch about the noise and the hassle. Oh, but that was probably nothing compared to the grief she would give him now. Now that she really hated him.

He thought of the gun again. The last time he had seen it was a Saturday just after Christmas. David was helping him steam and scrub and scrape layers of gaudy wall covering from his bedroom walls.

"There's paper inside the closet, too," the boy had said.

"Forget it. I hardly look in that closet."

"We ought to do it. I mean . . . the steamer is rented for all day and—"

"I don't want to clean out the closet. It's too much trouble." He threw down his scraper. "I'm getting something to drink. You want a Coke?"

"Sure. Thanks," the boy said, continuing to scrub as Jack left the room.

All the way to the kitchen and back Jack thought about the jobs he'd done with his own father, repairing fences and painting and digging holes, even though there was a hired man whose job it was to maintain the small ranch. There was something about boys and physical labor. They needed to work with fathers or uncles or someone equivalent. It was important.

When he returned to the bedroom Jack found David emptying the closet, eagerly pulling out clothes and boxes.

"Oh no!"

"I'm doing it all," David insisted. "You can just sit and watch. I know how to do it."

Then the boy picked up the hiking boot box that held

the gun and ammunition, and Jack lunged for it, which caused David to panic and drop it, spilling everything onto the floor.

Wide-eyed, the boy stared down at the weapon. "Is that your gun from when you were a detective?"

"It's one of them," Jack said, squatting to put everything back into the box. "It's the only one I kept."

"Tommy's dad has a couple of rifles and Reg's dad has a shotgun, but I've never seen a gun like that. In person, I mean."

"Yeah, well, there's no glamour attached to a gun. Remember that. A handgun like this has one purpose—hurting people. It's not the mark of a hero, it's a tool for the desperate."

The boy frowned in puzzlement. "Detectives aren't desperate."

"Sure they are. They're desperate to do their jobs and stay alive and keep the scum from taking over."

"But then . . . if you don't like guns, why do you keep it? You're not a detective anymore and you're not desperate."

"Good question," Jack had said, not wanting to tell the kid that there were different kinds of desperation.

And now he saw what he had been too stubborn or too set in his thinking to see before—that he *wasn't* desperate anymore. The desperation was gone, and David was the reason. The boy needed him. And, though it was difficult to admit, he very much needed the boy.

A surge of panic hit him then. Thea was just crazy

enough that she could decide to leave town without telling him. He wheeled and raced back down the path in the direction of his car. Whatever he had to do to appease Thea, he would do. Whatever he had to do to help her, he would do. Anything to keep David close and safe.

By the time Jack pulled the Bronco into his driveway he had decided to shower and maybe even dig into his closet for a decent shirt, then drive out to their house unannounced, without calling and therefore without giving Thea the chance to forbid his visit. It would be almost dinnertime when he got out there—not propitious timing given the disaster of the previous night—but he was determined to go anyway. He could invite them both out to eat as a sort of peace offering. Someplace special. Maybe the Benbow Inn.

He slid his key into the lock but the front door was already open. Odd, but he had been agitated when he left for the grove that morning and he must have gotten sloppy. It showed what happened to good sense when emotion took over. Emotion was dangerous. And he had to be careful because he was in the grip of something raw and powerful. He hurried inside. The red light on the answering machine was blinking but he dashed past, stripping off his sweaty clothes en route to the bathroom.

His back ached from the long run and the hot water felt good, especially where it beat against the scars, but he didn't allow himself to linger. In five minutes he was out and toweled dry. Pants on but still buttoning his shirt, he padded barefoot over the raw uneven subfloors, feeling remarkably alive, apprehensive and exhilarated, anxious and eager, ready to . . . what? Tackle the world again? What a joke that was. When had he ever tackled the world? He stabbed the play button on the answering machine, then went into the kitchen to sit and put on his socks and boots.

"Jack, it's Edmond. I'm calling you from the Paris airport. Mom's in a state about you, and you know how dramatic she can be when she's in a state. Why don't you do us all a favor; call her and pretend to be cheerful. I have a flight out to Kennedy and I'll be in New York for a while so I'll give you a buzz from there. And I give you fair warning—I am coming out to see you whether you approve or not so look at your busy social calendar and decide on a date. Maybe I'll even pry Dad and the twins out of L.A. and bring them along. Ciao."

His brother. When they were young he'd been closer to Edmond than to anyone else on earth, but distance and circumstance had eroded that. Then, after he left the force and changed his perspectives, he had avoided his brother, had avoided his entire family, denying himself all comfort and support. Now, the prospect of seeing Edmond was exciting.

He finished pulling on his boots. As the machine moved on to the next message he reached for the pencil beside his solitaire score pad and absently printed *Kennedy Airport. Mother. Dad?*

"Hi," said a muffled tentative voice that was barely audible over loud background noises.

Jack wrote *David* on the pad.

"It's me . . . David. I . . . ah . . . I just wanted to say . . . I'm sorry about Mom last night. She's . . ." There was a loud announcement that drowned out several words. Jack dropped the pencil, got up, and went into the hall, staring at the machine to listen harder. "Well, you know how she is. Anyway, I wanted you to know I don't blame you. It's not because of you. I gotta go. Bye." The dial tone sounded briefly before the mechanical voice of the machine announced the time as eleven a.m.

What was David doing leaving cryptic telephone messages from a public phone at eleven in the morning? Did school let out early again? Had the boy been stranded somewhere without a ride home? He tried to douse his worry with annoying scenarios.

There was a chorus of whirs and beeps as the tape went on to the next caller.

"Hi, um, this is Glory Stevens . . . the manager of the donut shop? Anyway, it's always so busy in the mornings when you come in and I was just wondering if you might like to get together sometime . . . maybe for lunch or something? I'm in the book. Or you can just come by the shop. Bye."

He grimaced and rolled his eyes at the thought of Glory Stevens leaning over him to refill his coffee, her breasts near his cheek, her spiky white-blonde hair catching the light. He'd amused himself many times by watching other male customers stare down her dress when she bent to pour their coffee; he'd seen both young and old make fools of themselves, trying to impress her with their wit as they ate their double glazed or chocolate frosted. She'd probably zeroed in on him because he was the only customer with a full set of teeth who ignored her. The problem was that it hadn't been a ploy. He wasn't interested. Not in her . . . not in any woman. Now he'd have to find another place for his twice-weekly coffee and roll.

There was another call and hang-up, then suddenly Thea's voice came through the speaker.

"Hello? Hello, Jack . . . it's Thea. Are you there? If you're there please pick up."

Again he focused on the small gray machine, listening intently.

"I know you're probably still angry about last night but . . . David didn't come home on the school bus this afternoon. Did he go to your house again? Please call me if he's with you. I'm worried."

There was a click and the time notation, then another call from Thea, this one more frantic.

"Jack! I found out that David didn't go to school this morning. Nobody saw him all day! He's still very upset with me, barely talking to me, but please, please . . . if he's with you . . ." Her voice broke. "Or if you could help me find him . . . please." She hung on for a moment without speaking, then there was the buzz of the disconnect.

Jack started to reach for the phone but there was one more message, and he waited, hoping to hear David's voice or Thea sheepishly announcing that her son was safe.

"Jack. . . ." She was crying. "Jack . . . he's gone. He's—" She stopped, then hung up.

That was it. There were no more messages. He jerked the receiver up and dialed her number. It rang and rang, five times, seven, a dozen times. He redialed to make certain he'd gotten it right. Again it rang unanswered. He slammed down the phone. Nearly two hours had elapsed since her second call. Anything could have happened in that time. David had probably shown up and everything was fine now. But if that was true then why wasn't there an answer? He tried her number again and the ringing went straight to that place in his gut that told him something was very wrong.

Damn. Damn. Damn. He should have been home. He should have been there when David called. The unlocked front door sprang to mind. David had been aware of the spare key. The boy could have come to his house after calling and used the hidden key to get in. He could have been waiting there alone in the house while Jack was out communing with the trees.

Jack rushed outside and looked under the strategic rock. The spare key was missing. It had to be David. David had been there waiting for him. He walked through the house, looking for signs that this was true, and he saw that the key had been left on his dresser. Indeed, someone had been there. What was going on? Where was the kid now? Was he in trouble? He felt maddeningly helpless for a moment, almost as frantic as Thea had sounded. The kid was not an experienced outdoorsman and if he had gone into one of the wild areas to brood he could be in serious danger. If he had walked out to the highway to hitch a ride, he could have been picked up by a psycho. Or hit by a car. If he'd taken a bus somewhere he could be standing right now in a bus station full of chicken hawks and pimps and other predators.

Think! he ordered himself.

Quickly he flipped through the phone book and dialed the hospital. A series of weary voices answered his questions, informing him that David Auben had neither been admitted as a patient nor treated in emergency and released. He tried Thea's number again, then looked up the police number and reluctantly dialed. Since moving to Humboldt he had avoided contact with local law enforcement because he wanted nothing to do with the buddies-in-blue mentality.

The desk officer referred him to a sergeant.

"Have you had anything about a boy, David Auben, white, thirteen years old, mother's name Thea?"

"And who am I talking to?" the sergeant asked in a carefully neutral voice.

"Jack Verrity. They're my tenants. The mother left several messages on my machine this afternoon. She sounded pretty worried. And now there's no answer at their house."

There was a brief pause. "You're the retired LAPD guy, right?"

"Yeah," Jack admitted. Being an ex-L.A. cop was the one defining part of his history that seemed inescapable.

"As a matter of fact she did call. I sent one of my guys out to her house, but nobody was home. And she hasn't called back so. . . . We figure no news is good news."

"I'm not sure that's the case here."

"Well . . . this isn't the first time the lady has panicked about her kid. She called just yesterday. That turned out to be nothing."

"Yeah, but I've got a bad feeling this time. Did you put him on the computer yet?"

"Heck no. Like I said—she wasn't around by the time my guy got there. And I'm not convinced the boy's actually missing."

"All right. I'm going out to her house. I'll let you know what I turn up."

"Fair enough."

8

Speeding down the highway through a pink sunset and into a flat gray dusk, Jack was gripped by an anguish that was new to him. When he was on the job he had always dreaded the cases involving children, but even in the worst, most gut-wrenching circumstances there had been a barrier, a thin protective membrane that kept him separate because the children were strangers. David was not a stranger. David was connected to him. And Jack had it all, every agony that he had witnessed so often in others—the panicky fear, the frenzied desperation, the nagging guilt. Yet somewhere inside him there was also that detached rational detective. So he was a man divided, one moment analyzing the facts like a professional, reminding himself that there was no proof of anything bad having happened, and the next tormented by possibilities, berating himself for not having seen what was coming, for having failed David.

He covered the distance in record time, slowing only when he made the turn into the shop's parking area. Darkness had descended. Insects sang and small nocturnal animals scurried and stars appeared in the black sweep of Humboldt County sky. There were lights inside the shop and a familiar red pickup sat in the parking area. The lesbos. He sprinted around the side toward the house. The carport was empty. The house was shuttered and dark.

"Jack, is that you?" he heard one of the women call.

"Yeah!" he answered, walking back around to the front of the shop. "I'm looking for Thea and David."

Both women had stepped out onto the long shop porch. They had separate last names but always appeared together and he thought of them as a unit— the lesbos. Kind of like the Smiths only more descriptive. He'd heard them refer to him as the Dick, whether based on his former occupation, his personality, or his anatomy he wasn't sure.

The small cocky one in the cowboy shirt was Jean. The round fluttery one in the caftan was Marsha. They had leased the shop from him and started the Sequoia Artists Guild and Gift Shop, taking in work and selling it on consignment in addition to stocking the miniature redwood outhouses and fool's gold jewelry that the tourists liked. Sometimes they paid him late and sometimes they annoyed him, but, all things considered, they were good tenants, and he liked the idea that the shop helped the area's artists.

Instead of hello Jean hit him with, "Why didn't you come help Thea earlier, when she needed you?"

"I just got her message. What's happened? Where is she?"

"David is turning into a typical male," Jean said scornfully.

"That poor woman went completely to pieces." Marsha's eyes were wide. "Completely to pieces."

"What happened?" he asked impatiently.

"He ran away," Marsha whispered as though the words were too awful to say aloud.

"Are you sure of that?" He was surprised to hear that Thea had confided in them; he had thought they barely spoke. "What did Thea tell you?"

Marsha clutched her pudgy hands to her ample bosom. "When we got here this afternoon Thea came out, really upset. She said he'd been mad at her and she was afraid he was staying in town or hiding somewhere out in the forest to punish her."

"She had called the police," Jean said, bluntly filling in pieces as her partner spoke. "And they *were not* taking her seriously."

Marsha nodded. "And she was sure you could help her find David but she couldn't get ahold of you. She tried and tried."

"Then I went to open the shop and there it was." Jean pointed. "Between the screen door and the wood door."

"There what was?" Jack demanded.

"David's note. He'd slipped it between the doors." Jean crossed her arms and glared at him, but then she always glared at him. "Why would he have put it here? His mother would never have found it and we weren't due to come in till Saturday morning."

Jack knew why. David wanted to make sure the note was found, but he didn't want it found too soon. He was giving himself a long head start before anyone began searching.

"Did either of you read the note?"

"I saw it over her shoulder," Marsha admitted. "There was something about his father being alive . . . finding his father . . . and she shouldn't worry."

"So Thea knew exactly where he was headed, then?"

The women looked at each other with questioning expressions, then Marsha shook her head and Jean said, "It didn't seem like it."

Marsha's face was solemn but her eyes were bright with the drama she had taken part in. "Thea ran to her house and I went with her to help. She had big tears running down her face like she didn't even know she was crying, and she was saying things, not really to me, just sort of talking to herself, things like, 'Where is he? Where could he have gone? Oh my God, where's my baby?' It was pretty bad—you know, like her heart was breaking and she was sort of confused and lost."

"But she left here," Jack said, trying to keep his voice level. "So she had to have learned something that sent her off in whatever direction she went."

Marsha nodded enthusiastically. "She went into David's room and looked around. Then she got crazy and started tearing things apart. I said I was going to call the police and tell them about the note and while I was in the kitchen dialing I heard a kind of cry . . . real creepy . . . like an animal cry . . . and then she shouted for me not to call them. That's when she must have found whatever she found. It was weird. Like she completely changed. She wasn't freaked out or crying anymore, but she wasn't normal either. She was spooky . . . really intense . . . like in one of those movies where the woman is walking up the stairs to get her head chopped off. I asked her why she didn't want me to get the cops and she said, 'They can't help me anymore.' "

"And then what? Try to remember every detail, Marsha."

"Then she started hurrying around, throwing things into a bag. No . . . wait. First she worked at her computer."

"What did she do?"

"I couldn't see. I was making her tea. But she was typing away for ten or fifteen minutes and she printed some pages."

"She must have told you something."

"Not about where she was going or where David was," Marsha said indignantly. "She acted like it was some deep dark secret. She just asked if we would watch the place, and I said, 'Sure.' I mean that was the least we could do, right, Jean?"

Jean nodded.

Both women looked at him expectantly.

"Thanks." He turned and started away.

"Are you going to look in the house?" Marsha called. "I could help . . . show you exactly what she did."

"No thanks," Jack answered. As he rounded the corner of the shop he heard Jean forbidding Marsha to follow.

It was not exactly breaking and entering, he told himself, because he was the legal owner and he had a key. He opened the kitchen door, calling "Thea! David!" just in case. Empty darkness greeted him. He stepped inside, listening, picturing the location of the light switches. And suddenly the old sensations stirred—the acute focusing that elevated every sense, the intoxicating electric rush of entering a mystery. This was who he used to be. This was the old Jack Verrity—the man he'd thought was dead.

He hesitated for a moment, asking himself whether he ought to go forward, whether the facts warranted this invasion of privacy. But the hesitation was brief. David needed his help. He knew that with absolute certainty. He did a quick survey of the kitchen, scanning the table and counters, hoping for a scribbled notation or a convenient notepad where he could do a pencil rubbing to reveal impressions. No luck. He pressed redial on the phone and heard his own answering machine pick up. He pressed the code to connect with the last unanswered caller, and that was his line too. He spread a large garbage bag on the floor and dumped the kitchen trash over it. Slowly, carefully, he picked through the detritus. There was nothing of value.

In the living room he glanced at the treadmill, positioned so that the user had a view through the barred windows out into the redwoods. He had not understood her obsession with putting metal grilles over all the windows—this was not the kind of place where houses had barred windows—but she had paid for it herself and the contractor said they could be removed with minimal damage so he had allowed it. He hadn't understood the treadmill either. She seemed to be a nature lover and had moved to the area because of the redwoods, so why didn't she go outside to do her running or walking?

He looked at the rows of glass-enclosed cocoons. He'd assumed they were David's and had been surprised to learn that this hobby was Thea's. There was a camera set up on a tripod, ready to catch the action when the butterflies and moths emerged. On the walls were large close-up photographs, some as big as posters, that she had taken of other cocoons and other transformations. Some were quite beautiful. Some were disturbing. But it was her fascination with the subject that intrigued him the most.

He crossed the room to stare at the flat, dull face of the computer monitor and realized that this was the first time he had ever seen it without the little butterflies flapping across the screen. Not once had he seen the machine completely off like this. Clearly this was a sign that she planned to be gone a while.

Overnight? Several days? Though he had always hated computers and even the idea of computers, he now wished he knew something about them. At least enough to figure out why she'd been using the thing just before she left. Marsha said she'd been typing for ten or fifteen minutes and had printed some pages. That sounded like she'd had a purpose. Certainly more than just shutting the thing down. Yet he couldn't imagine that she'd been performing any work tasks after just learning that her son had run away. It must have been something related to David or to going after David. He sifted through the papers on the desk and the contents in her trash basket without success, then went down the hall to David's room.

The kid was careful with his possessions and almost neat for a thirteen-year-old boy. Neater than Jack. Just the day before when Jack was in the hallway, the door to David's room had been open and the profusion of rocket models, constellation globes, and space books were in perfect order. Now the room was a mess. He could almost feel Thea's fury and panic in the chaos, affirming that she did not know where David was headed and had desperately searched for clues.

Which brought him back to the basic questions, because the answers to those questions would make it a lot easier to help. What was the real story? Had Thea not known where her son was headed because there was no living father to find? Or did David's suspicions have merit? Was there a live father out there somewhere? Possibly a father who abandoned them and whose whereabouts Thea herself had not known?

He sat down on the corner of David's bed, worrying over the puzzle pieces and trying to see how they fit together, trying to discover a place to start from. If Thea had been hiding, how did that fit in with the dead or missing father? Could it be that she ran away from him when David was an infant or when she was pregnant, possibly even without telling the guy she was expecting . . . and had stayed hidden all these years, either out of spite or out of fear, eventually losing track of the man's whereabouts? The possibilities expanded as he considered them and he had to remind himself that even the hiding part was based on a hunch. He had no actual proof of anything.

But he knew the smell of fear and was well acquainted with the symptoms of hiding. If he were a doctor his hunch would be called a diagnosis. Then again, even assuming his hunch was correct, Thea's hiding could be completely unconnected to the paternity issue. The father might very well be dead, just as the boy had been told, and the kid's suspicious discoveries could point toward some other secret. Jack considered Thea for a moment. Even a woman with alphabetized bookshelves could have a wild past behind her. She could have run from a creditor or an ex-lover or her own family. Or the law. She could be wanted. She could even be part of a witness protection program.

He exhaled heavily and looked around the room again. Panic. That was the key word. She had been in a panic and trashed the room looking for clues. Anyone might panic upon reading a runaway note from their missing child, but this felt like more. It felt more deeply rooted. And what did she find that sent her racing away into the night in spite of all her fears and inhibitions? What was she doing on her computer just before she left? And why had she said that the police couldn't help her anymore?

An hour later he had finished David's room and was still without answers. He gave the bathroom a cursory inspection, then headed toward Thea's bedroom. It was her private space, a room that had been pointedly off-limits anytime he was in the house. As he approached the closed door, it struck him that this was the ultimate invasion of her privacy and that he could still stop, call the local cops, and back away.

Maybe a few weeks ago that was exactly what he would have done, but today he did not even hesitate. He entered, crossing more than her bedroom's threshold—crossing an interior line. This was about David and more than David. This was about setting things right. This was about a boy who shouldn't have died and another boy who must not, would not, come to harm. And in some odd twist of fate that he refused to analyze, this was also about him, about who he was, or maybe who he still could be.

He scanned the room, seeing a haven, a comforting space to burrow into. A cocoon of sorts. All of the furniture was antique. The bed was big and high off the ground, with heavy carved posts. It was covered with a handmade quilt and piles of pillows. On each side of the bed old cabinets served as nightstands with stained-glass lamps on top. In the corner was a wooden rocker and footstool beside a small bookshelf full of hardcover volumes. Opposite the closet stood a large dresser, again solid and carved, with a beveled mirror so fogged by age that his image barely made a shadow. It was the room's only mirror. Why hadn't she had it resilvered so she could actually see herself?

As he moved toward the dresser a keen focused excitement rose within him: the thrill of the hunt, the challenge of the riddle, the detective's compulsion to dig through the secrets of others in pursuit of answers. And the thrill was more intense when the secrets belonged to a woman. Especially this woman, whose nature had completely eluded him. But then women were ever the mystery. All women. During his time on the job he had become so experienced in psychology that his behavior profiles and predictions were seldom wrong, yet he had never felt that he could fathom the female psyche. Men were open books written in plain straightforward language while women were coded messages, puzzles within puzzles with lots of tricks and traps and the answers recorded in invisible ink. Like his wife.

On top of the dresser was an intriguing feminine clutter: crystal bottles of perfume, a lacquered tray holding scented oils in stoppered jars, a velvet box brimming with interesting handmade jewelry, and more than a dozen fragrant votive candles. It was hard to connect all this with Thea. Then he opened the first drawer and was confronted with a gorgeous profusion of silk and lace lingerie. Perplexed and amazed, he stared for some moments, then dipped his fingers into the cool, smooth fabrics. These belonged to Thea?

Inside the other drawers he found the kind of clothing he expected—denim jeans and shorts, heavy wool sweaters, sweatshirts and T-shirts, flannel pajamas and lighter cotton nightgowns, basic cotton bras and panties, white cotton socks. There was not much and it appeared as though it had been neatly arranged but then disturbed, probably during the packing process. What he saw told him that she'd taken more than just a single change of clothing. He turned away from the dresser and went to the closet. There were a few loose cotton dresses, several empty hangers, and a beautiful blue silk robe that would have surprised him before, but now seemed to fit a pattern. On the floor were ragged sneakers and oiled leather hiking boots. At the back were several cardboard boxes that looked as though they were packed and sealed a long time ago, perhaps during a move, and then never disturbed again. He ran his fingers along the tape, wondering what was inside, but he turned away without breaking the seals.

A check under the bed turned up several long plastic containers, but they were packed with quilts and extra bedding. The first bedside cabinet held folders and manila envelopes and magazines. The second held lotions and miscellaneous clutter on the top shelf and a shoebox of prescription bottles on the bottom. He pulled out the box. Strangely, every label had the pharmacy information and the patient's name blacked out with heavy marker. Only the medication and dosage were readable. The one in his hand was a tranquilizer. He sorted through them all, finding most unfamiliar but recognizing a few sleeping pills and antidepressants. Years' worth of pills from many different pharmacies, judging by the varying label styles, and each label blacked over as though a crazed censor had been at work. Maybe he had been wrong about Thea. Instead of fearful and hiding, maybe she was paranoid and disturbed.

He shoved the box back inside the cabinet and surveyed the room. Did he really want to go through all her folders and open the sealed boxes in the closet? The thrill was dimming and resignation was settling in. It was entirely possible that there were no clues left as to David's plans or her destination. If so he would have to wait until she came back or contacted him or—No. No waiting. During his time on the job he'd seen too many runaways fall victim to the vultures. He couldn't let that happen to David.

But what then? Given his unofficial status he questioned whether a real investigation was within his means, but then he realized that what he was really questioning had nothing to do with status or means and everything to do with confidence.

Where was David? Was he safe? Was he frightened? He gripped his forehead in frustration, then roughly raked his hair back with his hands. Damn. He grabbed the top folder from the bedside cabinet and opened it. Inside were typed—or rather, printed—pages. Pages from her computer printer.

Butterfly: *Hi everyone.*

TimTop: *Hi Bfly!*

SamSon: *Hola, B.*

Bunni: *How you doing, gal?*

KathyXO: *Hi. We've been worried about you.*

Motorman: *Where have you been?*

Butterfly: *Haven't been anywhere. Just sleeping for a change.*

TimTop: *How strange!*

KathyXO: *Sleeping? What's that?*

Bunni: *My husband sleeps every night. He's such an odd man.*

KathyXO: *Husband? What's that?*

Bunni: *Male human. Grouchy in daylight, snoring at night.*

SamSon: *Uh-oh. Snide female talk.*

Motorman: *Let's gang up on them and list batting averages.*

Butterfly: *Speaking of gangs . . . where is the rest of ours? DrDon, Kitschy, JDVal, etc?*

KathyXO: *DrDon is on vacation and Riorita is having surgery. Don't know about the rest.*

TimTop: *Wish we could send Rio snail mail getwells. Anyone know her otherworld address?*

KathyXO: *We already looked into that. No one knows and her listing in member directory gives no clues. She's filled it in with all jokey stuff and song lyrics. I e-mailed a get-well. Figure she'll get it whenever she can turn on her machine again.*

Bunni: *Butterfly, the info u e-mailed me really made a difference. I know u went to a lot of trouble to find it and I can't thank you enough. Thank you. Thank you. Thank you.*

Butterfly: *Stop, Bunni. It was nothing. Research is easy for me.*

KathyXO: *This group is sooo wonderful. It really helps me get thru the day knowing i have u guys to turn to at nite.*

Bunni: *Anyone gardening yet? I've got spring fever.*

TimTop: *I live in a teeny weeny apt in San Francisco. No planting for me, but I have been enjoying spring in the park and cruising all the garden sites on the web.*

Motorman: *Got my trusty rototiller out 3 weeks ago. I planted green beans, potatoes, okra, tomatoes, sugar peas, peppers, onions, squash, and cukes.*

KathyXO: *Wow, can we come eat at your house?*

VIOLATION

Butterfly: Flowers? Fruit trees? You sound like you've got room 4 everything.

Jack turned the page. This had to be a printout of a chat. Reading it made the entire concept seem even more bizarre to him than it had seemed when she described it—that these people would hook up electronically and communicate through their computer screens without really knowing one another, without ever seeing each other or hearing a voice, apparently without knowing the most basic facts about each other. What kept them from lying? Motorman could be inventing his garden and TimTop could just be wishing he lived in San Francisco and DrDon could be a janitor rather than a doctor and Bunni's husband could have left her years ago and KathyXO could be a man wearing his wife's underwear. Apparently there was a directory, but it was controlled by the individual and so just another opportunity for evasion or pretense. These chat friends could be convicted criminals or transvestite hookers. What normal person would be up chatting to a computer in the middle of the night anyway?

The whole thing made him angry. There was enough wrong in the world already. This seemed to take away whatever hope there was left for civilization. And what in the hell did Thea need this stuff for? Why didn't she make friends the normal way?

For several pages the chatter went on. SamSon told

them all good night and Kitschy came to the party. Then someone called Delian typed hello and the whole tone of the conversation changed.

TimTop: *No point in me saying hi. I know who u want to talk to. That is—IF she wants to talk to u.*
Bunni: *Chill, Tim. Not our bizness.*
KathyXO: *Butterfly is my friend so that makes it my biz. Bfly . . . u don't have to talk to him if u don't wanna.*
Motorman: *Why don't you take a hike pal?*
Butterfly: *Stop everybody!*
Delian: *Will you talk to me, Butterfly?*
Butterfly: *I'm talking right now.*
Delian: *You know what I mean. Please? Meet me?*
TimTop: *Don't let him bully u, Butterfly.*
Motorman: *Tell him to get lost.*
Butterfly: *Thanks guys, but it's ok. Really.*

The printing ended and then started again on the next page with just Thea and Delian. He remembered something she had said . . . something about private rooms that people could go into. Had Thea gone into a private room with this guy? Then he smiled at the absurdity. He was assuming that it was a guy and he was assuming—well, he was assuming a lot of things. And he realized that he was feeling something very close to jealousy. He read more intently now.

VIOLATION

How are you Thea?

Fine. I missed you.

Did you?

Of course I did.

Are you angry?

More hurt. Confused.

Why?

Because . . . we were together several times a week for months and then suddenly you disappeared without any explanation.

You could just turn me off right now. Never speak to me again. Is that what you want?

No.

Are you on-line because you're having a bad night?

Yes. A terrible scene with my son and then I started into one of the nightmares.

Is David asleep now or is he still up too?

Asleep. I heard him on the computer till late . . . probably talking about me.

Cursing you to the stars.

Probably.

Which nightmare was it?

A new variation. This time there was a man carrying me and Sorry. Don't want to talk about it.

A man carrying you? That's completely new, isn't it?

I think he's been there in a vague way before but tonight he carried me and he spoke.

What did he look like?

I don't know. Big.

Tall, short, old, young?

I don't know. Just very frightening.

Someone you knew?

No. But he felt real.

Interesting. Are you still set against therapy?

I told you, I'm through with all that. I'm in charge
of my own life now.

And what was the scene with David about?

He started by being furious with me because he
wanted someone to eat dinner with us and there
were problems.

Someone? One of his school friends?

No.

Ahh. Your reserve tells me we could be discussing
Jack here.

OK . . . Yes.

You're not afraid to be honest with me now, are
you, Thea?

A little. You got so upset with me before.

That's in the past. You aren't going to cheat on our
agreement, are you?

It was nothing. David wanted Jack to stay to dinner
and I tried, but after just a few minutes of talking
to the man we got into an argument.

An argument? That sounds like a new level of
intimacy.

No. I told you. It's not like that.

Liar.

Oh God, can't you get it through your head that Jack is not anything to me!

What about your fantasies? What does he do to you in your fantasies?

He's not in my fantasies. My fantasies are completely separate from my life.

Don't we all want to act on our fantasies?

There is nothing going on with Jack. Absolutely nothing. Real or fantasy.

But what you have with me is real?

More real. Yes. Real in a different way.

Want me to help you forget your bad night?

I don't . . . Do you?

Just say yes or no, Thea.

Yes.

What are you wearing?

My long sweatshirt and cotton nightgown.

Go. Put on the silk robe. Nothing else.

OK . . . be right back. . . .

Here I am. I'm back. In the robe.

The long blue one.

Yes.

A beautiful color on you. Come put your head on my shoulder.

Thank you. I need to be close to someone.

You need me.

Yes.

Say it.

I need you.

Mmmm. I love the feel of silk. And you're so warm

underneath. Feel my hands through the silk . . .
oh yes . . . your nipples are hard. I'll suck them thru
the silk first.

Yes.

And I want to taste you all over tonight. Lean back.
I want your neck and your shoulders. I want your
earlobes.

Mmm.

Open your robe so I can feast on you with my
eyes. All your beauty, open to me, calling me. Inviting me in. Show yourself to me, Thea. Open yourself to me.

m

I want your mouth. I'm taking your mouth. Kissing
you softly, then harder, showing my hunger, cupping your breasts with my hands, nipples swollen
against my palms.

m

Is it Jack's face you're seeing now?

No!

Whose then?

No one. There is no face. There's just . . . you.

Good. Because you are all mine. You have always
been mine.

Yes.

Now I want you to go to your bedroom and drop
the robe on the floor. Lite the candles. Lay down
on the bed with oil right beside you on the nightstand.
Lay on your stomach first because I want you from
behind. Put the small pillow between your legs and

move your beautiful ass for me. Move until I can feel your wetness. Then turn over on your back. Drizzle oil on your belly and rub it around, caressing your breasts. Pinch your nipples hard. Close your eyes and slip that oiled hand down between your legs, two fingers inside, the heel of your palm tight against your clit. Me. That's me inside you. That's me moving against you as your pelvis thrusts to meet mine. We're moaning, moving together. Hotter and hotter. Breathing into each other's mouths with our flesh burning until we come together like stars exploding.

NOW GO!

"Fuck!" Jack threw down the pages. He realized immediately that it was an appropriate epithet for the circumstances because that was exactly what he'd just read. A computer fuck. Electronic sex.

"Sick!"

But why was it sick? Because he didn't like computers and because he didn't want Thea involved and because . . . just because?

And what was all that about him? Was this computer Romeo so controlling that he'd resented her mentioning Jack in some previous conversation? Who was this jerk? Delian. What kind of screen name was that? It was worse than the overtly stupid names because he suspected that it was slyly preening and egotistical.

In a fury he stalked to the living room and turned

on her computer. A large photograph of a mountain lion filled the screen. Scattered around the edges were small pictures and symbols. He had used a computer before but always in a situation where the program was already running and where there were written instructions to follow. He studied the keyboard and placed his hand tentatively over the mouse. A little white arrow jumped across the mountain lion in response to his mouse movements. He clicked a frog icon with MY COMPUTER under it. The result was not promising so he clicked the x and it vanished.

"Easy," he said aloud, trying to convince himself.

He tried CONTROL PANEL, scanned that screen and exited, then tried a picture of a pen nib labeled WORD PERFECT. From the empty, margin-lined screen that came up he guessed it to be her word processing program. The next symbol took him into a welcome message inviting BUTTERFLY to sign on and asking for a password. That was it. He clicked the sign-on button. Immediately a box appeared saying that a password was needed. He clicked the help button and read the hints and tips about passwords, about how they ought to be protected and never revealed. About how they should not be written anywhere near the computer.

Leaning back in the chair, he steepled his hands and considered the problem. Absently he read the clipped quotes and notes Thea had taped around the frame of her monitor. *"Our birth is but a sleep and a forgetting"*—Wordsworth was on the bottom. *"When we remember that we are all mad, the mysteries disappear and life stands explained"*—Mark Twain was on one corner, and *"We are the real countries—not the boundaries drawn on maps"*—Michael Ondaatje was taped on another. And centered across the top was one word printed with a heavy marker—*pteron.* Greek for something. He found a small tattered dictionary and flipped it open. *Pteron* was a Greek root word for winged. He smiled to himself. Thea and her winged creatures. He typed *pteron* into the password box, and was rewarded with a logo, then a message about initiating modem and bingo! He was into the service. Luckily Thea had not taken the password cautions to heart.

As soon as he had the option he clicked help and asked about members' biographies. Following the instructions, he entered the screen name Butterfly and got a profile for Thea.

Name: *Butterfly*
Location: *California*
Sex: *female*
Hobbies: *butterflies (I am a very amateur lepidopterist)*
Computer: *Gateway (do they really borrow Ben & Jerry's cows?)*
Comments: *My days are busy with raising a son and running a small computer research service so*

I am looking for good conversation and interesting friends in the late night hours.

Honest and unassuming with a little gentle humor thrown in. Reading it caused something in his chest. He could feel loneliness. He could feel a sad sweetness. It was not what he would have expected from her.

Next he typed in Delian.

Name: *Delian*
Location: *place is only a state of mind*
Sex: *male*
Hobbies: *rock climbing, poetry, Greek mythology, the exotic*
Computer: *IBM*
Comments: *What is this world we live in? Who are we as humans and as citizens of our time?*

What a pretentious crock of shit! How could Thea fall for this stuff? But then he recalled that the phoniest of his fellow officers were the ones who had always scored in the singles bars: Women didn't want sincerity. They didn't want a real person. They were searching for romantic fairy tales, high drama, and soulful bullshit.

He clicked the arrow on a printer icon at the top of the page, guessing at the function, and the printer hummed to life, spitting out a permanent copy of the biography.

"Delian," he muttered to himself. Except for the gender ID, which sounded right for the guy's behavior, Jack was willing to bet that the only reliable information in the profile was the brand of his computer. He scanned it again. Greek classics jumped out at him this time and his own years of European education kicked in to form a connection. Greek . . . the island of Delos . . . Delian. What a jerk-off geeky asshole. The guy was probably some dweeb who had visions of himself as a Greek god.

Jack used the mouse to rid the screen of Delian's biography, then clicked randomly, through weather reports, book clubs and kids' games, shopping, magazines and travel, at a loss as to what else he might learn. In accounts and billing he found a record of Thea's spending thirteen minutes on-line just before five o'clock. She had definitely logged on to this service during her frantic preparations for leaving, but why?

Again he resorted to the help button. After a frustrating period of groping for information, fishing it out of what seemed like a murky cyberwell, there was a reference to saving chat logs. Following that thread, he learned that Thea had filed away all her chats and copies of her outgoing as well as incoming e-mail messages.

Still fuming over Delian, Jack skimmed through the chats starting at the oldest, and saw the developing friendships between her and her fellow Night Owls through conversations that were very affectionate and emotionally open, but managed to reveal little factual personal information. He saw that the Night Owls were composed of a core of regulars, a scattering of semiregulars, and an ever-changing parade of characters who popped in for a few minutes or possibly a whole session, never to be heard from again. When Delian appeared one night it was clear that the group regarded him as a temporary visitor. It was also clear that he focused on Thea from the start. He returned every night after that, paying special attention to Thea, and then after two weeks he invited her to a private room where, much to Jack's disgust, the guy slowly, cleverly manipulated and seduced her.

Reading over the thing as a whole, it began to feel very calculated. It felt like the guy had been circling, a hawk waiting for the right prey, and like when he'd swooped into the Night Owls' room and found Thea he'd immediately begun positioning for the kill.

It would be easy to drop in and out of the group's chats using various names, since the service allowed the user multiple screen names and self-generated biographies that could be changed at will. The system was a Don Juan's dream. A guy could check out a woman and spy on her using other identities, then suddenly appear in a personality that was tailored to appeal to her. How could anyone believe that this was better than old-fashioned human interaction? How could Thea be so caught up in this? How could she have fallen for this jerk's act? But then, that was none of his "bizness," as one of Thea's on-line friends had put it. Her electronic affair had nothing to do with David's running away. Nonetheless, he pressed the print button to make a copy of all her chats, assuring himself that he had a good reason because his cursory scan might have missed vital information. Then he turned to her e-mail files: The very last one she had sent was a message to Delian.

Hi,
    I know you don't like me to contact you this way but it's an emergency. My son believes that his father is alive and he has run away to search for him. It's complicated. I've told you a lot but not everything and I don't have time to fill in the gaps now. I found a map of the area I grew up in hidden in his room so I think that's where he's going, but I can't figure out what he knows or how he knows it! His note said he had help and I think it had to be help from Jack. Who else could it be?
    How could anyone be so stupid and irresponsible, especially when David adores him and I trusted him. Is this all my fault? I don't know how to protect my son but I have to try. What else can I do but go after him tho I am terrified and I am not supposed to ever go back there. What else can I do? The police can't possibly understand unless I tell them the whole story and I can't do that and so they aren't taking it seriously enough.
    Please, please, if you're there write back to me.

David's note said that he would communicate
with me thru e-mail to let me know he was okay so
I will have my laptop and will be checking mail
often. I am so scared and alone. I don't have much
time. It's a long drive to the airport in the dark.
Got my ticket on-line and was lucky to find a flight
available for tonight.

I don't know if I can do this but I have to. I have
to. If anything happens to David Oh God, I can't
even finish that sentence. Please, if you're there,
write.

Thea

Jack cradled his head in his hands. With a heavy
sigh he scanned the titles of other recent outgoing
messages, hit the print button, then moved to the file
for incoming e-mail. There was nothing from Delian.
Where was she flying to? Where had David gone and
if it was flying distance then how did the kid travel?
Why couldn't she go to the police? And how could
she ever think that *he* was helping David on such a
destructive course?

With the printer spewing pages to take with him,
he shifted his thoughts. David also spent a lot of time
on the computer and Thea had said he did the chats
too. Maybe he had confided something to on-line
friends. But wouldn't she, as a computer expert, have
checked that possibility already? Regardless, he had
to try.

His eyes felt like they had sand in them. The computer had sucked hours away and it was very late. He signed out of the service but left Thea's computer on in case he thought of something else. As he walked down the hall he stretched his shoulders and eased the kinks out of his back, wondering how people spent so much time every day hunched over such miserable machines.

The chaos of David's room struck him anew as he entered. It was hard to imagine Thea tearing everything apart with such callous disregard. Keeping watch for chat printouts, he once again sifted through the pages that were strewn across the boy's desk. What he saw was mostly school projects. There were also folders filled with printouts relating to astronomy and dogs, the kid's two favorite subjects. There were no chats, however, and no copies of e-mail messages. Either the boy had been careful not to leave evidence or his mother had already found it and taken it with her. Jack tried logging on to the on-line service through the boy's computer but could not come up with the password. Unlike his mother David had taken the password cautions to heart, and Jack could find no clue to the magic word.

He tilted back in the desk chair, accidentally knocking several folders from the edge of the desk and spilling the contents across the floor. Ignoring the scattered pages, he stared up at the planets and stars that hung from the ceiling in mobiles, at the dog posters taped to the walls and the elaborate model of the solar system on the boy's dresser, and he thought of another boy whose walls were cracked and peeling and who hadn't daydreamed about the stars because he was too busy surviving on the earth. But somehow their eyes were the same. Hungry eyes that looked to him for help, that dared to invest hope in him. He had failed that other boy.

He glanced around the desk wearily. His thoughts were skipping now, sliding into a fog of exhaustion. He needed some sleep before he could continue with any efficiency. Schoolwork from the fallen folders covered the floor at his feet. He bent to scoop the papers together so he wouldn't step on anything. One of the folders was labeled "Essays and Creative Work—Ms. Bayer (Keep together and pick out best for class journal)." God . . . essays. He had been terrible at essays when he was David's age. Probably still couldn't write a decent essay.

He flipped through, reading pieces here and there, wincing at the boy's struggles with the written word. Then suddenly he came to something that raised the hair on the back of his neck. The essay was handwritten in an awkward cursive, obviously done in class because the kid typed everything at home. At the top was the eighth-grade heading with a recent date. The teacher had used a red pencil to scribble *Good content but what about paragraph and essay rules?*

My Daydreams

In my daydreams I have a dog named Scout who follows me everywhere. He keeps me from getting lonely and he protects me. He protects my mother, too. I go hiking and camping with my friend Jack and Scout goes with us. Scout likes Jack a lot.

Also in my daydreams I go on space missions with my secret friend. Nobody knows about my friend and nobody has ever seen him including me, but I could see him if I wanted. He is like a superhero, strong enough to climb mountains and drive a chariot to the sun, but he is a real human. He knows all about the stars and about the secrets of the universe and about old stories. He is there anytime I need him and he never thinks I am just a dumb kid. I talk to him through my computer

Jack reread it twice. *I talk to him through my computer. . . . He is a real human.* What if the "secret friend" was a real person David had met on-line? A real person who never treated David like a dumb kid—translation: a person who was more mature but did not talk down to the boy. An older friend. Possibly an adult. And what if this was the friend who helped him run away?

But that was a hell of a lot of supposition based on nothing, or at least nothing more than an ex-detective's suspicious nature, cynicism, and loathing for the whole process of digitizing and electrifying relationships. And based on his neck hairs.

I talk to him through my computer. . . . He is there anytime I need him.

The boy could have met anyone in those damn

chat rooms. Anyone. Any age, any disposition, any criminal background, any sexual appetite. What kind of adult men spent their time on-line in the company of young boys? The lonely and the insecure and the Peter Pans were certainly there. But according to newspaper reports there were also wackos and porn freaks and cyberpedophiles. From reading Thea's chats he had seen how easy it was to target someone and set a lure that had just the right bait. What if David was the victim of a creep who had befriended him, studied him, hooked him with bogus paternity facts, and was now reeling him in for the kill?

9

Waiting. What exquisite torture. Even for a great and patient hunter the hours waiting for David's arrival were an agony to endure. So many things could still go wrong. The boy could have a change of heart in midair and use one of those on-board phones to call his mother. He could say the wrong thing to a flight attendant, arousing enough suspicion for the airline to notify the police. He could choke on his in-flight peanuts or fall on his way to the bathroom. The plane could be hijacked by Texas separatists or blown to bits by a disgruntled graduate student.

Ah, but even the worrying was sweet. He had never had anyone to worry about and the novelty of it was something he could savor, turning each thought and anxious flurry into an almost sensual experience.

He made a final check of David's room, assuring himself that everything was perfect—the telescopes, the books, the antique model of the solar system, the night sky device with the seasonal domes, the mariner's clock that marked the phases of the moon and the position of the major stars, the state-of-the-art computer and the shelves of games and reference discs beneath it. He fingered the chain of keys around his neck, singled out the key to the newly installed dead bolt on the door, and gripped it tightly. David was going to be so happy in the room. He would forget that his other life had ever existed.

10

White-knuckled, Thea gripped the steering wheel, pushing the car faster and faster. The darkness was like water, like driving along the bottom of a deep and murky lake with the headlights illuminating only a few feet ahead and the windows and doors shut tight because one tiny crack, one weak spot would bring it all flooding in, all that suffocating, terrifying darkness. She couldn't let herself think about that. And she couldn't let herself glance toward the side windows and catch the eyes that were peering in at her through the dark glass.

This was the first time she had been in a car at night since she was seventeen years old. With a few exceptions it was the first time she had been out of her house at night since the rape. She focused only on David and the message he'd left and the horror he was headed into.

Mom,
  I can't live this way anymore. I know my father is alive

*and I am going to find him. You don't have to worry
because I have help with stuff and so I'm not going to
get kidnapped or anything. I'll probably e-mail you in a
few days.*

Love, David

That note had clamped a cold vise around her heart
and squeezed so hard she thought she might die. Her
son was out there alone, exposed to a brutality that
he did not know existed, facing dangers she could
not protect him from. But she had to protect him.
She had to find a way. She had to find him.

When she first read the note with Jean and Marsha
breathing down her neck, she had been shocked,
angry, frightened, and hurt, reacting solely to his act
of running away. He had left her. Had chosen to go.
Casting all her love and nurturing aside and declaring her unworthy. A failure. Declaring all the years
of sacrifice and joy insignificant. In effect declaring
that he did not love her or care about her, and that
he did not consider her important. But by the time
she'd run back to her house she had passed through
the initial heartbreak and descended into a special
hell reserved just for parents—plunged into a situation where her child's fate had been ripped from her
control. It was a hell that her own mother must have
experienced after the rape.

With Marsha dogging her steps, she had desperately sought to regain control, frantically trying to
outguess her son. How far would he have gone to

satisfy his need to act out? Would he have hitched a ride out on the highway? No. Not after that horror movie they had watched together on tape. He would not have hitchhiked . . . thank God. The bus maybe? She could imagine him using his savings to buy a bus ticket. But to where? Would it have been a random destination based on where the next bus was going or had he planned and bought a specific ticket? Mendocino? Sacramento? All the way to San Francisco? Which city would have attracted him as a place to explore and feel that he was on a father quest?

"We should call Jack," Marsha had said. "He'll know what to do."

"I've tried him several times this afternoon. The machine answers."

"But he could have come home. Want me to try again for you?"

"No. I'll do it," she'd said and dialed the number she now knew from memory. Marsha was right. From his years as a detective he would know how best to proceed. And surely, under the circumstances, he'd forgive her and help. As she listened to his phone ring she reread David's note.

You don't have to worry because I have help with stuff.

What did that line mean exactly? Help from who? What kind of help? She had spoken to both Reg and Tommy in her flurry of afternoon calls. Those were his only close friends and both boys had sounded genuinely innocent of conspiracy.

As it had all day, Jack's machine picked up. Dismayed, she concentrated on the note while his gruff message played.

I have help.

The machine's beep sounded and she started speaking. "Jack . . ." It was hard not to break down. "Jack . . . he's gone. He's—" But then she stopped.

Jack.

And she had put the phone down without continuing because Jack was the one person David knew who could have given him "help." Jack who had threatened her with his contacts and his investigative abilities.

With Marsha at her heels, she had started searching David's room: going through his drawers, feeling under the mattress, opening his computer files, trying to find something, anything that would give her a clue. She had insisted that he keep her informed of his on-line passwords so that she could retain some control of his computer use, but unlike her, he did not save chats or e-mail in a file so there was nothing for her to find in the electronic realm. At a loss, she'd stood in her son's room, looking at all his cherished possessions, weeping and keening.

"Shouldn't we call the police and tell them about the note?" Marsha had asked, and without waiting for an answer the woman had scurried away down the hall.

Then Thea had suddenly realized that her search had been based on her son as a thirteen-year-old. What about when he was younger? For years he'd been obsessed with hidden messages and treasures, begging for a little box with secret openings and a toy pirate chest with a hidden drawer, prying open other toys to make his own secret places, blissfully unaware that his hiding places were known. If he'd needed to hide something might he have reverted to those old trusty objects?

Within minutes she had torn into every toy left from that phase, and inside the supposedly sealed model of the Apollo 13 rocket she had found a folded piece of paper. And she had opened it to see a computer printout of a map. A map of the county she grew up in. And the shock of it had been like a physical blow, making her cry out and clutch her stomach.

Her knees had gone weak and she'd sat right there on the floor, staring at the map as the full horror sank through her. David hadn't run off to some nearby town to wander the streets, and he hadn't headed for the excitement of San Francisco. He was on the most destructive course imaginable. Somehow, some way he had found a trail that led him into her past—a trail that was not supposed to exist through any accessible means.

That did not exist!

She had used her own research expertise to check and had not been able to find any trace of it prior to their arrival in Sacramento six years ago. Not that she believed the task was impossible. There were undoubtedly ways to crack open anyone's past, and her

mother's trail-covering had been done with more
nerve than skill. But David knew only the basics of
information-gathering. He would never have accom-
plished this on his own. This was a task for a top-
notch hacker using shady means or a government
agency with access to secured records. A government
agency like the police.

What had Jack said in her yard? Something about
having contacts . . . Cops and journalists and people
who knew how to do things, he'd said. People who
made a profession of prying was what he'd meant.

She'd tried to recall every word he'd said but could
not because she'd been too upset at the time. He had
asked if she was hiding from David's father. That
was the key. He believed that she'd been hiding from
her child's father. David must have told Jack that
his father was alive and that she was the big bad
unreasonable woman who was keeping them apart.
And naturally Jack would have believed him, assuming the worst of her and siding with a thirteen-year-
old boy and a phantom man he knew nothing about.
That was the reason he'd been so friendly to her.
He'd wanted to get more information for David. All
that chatty conversation had just been to relax her
and make her let down her guard so that he could
blindside her with an interrogation. He must have
thought that a sneak attack would cause her to
admit everything.

And that explained why David just *had* to talk to
Jack after school. Maybe that was when Jack had

given him the map. Maybe that was when the final arrangements had been made. *I have help.* Had Jack bought a plane ticket for him? Had Jack called ahead and made room reservations? How much "help" had the man given? And how could he have done that when he seemed to care about David? How could he have given such devastating information to a vulnerable child? How could he have sent a thirteen-year-old boy off alone like that?

Anyone who cared about a child . . . Anyone with the tiniest bit of decency or common sense . . . No. As much as she distrusted men in general and as wary as she was of Jack in particular, she could not see him doing such a thing. Could David have used Jack to get information and help, without revealing his plans or arousing any suspicions? But if that was true then the information he found for David couldn't have been too shocking or damaging because that would have alarmed Jack.

How much had her son learned?

She'd ripped apart the room, looking for any small clue she might have missed. There was nothing. Just the map. Just that slender thread leading into the one place she was not ever supposed to go back to.

So she had driven to Jack's house to confront him, but he hadn't answered his door. She couldn't see into his garage to check for his vehicle, but she suspected it was there and that he was refusing to take her calls or answer her knock because of the scene they'd had. "Jack!" she'd shouted, banging on his door. "David's run away." Then she had pushed through his decaying side gate and into his backyard to look for him there, and she had pounded on the locked back door and she had pressed her face against the multipaned bay window and looked into an empty room with splintered raw flooring and dirty dishes on the counter. Then she had looked down at the table that was pushed up against the window. On it was a solitaire game in progress and a pad with *Kennedy Airport. Mother. Dad? David* printed in block letters amongst arrows and circles. Proof that Jack had known David was going. He had known and he had helped.

There was a window into the garage from the backyard and she ran to look inside. Jack's Bronco was gone. Had he taken David somewhere to catch a flight? Maybe even gone with David on the trip? Was he so desperate to be a detective again and to impress her son that he was blind to the consequences of his actions?

Oh God . . . her son . . . her child . . . headed for disaster and she couldn't stop him. And for a moment everything had spun away, leaving her suspended over the black void that had tried to swallow her before. Only now it was after her child too.

She glanced at the digital clock in the car's dashboard. What had felt like an eternity in the darkness had been only three hours of driving. She would make it to the airport on time to catch the flight, and from there she would take it step by step. She would get on the airplane alone and she would go find her son. And no amount of fear, no paralyzing panic attacks could stop her.

She stared out the windshield at the dark road ahead. "Oh God, please don't let him be hurt," she whispered, though she had long ago stopped believing in a God who listened or cared.

Jack went home to sleep. All the way there he hoped that he would find a message from David or Thea on his machine. There was nothing. After allowing himself five hours in bed, he got up, ready to tackle the investigation again. He recorded a new greeting on his machine, a personal plea addressed to David or Thea should either call, and then he flipped open the tape door to read the instructions, remembering that there was a way to access the thing from an outside phone and listen to messages. He had ignored all that before because he'd bought the machine to avoid speaking to people. Now he saw it as a possible connection to David.

He had already called the local police, alerting them as to David's runaway status and to the identities of the two women who found the note. He hadn't told them everything he knew, though. Just the most basic of facts. Maybe later he would dump everything on them, but he hesitated to give out provocative bits of information that he himself didn't understand yet. The sergeant promised that David would be put on the national computer and that was all he really wanted from them for now.

Questions plagued him. So many questions. Even the key was nagging him. Why hadn't David locked up and put the key back under the rock when he left? Had he been in such a hurry that he couldn't bother? Or was it that he had wanted Jack to know he'd been inside the house? But if so why not just leave a note? And why was the key on the dresser? If David hung around for a while he would have stayed out in the kitchen or den where there was food, television, and music. Logic dictated that the key would have been left out there somewhere, on the counter or the coffee table, not in the bedroom. Even if the kid had gotten bored and decided to poke around, he wouldn't still have had the key in his hand. The key would have been put down as soon as he came inside. So did that mean he had come in and gone straight to the bedroom?

Jack stood in the doorway to his room. The key had been on the dresser, which was the first available surface, the place where he emptied change from his pockets and tossed his wallet. If a person walked from the front door to the bedroom with the key in hand, the dresser would be the logical place to set it down. But why would David have gone straight to the bedroom?

He looked around. If the kid was tired and wanted to lie down wouldn't he have stretched out on the couch rather than the bed? Even to him the perpetually rumpled bed looked less than inviting, and David was fastidious. What could he have wanted in here? Clothes? Maybe something from the dresser? That was unlikely since the drawers held only the warm-weather items he wasn't using now. The clothes he wore every day came from the jumble of clean things piled on top of the dryer, and David knew that. Had even commented on it.

Maybe the kid was chilly and needed to borrow a jacket? There were a few jackets in the closet and, from his wallpaper removal, the boy was certainly familiar with the contents of the closet. He opened the door. His denim and leather jackets were accounted for and the sports jackets and suits he'd kept still hung at the back. In fact, there was not one empty hanger. The Irish fisherman's sweater his mother had sent for Christmas was spilling out of the gift box on the floor. Puzzled, he stood there thinking, not really studying the closet contents any longer but not closing the door either. And then suddenly, the loose ends connected. A Sherlockian moment, he and his partner would have joked, back when the job was still a heady experience and his partner was still a friend. And he bent down and pulled out the hiking boot box. His desperation box. And as soon as he lifted it he knew. The gun was gone.

Orion watched the boy explore the delights of the room. Such a facile, sharp mind. He had known from their electronic interaction that David was bright, but what he saw went beyond all his expectations. Without benefit of written instructions or verbal hints the boy had assembled the antique solar system, selected the correct insert for the stardome, set the mariner's clock, and positioned the telescope. He had then moved to the computer, where he now sat in the ergonomic chair, engrossed in the reference discs and games that were stacked on the shelves beneath the tower.

"Can I open them?"

Such guileless blue eyes. So full of trust.

"Certainly. They're yours, David. Everything in this room is yours if you want it."

"Why? I mean . . . sure we're friends and all, but why would you give me all this?"

"I want to see you happy. There isn't much happiness in my own life, but I can experience joy through you."

The boy considered this a moment. "Sort of like watching a TV show where people are having fun?"

That made him laugh and the sweetness of that spontaneous laughter spread through him, infusing him with a lightness and joy he hadn't felt for years. For so very many years. It took him back to golden days, kicking a ball through the grass with friends, all of life spread out before them like an endless party. Not just having fun at that moment but unaware that there would ever be a time without fun.

That there would ever be problems their parents could not fix.

Carefully the boy tore the plastic wrapping from a CD and looked around.

"There's no trash in here."

How could he have neglected something so basic? Of course the room needed a wastebasket. Remember the cage?

He had made the cage as a shop project in sixth grade. His boarding school hadn't allowed pets but he had thought that a beautifully made cage might soften one of the teachers into permitting something besides fish as a classroom mascot. So he had lovingly crafted the most beautiful cage imaginable, but he had forgotten to build it in such a way that it could be easily cleaned. PETS MAKE MESSES, the shop teacher had printed on the project evaluation tag. HOW WILL YOU CLEAN OUT THE SOILED LITTER? NEXT TIME HINGE THE BOTTOM OR DESIGN A PULLOUT TRAY.

A poor grade for the cage and still he hadn't learned.

"Just put it on the desk and I'll bring in a basket for you."

One after another the discs were opened, accompanied by wows, thank yous, and various other exclamations.

"How'd you get all this stuff?" the boy asked finally, taking in the entire room with a gesture.

"I ordered it on-line. You can buy anything with cybershopping."

"Jeez . . . you sound like my mom."

"Do I?"

How strange—that he should remind the boy of his mother.

"There's no phone line in this room." The blue eyes looked to him, so sharp, but so gullible. "I can't connect to the Internet, can I?"

"No, David. I'm sorry. But you'll find everything else you need. The bath is through that door, and over there behind the dresser is a small refrigerator full of snacks and drinks. There are clothes that should fit you in the closet and in the drawers."

"Whose clothes are they?"

"Yours. I bought them for you. If there's something you need that you don't see just say so."

"But . . . I don't understand. How'd you get all this stuff so fast? I just decided to come last night."

"Yes, well, it's a miraculous age. Twenty-four-hour order lines and overnight express shipping . . ."

Accepting the flimsy explanation, the boy nodded and surveyed the room in wide-eyed wonder. "Wow."

"There is one unpleasantry we have to discuss. Your door has to be locked to keep you hidden. No one else is home tonight but that's not always the case and we don't want our secret to get out, do we?"

"Okay. Yeah. I'm used to hanging around in my room a lot anyway."

How much more perfect could this be? The boy

was so pleased with the new toys that he had already forgotten his purpose in leaving home. There hadn't been one mention of the quest. And now it sounded as though there would be no complaints about the locked room either.

"It's late and you've had a big day. Why don't you get some rest. I'll smuggle you breakfast in the morning. What do you like? Eggs . . . bacon . . . waffles? Maybe an omelette?"

"I usually just have cereal, but yeah . . . if it's not too much trouble . . . waffles and bacon would be great."

"Good night then. Sleep well."

II

Thea claimed her luggage and rented a car in the bright light of a New York morning, though her internal clock insisted that it was three hours earlier and not even sunrise yet. She was exhausted. Other passengers had slept on the late night flight but she had been in a state of controlled panic, trapped in a small space with so many strangers, the nearest of whom was a man, and plagued by ragged blasts of emotion that came and went with her agonized thoughts.

Using the last of her energy reserves she navigated through the confusing maze of Kennedy Airport and out onto the correct highway. Then the exhaustion crept into numbness. Which was a relief. Like having the torturer go on a break.

Everything became distant and vaguely surreal, as though she were watching through the wrong end of binoculars. It was hard to believe she was there. David had done the impossible. He had forced her out into the world alone. He had made her confront all the old demons and take on a whole new set.

From the airport she drove east to the Southern
State Parkway and into the area she'd grown up in,
the piece of Long Island that was nearest to New
York City. In mileage, Nassau County was not far
from the city, yet it had more in common with Sacramento, than it did with Manhattan. To her and her
mother, and to others in their blue-collar suburbia,
that legendary city had been worlds away—a place
to imagine, often to be scornful of. A place to either
dream of or dread. Wealthy Islanders in the towns
to the north of theirs might have ties to Manhattan,
either through business or through theater tickets
and museum subscriptions, but people with lesser
incomes rarely ventured into the city. Aside from the
occasional school field trip her only experience with
Manhattan had been through the Juilliard application
process. Which all seemed a little odd to her now
that she was older and removed from the place.
Looking down out of the airplane window the distance between Manhattan and Long Island had appeared insignificant. From the air she had seen the
city's towers rising like stalagmites just ahead while
the green finger of Long Island stretched out below,
pointing toward Europe like an arrow tracing origin
or maybe blame. Yet, the island of her youth had
been completely removed from the city and the general consensus had been that Manhattan was distant,
exotic and unapproachable. Not to mention dangerous.

She exited the parkway and headed toward Sackville, which, she had noted on the map, was not actually a town but a village within the greater town of Hempstead. Studying the map of the island had been a surprise. When she lived there she had not been aware of the confusing designations of town, village, municipality, and hamlet or to the legalities of organization and jurisdiction. Hers had been a teenager's reality. She had studied the nation and the world in classes but was oblivious to local geography or politics.

She drove through dimly remembered areas and then into her old neighborhood. When she found her former address she pulled over and stared out the window. It was a street of tiny untended houses, saved from abject shabbiness by the grace of large old trees. The two-bedroom one-bath rental that had been her home during her high school years was even smaller and sadder than she had pictured it. She felt no nostalgia or sentiment as she looked at it. If anything, what she felt was relief at having escaped.

Reluctantly she got out of the car and went up to ring the bell. A man in a white tank-style undershirt answered and her heart rate soared. He squinted at her through the screen door, absently scratching his furred chest with a tattooed hand.

"Yeah?"

"I'm looking for my thirteen-year-old son. I used to live in this house and I thought he might come here."

"Nah." He shook his head.

"Does Mrs. Mazziola still own the house?"

"Nah. Her kids put her in a home. We rent from them."

"Do you know if there's anyone left on the block from back then?"

"There ain't nobody. Whole block's rentals now. People movin' in and out . . . just like us."

"Is there anyone else living here with you who might have seen my son?"

He turned and called, "Angie, you seen a kid around whose mother used to live here?"

"David," Thea said to the man's back. "His name is David."

"A kid named David, Angie! You seen a kid named David? Will you get the fuck out of there and answer me!"

He hesitated a moment, then stomped off into the house, leaving the door open. Thea retreated several steps and wondered if she should leave, but then he reappeared.

"Nah. She don't know nothin'."

Before Thea could ask anything else, the door closed.

She walked back to her car, angry at herself because it seemed to her that she had handled that simple task badly and because the idea of finding David on her own suddenly seemed naive and improbable. The plan had been so clear in her mind— go there and get David. Now she realized that she didn't even know where "there" was. The map she'd found in David's room had been of Nassau County. She had assumed that meant he was headed for Sackville and she had pictured tracking him through well-known streets and old high school haunts, but now she realized that her son might be anywhere in the county. Her dazed numbness gave way to a leaden despair.

She could not possibly find her son in so large an area, particularly since she did not know what his starting points were. Did he even have her old address? Did he have her birth name? Did he know about the rape but believe she'd been pregnant beforehand? Did he have Ronnie Rusket's name but not know the man was a criminal? Did he have Rusket's old address? If so he was one up on her because she didn't. Had he discovered everything, right on up to the location of the prison where Rusket was serving his time?

"Oh God . . ."

She buried her face in her hands, tormented by the questions. Exactly what had Jack been able to dig up? If David had known anything very disturbing then wouldn't his note have had a different tone? And surely Jack would have put a stop to the trip if he had learned much of the story. The man couldn't possibly be aware of the Pandora's box he was opening. He had to still believe the fantasy about a poor abandoned father . . . and for him to believe that he couldn't have learned much of the story.

Maybe . . . maybe all they had was a link to Nassau County. Maybe David had made this trip out of desperation because Jack's investigation hadn't turned up anything more. In which case she still had time to stop him. If she could find him.

She drove to a commercial strip, found a pay phone, and called Jack's number in California, ready to demand the truth from him. His machine answered. As soon as she heard the recorded hello she hung up. It was early in California and from what she knew of Jack he was usually still in bed at this hour. Had the machine been on yesterday and today because he was gone? Because he had actually made the trip with David? She stood at the pay phone a moment, so weary that she could barely sort through the options left to her.

She had to have help. Logically that meant going to the police, but she was afraid of them because they were Long Island police and they might remember the Rusket case and guess who she was. Then guess who David was. But if she handled it carefully and told them just enough, shaded the facts just enough, then maybe she could protect her identity yet still persuade them to search for her son. It was a risk. But what were the alternatives? She had to involve the police. Of course, then she had to figure out which police. There were a number of small stations scattered around and she did not know whose jurisdiction the problem fell into. A red light stopped her and she studied the map. The cluster of buildings

identified as county court and county police headquarters was in Mineola. That sounded like as good
a start as any.

She drove north and east, toward the center of the
rectangular-shaped county. When she was young she
had thought the central neighborhoods were so wonderful, each of the houses glowing with the promise
of happy carefree families. Though these areas were
still well kept and pleasantly tree-shaded, she now
saw them without the glow and she realized that the
families in them, though securely middle class, were
not necessarily happier or freer of care than the poor
families where she had lived.

At the county center she parked among ponderous
stone buildings set back behind broad lawns. It was
hard to believe that she had been the focus of important proceedings in one of these imposing court
buildings, yet she knew that she had. In an odd way
she was grateful that she had been spared from
that trial.

*The sleep of the just. Ha. More like the sleep of the
damned.*

Inside the police building a uniformed officer
leaned out of a cutout in the wall and said, "Can I
help you?"

"Yes . . . I need to speak to someone about a missing boy."

"Have you been to your local police?"

"I don't have a local police. I'm from California."

The officer wrinkled up his nose and scratched his head. "Where is the missing boy from?"

"California. But he came here."

"To this building?"

"No. To Nassau County."

"You need the Juvenile Aid Bureau. Your local police are supposed to call them for you."

"But I don't have a local police."

Another scratch of the head. "I can notify Juvenile for you and they'll give you a call."

"No! I've just flown clear across the country and I'm not waiting for someone to give me a call!"

She was startled by her own vehemence.

He turned slightly, looking over his shoulder to listen to someone who was not visible and whose voice was faintly audible but not intelligible, then he swiveled back to face her.

"Take it easy. How old is the missing boy and what's your relation to him?"

"Thirteen. Barely. I'm his mother. But . . . he's not completely missing. I mean, he ran away, but he left a note and this is where he was headed."

"Your name?"

"Thea Auben," she said, then spelled it for him as he wrote.

"Address and phone?"

"In California?"

"Where you're staying here."

"I came straight from the airport. Is there a motel close? That's where I'll stay."

"The Country Inn is just a couple miles east on Old Country Road. It's the closest."

"That's where I'll go then. Put that down as my address."

"Okay." He finished scribbling. "Just stay calm while I get this figured out."

She waited near the wall, moving back and forth in tight little steps that weren't really pacing so much as shifting. David would be easy for the police to spot and pick up. This was automobile land and a young boy walking along a commercial thoroughfare with his pack on would stick out and be noticed. She had done the right thing by contacting the police.

"Ms. Auben?"

She turned to see a pleasant face and kind eyes, hair going gray and a midsection going soft. A man, yet she did not feel the least bit threatened. Who would, though, inside a police station?

"I'm Jim Michaels, a detective with the Juvenile Aid Bureau. This isn't the way we usually do things but I was in the building on another matter."

She nodded, though she had no idea what he meant.

"My partner's borrowing an office for us to talk in so come on with me and we'll see what she found."

She followed him through corridors until a short round-faced woman appeared and waved at them.

"I'm Loreva Wilson," the woman said, briskly shaking hands. "We're in here."

Thea followed the woman into a small interior office and sat in a chair beside the desk. Wilson sat by the wall and Michaels took the creaky tilt chair behind the desk.

"Start from the beginning," he said.

She drew a deep breath to organize herself. "I'm not crazy," she insisted, worried that they might think she was.

Michaels blinked twice, glanced at his partner, then, too carefully, responded with, "No one said you were."

It was a bad beginning. Now they most certainly thought she was disturbed.

"My name is Thea Auben. I live in California now but I'm originally from the Island. My son David is thirteen. He's a very good student and he doesn't get into trouble but he's been upset lately. And then yesterday he ran away. I found a map and I'm sure he came here. So I got the night flight and drove straight from the airport."

"Is he on the computer?"

"What do you mean?" she asked, thinking that the policeman was referring to David's on-line habits.

"Did you report this to your hometown police? In California."

"I called them, but then I found David's note and I had to leave to catch the plane before they came to my house."

He turned toward Wilson as though passing her the lead.

"There's an organization," the woman said. "The

National Center for Missing Children. And there's a computerized registry. I'll go check to see if he's on the computer."

Michaels stood. "Would you like a cup of coffee while we wait?"

"Yes, thank you."

"Milk . . . sugar?"

"Milk, please."

Then they both left the room and she was alone. Maybe she shouldn't have contacted the police. Maybe that was the worst thing she could have done. What if it all came spilling out? She buried her face in her hands.

"You okay?"

Startled, she looked up to see Michaels carrying coffee in a plastic foam cup and a pink frosted doughnut on a paper napkin.

"You look like you could use this," he said as he put the doughnut on the corner of the desk.

The kindness triggered the tears she had been holding back and she used the napkin to blot her eyes.

"Eat," he said. "If you don't put food in your stomach the worrying will burn a hole right through it."

She ate the doughnut without tasting it, while he sipped his coffee. Though she was trapped with him in the small office she was not nervous at all. Whether this new horror had wiped away old fears or whether it was because he was a detective or whether his kindness had worked some kind of soothing magic on her she didn't know. But rather than being threatened by his presence she felt comforted. It was odd and puzzling. Then Wilson returned and handed him a sheet of paper.

"Yeah," he said, reading the sheet. "They got him on all right. I was afraid . . . since you said you left without waiting—"

"Yes. I did. But it's okay, right? He's there." Not that she understood why the computer mattered. That wasn't important. She simply wanted them to go forward.

"Right."

She pulled a large folder out of her bag. "I'd like to find him as quickly as possible and take him back home."

The detective cocked his head and pulled on his earlobe several times. "What have you got in that folder there?"

"The note he wrote, his picture, his birth certificate, his last report card. I didn't know what all you might need."

"Have you got any identification for yourself?"

"Just my driver's license."

He leaned forward expectantly so she pulled it out of her wallet and handed it to him.

"Just a minute," he said, carrying the license away and leaving her to wait in Wilson's company.

He thinks I'm crazy. He's taking my license to check up on me because he thinks I'm crazy.

She twisted the hem of her jacket in her fingers and willed herself to stay in the chair as Wilson scrutinized the contents of the folder.

"Looks like he's a math and science whiz," the woman commented, holding up the report card.

"Yes. I wanted you to see that he's not a dropout or anything . . . he's just confused."

Michaels returned, handing the license back to her without comment as he resettled himself. He scanned the items that his partner had fanned out across the desk, then nodded at the print of David's school portrait. "That's the same one they have on the computer."

"It is? I didn't give them one."

"Somebody did."

David had not exchanged pictures with his friends because that was considered dumb. He had given out only one picture—to Jack. But it was Jack who helped David run away so he wouldn't be handing out pictures to the police. Had the police gone inside her house and searched it?

Michaels studied the photograph as though it might tell him something, then said, "We'll have copies made and put the word out."

Wilson passed him the note and he smoothed it down on the desktop with his fingers. The words jumped at Thea even though they were upside down.

"Do you know who's helping him?" Wilson asked.

"I'm not sure," Thea answered, unwilling to mention Jack because she had heard too much about cops sticking together and she worried that Jack's being an ex-cop might work against her.

"Not sure?" Michaels' brow furrowed. "Does that mean you have people in mind?"

"No. No."

The man was looking at her too carefully again. "What do you make of the note . . . overall?" he asked.

She studied her hands. Now she had to decide how much of what story to tell them. She had never been a good liar. Her mother had been the one to spin the stories.

"David has been yearning for a father," she explained haltingly. "He never knew his." Deep breath. "We told him that his father died before he was born."

"We?" Wilson pressed.

"My mother and I. We all lived together until about eighteen months ago when she passed away. It was terrible for David. And that was the beginning of his confusion."

"How so?" Michaels asked.

"Her death was hard on him, of course, but there were things she said at the end. . . . She was on heavy pain medication, rambling, talking to God, mistaking me for her sister and David for a priest. And she kept begging for forgiveness, asking if she'd done the right thing."

Please, father, forgive me for all the lies. They were told in love.

"I tried to soften what she said, and explain it away. But that's when the questions were planted. David has been after me for answers ever since."

Wilson appeared skeptical, like a disapproving schoolteacher.

"And what *are* the answers?" Michaels asked softly.

The detective's manner was professional and neutral, but there was compassion in his eyes. She wanted to trust him. Her instincts told her that she could trust him. Except that he was a man and you could never be sure about men. Not really. Didn't she still believe that?

"The man who—" She cleared her throat and started again, forcing herself to use the phrase "David's father" though it galled her to do so because the male body that produced the sperm that caused David's conception was in no way a father. "David's father did not die before I gave birth. And now David knows, or thinks he knows that his father is alive, and he's come here to try to find him."

"In that case it looks like we should start by talking to the father," Michaels said.

"It's more complicated than that. The man never knew I was pregnant. And, though David apparently believes the man is here, he's not."

"You're certain of that?" Wilson asked, judging her harshly, assuming that she had cheated some poor man out of his son.

"Yes." Thea looked from one face to the other. "He's in prison."

As soon as the words had been blurted out she regretted them, but they had a positive effect. The manner of both detectives softened immediately.

"Oh," Michaels sighed. "I get the picture. You've been trying to protect your son and keep him from finding out that his father is a felon."

Wilson nodded knowingly. "And you wanted to wipe the guy out of your life, too, right?"

"Yes." She knew that she had told just the right part of the truth. They would help her now.

12

With the gun weighing on his mind, Jack drove back out to Thea's house. Somewhere there had to be a clue to her hometown—the direction both of them were apparently headed—and he was willing to look through everything, tear through everything, in pursuit of that elusive clue.

Did she know that David took his gun?

Why would the boy have wanted a weapon? Protection on the trip was one answer. But it was so hard to believe that a sheltered kid like David would think of arming himself.

He ignored the kitchen and living room this time, certain that what he sought would be packed away out of sight and recalling that the only unexplained boxes were in her bedroom closet. They were just as he remembered: three cardboard cartons, sealed with tape, and shoved far into the back corner, where they were nearly hidden. He pulled out all three and put them on the bed. The tape was strong and applied so thickly that he had to use a knife to open the first one. As he folded back the flaps a faint scent rose from the contents, reminding him of childhood and his mother cleaning out his grandmother's dresser after her death. He knew immediately that he had opened a box of mementos from Thea's mother.

There were snapshots of people in chairs and of babies in the grass that could have been taken anywhere. There were childish artworks and tiny infant gowns and dried flowers. There were letters tied together in a ribbon without the envelopes. They were from a man named Davy to a woman named Anna. The man was away at war, though the particular conflict was not specified and the dates at the top gave month and day but not year.

Dearest Anna,

How are you? Is the morning sickness over now? I hate it that I am not there to take care of you and that you are scrubbing up for people who treat you mean while you are in such a condition. When I come home that will all change. I think you are right and we will have to get married real quiet-like what with the baby and you already using my name and people thinking you are a married woman. Don't worry about God because he is watching all this and he understands.

The fighting today was real bad. Two of my friends got hit and I don't know if they will make it. The only thing that keeps me going is thinking about you and how it will be when I get back and we are a family. I agree with you about moving away from Rochester. There's no one in the town with any kind thoughts for us so we will make a new start. Would you like to live closer to the ocean? I have always wanted to live near the ocean.

Sincerely Yours,
Davy

All the letters were similar until the last two.

Dearest Anna,

A very kind nurse is writing this for me because I'm hit. I have been having dreams about you. Why do you say that you are ugly when pregnant women are beautiful and I know that you are beautiful? Do you dream about me? I hope you never forget me. If the baby is a boy will you name him after me?

I love you and I am trying to get well and come home to you but God might have other ideas.

Your husband in God's eyes,
Davy

Dear Anna,

I am the nurse who took care of Davy and wrote the letter for him. He died in my care and I don't think he suffered too much. It breaks my heart that he will not go home to you or see his child but you have to believe that he is watching over you with the angels. This war has taken so many good lives, including my fiancé, and so I know a little of how you must feel right now and that is why I had to write. He loved you very much and you are all he talked about. Take care of yourself and your baby for him.

Sincerely,
Althea Sikes

Jack considered the names—Althea, David, Anna. Anna must have been Thea's mother and Davy was her father. From reading the letters he saw that Thea had been named for the nurse. David was named for his grandfather, who died in some faraway war. Then he thought about the sketchy tale David had been told: that his father and mother were engaged and due to be married but that his father died in an accident. It was clear to him that David had been told a story that was reminiscent of his grandfather and grandmother's tragedy. The story of Davy and Anna.

In addition to the names the letters contained the mention of Rochester, of coming home to Rochester. A city, obviously. Rochester, England? Rochester, Minnesota?

In the living room Jack found a few general reference books. Thankfully Thea did use a few books for her fact-finding. In addition to the two cities he knew, there were also Rochesters in New Hampshire and New York.

After adding all this to his notes he cut open another box. This one was filled with remembrances of David's babyhood. Impossibly tiny clothes and miniature sneakers and little caps. Album after album of photographs. He hoped for a birth certificate but didn't find one. He hoped for some reference to David's biological father—something like the letters that Davy wrote to Anna—but there was nothing. He flipped through the volumes of baby pictures, looking for something that might give a hint of place. It was remarkable how well documented the kid's infancy was. There were several poses photographed and labeled at regular weekly intervals. Most were of the baby alone. Some included a fiftyish woman who was an older, harder version of Thea and had to be her mother. A few had various uniformed nurses playing with the baby. He looked through them for several minutes before it struck him that not one shot included Thea. Not one.

Where was Thea? Was she always stuck behind the camera? Didn't someone ever suggest that she be photographed with her child?

The pictures with the nurses started when David was a wrinkled newborn and continued for three months, according to the dates on the back, yet they were all taken in an institutional setting that looked like a hospital. The baby was still in the hospital or having to visit the hospital at three months old. One of the shots with a nurse was outdoors and there was a long brick building in the background. Against the brick were letters that he could not make out. He remembered seeing a magnifying glass in David's desk drawer and hurried to get it. The letters popped out under the lens.

WYNKOOP IN

Despite having some scraps of hard information in his notes now, he was still frustrated. He opened the final box. On top was a large manila envelope full of greeting cards. None had envelopes so there weren't any postmarks to study, but he looked them over anyway. The majority were get-well cards with one or more first names signed. There were a few graduation cards and then a congratulations card with a little note that read, "Dear Althea, I am proud to have had you as a student. I always knew you would get the Juilliard scholarship. Please come show me the new flute when it arrives. Mr. Levy."

A flute? Thea played the flute? He had never seen any indication of musical interest. She didn't even own a stereo system, and she certainly hadn't supported her son's playing an instrument. And Juilliard . . . Wasn't that the name of a famous music school in New York City? So . . . did that mean Rochester was Rochester, New York? Possibly. But then a prestigious school like that probably drew students from all over—from Rochester, Minnesota, or even from Rochester, England.

He shook his head in amazement over this piece of Thea's history. If her musical ability had been such that she'd won a prestigious scholarship, what had happened?

He lifted out a layer of abstract watercolor paintings and beneath them was a row of books, all of the same size, with colorful covers, the sort sold as blank and commonly used for journal writing. His pulse geared up a notch. Each book had a number printed on it in marker. He opened number one.

I am alive. The sky is blue. Today is meetloaf day.

And he closed the book in disappointment because it was obvious that these volumes were of a child's early writings. David's or perhaps Thea's. He pulled out the last book, flipped the pages, and saw that it was written in cursive, indicating that the kid was older. Still, he doubted there would be any information in the pages.

He slapped the steno pad against his palm. So little information. But he knew who could tell him how to take those scraps and come up with a lead. The question was, did he want to make the call and reconnect with someone from his own past? Several minutes passed. He thought of David and how vulnerable the kid was in this world. He thought of the gun. And he fished the tattered business card from his wallet and went to the phone.

"Alert Services, may I help you?"

"Alert Services? I thought this was Wally Goon's number."

"Mr. Goon is our president."

"Oh. This is Jack Verrity."

"May I say what your call is in reference to?"

"You may say that it's Jack Verrity."

"One moment please."

"Alert Services," Jack muttered, rolling his eyes.

"Jack!" Wally's voice came through the line with such enthusiasm that he had the urge to hang up. "What a great surprise!"

"The card you gave me says 'Walter Goon Detective Agency.'"

"Yeah. Yeah. But I've moved up in the world. Needed a classier name. Even I had to admit that Goon Detective Agency had the wrong ring to it."

"I always thought you should call it the Goon Squad."

Wally Goon's characteristic laugh had always made Jack think of a choking victim.

"Very clever, Jack. I like that."

"So business is good, I take it?"

"You bet. As life in L.A. gets nastier I get richer. The big thing now is bodyguards. I've got a dozen top-notch bodyguards working for me and I keep them placed most of the time."

"Amazing."

"Beats life on the streets. How are you doing, old buddy? Last I heard you were trying to be a mountain man."

"That's stretching it. I did move north. Redwoods and fishing and lots of peace and quiet."

"Yeah . . . I had a meeting with a studio exec last year and I ran into your brother—your half brother, I mean; the stuntman, not the antique dealer."

"Kyle. Ledoux. I consider him whole, not half."

"Right. Kyle. He said you'd been having a rough time of it."

"Well, remember—he falls on his head for a living."

Wally Goon laughed. "Wish you'd come work for

me. You'd be a natural in this biz, Jack. You were always into that 'knight in shining armor to the rescue' stuff and as a private that's most of what I do."

"I'll keep it in mind if you ever open an office up here in God's country."

Another laugh. "Okay, go ahead, tell me why you called."

"Do you do any missing persons work, Wally? Or skip tracing?"

"Sure. The basics never stop."

"I'm looking for a previous address on a person."

"What info you got?"

"First and last name. Birth date. Present address. Deceased mother's name. And some odds and ends."

"Like?"

"One child, a boy, born thirteen years ago in a hospital with 'Wynkoop In' as part of the name. And she won a music scholarship to Juilliard."

"Sounds easy. Give me an hour."

"No. I'm not asking you to do it. I just need you to point me in the right direction. I'm a little out of touch up here."

"Don't be ridiculous! That's a five-minute job on the computer. The only reason I'm saying an hour is that my resident nerd is having a Star Trek moment right now."

"What?"

"Don't ask. It's too weird for words."

"You do everything with a computer now?"

"You bet! It's a new age, Jack. Our lives are in

those databases now . . . everything about every one of us. Trouble is I can't use the damn things to save my life. Everybody just assumes that because I'm Asian I'm a cyberwhiz, but I have to rely on a weirdo Trekkie hacker who listens to audiotapes of figure skating while she works."

"I'll hire you then. Give me your standard rate."

"Just read me the info and we'll talk about it after we see what comes up."

Thea checked into the Country Inn Motor Hotel and immediately set up her computer to look at her e-mail. There was nothing from David, but Delian had left her a message. She opened it.

My Dear Thea,
   So sorry to hear about your troubles. You must be frantic. I know how important your son is to you. You say the police won't take you seriously because you can't tell them the whole story. . . . Does that mean you've tried to talk to them and they wouldn't listen? Where are you now? What are you going to do? Is there anything I can do to help you?
                                        Delian

Quickly she typed an answer and sent it:

Del,
   There is nothing you can do except be there so I have someone to talk to. I have never felt so alone. You'll have to wait to hear more because I am

absolutely exhausted from an all-night flight, no sleep, and so much worrying. If I don't lie down now I'll fall down. I'll E you tomorrow morning with an account of everything.

                              Thea

She was utterly drained, both physically and emotionally. With sunlight pouring in around the edges of the heavy window coverings, the room was not as frightening as she had anticipated, but night would be different. Despite the fact that the room's single window was three stories above the ground and she had figured out how to wedge a chair under the doorknob to supplement the dead bolt and chain, darkness would bring the fear. So she knew that she had to sleep as much as possible now.

She got into bed and lay there.

"Please," she whispered into the pillow, "please let David be safe and don't let him learn anything that will hurt him." It was almost praying—something she had not done for a very very long time.

Jack headed back to his house with an assortment of photographs, three of the journals, and all the printouts of Thea's chats and e-mail. He had faith in Wally's Trekkie hacker and wanted to start packing right away.

His suitcase was out on the bed but he had not put anything in it yet when the phone rang.

"Jack . . . Wally."

"What have you got?"

"Not much, buddy. Something's hinky. Althea Auben has a California driver's license with no driving infractions, an unlisted telephone which I can give you the number to, an address up there in your area, and a previous address in Sacramento, but other than that she has no trail. Nothing prior to her surfacing in Sacramento. No credit cards or credit history. No lawsuits, liens, or filings. Never made a campaign donation. No magazine subscriptions. No professional licenses. And the giant, hinkiest, reddest flag of all—couldn't come up with a social security number on her. And the Juilliard lead went nowhere."

"What about the mother?"

"Anna Auben was born in Rochester, New York, and got her social there. Nothing on her as an adult in Rochester. Nothing on her anywhere that we can find until she turns up in Sacramento six years ago, gets her first California license, lives at one address for four years, and then dies of liver cancer."

"They must have used a different last name for a while until the mother switched them back to her birth name."

"Yeah. That's the only explanation."

"Think we could be talking East Coast here, what with the Rochester and Juilliard links?"

"Bingo, buddy. Because we did have one score. An on-line search for medical facilities with Wynkoop In

as part of the name turned up the Wynkoop Institute
in New Jersey."

After saying good-bye to Wally, Jack opened the
yellow pages to look up the airlines. The phone rang
again and he lunged for it, hoping to hear either Thea
or David on the line.

"*Comment ça va*, brother? Greetings from Manhattan."

"Edmond . . ."

"You sound as though you were expecting someone else."

"Not expecting. Just hoping."

"Hope is good. I'm in Manhattan. I'll give you the
number and you can call me back later."

"No. Talk. How was your trip? How's business?
What are you pursuing?"

"Fine. And fine. And I am in pursuit of furniture
that I believe could be the work of John Hemmings.
That's highly confidential of course."

"Should that mean something to me?"

"Certainly it should."

"Give me a hint."

"He was related to Sally Hemmings. Does that ring
a bell?"

"Vaguely. Wait . . . Thomas Jefferson's slave who
we are not supposed to believe was his mistress?"

"Bravo."

"The hypocrite."

"It was bad form on his part, but he was reputedly

quite generous to the Hemmingses and without him they would have been just ordinary poor people and the chairs would not be worth a fortune."

"Sure. He was very generous—letting the man do all that beautiful woodworking for the master's pleasure and letting the woman live out there in her little slave cabin within convenient sneaking distance for nighttime visits."

"Oh, now. Forget that DNA nonsense. There's no real proof. . . ."

"There's no real proof that anything bad happened to Amelia and Fred either."

"*Mon dieu*, Jack—you are sounding remarkably spirited. Almost like your old self. What's happening?"

"Actually, I think I'm heading to New York or New Jersey."

"No! You are leaving the land of chain saws and the *mal soigné*?"

"Yes. How about a visit?"

"I'm overwhelmed. Genuinely. Is there anyone there to feel your forehead?"

"I'm not sure what my exact plans are but I'm driving to Frisco tonight then catching the earliest available flight tomorrow morning. Afterward, if you're available, I thought we'd meet. Maybe even for dinner if I get lucky on timing."

"Why don't we just meet here . . . where I'm staying. I've got a friend's apartment all to myself and it's got glorious views of the Hudson. We'll order in. That way it won't matter what time you arrive."

"Great. I'm looking forward to seeing you."

"Excuse me . . . am I speaking to the correct party? Is this Jack Verrity? The man who's been suffering from the *mal du siècle . . . the Weltschmerz*?"

"All right, you've got me. Translate."

Edmond sighed over the line. "Simply put, it is world-weariness, brother. And I was beginning to worry that you had a terminal case."

"Okay. Enough frivolous talk. I need to make arrangements."

"Wait. Tell me what this trip is about."

"It's . . . Have I ever mentioned Thea or David Auben to you?"

"No."

"They rent from me."

"You run a boardinghouse?"

"No. Remember I bought Uncle Tap's place and lived in his old house a few months—"

"How can I forget. I visited you there. You had such visions of yourself as a hermit bothered only by traffic and the annoyances of leasing out a business, but after a mere three weeks of residence you were already restless and clutching at excuses to drive into town."

"Yeah . . . Well, when I bought this house in Eureka, the market was down and the realtor convinced me to keep Tap's place awhile. I've had it rented out to a woman and her son . . . a good kid . . ."

"Thea and David."

"Yes. He's run away."

"Oh." All the lightness fell from Edmond Verrity's voice. "That's too bad."

"I'm trying to find out where he went. I want to bring him home."

There was a silence.

"He's close to the same age, isn't he, Jack?"

"What makes you ask that?"

"Just tell me, is he close to that boy's age?"

"Yes."

13

The boy's every movement and expression was fascinating. He could not stop staring, watching in wonder. There was such awkward beauty in the lithe form, and such innocent purity. Was a hunter supposed to be so entranced with the prey? No, but then he was not an ordinary hunter. In fact, he wasn't a hunter at all. He had always hated hunting. All that tramping around in the woods had been incredibly boring and the only reason he had ever gone was because it was the one thing his father was interested in doing with him.

The whole Orion-great hunter thing had become a nuisance. When the boy asked whether to call him Orion, he had said no. He didn't want to get that screen pseudonym stuck in the boy's mind. Yet, it was too soon to take any chances. So he'd come up with the name his father had called him when he was small. "Call me Sport," he'd said. "It's a nickname of mine . . . only used by people who I'm close to."

He tore himself from his watching and spun

toward the computer. "It's time to send your mother an E, David. She's probably been waiting to hear from you."

"Okay." The boy sat down in front of the monitor. "But how are we going to send it? We're not on-line here."

"You'll write it to disc and then I'll take it to a computer that is on-line and send the message from there."

"Cool. Okay."

He watched the boy open the software program.

"Can I tell my mom about how neat the plane ride was and—"

"Careful now, David. We don't want her to get any clues from these messages."

"Yeah. Okay. I'll just say I'm fine."

"Good. And you might want to remind her that you're doing this because she wouldn't help you."

"Yeah. That's right."

"You're a man now, and you're on a man's mission."

"Right."

"And maybe you should warn her that any effort by her to stop you or involve the police will just make you take evasive action and will prolong your mission."

"Okay."

The boy's fingers flew over the keys.

"How's this?" Blue eyes looked to him, seeking approval. "Is it okay that I asked about school?"

He read over the boy's shoulder. "It's just right. The school part is fine, but you know she won't be able to answer you."

"She won't?"

"Think about it, David. If I sent this the standard way from one of my e-mail addresses there would be a trail leading back to us."

"But if the return is just Orion . . . You haven't put a real name or even a state in your on-line bio."

"Under ordinary circumstances that does give you complete anonymity, but these aren't ordinary circumstances. Who knows what sneaky tricks your mother might resort to. She might get the cops to subpoena my server's subscriber list. She might hire some underground hacker to track me."

"My mother is not sneaky."

"She's been lying to you, hasn't she?"

Silence.

"Hasn't she?"

"Yes."

"So you see then . . . we have to use strict security precautions. I've got it set up so the message will be sent to a decoy, then routed and rerouted. By the time it gets to her it will be untraceable."

"Wow. How does that work?"

He didn't know how it worked because he had paid a hacker to set it up for him. "No time for explanations now. Are you finished? Is that ready to send?"

"Ummm . . . can I tell her to take care of my cactus?"

"You have cactus?"

"Just a few. It's hard to keep them healthy in our house because there's so much shade."

"Would you like cactus for your room here?"

"Sure! I especially like the ones that look like they have a red brain growing on top."

He laughed. Laughter was a gift the boy had brought him. A gift so unexpected and so precious that he felt a swelling of gratitude every time it was given. There were indeed many things that could not be purchased or demanded, and simple ingenuous laughter was one of them.

"Can I tell her about the space rocks?"

"I don't—"

"Please? Please? How can that give any clues away? They're just the best . . . the most awesome . . . and I want to tell her. She'll be really impressed and maybe she'll understand that I'm in a good place, you know?"

Laughter. "Go ahead and write what you'd like to say, and I'll take a look at it. But I might wait and include it with a later E."

Again the boy typed intently. When the addendum was finished he moved up close and read.

PS—my friend has a space rock collection! Is that
so cool or what? He's got Mars rock and moon
rock and pieces from the Mbale, Uganda meteorite

hit. Also pieces of the Ahnighito (look it up in my
books if you don't remember what this is) and even
a piece from the Peekskill, New York hit (remember that was a hit on a car in 1992). And there is
more too. Can you believe it? He says he's going
to give me some of them. Isn't that awesome? Love
again, David

"Hmm. Pass me the keyboard."

"You're deleting it?"

"No. Just making a few changes."

Quickly he took out the reference to "my friend"
and changed the part about "he's going to give me
some." Then he added a line to salt the woman's
wounds a little.

PS—there is a space rock collection here! Is that so
cool or what? There's Mars rock and moon rock
and pieces from the Mbale, Uganda meteorite hit.
Also pieces of the Ahnighito (look it up in my
books if you don't remember what this is) and even
a piece from the Peekskill, New York hit (remember that was a hit on a car in 1992). And there is
more too. Can you believe it? I might get to have
some of them, something that would never happen
to me if I stayed home with you. Isn't that awesome? Love again, David

"There. That'll do it." He handed the keyboard
back to the boy.

"Uhh . . . I don't know about that last part. That's kind of mean, don't you think?"

"But it's true and she has to be shaken up a little. She has to realize that she can't possibly give you everything you need. Agreed, partner?"

Shrug. "I guess so."

"How do you think your mother will react when she gets this?"

"I don't know. She's either completely spaced and not paying attention to anyone or she's flipping out, so I guess it depends on which mood she's in."

"You didn't bring a picture of your mother, did you?"

"No."

"Describe her for me."

Shrug.

"Come on, David. I'm genuinely curious. Please try. . . ."

"I don't know . . . she looks like a mom, but she's younger than my friends' moms. And she's sort of . . ." The boy's mouth stretched and compressed in an agony of embarrassment. "The other kids at school say she's cute or something. But it's not like she looks like a model or a movie star."

"Do you resemble her?"

"No.

"Hair, eyes, complexion?"

"Her hair is like mine, I guess . . . kind of light brownish."

"Does she have blue eyes like yours?"

"Not really."

The boy's discomfort was so great that he had to stop, though he still had questions.

"That's it then," he said. "Give me the disc and I'll send out the E tomorrow morning."

"Why not now?"

"Don't question me, you little bastard! I won't have you questioning me all the time!"

Silence.

Careful, he cautioned himself.

"Ah now . . . don't look so crushed, David. You have to learn to trust me. Trust. That's the glue between men like us. Absolute trust."

14

After a miserable sleepless night huddled in the hotel bed, Thea hooked her laptop computer to the phone line, dialed into her service, and checked her e-mail. There was no message from her son. No message from Delian either, but then he was probably waiting for word from her. She would write him later, she thought, anxiously checking the clock. Michaels and Wilson were due at their desks soon and she wanted to be there to hear what news they had of David.

She went to a McDonald's for breakfast, then headed toward the building that housed the Juvenile Aid Bureau. As she drove it occurred to her that Delian was out there waiting to hear from her, eager to hear from her for something other than a fevered late night session. Finally, he was inviting the sort of contact she had yearned for; yet now she no longer felt the urgency to connect with him.

Michaels smiled when he saw her. "We've had some sightings," he said instead of hello.

Her knees went weak with relief and she gratefully sank into the chair that Wilson pulled out for her.

"We blanketed the county with that picture," Michaels said. "David was positively identified by the manager of an ice cream parlor and a convenience store clerk. We're talking positively . . . even down to a T-shirt with 'Beam me up, Scotty. There's no intelligent life here.' "

"His favorite shirt," she confirmed, almost giddy with hope.

"These places aren't close together, but he hit them within five minutes of each other." The detective rubbed his eyes as though he'd just awakened. "He couldn't have done it walking. No bus. And we don't have street taxis who cruise out here. The only way you're going to get a taxi or car service is to call one of the companies and give them both pickup and delivery information."

"They're small companies and they keep logs," Wilson put in. "No fares were taken to those addresses. No thirteen-year-old boy was taken out alone at all on that day."

Thea waited, barely breathing.

"He's getting rides," Michaels said. "Hitchhiking is pretty unlikely here. We think he's with somebody who has a car. That means an adult or at least someone old enough to have a license."

Jack. Now it was certain. Jack had come all the way with him. Damn the man. But along with the anger came an enormous relief. Her son was not alone. He was with someone who would take care of him.

She looked up and realized Wilson was watching her, gauging her reactions.

"Nothing from any area hotel clerks," Wilson said. "That doesn't mean much though—David could be staying out of the clerk's sight. But there again he would have to be with an adult, someone who could check into a room without drawing any attention."

Wilson eyed her for a silent beat. "Makes you wonder whether he's staying at somebody's house."

"Would David trust a stranger?" Michaels asked.

"No. He's very aware. I taught him to be aware."

Wilson got up from her chair and moved around to perch her hip on the front of her desk. "You have to ask yourself, what adult would the kid have contacted? Old neighbors of yours, distant relatives, friends of friends? Who would he have hooked up with?"

"There's no one. There's really no one."

"And what about the father . . . ," Wilson said. "This con you're hiding from . . . does he have relatives or friends in the area?"

"I don't think so." Which was true because her rapist's mother had died during the trial and his wife had left him and moved away and his brother had been killed while in jail on a drug charge. Her mother had showed her a newspaper clipping that detailed the rapist's sorry history.

Michaels heaved a frustrated sigh. "You're not holding out on us, are you?"

If she told them her son was most likely in the company of an ex-policeman would they stop looking?

"All I want is to get my son back," she said. "And I will do everything and anything to make that happen."

Jack Verrity had the in-flight magazine open to a map of his destination and was trying to fix the area's geography in his mind, though he thought that he ought to recognize the shapes below him from the years he had spent flying in and out of New York's Kennedy Airport. After his mother remarried and moved to France, he and his brother had been shuttled back and forth between his father in California and his mother in Paris, always with a plane change and customs check at Kennedy. He peered out the window, trying to spot the airport, which, according to the map, was stuck out on Long Island's Jamaica Bay, a location that made it accessible to Manhattan but kept the air traffic patterns over the wildlife preserves and homes of the island's southern shore rather than the office towers and town houses of New York City.

He squinted into the bright sky. Where was the sun anyway? Which direction were they traveling? As if in answer the plane banked and turned for approach. Long Island loomed ahead and he realized he'd been staring out at New Jersey before. He glanced back down at the map and the bits of trivia printed for the area.

Long Island, he read, was the largest island of the continental United States. It was long all right—118 miles or 190 kilometers, according to the map—but there was no "islandness" to it, even from the air. It was too long, jutting out into the Atlantic like a permanent erection. He could see the western knob where the airport was located, anchored to New York by a series of bridges and tunnels, and from the plane window he could see both the North and South Shores, scalloped by bays and inlets and islets, but the thing stretched on and on so that he couldn't see the eastern end. Besides, islands were supposed to be more island-shaped. He checked the map again. Now, Staten Island . . . that was a better island. Though it looked to him like Staten should belong to New Jersey. And then, of course, there was the legendary island, the armpit of islands—Manhattan—bristling with bridges and tunnels to suck people in.

He was looking forward to seeing his brother but not to staying in Manhattan. As an adult he had visited New York City a few times, meeting his mother, brother, and the twins there because it was a convenient midpoint for all of them to gather. But Manhattan was an assault to him. It lacked the grace of Paris, the calm of Eureka, the charm of San Francisco, the dignity of London, and the freewheeling lust of Los

Angeles. It made him feel like he was not nearly cynical enough. As far as he was concerned the city had only one virtue and that was great music; otherwise it was dirty, noisy, and brutal.

The captain's voice came over the public-address system, thanking everyone for flying with his airline in the requisite pilot drawl. Jack turned the magazine in his lap and traced the route from Kennedy to New Jersey with his finger. If the car rental went smoothly and the traffic wasn't too heavy, he could be at the Wynkoop Institute by late afternoon and still meet Edmond for dinner.

When she left the Juvenile Aid Bureau, Thea went straight back to her hotel and used the yellow page listings to call every other hotel in the county and ask if Jack Verrity was registered. He wasn't. But then Jack had been a detective and therefore knew all about using assumed names and false identities and hiding a thirteen-year-old boy.

It was midmorning and the whole day stretched out ahead of her so she got back into her car and drove, looking at boys on bicycles, peering at boys in cars. And looking for Jack. She knew it would be a miracle if she found David that way, but she could not just sit in the room and wait, and she wanted to go out. She was strengthened by her own daring. Nothing had killed her. Nothing had overwhelmed her. And she had the strange feeling that she'd been asleep the whole time she was gone from this place, and that now she was waking up. The fear was still alive inside her, but it was not controlling her anymore. It was no longer the center of her existence. And with that shift the world took on a vibrancy and color that amazed her.

She drove north until she ran into the water of Oyster Bay Cove and then back south all the way to Sunrise Highway. The county was just as she remembered, neighborhoods and villages blending into one another, forming towns that blended into one another, with a giant shopping mall right in the center. It was less delineated than the picture in her memory though. When she was young it had seemed very rigid to her. North was rich, south was poor, and the middle class hovered in between. North meant civility and boys who danced in evening clothes. South meant keg brawls and boys who mooned each other out of car windows.

She'd been a South Shore girl who looked to the North Shore as the land of dreams. The land of Gatsby mansions inhabited by the cultured and the beautiful. The home of kids with perfect teeth who went to prep or elite boarding schools and spent their winter breaks skiing in Aspen or Europe. The golden boys and girls. Kids who looked down upon the lesser beings to the south, but who would occasionally come slumming, in search of trouble. And they usually found it—just as South Shore boys going north found trouble. The only neutral ground was the mall, where all classes tenuously shared the turf.

Disdain and contempt had flowed in both directions, but beneath it all, the girls she'd known had dreamed of meeting a North Shore prince and being swept away to a mansion. And even with her music, even though she hadn't been the typical girl at her high school, where tanning was considered a legitimate hobby and the ultimate goal was a big wedding at a fancy catering hall, she too had fantasized. Sometimes she had felt a bit like Cinderella, studying and practicing, then doing all the housework and cooking while her mother worked multiple jobs, and it was sweet to imagine being lifted out of her life.

Her musical ambitions and her strong faith in her future had not saved her from fantasies. She had been a product of fairy tales and grand romantic epics. Even her parents' story had been one of tragic romance. That was what she had yearned for and found lacking in the boys who surrounded her, and that was a quality that she'd been certain those unknown boys, those golden boys, possessed. She'd imagined that somewhere north in that other world was her soul mate, a sensitive intellectual who would never yell "Yo, baby!" out a car window, a boy who'd know the difference between Mozart and Metallica and who would think a day at a museum was preferable to a day at the drag races, a boy who would look beneath her shyness and cherish her.

And that was how she had felt on that liquid June day. That last day before her entire life changed.

VIOLATION

"Come on, Thea . . . ," Rosalie had urged. "You know you want to go."

"Are you sure we'll be welcome?"

"It's not like a formal thing, you know. My cousin met some Lattingtown boys at the mall and they said for her to come and bring a couple of her girlfriends. That's me"—Rosalie poked her with a sly grin—"and you."

"I don't know . . ."

"Thea! This is a real North Shore party. We can't miss this!"

She had gone to school with Rosalie since first grade. They had become especially close because they had also started music lessons together. When they reached their teens Rosalie quit music and became one of the daredevils in their high school, but still, even though they gradually lost most of what they had held in common, they remained friends. It was Thea's only deep and lasting friendship.

On her first free day after graduation, a day that felt truly free in a way that no day had ever felt before, Thea had finished the housework early and gone with Rosalie to Jones Beach. And it was there, lying on towels on the sand, laughing about high school being forever behind and Manhattan being in front—both of them headed for exciting and slightly scary schools, though Thea's direction was music and Rosalie's was court reporting—that Rosalie had told her about the party. And they giggled together, imagining what kind of beach party rich kids would have. Real rock stars. Valet parking. A white tent and ice carvings, waiters wearing black tie and tails with their bathing suits. The fantasy expanded and kept them laughing for hours.

And Rosalie concocted an elaborate plan to tell her mother she was spending the night at Thea's while Thea told her mother she was sleeping over at Rosalie's, freeing them both for the entire night. Thea had laughed, giddy with the thrill of it though not actually believing that Rosie was serious.

But now Rosalie was on the phone acting like it was all set.

"I've never lied to my mom about anything important like this," Thea told her. "Why do we have to stay out all night? Can't we just come in a little later than curfew?"

"No way. This is a major event, Thea. It's gonna go till dawn and I don't want to miss anything. And besides . . . we're bumming a ride. We can't ask my cousin to leave early to take us home."

"Oh, Rosie . . ."

"Don't you dare back out on me now. This is special and I asked you because I wanted you to have something special and I already told my mom I was sleeping over your house. I'm counting on you! You promised and it's too late to get somebody else to go with me."

And Thea had looked around the dingy home she shared with her mother, cigarette burns on all the secondhand furniture because her mother often fell asleep watching television with a smoke in one hand and a drink in the other, and she had felt the pull of that other more golden shore, felt a thrill that sent little prickles of electricity running up and down her arms.

"Okay," she'd said. "But I don't think I can look at my mom and lie."

"Call her right now at work. You can tell her over the phone and then just leave the house before she gets home. That way you won't have to look at her."

Where was Rosalie now? she wondered. What if Rosalie had spent years looking for her and had tracked her to California and contacted her son and invited him to come to see where his mother grew up?

What a fantasy that was! She shook her head at the sheer lunacy of the idea.

After Massapequa she realized that she was automatically driving toward her old home and that it was logical to keep looking in that area for David. As she cruised the streets she had no nostalgic feelings of homecoming and in fact felt a residue of bitterness. Any good memories were formed in spite of the place. She passed the high school and recalled hating it there, being a complete misfit. She would have been miserable if not for Rosalie. Rosalie . . . That was the only part of her past that mattered. She would like to see Rosalie. She would desperately like to see Rosalie.

The thought took hold and grew. She saw a pay phone and pulled into a parking lot. Rosalie's old number was one of the memories that hadn't been lost or destroyed, and she dialed it as automatically as if she were seventeen again, hoping to hear Rosalie's mother's answer, hoping to learn where her friend was now. But it was an unfamiliar man who picked up and impatiently told her that he'd never heard of a Rosalie. She tried information for any listings under the name of Stuvik, but there were none. Rosalie had loved the Island and could very well still live there, but she had no doubt married and if so would have taken her husband's name. Rosalie had not been the type to make an identity statement and she had probably married an old-fashioned sort of guy. At least that was the way Thea imagined it.

She thought of her friend's plans for court reporting school. It had sounded incredibly dull to her, but Rosalie's enthusiasm had been boundless. The county court buildings were in the complex near the police headquarters. Rosalie could be working someplace like that. If she had remained in the area and had indeed become a court reporter then she very likely had a job in one of those buildings. Immediately, Thea turned the car back toward Mineola.

Inside the most promising building on Courthouse Drive, Thea asked where to look for a court reporter and was sent in the general direction of the judges' secretaries. A number of women were busy at desks. She approached the nearest and explained that she was looking for an old high school friend who might be working as a court reporter and whose name used to be Rosalie Stuvik. The woman pointed toward a desk at the far end of the room.

"Ask Ada," the woman suggested. "She's been here forever and she knows everyone."

Thea approached the precisely organized desk, behind which sat a formidable sixtyish woman. There was no welcoming smile or inquiry but the eyes behind the oversized Lucite-framed glasses were attentive as Thea explained her purpose. Without revealing whether she knew Rosalie or not, the secretary stood, straightened the bow at the neck of her blouse, and said she would relay the message. Two steps from her desk she turned back.

"You didn't give your name."

"Althea. Just tell her Althea . . . her old friend from high school."

The woman blinked and seemed to focus even more intently on Thea, sending Thea into acute self-consciousness and a flight reaction that was barely controllable.

"You can sit down," the secretary said, pointing to a grouping of chairs near a window.

Ten minutes passed as Thea waited, wishing she hadn't come, thinking it was a stupid idea.

"Thea! Oh my God . . . Is that you!" A rounder, more sedate version of Rosalie came toward her, then stopped, face stricken as though seeing a ghost.

"It's me," Thea said, so nervous that her voice was a whisper and her knees quaked as she rose from the chair.

Rosalie lunged across the remaining distance, and Thea was enfolded in sturdy arms and the combined scents of perfume and peppermint and hair spray.

"I didn't know you were still alive," Rosalie said, crying into Thea's hair.

It was a strange moment. Thea felt stiff and unreal

in the other woman's embrace, as though she were a wooden figure. This was the first physical contact she had had with another adult since her mother died.

"Can we go somewhere?" Thea whispered, aware of the curious eyes around them.

Rosalie pulled back, smiling and dabbing at tears with her fingertips in an effort to preserve her mascara. "My judge just called lunch recess. I've got two hours."

Rosalie Stuvik had become Rosalie Flynn, proud mother of two small children, proud owner of a home in Levittown. Eagerly she had produced pictures of a girl and boy from her wallet and they lay on the table, smiling up at Thea.

"My husband's great," Rosalie said, rattling on and digressing as she always had. "Some of the other girls we knew weren't so lucky. . . . Forget about it. Bridget and Natalie . . . whoa . . . what jerks they married! Let me tell you, I was in both their weddings and I knew before the ceremonies that they were in big trouble. But I found a really nice guy. Maybe you remember him . . . Jimmy Flynn? He was a friend of my brother's."

Thea shook her head. She did not remember any of Rosalie's brother's friends, probably because she'd always ducked her head around them and willed invisibility.

Rosalie grinned and gave a dismissive wave. "Why would you? He was kind of a dork back then."

They were seated in an out-of-the-way booth at a busy restaurant, each with the lunch special in front of her. After the initial burst of emotion they had been awkward with one another, and by silent consent the discussion had focused on Rosalie. Thea knew that her friend was waiting for her to tell her story, but she had not been able to.

"You look so good!" Rosalie cocked her head in assessment and gave an approving smile. "Some girls get better. Some don't. You should have been at the ten-year reunion. Was that ever interesting!"

"You look good, too," Thea offered.

"Oh, get out of here. I look like a mom."

"But a cute mom," Thea said automatically, the old high school response popping into her head like a musical phrase. "All I got was a cheese sandwich," one of them might say, looking into a lunch bag, and the comeback was "But it's a cute cheese sandwich."

Rosalie laughed, then tentatively said, "So . . . *you* have a different last name, too. What's your husband like?"

Thea hesitated. It felt almost like a homecoming to be in Rosalie's company. She imagined that if she'd had an aunt to visit or a close female cousin this was how it would feel, and she sensed that the gulf separating them could be easily bridged, yet she was afraid to reveal too much, even to her old friend.

"I'm not married, Rosie. Auben was my mother's

birth name. We started using it a while ago. I do have a son, though. David."

"That must be tough, being a single mom and all. But there's a lot of divorced people our age . . . that's for sure."

Thea let the assumption stand without correcting it and Rosalie sailed on.

"How'd you manage a divorce with your mother being so Catholic?"

"My mother's dead. Cancer."

"Oh. Sorry."

They each focused on their food. Thea suddenly felt even more alone and bereft than she had before. Warmth and comfort were sitting just across the table, yet she was afraid to open up and make the connection.

Abruptly, Rosalie put down her fork and leaned toward Thea, face screwed up as though she was fighting tears. "You don't ever have to talk about it with me, you know. Never. Not one word. I understand having something that you can't talk about. But there's a few things I have to say to you. Things that used to wake me up in the night, you know? And I've got to tell you."

Thea waited, wishing she could disappear. Wishing she'd never found Rosalie. She had spent years forming an image of herself that was entirely separate from her identity as a victim and she did not want to be a victim in her friend's eyes.

"I don't understand why God let that happen to

you, Thea . . . unless he was using you to punish me. Why else would that happen? Why? You were so smart and talented and so good. It couldn't have been you he was mad at."

"Rosie . . ."

"I went to church every single day for a year, praying for you, asking God to please do something bad to me and let you be okay. Then, gradually, I fell back to going once a week and I stopped having nightmares and I stopped bursting into tears and my life got completely normal again, but I knew your life could never be completely normal again and so I hated myself. I mean, it was my idea to go to that party. It was me who told you to lie to your mom. And then, when I couldn't find you after the party, I was mad at you for leaving me and all I was worried about was whether I was in trouble. The sins were all mine, but nothing bad happened to me. There I was going to school, then getting a good job, then falling in love and having kids while you . . ."

"Stop it," Thea said, more brusquely than she intended.

Rosalie looked wounded.

"I mean stop punishing yourself. Stop blaming yourself." But in truth there was a time during her recovery when she herself had blamed Rosalie. That anger had been during one of the early stages when she had hated the world and everyone in it—all of which was so distant in her mind that it was almost a surprise to remember it. "Rosie . . . if I've been able to get over it, then you should too."

"You're over it?"

"Of course I'm over it. That was years ago. Three quarters of my life ago."

"But . . . You can't just . . . forget something like that. Can you?"

"Why not? Bad things happen to people all the time. Worse things than what happened to me. You get over it. That's what life is about—putting things behind you, learning to protect yourself, and going on."

They picked at their food. Thea had a heaviness in her chest. She wanted to pull out a picture of her son and weep on her friend's shoulder. She wanted the nurturing and emotional support that had been missing since her mother's death. But it was as though she faced this mature version of her friend across a great echoing chasm with no bridge in sight and without the energy to shout across it.

Rosalie lifted her eyes, and her expression was touched with wonder. "How did you ever do it, Thea? How did you come through so strong and sane? I never imagined . . . after seeing you in the hospital . . ."

Thea shrugged and attempted a smile. "I have my bad days. And I've got some pretty annoying phobias . . . night terrors, day terrors, dark-glass terrors, leaving-my-house terrors . . . I'm not much fun to be around."

"Think about what a comeback you made though. Sweetie, if you had seen yourself after all that surgery—"

"Like a cross between Frankenstein's bride and a cauliflower, no doubt."

"And now here you are, looking terrific and making jokes and raising a son all by yourself. I'm amazed. I am just so impressed."

"Oh please . . ."

"Tell me about your son. How old is he? Do you have pictures?"

Thea stared at the tabletop. The wood grain blurred and before she could stop herself tears were falling. Without a word Rosalie moved to her side of the booth and once again she was held against the warmth of another human body.

"He's thirteen, Rosie." The words hurt her throat as she forced them out. "He's thirteen."

"Oh my God," Rosalie whispered, absorbing the full implications. "Oh sweet Jesus. How have you been able to bear this?"

The story was difficult, and Thea found she too could not tell everything. She had spent too many years suppressing it. There were things she dared not dredge up, and she simply did not have the strength for a very complete unburdening. So she skipped through it, giving an edited and condensed version.

"I thought they gave morning-after pills to rape victims," Rosalie said.

"Now they might—if you're lucky and have a concerned doctor, and if you're not at a Catholic hospital. But not fourteen years ago."

"And nobody ever worried or tested you for pregnancy?"

"I guess not. Or . . . who knows . . . maybe they tested too soon or maybe the results were overlooked. My mother said that they were fighting to save my life . . . eight hours of surgery and then later more surgery and . . . things were overlooked."

"That's for sure. Nobody could believe they lost the rape evidence."

"What?"

Rosalie covered her mouth with her fingertips. "I keep forgetting that you weren't at the trial."

"You were there?"

"As much as I could be. And I followed it closely. Then a few years ago"—she shrugged as though apologizing—"I became friends with the court reporter who worked it and she loaned me transcripts to read. That evidence was a pivotal point for the defense. Apparently the hospital did a rape kit when you were brought in but then during all the emergency procedures it was lost. Rusket nearly got off because of it."

Thea nodded, though she didn't know exactly what a rape evidence kit was and the legalities that Rosalie was so familiar with were completely foreign to her. Her mother had always insisted that it was unhealthy to look back at the trial; that she should be satisfied justice was done and the vicious monster who'd attacked her was locked up. She had convinced Thea that reading about the trial or delving into it in any way would upset any delicate mental balance she had achieved. Now, Thea suddenly questioned her mother's wisdom. This discussion of the trial was not upsetting and she realized she wanted to hear more. In fact, she needed to hear more.

"Could you tell me about it?" Thea asked.

"I can do better than that. I can borrow a transcript for you to read."

"Thank you."

"I wish there was something else I could do. I wish there was something else I could have done. You know, I visited you in the hospital here, and then in Manhattan. I talked to you, sang to you, and then one day I went in as usual and you weren't there anymore and no one could tell me where you'd been moved to. And so I called your mother's number and they said it was disconnected. And I went to your house and it was empty."

"It happened that suddenly?"

"Oh yes. It was like both you and your mother had vanished. And I begged the nurses to tell me the truth because I was certain you had died but they swore you hadn't. They said you'd been moved because it looked like . . ." She hesitated. "Because it looked like you would never come out of the coma and your mother wanted you in some kind of special facility away from the public eye. I couldn't find out where though. I tried everything. It was crazy. Then one of the doctors told me I should respect your mother's wishes—that obviously she wanted you to be left in peace and she didn't want you to be the object of all kinds of tabloid stories and reporters' snooping and that if I was really a good friend I should remember you as you were and stop looking for you. So I did."

It was strange hearing the story from a different viewpoint. Thea had only heard her mother's version.

"My mother said she was with me almost every minute, sleeping on a cot, eating from a tray, and she realized I hadn't started my period. She didn't tell anyone. Instead, she bought one of those home pregnancy tests and did it herself so it would be a secret."

"Your poor mother."

"When it came up positive she thought it was a sign from God. She thought that he was going to leave me in the coma but give her a baby that would keep my spirit alive."

Rosalie nodded.

"Never in a million years would she have consented to an abortion for me, because the pope wouldn't have approved. And, of course, I wasn't in any shape to have an opinion."

"Would you have wanted one?"

Thea sighed heavily. "I used to ask myself that question. But it's impossible to know now with

David so real and so much a part of my life. And . . .
as it turned out, having David is what kept me from
swallowing an overdose of pills on a number of occasions. Then other times, having David made me want
to go swallow the pills. I would look at him, look
into his little face and see the eyes of my rapist staring back. And I hated my mother for having forced
me to carry that monster's child while I was helpless
and I hated her for making that decision when the
doctors told her it might kill me to continue the pregnancy. But . . ." She smiled ruefully. "That was what
you might call my disturbed phase. When I finally
came out of that I got to where I could look at him
and see only my child. Mine. Just mine. The only
thing in the world that had meaning for me."

"Oh Thea . . . When you vanished out of the hospital, never to be seen again, I assumed—everyone who
knew you assumed—that you never woke up."

Woke up. Everyone thought that coma victims simply woke as though from sleep when instead it was
a long and arduous process, like crawling up a
mountain blind, struggling for finger- and toeholds,
sliding backward over the rocks periodically and
then struggling forward again, all the while never
knowing how much farther the top was or whether
it was possible to get there at all. Some days her
brain had functioned and some days it hadn't. Some
days she hadn't known who she was and some days
she had thought she was still in high school. She had
tried to fight . . . to hold on, but there were days

when she did not care—when she curled into a fetal position and shut out the world, wishing she would die. No part of it, however, had been remotely similar to waking from sleep. It had been a painful, frustrating, devastating journey, and in ways she was still on it. But that seemed like such a monumental load of explaining that she did not even try.

"How in the world did your mother do it alone?" Rosalie asked. "Keeping the secret . . . getting you moved . . ."

"Apparently donations poured in from complete strangers and there were a lot of people from the original hospital—doctors and nurses, even trustees from the board—who helped her. After my last surgeries in Manhattan I was transferred to a brain trauma facility under a false name. Then, I was moved again—to the place where I eventually gave birth. I don't know how she managed it exactly but each time I was moved I had a new story and a new name. Luckily I had brain damage as an excuse, because I had a hard time playing along and keeping stories straight."

Rosalie was quiet for a moment, puzzling over everything.

"You know, when I sat there in court staring at Ronnie Rusket I pretended I was staring for you. I wanted him to feel your eyes on him. I wanted to make you a presence in that courtroom. It made me sick the way everything revolved around him and all the stories in the papers were about him and his background and whether he was innocent or guilty. It wasn't about you at all, or what he did to you. What he stole from you. You were barely mentioned. I know some of that was because they were trying to shield you and keep your name out of the press and all that . . . but still . . . it was wrong. And then they tried to say bad things about you."

"They did?"

"You'll see it in the transcript."

Thea nodded.

"Well . . ." Rosalie glanced at her watch regretfully. "I hate to say this but it's time for me to go back." She gathered her children's photographs off the table. "You didn't show me a picture of your little guy. Surely you've got one in that big bag of yours."

With that Thea could no longer block out the present.

"I haven't told you everything yet. I'm here because my son ran away . . . to come here." Thea drew a ragged breath. "We always told him his father died before he was born and we showed him an old picture of his grandfather—my dad—and basically used my dad's story. Now David has figured out that it's all been a lie, and he's here to look for his father. I don't think he really knows anything, not even that my birth name was Fremont, but he's with someone . . . some adult who's helping him, and I'm so afraid of what he might learn if I don't find him soon. It would devastate him to know."

Rosalie appeared too stunned to speak.

"I've been to the police—to Detectives Michaels and Wilson in the Juvenile Bureau—and they're helping a lot. But they don't know everything. I can't afford for people to know all this and for the word to spread and somehow get to my son." Thea leaned across the table, looking intently into Rosalie's eyes and gripping her wrists so hard the woman winced. "You have to keep this secret, Rosie . . . for me . . . and for my son's sake."

"I swear," Rosalie breathed, pulling a wrist free and pressing her hand over her heart. "On my own children, I swear." She sighed. "My God, Thea. I can't believe how tough and strong you are."

Me? Thea thought in amazement. *Me, strong and tough?*

"Will you watch for him, Rosie? Here's his picture." She reached into her cavernous bag. "It's a copy that the detective made, so you can keep it."

The expectant look on Rosalie's face froze. She stared down at David's reluctant smile, at the lank light brown hair that he wouldn't let Thea trim and the bright blue eyes and the fair, fair skin with the childish dusting of freckles across his nose.

"Thea . . . ," she said in a voice that was both fearful and incredulous. "Your son. . . . Well, I mean . . . the rapist was . . . is . . ." Her lips compressed and pulled inward as though she were trying to make her mouth disappear. Then she looked up from the photograph to meet Thea's eyes.

"Ronnie Rusket is black."

15

Thea maintained her composure long enough to say good-bye to a very worried Rosalie; then she dashed into the restaurant bathroom and vomited her lunch into the toilet. She huddled there, trembling and terrified, counting to her safe place. *Ronnie Rusket is black. Ronnie Rusket is black.* Rosalie's words echoed in her brain like the refrain to a loathsome song.

The man who raped and beat her, the man who terrorized her and forced his penis into her so violently that she was torn and bloody, the man who smashed her skull in with a rock and left her to die—that man was Ronnie Rusket. It had to be Ronnie Rusket, because he was convicted by the court and sent away to prison.

But if Rosalie was right . . . Of course Rosalie was right! She went to the trial. She looked straight at the man. And if she was right it was impossible for Ronnie Rusket's genes to have combined with hers and produced such a fair-skinned, blue-eyed child. It was impossible that Ronnie Rusket had impregnated her.

How could her mother have kept this secret?

And it was so much more than just a secret from her—it was a vital evidentiary secret that was kept from the court. Her mother had not been formally educated, but the woman had enough life experience to realize that Rusket could not possibly be the biological father of her grandson. Had her mother been so obsessed with hiding David that she had ignored such a terrible injustice?

No. She could not believe that. Whatever her flaws, Anna Auben Fremont couldn't have knowingly sent an innocent man to jail.

Could it be that her mother never learned the color of Ronnie Rusket's skin? She was not sure of the time frame but she thought that Rusket's arrest took place after she'd been moved to Manhattan for her second surgery, and her mother would have been huddled there in the hospital with her, distant from Long Island and the furor over the arrest, cut off from everyone. In the local newspaper coverage there had not been a hint of Rusket's race, and the story had not been sensational enough to make the city papers or the television news. By the time the trial was held she had been deeply comatose and hidden away under an assumed name in a far-off long-term-care facility with her mother in constant attendance, and the prosecution hadn't wanted her mother to come back and testify (had her mother said that exactly or just implied it?). God, it was so vague in her mind, because her mother had been infuriatingly evasive about it all.

"It's not healthy for you to dwell on the past, Thea, and I won't talk about it."

At the sink she splashed cold water on her face and rinsed out her mouth. Her mother could not have known. That was all there was to it. She hadn't known.

When she was able Thea went out to her car, but then she sat behind the wheel staring out at nothing, asking herself the harder questions. If Rusket did not impregnate her, then who did? She had been a virgin. There was no question that David was conceived during the rape. Was she raped by two men that night—Ronnie Rusket and a white accomplice? That sickened her. But it was better than thinking an innocent man was in prison.

She leaned her forehead against the steering wheel and squeezed her eyes shut.

He can't be innocent. There was overwhelming evidence.

Images flashed in her brain: staring eyes, and a face . . . or faces. They were indistinct though, like faces glimpsed through fog. Nightmare images.

She had come out of the coma in a state of utter confusion, with no memory of the violent attack. The confusion had been intensified by the new identity and information her mother had spun around her, believing she would never wake up to be troubled by them.

"You were in a car wreck, Allie."

"Allie? Is my name Allie? I thought it was—"

*"We started calling you Allie for short. Don't you re-
member? You were tired of Althea."*

"Was I?"

*"Yes. And we're not going to use Althea or Thea any-
more. Understand? If any of the nurses or therapists ask
you your name, you say Allie, understand? No other
names but Allie."*

So much confusion. But she remembered only bits
and pieces of it because those first months had not
been well recorded by the sputtering synapses of her
awakening brain. She wasn't sure what she had
known when. She did know that she'd had terrors
and nightmares right from the beginning, before she
had a clue as to what had actually happened to her.
And she knew that she had rejected the baby, insisting that he couldn't be hers.

*"Someone come get this baby! Why do you keep leaving
his crib in here? Whose baby is this anyway?"*

She might have continued to reject him if she had
learned the facts of his conception, but that knowledge came much later, and so she had had that window of time, bewildering as it was, to fall in love
with the infant whose very existence was a mystery
to her. For months she was told the same vague story
that the medical staff had been given—that she and
the baby's father had been in a terrible car accident.
That she had been recently married.

*"But I don't remember being married. And I don't re-
member this boy who you say I was married to."*

"You weren't married," her mother had finally hissed. *"I just told them that so they wouldn't think you were a bad girl."*

"But, Mom . . . I don't remember even having a serious boyfriend. How did I end up . . . you know."

"Well, he wasn't really a boyfriend. . . . He was a boy from that night," her mother had confided, her lips pressed tightly together and her eyes glancing upward for support.

"Are you kidding me? I went to that party and had sex with someone I'd just met?"

"Don't be crude, Thea. Just forget all that and concentrate on how beautiful and wonderful our baby is."

"Did the boy really die in the car accident?"

"The boy is . . . beyond anyone's help now."

"I wonder what he was like. Have you talked to his family?"

"No!"

"Wait a minute. Now I'm beginning to see. That's part of the reason you're hiding us. It's not just because you're covering up your unwed daughter's sin. It's because you don't want anyone to make claims on the baby."

When the nightmares came Thea was told that this was normal for recovering patients of traumatic brain injury or TBI. When the visions from the nightmares invaded her waking hours she was told that this too was a result of the injury. Of course, the therapists who gave her these assurances had no idea that she had been a victim of violence. She'd been months out of the final treatment facility and living with her mother and young son in Sacramento, increasingly tormented by terrors and phobias and haunted by images that she thought were being manufactured from her misfiring imagination, when her mother sat her down one night.

"I've been praying and praying about this, Althea. I thought that you'd get over all the frights and that handling it the way I did was best, but you're getting worse now instead of better and my prayers have led me to see that it's time."

"Oh no. What is God putting you up to now, Mom?"

"Don't make fun of our creator. This is about . . . your getting pregnant. About what happened that night."

"Are you going to tell me that I didn't have sex? That it was an immaculate conception?"

"Your attitude hurts our Lord and it hurts me."

"I'm sorry. What is it?"

"There were good reasons for everything I said and did. I had to protect you and David in many different ways and I did the best I could. So that we could keep David. And so that you would love him."

Thea waited with dread creeping into her belly.

"There was no meeting a boy at the party. There was no car accident. You were . . . abused. Forced. And then he hit your head with a rock."

"What?"

"That night a man named Ronnie Rusket—"

"I was raped?"

"The police think he was watching the party and—"

"I was raped! I was raped and beaten that night! That's what all my nightmares have been about. How could you

*have kept this from me and let me think I was crazy?
Let me think all the fear was from brain damage? How
could you?"*

"Just calm down. You'll give yourself an attack."

But she'd had one of her panic attacks anyway
because suddenly everything had fallen into place
and she knew that all the horrible images were bits
of reality, fragments of memories that had been shattered when the rock smashed into her brain. The terror was real; it was not just a troublesome symptom
of her damaged brain. From that point on she had
accepted that the tilted axis of her life could never
be righted. The horrors in her brain could not be
exorcised, because they weren't just imagination. The
evil was real. The ugliness was real. The depravity
was real. And it was all waiting right outside her
door.

But now, after so much fear of remembering and
after so much effort at suppression, now she was
certain that nothing could diminish her love for her
son, and she felt something new: an urge, almost a
compulsion to learn exactly what had happened. And
a need to know the face of the man who did it.

She drove, agonizing over whether she should go
straight to the detectives and tell them everything.
But she was afraid that revealing the full story to
them would be like opening a floodgate. They would
be required to put it in a written report and their
colleagues would know and one person would tell

another and out the story would fly. According to
Rosalie the local paper had reveled in the Rusket
trial. This new development might stir a reporter's
interest and put her son at risk of seeing the horrible
truth about his paternity in headlines.

Did Rusket have an accomplice?

What other explanation was there? Someone had
to have impregnated her.

*Where is he? Who is he? Have I passed him on the
street? Does he remember my face? Does he, too, believe
I'm still in a coma?*

A chill went through her.

Does he know I had a baby?

No. He couldn't. Rosalie hadn't known and Rusket
couldn't know and this phantom monster had no
way of knowing either. He couldn't possibly know
anything. Her mother had been so extraordinarily
careful. It suddenly struck her that an undiscovered
accomplice had as desperate a secret to keep as she
did. Perhaps more desperate. He needed the past—
his guilt as a rapist—to stay buried.

Rosalie had promised to get the transcripts for her,
but she had to have some answers now. If not from
the official trial records then at least from the news
articles that were written while she was in her twi-
light state. She could hook up her computer and do
an on-line search through major news archives, but
she remembered her mother saying that the story had
generated only local coverage, and small newspapers
were not carried by any information sources. That

meant she would have to go to a library. She pulled to the side of the road and took the maps and guides from the glove compartment. There was a library noted that was not too far from her hotel. She decided to stop by her room and check for an e-mail from David again, then go directly to research in the periodical section.

Thea entered her room hoping to see the red light on her telephone signaling a message from the detectives, but there was no light. No miracle. Once again she plugged in and set up her laptop. Why had her son specified e-mail in his note rather than simply saying he would call her?

The detectives had asked that very question and she had assured them that it was not unusual because her son was so immersed in electronic communications that he was more comfortable with e-mail than telephones. She had gone on to say that David had probably taken it for granted that New York would have cybercafes and copy shops that offered cheap on-line access by the minute. Maybe he had also believed that e-mail was less traceable than phone calls.

Now, as she connected to her service, her assurance wavered. Despite David's computer mania, his using e-mail did seem illogical.

Her heart leapt when she saw the mail symbol flashing. It could be Delian, she warned herself, but she clicked open the message and saw:

Dear Mom,

I told you I would be fine and I am. Don't try to look for me or stop me because it will just make me hide from you more. I am doing something that you would never let me do which is find out the truth. You made me do this because you wouldn't be straight with me. I hope you aren't getting all crazy and calling the police and making this into a missing kid kind of thing because it's not. I'M NOT A BABY and I'm not missing. There is a lot to do where I am and it's going to be pretty cool here. Is the school mad? Are they going to let me graduate?

Love, David

PS—would you please take care of the cactus on my windowsill while I'm gone? Don't water them too much! I usually check the national weather and only water when there is rain in the Arizona desert.

She read it several times, relieved and grateful at first, then furious. How could Jack facilitate this? Not only helping but making it fun! Encouraging David to think that this was a grand and heroic quest.

Jack had always seemed so stable and reliable in his treatment of her son. But then . . . he was a man. And like all men he was unfathomable, unknowable, governed by instincts and needs that she couldn't understand, by dangerous urges and an inborn aggressiveness, and by a bravado, a certainty—a sense of entitlement—that allowed for intimidating and repellent acts. Men were never to be trusted. Men were the source of terror and misery. She should have sheltered her son better. Not only would he suffer from this man's arrogant thoughtlessness, but he would no doubt learn the behavior.

She read the message again, then examined the return e-mail address at the top. It had been sent through something called whizbox.com. She copied the address, saved David's message to disc, and then sent a note to whizbox asking where they were located and how their service worked.

Her finger was poised at the laptop's touch pad to close the program when she realized that there was another unread message. It was from Delian saying he was worried and she should let him know how she was doing. Though she was in a rush to leave for the library, guilt made her compose a brief response. Just days ago she had wanted to lean on him for support, but now communicating with him had transformed into an obligation that she could barely spare the time for.

Del,

Sorry not to have replied sooner. Have heard from David by e-mail so at least I know he's okay. Juvenile detectives here are helping. Two sightings of David confirmed. I'll get back to you.

Thea

Dread hatched in the pit of her stomach as she parked at the library. This was it. After all the years of denial and hiding, she was going to stare her nightmare in the face.

She sat down at the microfilm reader with a stack of reels and began the search, fast-forwarding to June 28. The big story was about a terrible car accident that killed one area teen and injured four others. It featured a photograph of distraught parents arriving at the hospital and another photo of the smashed automobile. Then there was a related story about a proposed crackdown on wild parties and teen use of alcohol and drugs. There were articles about zoning and development, articles about traffic problems, and articles about local politics. On the third page, with stories about water quality in the Long Island Sound and area anger over beach closings, she found the headline FIRE DESTROYS HISTORIC MANSION; TWO INJURED. And she almost laughed because it was not what she had imagined at all. The girl with the caved-in head was an afterthought—relegated to page three and not nearly as important as the mansion that was burned.

LATTINGTOWN, L.I.—Two people were injured in an early morning fire that demolished one of the North Shore's finest historic buildings, a house previously owned by the Vandeveer family. The injured are Ronald Malcolm Rusket, 21, a resident of Valley Stream, and an unidentified female who is estimated to be between 16 and 18 years of age.

VIOLATION

Firefighters responded to the 3:00 a.m. blaze when they were summoned by a Lattingtown man. The man, whose name was not available at press time, told firefighters that he was out searching for his lost dog and saw smoke and flames through the trees. The firefighters found Mr. Rusket and the unidentified girl collapsed on the ground outside the mansion.

The house, which was originally named Windmere, had come to be known to historians as Vandeveer House after the original owners. Local residents commonly referred to it as "The Castle" due to the gothic architecture. Recently it has been the center of a battle between the Island Preservation Foundation and the North Shore 2000 Development Group. Neither organization could be reached for comment; however, a police source said that the house had been a magnet for teens and vandals. A fire department spokesperson announced that the mansion was completely destroyed and that the blaze is being investigated.

She plugged coins into the machine and made a large copy of the entire page because she couldn't get the controls on the machine to do anything else. Then she scrolled forward to June 29 and found ARSON SUSPECTED IN CASTLE BLAZE.

LATTINGTOWN, L.I.—Arson is being investigated as the cause of the blaze that destroyed one of the North Shore's finest historic homes yesterday. Firefighters were summoned at 3:00 a.m. but were not able to save any part of the mansion.

Injured in the predawn fire were Ronald Malcolm Rusket, 21, of Valley Stream, and a female companion. Police will not say whether the female has been identified but a spokesman for Vale Memorial Hospital reports that the woman has undergone brain surgery and is in extremely critical condition. Mr. Rusket was treated for smoke inhalation and released.

"They were having one of those parties where they sneak onto a private beach when the owners are out of town, and they were racing their cars on the roads," said Mr. John Nelson, the area resident who called firefighters. "Some of those drunk kids must have gone up to The Castle and started the fire. It's happened before," reported Mr. Nelson.

She fed the machine her coins and began the copying process, thinking that the gap in identifying her must have come because her mother thought she was safely asleep at Rosalie's house and Rosalie thought she had left the party on her own and her purse had disappeared or been consumed by the fire. She was surprised at how easy it was for her to read the articles. They were neither frightening nor disturbing and her dread had been replaced by an intense curiosity. She moved on to the next day's coverage and saw HERO SAVED UNKNOWN WOMAN FROM FIRE.

LATTINGTOWN, L.I.—Ronnie Rusket, 21, of Valley Stream, is being hailed as a hero for saving the life of a woman in the June 28 fire that destroyed an area landmark.

Mr. Rusket, who is recovering at his mother's

home, saw smoke through the trees. When he went to investigate he heard moans coming from inside the burning house. He entered the house through an uncovered window and located the unconscious woman.

"I threw her over my shoulder like I'd seen the firemen do in the movies," Mr. Rusket said. "That smoke was so thick I thought I'd never make it back out but I guess God was watching."

Authorities are still not releasing the name of the woman though it has been confirmed that her identity has been established. A reliable source reports that the woman has been airlifted from Vale Memorial Hospital on Long Island to an undisclosed hospital in Manhattan where she will undergo further surgery. Questions remain as to what the woman was doing inside the house, whether she was alone, and whether she was involved in starting the fire.

Several area churches and organizations have started a hero fund that will be presented to Mr. Rusket in an upcoming ceremony.

Thea made the copy and hurried on to read RAPE AND ASSAULT IN CASTLE FIRE.

LATTINGTOWN, L.I.—Police have revealed that the woman injured in the June 28 fire that destroyed the mansion known as The Castle was the victim of a brutal sexual assault. She is a 17-year-old resident of Nassau County and a recent high school graduate.

Medical sources report that the victim has undergone a second major brain operation and is comatose. Dr. William Guerin, the noted neurosurgeon who performed the initial eight-hour surgery, said,

"For this type of brain injury the incidence of recovery is so small that I cannot give a percentage on it."

Sgt. Henry Wall, a police spokesman, said that an extensive investigation is in progress and area teens who attended the beach party that night are being questioned as to whether they saw anything suspicious.

"We're looking at every possibility," Sgt. Wall said. "The girl could have been assaulted elsewhere and then taken to the house or she could have been attacked at the house. Either way, it appears that the fire was set to cover up the crime and that the attacker intended for his victim to die in the fire."

Friends of the young woman expressed surprise at the crime. "She was the quiet type who never hung around or went out much," said a fellow student. A former teacher reports that the victim is a very talented musician and has a scholarship to study music at Juilliard in Manhattan. Her goal is to play with one of the noted symphony orchestras.

Suddenly her chest ached and there was a burning in her eyes that she could not blink away. The next story was one that her mother had showed her years ago—the one where the police finally announced that Ronald Malcolm Rusket was the main suspect in the ongoing drama. She copied it, then skipped through the subsequent days, copying the pages that contained headlines without reading the stories. Then she changed reels, intending to copy the coverage of the trial in the same way, but before she found the first article a tightness gripped her chest and the air in the library seemed stale and overheated.

VIOLATION

She escaped out into the fresh air and breathed deeply as she carried the copies to the car.

Not quite as tough as you thought, huh? her interior voice needled as she turned the key and slammed the car into gear.

16

The car rental was a problem and then there were traffic jams and it was nearing six by the time Jack turned into the Wynkoop Institute's parking lot. He took out the pictures he had brought with him and indeed it was the same building. The only difference was the size of the trees. They had grown since the photo was taken.

Using the rearview mirror, he put on a tie for the first time in years and was amused at the way his fingers recalled the maneuvers. He got out of the car, pulling on a navy sport coat that had been at the back of his closet ever since he moved to Eureka, and slid the pictures into the breast pocket. He had no idea how he would play the scene. Even if he'd had the weight of a police department behind him he doubted that the Institute would be very forthcoming about a previous patient, and he did not have the weight of a police department. He had no official standing at all.

Instead of going to the front he slipped around the

side of the building and saw a carefully manicured expanse of lawn and a curving series of terraces connected by ramps. No one was in the area. If this was a hospital then it had to be one of those exclusive ultraprivate places. He edged along the back wall, through the groupings of potted plants and the scattering of chairs and chaise longues. There was a large pair of French doors. He tried them and they were unlocked. If he could find a storage area for old records . . . Surely they still had to keep charts and medical reports. Everything couldn't be on computer, could it?

He stepped into a large open room with a piano and a scattering of chairs in it. This was not the bustling health care facility he had expected. He wondered if it was one of those specialized birthing centers he had read about. Noises came from other parts of the building and he caught a faint whiff of food. Dinnertime. Instant mashed potatoes and red Jell-O for everyone. Even to his cast-iron palate, the food he'd been served in the hospital had been abominable . . . or abdominal, as his father had pronounced it.

He crossed the floor, heading for one of three doorways. A food cart rattled down the hall toward him and he had to duck back to avoid being seen. When the hall cleared he slipped out. Most of the numbered doors were closed. Many of them had name tags slid into metal holders beneath the numbers. He tried the knob on one and it opened. Softly he knocked. When there was no answer he peeked in. Inside, looking very small and contorted on the bed, was a patient so strung with wires and tubes that he looked like part of the machines humming by his bedside.

"Sorry," Jack told him, but the boy was beyond hearing. It was not a scene from a birthing center.

Farther down the hall was an open door and he saw a man seated beside the bed of a motionless woman. "It was a beautiful day out today, Darlene, and the kids helped me work in the garden. I think Kevin might have gotten a little sunburn but I swear I remembered to put the sunscreen on him just like you always say to." The man started crying and Jack quickly moved on. This was definitely not a maternity hospital. It looked like a warehouse for hard luck cases. Maybe it had changed management over the years. That was probably bad news. After searching for several minutes he decided to forget the stored records approach and try something else.

He circled back to the patio doors, let himself out, and went around to the front as though he'd just arrived.

"I'm here to see your facility," he told the receptionist. "For a patient."

"We take very good care of them here, sir."

"I'm sure you do."

Within moments a smiling man in a white coat appeared to greet him.

"I'm Dr. Connor."

"Jack Verrity."

They shook hands.

"Let's go to my office, shall we?"

As he sat opposite the doctor's desk Jack scanned the room. It was very showy. Lots of leather-bound books, awards, and certificates. A sleek computer sat off to the side on its own small desk. There were no file cabinets. What was wrong with people?

"How did you hear about us?"

"I read something on the Internet and thought it sounded like a great place."

"Ah, yes." Connor beamed. "Our new web page. I am delighted to hear that it is already being noticed."

Jack smiled.

"May I inquire about your patient?"

"My aunt. She's actually younger than I am."

"I'm very sorry." The doctor produced a booklet from his desk drawer. "This will give you more information on our facility."

Jack thumbed it. The letters TBI jumped out repeatedly from the text. "Yes, well, I was wondering if I might also have a tour?"

"Certainly! However, I was just leaving and I am afraid I can't delay. Dr. Jennings will be here shortly if you can wait a bit?"

Jack glanced at his watch. "I don't have much time. Isn't there a nurse or someone who can show me around?"

"Let me see."

Connor left the room and came back with a woman

dressed in what might have been a nurse's pantsuit except that it was bright pink.

"Bren can show you our facility."

The woman smiled nervously.

When they were outside the office and headed down the hall, Bren glanced at him. "You'll have to bear with me. I don't usually do this kind of thing."

Perfect. Bren would not have a set spiel and could be easily steered into digressions. He trailed along behind her through the recreation room and the music room and the hydrotherapy room, asking simple questions and hanging on her answers.

"So what types of patients does this place take?" he asked finally.

"TBI of all kinds. Mobile, immobile. All stages of coma. Everything. As long as they have a traumatic brain injury."

"Did it used to be something else? Like a birthing center?"

"No. It's always been dedicated to TBI."

He kept his expression neutral, wondering what to think. Had David's brain been injured at birth and he'd been sent here?

"What age range is treated?"

She shrugged "Every age."

"Even babies?"

"There hasn't been a baby since I've been here, but I'm sure they would take one."

"I can't help noticing, since some of the doors are open, that everybody looks very . . . sick."

"That's what you get in a long-term facility. We do a little rehab here but that's not really our function. If a patient ever recovers to the point that they need intensive rehab then they're transferred to another facility."

"Anyplace in particular?"

"Wherever the family chooses."

"Do many patients leave here?"

"Not many," she said regretfully.

"It's all very clean and cheerful. Very impressive. I haven't seen much staff around though."

"Oh. They're having dinner. Most of our patients are on tube or IV feed so once that's done the staff has dinner together in small groups. It's our time to discuss any patient problems or make suggestions."

"Could I peek in at them? See what kind of people work here?"

"Umm . . ." She mulled over the request. "I don't see why not. I could even introduce you."

"No. No. Let's keep it low-key. I don't want to disturb their meal."

She led him to a doorway and gestured for him to peek in. The room was set up like a small cafeteria with people seated at long tables. He looked from face to face. A jolt went through him when he recognized a nurse from the baby photos of David.

"It's a very good group," she assured him as he pulled back from the doorway.

"What are the shifts like? This isn't one of those

places where they force the staff to work twelve hours straight or anything?"

"Oh, no! We have eight-hour shifts. I come on at four and go off at twelve."

"I won't keep you any longer, then. I've seen enough."

"Who knows." She smiled. "If you bring your aunt here maybe I'll be her nurse."

"Who knows," he agreed, responding to her subtle flirtation with a smile. "Is there a pay phone I can use before I go?" He remembered seeing one in the cafeteria and another in an alcove adjoining a tiny service kitchen.

"Sure," she said and took him to the alcove.

He was hoping for the cafeteria but still, he could see the cafeteria door from the alcove. "Don't let me keep you, Bren," he insisted, deliberately using the intimacy of her first name. "I know your dinner was interrupted to do this, so please, go back before it's over."

She blushed a little, gave him one last smile, and retreated down the hall.

He dialed Edmond's number.

"It's me," he said in response to his brother's hello. "I'm in New Jersey. On my way to you soon."

"Soon? As in soon enough that I should go ahead and order dinner?"

"No. Not that soon. I need to talk to a particular nurse here and if I can't catch her in the halls I may not make dinner at all; I might be lurking in the parking lot until shift change at midnight."

"I see. Take care, please. Bad things happen to those who lurk in dark parking lots."

From down the hall he heard voices and he glanced over his shoulder to see a group exiting the cafeteria. The baby-photo nurse was among them.

"Gotta go," he said, thumbing a disconnect without replacing the receiver. As the woman passed he leaned out from the alcove, still holding the phone receiver, and said, "Excuse me."

She turned and smiled quizzically. His luck was good and her companions kept going.

He held up one finger and did a charade of silently asking her to wait, then pretended to speak into the receiver another moment until the other nurses were out of sight.

"Sorry," he said as he finally hung up. "You are exactly the person I needed to talk to."

"Me?"

"I know you have to get back to work, and I don't have much time either."

He pulled the photograph from his pocket and handed it to her. She studied it, appearing pleased at first, then suddenly frowning.

"What do you want?" she asked suspiciously. "You're didn't come here for a tour, did you?"

"That baby is now a thirteen-year-old boy and he's run away from home. I'm trying to find him before anything bad happens."

She sighed heavily and leaned against the wall.

"I did come here pretending to want a tour," he

said. "Not knowing what I might learn here. I saw you and recognized your face, and I knew that anyone who was so obviously loving to a baby would want to help that same child if he was in trouble now."

"How can I help? I haven't seen them since just after that picture was taken."

"You can talk to me. Answer some questions. It's possible he's headed here."

"Why?"

"You tell me."

Her eyes darted up and down the hall, then she stepped through the alcove and into the small service kitchen, busying herself with measuring coffee into a filter.

"I'm not really surprised to hear this. Poor little Davey. It was a difficult beginning and I suppose it was bound to have consequences. Especially with that grandmother of his." She glanced sharply at him. "Who are you finding him for anyway?"

Her disapproval of the grandmother was apparent so he took a chance and said, "The father's side," trying to keep it vague enough that it would fit in with whatever she knew. "The maternal grandmother is dead now."

"Oh." She sighed again. "I'm sorry about her death but I'm glad to hear the father's people became involved. It never seemed right to me that they should be so estranged. I mean . . . I know the car accident and their son's death was a terrible blow, but how could they just walk away from their son's child?"

He gave a small nod of agreement but otherwise kept his face still, though this new information was giving rise to lots of questions. A car accident? Dead father? The baby with a head injury from the accident? Where was Thea in all this? And if this was the true story why had it been kept such a deep dark secret? Why hadn't David been told the truth?

"How old was Davey when he was brought here?"

"Oh, they sent him over at two days." She paused in her coffee making and smiled warmly at the memory. "He had this whole place gaga over him. What a treat. Having a sweet little newborn to fuss over in the midst of so much hopelessness and suffering."

"So he was . . . responsive?"

"Of course. You aren't one of those men who think newborns are just lumps, are you?"

He grinned, leaving her to take it any way she chose. But he was confused about what she was telling him. If David was responding and doing cute baby things then why was he a patient in this place?

"He was here almost all the time. Keeping him close to her where she could smell him and hear him cry was better therapy than anything else. And after the breakthrough during delivery—we all had such high hopes."

"Tell me about the breakthrough." He was careful, barely allowing himself to breathe, when inside he was screaming, *What?*

"Not much to tell. She was pregnant at the time of the accident, you know, and all the doctors recommended termination, but her mother . . . I thought I'd never forget that woman's name, but now . . . wait, don't tell me . . . Mary! Right?" She smiled. "Mary insisted that she'd already lost her daughter and that God was giving her a grandbaby in return, so she wouldn't give permission. Even though it's dangerous for the mother and it makes treatment so problematic—considering the fetus's health and all that. I mean, I'm not radically in favor of abortion or anything but that decision seemed kind of sick to me. Jeopardizing what slender chance her daughter had, and using her daughter's body that way. It would have been different maybe if the pregnancy was advanced, but she was two months along at the most when we got her here. And there was the additional concern of what the fetus had already been exposed to with all that complicated surgery and anesthesia the mother had undergone."

Inside his head he was shouting, *Thea! It was Thea with the brain injury! Oh God . . . Thea gave birth to David while she was in a coma. That is the secret she was hiding from her son.*

"I guess maybe the mother did have a pipeline to God though, because she got her miracle. The pregnancy was successful and the daughter remained stable and the baby was born fine."

"But what about the breakthrough?" Jack asked, urging her along with the story.

"Oh . . . well . . . she'd been in stage one coma—no reactivity or perceptivity at all. An obstetrician was coming by and seeing her regularly, and he had a cesarean scheduled. About a week before we were supposed to transport her to the hospital, she started exhibiting stage two behaviors—reacting to touch and sound, but in a very inconsistent and vague way . . . kind of like a sleeper who will react to being poked, but he doesn't wake up and the reactions are unpredictable. He might turn over or he might mumble or he might wave an arm. You know he's going to react, but the actions are not focused or purposeful.

"We were excited but cautious, knowing that it could mean absolutely nothing or . . . it could mean the beginning of an emergence. We started monitoring her more closely. I was the one who found her thrashing in the bed. It was the middle of the night and by the time I got the duty doctor in there the baby's head was crowning. The OB never made it at all. We delivered him." She beamed proudly. "Two nurses were supporting her back, holding her so that she was in a semi-upright position, like she was going to push, only of course she wasn't because she was comatose. And suddenly, she jerked forward, and her eyes focused, and she looked down between her legs at the blood and the baby's head and she screamed." The woman gave an involuntary shiver. "I'll never forget that scream. Never."

Jack shuddered internally. It was almost too disturbing to imagine.

"We had to send the baby over to Neonatal at the hospital for a few days, but the doctors decided to keep her here. She was weak, but okay. And they were eager to start working with her and gauge the level of her responsiveness."

"And that was it? She was just awake and normal from then on?"

The woman moved from the coffeemaker to an ice machine and began filling plastic glasses with ice.

"That's movie stuff. Oh, I guess it does happen once in a blue moon, but the average coma patient— if and when they come out—comes out gradually. Very slowly and usually very painfully."

"Physical pain?"

"Certainly. What do you think it's like to rebuild all that muscle tissue, to regain balance and range of motion? But I was more referring to emotional pain. It can be devastating for an adult to become aware of themselves as helpless and infantile, robbed of memories and skills."

"Did she have a difficult time?"

"The rest of her stay here she was at stage four with occasional progressions into stage five."

"And those stages are . . . ?" Jack prodded.

"Four is the most awful, in my opinion. I've heard other nurses refer to it as the nightmare state. The patient is confused, disoriented, and very active, sometimes frenzied so that they have to be restrained. They get angry or scared for no reason, and they'll do and say the most bizarre things. It's like they're half in the conscious world and half trapped in a nightmare. Stage five is a significant improvement. The internal turmoil lessens and they're alert and responsive. If they do get agitated it's usually focused on what's happening around them, and their level of confusion."

"When she was in her occasional stage fives did she remember anything about how she got there?"

"Oh no. Five is way too early for that. They can't learn much and they can't remember much and they can't express themselves. I just always hoped that she went on improving after she left here."

"She was sent home?"

"Oh no! Her mother moved her to a specialized rehabilitation facility. That's what she needed . . . a place with resident therapists to work with her on every level."

"How long would she have needed that?"

"There's no set timetable. She had to develop self-care skills. She had to learn to walk and write and speak normally. And she had to work on short-term memory skills, long-term memory recovery, paranoia and anxiety control, judgment and abstract reasoning . . . the list goes on and on."

"Tana!" a voice called from down the hall.

Motioning for him to stay back out of sight, the woman leaned through the doorway. "I made coffee and now I'm doing the ice water," she called in response.

"It's not your day to do that."

"It's not? Oh, well, tell whoever's posted that it's done."

She ducked back into the tiny kitchen and shot him an angry look. "I could be fired for talking to you like this."

"I'm sorry. Just a few more questions. Where was she sent from here?"

"You know, that was the weirdest thing. The mother arranged everything. A private medical transport came. The mother demanded that the records go with them rather than being sent to the new place through normal methods. And when a few of us got together and called the new place a week or so later to check on the baby they weren't there. The staff there said the mother had canceled. Told them she had made other arrangements."

"Did you try contacting the hospital that sent her here?"

"Somebody did . . . thinking that they might have kept in touch with the surgeon and maybe he would have information. But that was a real hassle. Have you ever tried to get any 'nonroutine' information out of a big-city hospital? Forget it. They couldn't find any records. They didn't know the surgeon. And they didn't give a shit, if you know what I mean."

"Yeah. I know. Do you remember what hospital it was?"

"Not exactly. But it was in Washington, D.C."

"That was the hospital listed in the medical records that came here with her?"

"Yes."

"And what name was the daughter using then?"

The woman frowned. "Allie. What else would she be using?"

"I mean her last name. It's been changed since."

"Oh, she's remarried? Let me see . . . Her last name was Reagan, just like the president. But you should know that. That was her husband's name."

"I thought she might have been using her mother's name."

"No. She was definitely Mrs. Reagan. I don't understand, though, how my telling you this can possibly help you find the boy."

"Everything helps. I believe he's trying to dig out the truth about his past. The family never told him anything about his birth."

"Oh."

"Here's where I'm staying." He scribbled Edmond's number on a coffee filter. "If David should show up here asking questions will you give me a call? Don't tell him though."

She nodded and slipped the folded filter into her pocket.

"Tana! Aren't you done yet?"

"Coming!" she called, hefting the tray of ice-filled glasses and the pitcher of water. "After I'm gone you can leave through the front. Good luck finding Davey. The poor kid."

17

Thea had locked and bolted the hotel door. She had wedged the desk chair under the doorknob. She had looked out the window to reassure herself that there was still a three-story drop to the ground and then she had made certain that every inch of the dark glass was covered by the heavily lined curtains, but tonight nothing could comfort her. She was gripped by a new level of fear—something rawer and more violent than her panic attacks, primal adrenaline-fueled alarm. She was in a cave, waiting, and just beyond the campfire, beyond the circle of firelight, a predator prowled and watched.

There was another rapist.

He could be anyone. He could be anywhere. And she was a threat to him.

She dragged the stuffed easy chair into position and stood on it to unscrew the air vent grille. Inside was the terry-cloth bundle she had hidden there. Gently, she carried it to the bed and unwrapped the towel. It was a gun. Jack's gun.

She had been at his house, infuriated by the note she saw through the window, and she had remembered David's mention of the spare key. At first she'd intended only to go in and look around for any other clues leading to David, but as soon as she had the door open she thought of the gun. David had come home awestruck one day and told her that he'd seen the police gun and that Jack kept it in a hiking boot box in his closet. Stepping across the threshold into his stripped and barren house she had been seized by the compulsion to have that gun, to carry it with her to Long Island, and she had rushed into the bedroom, slipped the gun and ammunition out of the box, and stolen for the first time in her life. Only later, miles down the highway on her way to the airport, had she realized that she'd raced away without replacing the spare key or locking up. She wondered if Jack ever took the gun anywhere himself. But then men didn't need special weapons. They had fists and rocks.

With the gun tucked beside her she sat on the bed, her back pressed against the headboard, knees up, watching the door in silence—no television or radio—so she could hear approaching footsteps and not be distracted from her vigil. There was an accomplice out there, a second rapist, and he could know about her by now. He could have seen her in the county court buildings or at police headquarters or driving down one of the many streets she had cruised in search of her son. He could have been at the library. He could have followed her to the hotel and he could be waiting until she fell asleep.

The phone rang and she jumped, then fumbled the receiver to her ear.

"Hello! Hello!"

"It's Rosie. Are you okay?"

"Hi. Sorry. The phone spooked me."

"Any news of David?"

"No."

"Why don't you leave the hotel and come stay with us," Rosalie suggested. "I know it's kind of late tonight but maybe tomorrow morning? We have a foldout couch in the den that you're welcome to use as long as you like."

"Thank you, but no," Thea said. There was at least some security in the hotel room with the heavy drapes and the window high above the ground and the dead-bolt locks. Rosalie's den might not be secure at all. Rosalie's husband might be frightening. And she didn't want to have the gun in a house with small children.

"If you're saying no because you're trying to keep out of sight . . . I have bad news for you. My brother called. He heard that you might be in town and he wondered if I knew anything."

"How did he hear?"

"Don't you remember how things are? Gossip travels like wildfire. Judge Napoli's secretary probably figured out who you were and started the story. Judge Napoli presided over the Rusket trial so his secretary knew a lot about it, and she knows that the victim was a friend of mine. Unfortunately she's the woman you asked to find me at the courthouse, and she's a gabby old busybody."

"What am I going to do? This can't get into the papers! Oh my God!"

"Stay calm. I told my brother you were gone and I'll tell Napoli's secretary the same thing. Nobody knows about David. And nobody knows that your name is Auben now so you should be safe registered at the hotel. Just be careful where you go and who you talk to. And don't come to the courthouse again."

"Did you tell your husband about me?"

"Just that I'd seen you and I was going to invite you to stay with us. I didn't say anything about David or why you were here."

"Thanks."

"But Thea, I'm afraid you're sitting on a volcano with this."

"I know. And I have to talk to someone about . . . about Ronnie Rusket not being . . .''

"Oh Jesus, don't say it. Don't even think about it. Your son is all that's important right now."

"Yes. I have to find David and get him safely away from here and back to California. Then I'll do whatever I have to do."

"Thea . . . maybe what you ought to do is just keep quiet. Do you know how terrible it will be for you if you break that story open? You'd have to be here for questioning, and they'd pry into your life. They'd either want to try to prove that you slept with someone else or they'd have to reopen the whole damn case."

"But he could be innocent, Rosie."

"I seriously doubt that. He already had a record."

"Did he?"

"Juvenile offenses, but that's how they start. And he admitted the arson."

"But even if he is guilty, still—there had to have been someone else with him. Someone with light skin and eyes. Someone who's out there free."

"And someone who's going to stay free because there's no evidence and if Rusket hasn't ratted him out yet, he's not going to now. He's either been paid off or he's afraid."

Thea sighed.

"Is it possible," Rosalie said in a very small, very tentative voice, "that you had sex with some guy and can't remember it because of the head injury?"

The question both hurt and offended her, but Thea knew it was fair. "I was a virgin up to that night. And then, wasn't I with you the whole time at the party?"

"Up until you left."

"I certainly wasn't sneaking off to be with some boy. No boy had spoken a word to me that night. As I remember it no one was very nice to either of us except for that one snide group of loser girls who kept insisting that we share their vodka and smokes and then made fun of me for nearly choking to death."

"Yeah," Rosalie agreed ruefully. "We were pathetic, weren't we? So glad to be included . . . even though those girls were repulsive and we both hated vodka and didn't smoke. I can't believe how stupid we were."

"We were stupid to have gone there at all."

"True. So . . . were you sick that night or just escaping?"

"Sick. Woozy. Miserable. And really disgusted with myself. I had thought I was so smart. In control. A few sips and a few puffs—no problem. What an idiot I was."

"Then you really did go to my cousin's car?"

"Yes."

"What do you remember after that?"

"Eyes. Eyes looking at me through the window. Faces smashed against the dark glass."

"More than one?"

"I don't . . ." Thea cupped her forehead in her hand and closed her eyes. "That image of the eyes and the dark glass has been so terrifying to me that I think I've always just assumed that my imagination was exaggerating it. Distorting it the way nightmares do. I mean there are times when I dream that dozens of eyes are looking in. So . . . I guess I can't give a good answer to that."

"Your memories . . . are they permanently messed up or do things come back sometimes?"

"I've tried to block them for so long but bits and pieces have crept in anyway. Now that I'm finally trying to remember, nothing is coming at all. It's like I'm walled in . . . cut off . . . I don't know. Maybe they're unrecoverable."

"What are you going to do?"

"What can I do? Find my son."

"And pray the rapist doesn't find out you had a baby."

Thea's heart plummeted at hearing her worst fear given voice. "Oh, Rosie . . . ," she cried.

"No! I can't believe I said that. It won't happen! It can't possibly happen. Think about it, Thea. The guy could be living anywhere, and even if he's still on the Island he could be in another county. Or he could be in jail or even dead . . . hit by a car or killed in a bar fight. And even if he's here—even if he's living nearby—he probably won't ever know you were in town."

Thea looked down at the gun beside her on the bed.

"I could suddenly remember his face, Rosie."

"That doesn't sound likely. You're not remembering much of anything."

"But he doesn't know that, does he?"

Several hours later Jack was with his brother in a Riverside Drive apartment that was once the living area of a mansion, surrounded by empty take-out cartons from an Indian restaurant and finishing his third beer.

"That's an incredible story," Edmond said. "And you think that each time there was a patient transfer the mother was changing names and fabricating prior hospitals and fiddling with the records?"

"What other explanation is there?"

"But why?" Edmond asked, gathering the remains of their dinner. "I can understand keeping the truth from the boy, though I don't see why it should be so terrible for him to find out now. But it sounds like this mother-grandmother person was doing a lot more than necessary just to keep the child from knowing about the past."

"Right. She was covering up their tracks as they went. So that they couldn't be traced. I think it has something to do with the biological father."

"Who died in the car accident."

"So everyone at the Wynkoop Institute was told. But the Institute was also given false names, so it could be that the entire accident story was a lie and there was no dead father."

"What about the medical records that traveled with her? Wouldn't the cause of injury be mentioned somewhere?"

"I don't know. But I suspect that it would be easy to alter or leave out a few lines in a written record, while still keeping the essential medical information intact."

"Knowing you, you have a hunch."

"My hunch is that Grandma wanted to hide this baby from Daddy or Daddy's side of the family and she was willing to do a lot of sinning to do that. The trouble is I'm still no closer to finding David. I called a friend in L.A. as soon as I left the Institute and he checked out the names they used there. The names are definitely air. They weren't used anywhere else. So even with all this new information I'm still stuck." He carried his beer bottles to the sink. "I guess I'll run up to Rochester tomorrow and poke around."

"You don't sound too enthusiastic."

"I know. It feels wrong. I think the grandmother left there when she was young and never looked back."

Jack opened his suitcase and took out the filled grocery bag and the long hard-sided case that he had brought with him.

"Did you bring your own snacks?"

"I wish I'd packed some Red Nectar. That beer you bought is swill."

He put the paper bag on the coffee table and carefully slid out the contents. It was everything of interest that he'd gathered from Thea's house. In the case was her flute. He had opened the case and looked inside and that was all it held. He wasn't sure why he'd brought it. Somehow it had just felt wrong to bury it in the box again.

"What have you got there?"

"Stolen goods from Thea's house. I haven't had time to go through it all yet."

"Excellent." Edmond looked over the material as though selecting a truffle from a box of candy. "We'll play sleuth. I'm Colonel Mustard."

He reached for the folder of printed pages and Jack snatched it away, protective of the sexual content in Thea's chat logs. "Here." Jack handed over the three journals. "I think these are David's childhood memoirs. They should be fascinating."

Edmond opened the first book. "How old was he when he wrote these?"

"Don't know. They're numbered rather than dated. What does that handwriting look like to you? Maybe fourth or fifth grade?"

"Yes, it's either very young cursive or it's someone with a medical degree."

Jack settled back to read but thought about his brother instead. Edmond was charming and droll, one of the most engaging men he had ever known, and he felt incredibly lucky to have him as a brother. Yet, he had managed to avoid seeing him for most of the past three years. That struck him now as a terrible waste of whatever time he'd been allotted on earth. What had he proved by denying himself his brother's company?

"This doesn't sound like *my* childish thoughts," Edmond said, studying the book. He glanced up at Jack. "Take a listen," he said, then lowered his eyes and began reading:

"All vertebrate brains, both human and animal, have the same three parts. They are the brain stem, the cerebel-

lum, and the cerebrum. The brain stem controls basic functions like breathing and it is at the top of the spinal cord.
The cerebellum takes care of balance and movement. The
cerebrum is where intelligence happens.

"A fish has a big brain stem and a big cerebellum and
a tiny cerebrum. Lizards have small brain parts that are
about equally sized. A bird's cerebrum is slightly larger
than the other two parts because birds have such good
vision and optics are connected to the cerebrum. In dogs
the cerebrum is a little larger, and then in humans the
cerebrum is gigantic.

"Humans have great intelligence and complex emotions.
But we are still animals. We have those three brain parts
just like fish and lizards. If something goes wrong in the
cerebrum then we can be reduced to the level of a guppy
or an iguana. And even when our cerebrums are working
fine, we are underneath it all just guppies, because no
amount of intelligence can overcome those more basic parts
of the brain. Where does fear come from? I'll have to remember to ask."

Edmond raised his eyebrows. "What sort of child
is this?"

"A science whiz. Who can explain it?"

"With a big cerebrum no doubt," Edmond said as
he settled back into reading.

Jack scanned page after page of computer chat that
seemed as inane to him as any cocktail party conversation he'd ever heard. Then he came to a rendez-
vous with Delian.

"Listen to this!" Edmond demanded.

"No. You read yours and I'll read mine. Then we'll compare notes later."

Edmond gave him five minutes of silence, then said in an uncharacteristically serious tone, "You have to hear some of these passages now, Jack."

Jack relented and put aside his chat log reading.

Edmond took a drink of his wine, then held the book up. "Just a selection," he said, and his cultured voice made it sound as though he were introducing a poem.

"*The normal brain is beautiful in PET scan pictures. At rest it is like the sea, lovely deep sapphire and light Caribbean aqua, with areas of the palest green like water that is full of microscopic plants, and small yellow spots like morning sunbeams. Then there is a brighter yellow area with an angry red center. Is this where nightmares happen?*"

A chill skimmed across Jack's skin as his brother turned the page and continued reading.

"*I saw a picture of a brain listening to music. The dots and splotches looked like a human face. Two dark blue eyes staring. Yellow hair. Green and yellow nose and cheeks. A big red mouth wide open. And a red shape on top of the yellow hair that looks like blood. My brain doesn't understand music anymore.*"

Several pages were skipped.

"It's Thea," Jack breathed. "It's her journal during therapy!"

Edmond nodded and went on reading.

"*I love the baby more every day so the part of my brain*"

that loves is still functioning. What is damaged? When I pick up my flute but cannot remember how to make music is it because those brain cells died or is it because music is beautiful and all the beauty in my mind was killed?"

Another few pages.

"I cannot remember things. Lists of objects. New numbers or names. I can remember my locker combination from high school but I cannot remember the number that is on the door to my room. I get lost. They have a beeper on my wrist so they can find me. I can walk but I can't dance. I am afraid and I can't remember why."

Edmond glanced up, his expression somber and sad, then lowered his eyes back to the page.

"Only eight episodes today. I am improving. I have gotten pretty good at counting to a safe place. The place that I go to is Carnegie Hall. On one I sail through the air to Manhattan. On two I take a seat in center orchestra. On three the musicians lift their instruments. And on four I am enveloped by the music and I am safe.

"My mother wishes that a lot of my memories would stay lost. She said that it would be better if I never remembered some of the things that happened to me. Why? She won't tell me. I had a computer class today and I made a mistake and erased my disc. When my brain loses things have they been erased forever or are they floating around in there waiting to be recovered?"

The page turned.

"Today my therapist brought me more to read about the brain. She brought me articles about Dr. Llinas, the researcher. I wrote his name in ink on the inside of my

wrist so I won't lose it. He thinks that humans are the only self-delusional animals. We confuse facts and fantasies. We get lost in our thoughts and we hide from ourselves. He must be a very great man. I wish he would look into my brain and take out the bad parts."

Another page turn.

"My mother took me out of Miller Rehab Center and we moved from Oklahoma City to Denver. I miss my therapists. She says maybe I can have outpatient therapy now but she doesn't believe I need therapists anymore. She thinks I'm not trying hard enough. She told me today that God had punished me for pride and arrogance. I told her that there was no God but if there was I hated him. She got so angry she threatened to keep the baby away. I hate her sometimes. She thinks she is God!"

Another page.

"I understand my brain better now. Our natural state is dreaming. We dream interior worlds. When we are awake we are bombarded with sensory input. Our brains are forced to process the data and create a reality separate from the dreams, but the dreaming is always there, waiting to break through as fantasy or fleeting image. Our brains were made for dreaming. We impose the order of thinking on them. And we fool ourselves into believing that we are rational, predictable, and capable of absolutes. We dream that we are thinkers."

Edmond paused and drew a deep breath.

"Today my mother told me I was raped. A man held me down and hit me and forced open my legs. She showed me a newspaper article, but she wouldn't let me keep it.

She wanted to show me it was true but she doesn't want me to read it again.. She wants me to forget it all now. Finally, my nightmares make sense, and they have a name. I don't want to forget the name. I have to write names down or I lose them. But she's right—I don't want to remember any more about the rape. And I don't ever want to know if my baby looks like the man."

Gently Edmond closed the book. "Those are just some of the passages that struck me. There are others that are even more painful to read. She must have been assigned to write every day as part of her therapy, and on some days she was barely lucid, while on others she was so angry that she just made slashing marks with the pen."

Jack started to speak but had to clear his throat before the words would form. "I should have looked more carefully at those." He cleared his throat again. "Were there any clues?"

"Only clues to the depth of the woman's agony and the richness of her soul. How can you know this person, Jack, yet not have had a sense of her heartbreak?"

"Oh, get off it, Edmond. I'm not a psychologist and neither are you." Jack reached for the flute case and opened the lid.

"Beautiful," Edmond said. "Looks like solid silver."

"I wonder if she ever played again." Jack lifted out the pieces of the instrument and held them up, trying to see how they fit together. A cylinder of paper fell out. Edmond plucked it from the floor, and Jack carefully put the flute down as his brother smoothed out the paper on the coffee table. The name Ronald Malcolm Rusket was written on it over and over in slanted lines that disintegrated into slashes at the end.

"What are you doing?" Edmond asked as Jack lunged for the phone.

"It's three hours earlier in California. I'm hoping to catch Wally Goon still in the office."

"Alert Services," a recording of a modulated female voice answered. "The office is closed for the evening and will reopen at nine o'clock tomorrow morning. You may leave a message at the tone. In the event of an emergency—"

"Wally!" Jack shouted. "It's Jack Verrity. If you're there, pick up. If anyone is in the office please pick up!"

"Okay. Okay, Jack. Stop shouting."

"Wally. I'm glad I caught you."

"No one else is. We were all just walking out the door and I have five people glaring at me right now."

"This is really important. There's a kid in trouble, Wally."

"Okay, you said the magic word—kid. What do you need?"

"A check on another name. Ronald Malcolm Rusket."

"Sure. Can I get back to you in the morning?"

"Would you see what you can find now, Wally? If

nothing pops up immediately then I won't ask for a deeper check till morning."

"All right," Wally agreed against a chorus of groans from the background. "I'll call you back in a few minutes."

"No, I'll stick with you," Jack said.

"Come on, Phyllis," he heard Wally plead. "The guy is single and good-looking. Next time he's in town I'll make him take you to see the Ice Capades or something." Then he was put on hold and assaulted by a painful rendition of "My Way."

"Jack! Got it! Ronald Malcolm Rusket, a.k.a. Ronnie, a.k.a. Atomic. Home address Valley Stream, Long Island, in the state of New York. Presently a guest of the penal system. Rape and attempted murder."

"Name of the victim?"

"No slips. They protected her identity. You got a fax where I can send you all the details?"

Jack looked up at his brother and mouthed, "Fax?"

"Always." Edmond pointed to the phone Jack was using. "Give him that number."

"Just wait one minute and then fax it to this same number," Jack told his friend.

Jack moved away from the telephone so Edmond could connect his portable fax machine. Thea. At last he understood. Thea was brutalized and beaten. Thea was raped and terrorized. That's why she was in a coma. That's why she screamed when she came back into the world and looked down and saw the bloody head of a baby between her legs. That's why she was such a mess of phobias and fears. And that's why there was no father for David. The child had been conceived in hell.

18

As soon as he entered the room he knew that David was unhappy or upset. Instead of being engrossed with the computer or occupied with one of the other toys in the room the boy was sitting on the edge of the bed, hunched and dejected.

"What's going on here?" he asked.

The boy shrugged.

"What's wrong?"

"I'm not . . . you know . . . *doing* anything."

"How about we do a little sky-watching then. See if we can find that Pistol star you were talking about."

"We can't see that with our telescopes."

"Hey . . . what's got you down? You haven't played every one of those computer games and read all those Carl Sagan books already, have you?"

"No." He shrugged. "It's . . . well, I've been here like . . . days, and I'm having a great time, but I haven't started looking for my dad yet."

He moved up beside the boy.

"Oh, David . . . I'm sorry to have to tell you this now when you're already upset, but there's a new problem."

"There is?"

"Your mom is here."

"Here!"

"In the area. Sniffing around. Crying to the police and getting them all stirred up."

"How do you know?"

"Contacts at the police station."

"Oh man. How'd she figure out where—"

"You tell me."

The boy winced. "She's real smart. You know, she never went to college but she's taught herself so much stuff out of books and off the computer that she always knows more than my teachers."

"I'm sure she is smart, David. But you gave her a big clue. You left that map I sent you and she found it. That was really stupid."

"Oh man! I'm sorry! I forgot all about that. But how could she have found it? It was really hidden."

"Like you said—she's smart. Are you sure you didn't make one file copy or one printout of any of our chats or e-mails?"

"I swear. Cross my heart."

"We'll be okay then. This changes things, though. We were going to start your search tomorrow, but we have to be more careful now and lay low a while."

"Man. Oh, man . . . If she catches me I'm dead. She'll probably lock me up forever."

"I won't let her catch you."

"I can't believe she's here! She's got this thing about staying home after dark. And she *never* goes anywhere alone. I can't believe she came!"

"She did."

"She must really be worried about me."

"No. She just wants to stop you from learning what you have every right to know."

"Yeah."

"You're missing her a little, aren't you?"

"I guess."

"Do you think your mother would like me, David?"

"Umm . . . I don't know."

"You said she hates everyone."

"It's more like she's afraid of people or doesn't trust them."

"And she'd be that way about me, too?"

"I don't know. She's that way about Jack."

"The famous Jack. If she doesn't like Jack then you're sure she won't like me, right?"

"Yeah. I mean no. Maybe she'd like you."

Things were so much more complicated than he'd thought they would be. He hadn't imagined he would become so attached. Certainly he had thought it would be interesting to have the boy around, but he'd considered David a pawn, not the final prize.

Now, he wished he could go back and do things

differently. But wasn't that a joke? If going back were possible then he would change what had happened so many years ago.

The blue eyes were waiting, focused on him in a way that went under his skin and straight into his heart.

"Let's figure out how to handle your mother. It's time to compose another message."

19

Morning. Thea woke with a start, surprised to have fallen asleep at all. Her head hurt and her eyes were scratchy and her body ached from sitting up all night. She soaked in the tub until she felt human, keeping the gun within reach on the floor. A shower would have felt better but that was out of the question—all that noisy water masking the sound of an intruder and the shower curtain pulled so that she couldn't see the bathroom door opening . . .

She left the hotel only after watching the parking lot for some minutes. There was no man lingering near her car. She bought coffee and a bagel at a drive-through, then went to see Michaels and Wilson, checking her rearview mirror constantly to see if a man was following her. Though it was early they had already gone out on a case and none of the other officers could or would give her any information. Like little tape recorders each person she asked advised her to go back to her hotel and wait for the detectives to call. Stubbornly she took a seat in the reception area and waited. The personal contact was important to her. She didn't believe they would try as hard if she only spoke to them on the phone.

An hour passed. She heard pieces of conversations that were fraught with mounting tension. Something was going on. Finally she could stand it no longer and asked a female officer if it concerned David.

"No," the woman said gently. "It's a double homicide involving an important family. Nothing to do with your son at all."

The words "double homicide" spoken with such matter-of-factness chilled Thea, and she could no longer sit there listening to the buzz. She left the building and walked to her car, casting her eyes about for an attacker yet at the same time feeling very lucky. Her son might be stumbling toward a traumatic revelation but at least she knew that he was physically safe in Jack's company, while some other mother or sister or daughter might be identifying the victim remains from a double homicide right now. But the luck felt tied to something—as though it required some penance or punishment, some extreme action before it would blossom and offer up her son.

What can I do?

No answer came to her.

She glanced at her watch. She had nearly three hours before she was due to pick up the transcripts from Rosalie. She could drive around again, but that seemed so futile and passive. Jack wasn't just out driving David around—he was investigating. She had to think of it from Jack's point of view. Where would he take David to look for information? Again that took her back to the question of what they already knew, but she didn't let the uncertainty sidetrack her.

How would a detective approach the problem? He might look for David's birth records . . . but she knew there weren't any to be found on Long Island. That meant that they could only proceed through investigating her. Had they learned yet that her last name had been Fremont? Maybe they were going from high school to high school looking at yearbook pictures in a quest for her former name. But if they did discover her name, where would that take them? What exactly was left of her to find? She hadn't been born there herself so no birth information was on file. She hadn't reached voting age there, or had her own bank account or credit card or local charge account. No one at her old address could tell them anything. She'd done a lot of baby-sitting, but that hadn't generated any official records. She hadn't ever been arrested or even ticketed. She had gotten a driver's license and, though long inactive, that linkage of photo and name was probably forever, but, assuming it was accessible, it would reveal nothing to an investigator beyond the fact of her having driven. There would be school records—if indeed schools kept their records for that long.

The name Fremont would allow them to poke into

her mother's history, too, but she couldn't imagine that they would find anything of interest. Her hard-working but uneducated mother had been deter-mined to support them without public assistance and so had been forced to work on the margins—cleaning houses and offices, doing home care for the elderly, sewing piecework for an exclusive stuffed animal company—never officially employed and so never accumulating a paper trail. The old parish priest who'd known her had surely gone to his reward. Her mother's sister, Aunt Dot, had died twenty years ago, and her mother had had no friends or confidants who would be traceable. And any other of the surviv-ing relatives from the Rochester area were distant, in blood and in years and in concern, because her mother had been a black sheep even before she ran off with a boy and lost touch.

The biggest question was, would the name Fre-mont lead them to the rape? If they didn't learn of the rape they couldn't possibly figure out who Da-vid's father was.

The newspaper had never published her name. She was certain of that because she'd done a search using Althea Fremont at the library before she'd looked up Ronnie Rusket or The Castle, and there had not been a single reference under her name. That left two areas of vulnerability—legal and medical. Not only were there the trial transcripts, but anyone with a good memory who had been connected to the trial was a

danger. And then there were all those medical records and the doctors and nurses at the hospital.

But . . . would a person . . . a detective . . . who
was nosing around in her ordinary seventeen-year-
old life find any clues or hints that would lead them
to Vale Memorial Hospital or to the legal system?
Because if there was nothing that pointed in those
directions, then she might be safe.

She knew what would happen if Jack and David
found their way to the courthouse. Someone like that
judge's secretary would probably remember her
name and steer them right into the rape. But what
about the hospital? What was available there? Maybe
she ought to find out.

After an hour of speaking in circles to a succession
of hospital records clerks, Thea had not learned a
thing. They were overworked. They had bill collec-
tions to worry about. They were not eager to hunt
for fourteen-year-old information. Then when they
realized that she was asking for confidential information on Althea Fremont but had no identification to
prove that she was Althea Fremont, and pretended
that she had no ID at all because she didn't want
any more links to the name Auben, they gave her an
abrupt no.

Angry and frustrated, she left the office and went
out into the main hallway. And stopped. Why was
she upset? This was good! Anyone else attempting
to pry information out of Vale Memorial would have

hit the same brick wall. None of the clerks would even confirm that an Althea Fremont had been treated at the hospital.

She wandered down the corridors in search of coffee, still fighting the headache she'd had since waking.

"Is there a coffee or soda machine nearby?" she asked a passing orderly.

"In the hall outside the emergency room. Take the next left."

The emergency room. That was where she had been taken that night, broken and bleeding, already settled into her long long sleep. Would there be someone in emergency who remembered her?

She went into the waiting area and was assaulted by the sounds of crying children and the sharp smells of cleanser and sickness. It was unfamiliar. She had thought it might be upsetting to visit the place but she had no memories or feelings about it at all.

"Sign the book," the triage nurse ordered as she approached his desk.

"I'm not here for a medical reason."

He looked up at her impatiently.

"I need to talk to someone about a patient who was brought in here fourteen years ago in a coma. Is anyone still working here from that time?"

"A few," he said, tapping a large notepad on the corner of his desk. "Put down the name and the date. I'll send it back to the desk and they'll ask around."

She wrote "Althea Fremont," put the date of the

rape underneath, and then added "rape victim in a coma" to jog people's memories. Then she sat down on an out-of-the-way bench to wait. Twenty minutes later a woman in a green scrub suit walked out the swinging doors and scanned the crowd. The triage nurse pointed in Thea's general direction and said a few words.

Thea watched the woman cross the floor. She was tall and strongly built. Purposeful. Not a person to be trifled with. Beneath a fringe of gray hair her round face was weary and more than a little apprehensive. Her name tag read K. Falk.

"Reporters are supposed to go through the public information office so you're wasting your time back here," the woman warned.

Thea rose. "I'm not a reporter. Were you one of the nurses?"

"I was. Who are you?"

Thea glanced around at the jammed emergency area. "Can I talk to you privately for a few minutes?"

"Not without telling me who you are and what you want."

"I'm . . . a relative."

The woman studied her, frowning. "You're lying."

"Never mind," Thea said, turning to go.

"Wait," the nurse breathed, staring now as though looking straight through Thea's eyes and into her traumatized brain. "You're her, aren't you?"

Thea forced a laugh to demonstrate how ridiculous an idea that was.

"It is you. Your mother put up your picture so that we would all know who you were beneath the bandages and the swelling. After you were gone that picture stayed on the bulletin board for months. No one had the heart to take it down."

"Oh . . ." Thea shielded her eyes with her hand to cover the sudden onslaught of tears.

The woman took a firm grip on Thea's arm. "I'm taking my break," she called to the triage nurse as she steered Thea away.

They entered a crowded elevator car and Thea kept her head down, swiping away her tears with the back of her hand. No one paid any attention. It was, after all, a place for the sick and dying. For raw grief.

Two floors up the woman led her through a door marked STAFF ONLY and into a small empty lounge with a pay phone and turquoise Naugahyde couches facing each other over a battered coffee table.

"This place is usually deserted so we should have privacy here," the nurse said.

They sat down opposite each other.

"I'm Karen. Karen Falk. I was in emergency when you came in and I took care of you in ICU."

"You're right. I am Althea Au—Althea Fremont. But please . . . I'm begging you . . . don't say a word to anyone about seeing me."

Falk scrutinized her with puzzled concern. "Not even the others here in the hospital who took care of you?"

"No one. Please. I can't explain right now but it is

vital that no one else finds out. I should never have come here. It just did not occur to me I could be recognized."

"Is all this secrecy something to do with the police?"

Thea hesitated a moment. "Yes."

The woman nodded as though something had been confirmed for her, but then she broke into a wide smile. "I can't believe this! You look wonderful. I thought . . . with the TBI you had and the surgery . . . And we were told later that you were long-term stage one."

"I was stage one for about nine months. After that I started to surface. A year of rehab, lots of therapy, and here I am."

"Well, you are an amazing testament to modern medicine and the recuperative powers of the human organism. You can't imagine how terrific it is for me to see you. I wish I could share it with the other nurses."

"I'm sorry. Maybe it will come out later, but for now . . ."

"This would be such a positive story. A story with a happy ending."

"A happy ending?" she asked, wondering if the woman could see into the future.

"All right then, a complete recovery from TBI. In nursing that's a happy ending."

"I am happy." Thea smiled. "Except for night-mares. A touch of paranoia. Fear of the dark and fear of men. But hey, I knew a woman who had all that from watching *Psycho* when she was twelve."

The nurse gave her an appraising look and Thea shifted in the squeaky couch, uncomfortable beneath the scrutiny.

"Do you have any memories of being brought in?"

Thea shook her head.

"I could tell you what I remember."

"Thank you. I'd appreciate that."

"It's natural to want to know," the woman assured her. She paused for a moment, collecting her memories. "That was the shift from hell. People talked about it for years. We had all the usual summer Saturday night stuff plus a near drowning and a drug and alcohol case from the beach party. Then came the car accident. Five boys. All of them in bad shape. I was strictly ICU then but the ER staff put out a general call for help and since we had a light load in ICU I went down. One of the boys died just as I got there. And then, in the middle of all that chaos, the paramedics brought in you and the man from the fire."

"Ronnie Rusket?"

The nurse nodded. "No one knew yet that he was your attacker. You were completely unconscious and he was raving. Both of you reeked of smoke and you were covered with black soot."

"What did my head look like?"

"The actual injury was hidden by your hair, which was matted with blood and soot."

"Did you think I would die?"

"Yes. But then your first miracle happened."

"What was that?"

"Dr. Guerin, of course."

"He was my surgeon, right?"

"He was your miracle." Karen Falk frowned. "Didn't your mother tell you the whole story?"

"I guess not."

"Guerin is a legendary neurosurgeon . . . one of the pioneers in the new treatment methods for TBI. He practices and teaches in Manhattan and spends most of his time there, but he has a house on the North Shore. And that night, my dear, Dr. Guerin's son was in the car accident . . . and the doctor rushed to the emergency room to be with his son . . . and he was right there when the ambulance brought you in. He took over and saved your life."

"I lived because someone else had an accident?"

"Because you were given a miracle."

"Did Guerin's son live?"

"Yes. He lost his foot, but he went on to become a doctor . . . a really fine doctor, I hear. Not everyone had the chance for a happy ending that night though. One boy died. One was paralyzed and one disfigured."

Thea nodded. "I was the lucky one that night, wasn't I?"

"Very, very lucky."

"Yes."

"You were in my ICU for three days. Your mother

was there all the time and you had a girlfriend who came a lot. Visiting was very limited outside of your mother. Then there were further complications and you were transferred to Manhattan so Guerin's team of specialists could take over."

"And what about Rusket? Did you see him while he was in the hospital?"

The nurse glanced away.

"What?" Thea pressed.

Karen Falk sighed. "He came to see you. Before we knew what he'd done. . . . Well, I hate to tell you this but, thinking he had saved you, we let him in for several quick visits. He stood there beside your bed and prayed for you to wake up."

Thea shuddered.

"Sorry. If you hadn't asked about him I wouldn't have told you."

There were so many questions that she knew she should be asking the woman yet Thea could not think of one of them. She drew a deep breath and studied her hands.

"Take it easy." The nurse reached across the distance separating them to pat her hand.

"You didn't seem surprised to hear that the police are involved in this again," Thea said finally.

"No. There were so many problems with the physical evidence that I figured sooner or later there would be more poking into this. I'm the one who was blamed for losing the rape kit evidence. But I know I didn't misplace it or accidentally pitch it into the dirty laundry. I've been a volunteer rape counselor for twenty years and no one is more careful or conscientious with rape evidence than I am."

"What do you think happened to it then?"

"I have no clue. If it weren't such a crazy idea I'd think that someone had purposely gotten rid of it." She shook her head, shaking away aggravations from the past. "What brought on the renewed police interest? Is some lawyer trying to get the court to question the conviction?"

"I can't talk about it," Thea said apologetically. "But could you tell me how and when it was discovered that I had been raped?"

"You sure you want to hear this?"

"Yes."

"I was cutting your clothes off. Do you remember what you wore that night?"

"I think it was a pair of cotton shorts and a knit top. I didn't have a lot of clothes and it was my favorite outfit at the time."

"And underwear?"

"Of course underwear."

"Well, everything was black and sooty on the outside from the fire but when I cut your shorts open there were bloodstains. Both on the inside of the shorts and on your skin. And you didn't have on any underwear. I could see that you also had extreme vaginal bruising and tearing. Right away I called for a gynecologist to do an exam but Dr. Guerin was already rushing you into surgery so it had to wait.

When the GYN finally tracked you down in post-op the nurses had cleaned you up and scrubbed all the soot off, destroying a lot of potential evidence, including whatever was under your fingernails. Luckily, they hadn't washed everywhere. I was asked to assist and we did swabs and combings and all that. The GYN said you had semen at every orifice."

Thea stood and crossed to the narrow window, willing herself not to be sick. "Did you see anything to indicate that there might have been two men . . . that Rusket might not have done it alone?"

The nurse considered the question a moment. "It was so long ago . . . but I do remember wondering about the marks on you. Especially the next day when all the bruises really came out. See, you had hand-shaped bruises so many places and . . . well for instance I remember perfect finger marks—the marks that happen when an attacker is holding a struggling victim—on your upper arms. The fingermarks were pointing down so that means your attacker had to be either behind or above you to grab your arms like that. You also had marks on your thighs and ankles that looked like they were made by hands holding you from the side. Well . . . what was going on? What positions was he in? Even assuming that he raped you vaginally, orally, and anally it's hard to imagine him holding you down with a hand around each ankle, or by clamping your forearms that way."

Wincing internally over the graphic images and

swallowing hard against her nausea, Thea tried to sound cool and detached. "So you're saying that the presence of another man would help explain the marks you remember?"

"Exactly. If you think about it, one man holding your arms or ankles while the other man—well, you get the picture. It makes a lot of sense. On the other hand, Rusket might have just been into Olympic contortions and lots of position changes. We'll never know if there was semen or pubic hair from two perpetrators because all that evidence vanished."

Thea nodded understanding.

The nurse looked at her watch. "I don't have too much longer."

"That's all right; I should be going anyway. I actually just came here for information from Records but I couldn't tell them who I was and . . . well . . . they weren't very helpful."

"You can have your current doctor get medical records for you."

"It's not really medical. I wanted to know what they have about my transfer and whether they have records of care facilities that I was in later."

"Why?"

"Some things have been happening. I live under a different name now and I'm worried about whether someone from here might be able to track down my location."

"Oh," the nurse said, instantly sympathetic. "Is Rusket up for parole?"

"Not yet, but one of these days . . ."

"So you're worried about whether you can be traced through your records."

"Yes. And what incidental personal information they might have."

The nurse winked. "Stay put. I've got a pal in Records and I'm going to run up there and see what I can do."

Fifteen minutes later Karen Falk was back, smiling. "No name on the records but Fremont, yours and your mother's. No other addresses listed. And here's what's great—there must have been a mistake or an omission because there's no record of you being transferred anywhere at all. Looking at the file it reads like you were discharged and sent home. Even if James Bond cracked the files he wouldn't learn diddly."

"Thank you."

"Come on. I'll walk you to the front door or you might never find your way."

"I guess I should thank you for taking such good care of me, too."

"You were easy, sweetie; it's the conscious ones who are hard. Besides, you had everyone pulling for you, so I had to do a good job."

"It's nice to know people cared."

"Did they ever! Cards and gifts from complete strangers flooded in here. And money. I noticed on your records that your mom didn't have insurance but that the entire bill was covered by donations."

"A lot?"

"More than I'll ever see."

"Did you follow the trial?" Thea asked as they reached the door.

"Sure. Even went once."

"Did you think he was guilty?"

Concern filled the woman's eyes. "You don't have any memory of the rape, do you?"

"No. I suppose that's good and bad. The thing is . . . I don't have a face for him."

"Just because you can't remember his face doesn't mean he isn't guilty. I work with rape victims who have no head injuries yet can't recall their attacker's face. Any kind of trauma—emotional as well as physical—can distort or block memories, and your situation is intensified and complicated by the brain injury."

Thea shrugged and attempted a smile. "So you don't think I'm nuts."

"Althea . . . forgive me for being so direct, but did you have counseling for the rape while you were undergoing TBI therapies?"

Thea shifted her gaze, unable to meet the woman's eyes. "I couldn't remember most of the rape so my mother said I should just pretend it never happened. It's not hard to do when your memories are scrambled anyway."

"You try to make a joke of it—about being crazy, about having nightmares and paranoia. Fear of the dark. Intense fear of men. But those are classic post-rape symptoms. Straight from the textbooks. And you don't get well by wishing them away or ignoring them. Or accepting them and making fun of yourself."

"I'm beginning to understand that."

"You'll never heal. You'll never get your life back until you take active steps."

Thea nodded.

"Call me if you need anything or even if you just need to talk. I could give you names of therapists . . . but I guess if you don't live nearby that wouldn't help. Call around when you get home—talk to the rape hot line or whatever your community has, maybe victims' services or a rape unit—and get names of therapists who specialize. You need someone with lots of experience because your case is so extreme. The brain trauma alone can produce changes in perception—anger, paranoia and panic attacks. Then when you add in the unresolved rape trauma you have some very tangled problems to sort out."

Karen Falk smiled and enfolded Thea in a tight hug, the second hug she'd had in as many days. This one did not startle or discomfit her as much as the first had but still it felt unnatural . . . this thing that was her body being held so tightly by another person.

They said good-bye at the front door and Thea hurried across the expanse of parking lot, clutching her purse tightly to her side, reassured by the comforting weight of the gun. Once she was locked safely into her car she took a moment to peer in all directions for threatening or suspicious men. The second rapist. *The other rapist.*

This was what she would be doing for the rest of her life—watching for an attacker. Waiting for him to find her. The other rapist might be dead or in jail or living in Mexico, but she would never know and so she would never feel safe again. The pathetic amount of confidence and normalcy she had achieved would be swept away by the fear.

Then it came to her . . . what she had to do.

You have to find out who the other man is and you have to stop him. Whatever it takes . . .

She had to wipe him out of their lives forever and if it took the gun to do that then so be it. That was the task set before her. That was the trial she'd been given to reclaim hers and her son's lives.

20

Jack drove from the Upper West Side of Manhattan, where he had spent the night with his brother, to Mineola, Long Island. Edmond, who had vacationed on the eastern tip of the island, had warned him that it was the suburban opposite of New York City, adding that there was a reason the island had a town called Hicksville.

From Wally Goon's fax Jack knew that Ronnie Rusket had been from a South Shore town, that the rape had taken place on the North Shore, and that the trial had been held in the Nassau County Center at Mineola. He still did not know exactly where Thea had lived or what name she'd grown up with. Having no obvious place at which to begin his search for David and Thea, he headed straight to the county police as his starting point. Because of Edmond's description he expected a police department that was quietly suburban and friendly, but when he arrived at the County Center he saw news vans jamming the parking lots and packs of microphone-toting reporters roving about as though hungry for something. He parked and threaded through the media to get into the police building.

"Is it always like this?" he asked the officer at the desk.

"No way. We've got a big case going and they've flooded in from everywhere. They've been promised a statement and it's got them foaming at the mouth."

Jack took the news like a punch, afraid that the "big case" concerned David and Thea.

"What exactly happened?" he asked.

"Double murder. That's all I can say. It's not the type of thing we're used to dealing with around here."

Jack nodded. "I'm from California. My nephew ran away and was headed for this area. I came out to try to help my sister and she said to meet her, but I'm not sure if this is the right place."

"You probably want the Juvenile Aid Bureau." The officer flipped some pages and began copying a phone and address onto a slip of paper. Then he cocked his head and tapped the pen against his lip. "Wait a minute. California? It was me that talked to your sister."

"You did? How was she holding up?"

"She was pretty stressed, but she's got good people on the case for her." He handed Jack the slip of paper.

"So, this isn't the right building?" Jack made a show of looking at his watch. "Damn. My plane was late and then I got lost trying to drive over here and by now she's probably given up on me and gone back to her hotel, and I don't have a clue how to get there."

"Take it easy. I know exactly where she went and you're not ten minutes away. Just get out on Old Country Road and go east. You can't miss it."

Jack couldn't ask which hotel because then the officer would wonder why his beloved sister hadn't even told him where she was staying.

"You're sure I won't miss it?"

"Positive. They've got a big sign shaped like a wishing well."

Jack thanked him and went back outside, where he was descended upon by reporters.

"Hey," he said. "I'm just a citizen visiting the police building."

As they melted away in disappointment he spoke to a young camera operator. "Who got murdered?"

"A shipping big shot and his wife. Got it in their mansion."

Jack nodded and moved away, reassured that it couldn't possibly have anything to do with David or Thea.

He found the wishing well sign easily and went to a pay phone beside the Country Inn Motor Hotel. Then he called the hotel and asked for Ms. Auben. To his surprise, it worked. She had registered under her own name, probably feeling safe because she hadn't been known as Auben when she'd lived on the Island.

They wouldn't give him her room number but they put through his call. The line rang unanswered so he went inside to the desk, announced that he was meeting his sister, Ms. Auben, and asked for a room near hers. The friendly clerk told him that Thea was in 269 and that he could have 267. As he went down the hall to his room he passed a maid with a cleaning cart and he paused to smile and say hello. Maids were always worth befriending.

After settling in his own room, he peeked out into the hall to make certain the maid was gone, then went out to knock at Thea's. No answer. With his door ajar so he would hear her arrival, he sat down to read the rest of her chat logs and wait for her, but at the end of an hour he was restless. He examined the little folder that his key came in. The 267 was written across it in thick black strokes. He went back out to the desk and browsed through the tourist brochure rack until the clerk was occupied, then he reached over the counter and took the black felt-tip pen. Back at his own room he changed the 7 to a 9 so that it read 269. Then he put his key in his pants pocket, placed the key folder conspicuously in the breast pocket of his shirt, slipped off his shoes, and searched the halls for the maid he'd smiled at. She was working toward the back of the building but she was happy to help the poor embarrassed man who had locked himself out of his room in his stockinged feet.

He doubted that she had taken note of which door he'd entered when she passed him earlier but just to be certain he feigned ignorance.

"I know it's one of these," he told her and was pleased to see exasperation behind her shy smile.

When it was clear that she didn't know either he said, "Oh wait, look here . . . ," pretending to discover the folder in his pocket. "Two sixty-nine," he read, waving it in front of her face.

Without a word she opened Thea's door for him. He thanked her and gave her a tip.

Thea's room was a mirror image of his own. Quickly he scanned it. On top of the dresser was a stack of photocopies. He crossed to examine them and saw that they were old news articles about her rape. The realization caused an ache in his chest. How must it feel to read about your own brutalization in an impersonal newspaper account? He sat down to read. The type was tiny and he recognized the sheets as being printouts from a microfilm machine. Rather than enlarge just the article, she had printed the entire newspaper page.

They were in chronological order. As was customary with press coverage of breaking news, the initial reports were wrong. The first story was primarily about the fire, the loss of the mansion, and the building's history, with a mention of two people's having been injured—Ronnie Rusket and an unidentified female companion. The second day's report led with the arson investigation, then again listed Ronnie Rusket and a female companion as having been injured. It did go on to say that the female had undergone brain surgery at a local hospital, but then it deteriorated into quotes about wild teenagers. The third day's article had Ronald Malcolm Rusket as a hero who had saved the still unnamed female from burning to death. Jack guessed that the police were already suspicious and working the rape angle. That was why her name had not been released—they were already treating her as a possible victim. Finally, on day four the police clued in the press and the headline trumpeted RAPE AND ASSAULT IN CASTLE FIRE. He read the article twice, wincing at the neurosurgeon's statement about the incidence of recovery being so small that he couldn't give a percentage. He memorized the police sergeant's line *"It appears that the fire was set to cover up the crime and that the attacker intended for his victim to die in the fire."* And he sighed heavily at the story's last sentence: *Her goal is to play with one of the noted symphony orchestras.*

Oh Thea. Everything he had thought before was eclipsed by a deep and enveloping compassion. He had come for David, but now he was there for her, too. And suddenly he felt a change so great that he glanced toward the hotel room's mirror, expecting to see a physical difference. The youthful idealism, the passion for justice, the pure white-hot heart of the protector was rekindled in his breast; he felt transformed, his hard, ugly shell cast away.

He would make the world right again for this boy and this woman. He could do it.

Strengthened, he pored over the rest of the news articles. The rape was competing for space with ongoing coverage of a fatal car accident involving prominent area residents. The accident victims' medical ordeals and the anguish of the families was probed and dissected. Only on days when gruesome details of Thea's case were released—skull slivers driven into her brain or theories about the duration and viciousness of the rape—had the coverage of the tragedies been equal.

He analyzed each of the later stories. From personal experience he knew that police were never completely forthright with reporters and that reporters did not necessarily get the facts they were given straight, even as a case progressed and there was more time for accurate and considered journalism, but he did not have a pipeline into this police department so the news articles were the only accounts he had access to.

For several weeks the coverage waxed and waned; sometimes articles would not appear for days and sometimes they focused on a peripheral theme such as the problem of teens breaking into abandoned mansions. One long feature article, though not helpful in terms of investigative information, kept pulling him back until he knew paragraphs by heart.

Darian North

Between Life And Death
By GINI STOVER

The victim of the brutal rape and beating on the night of June 28 is alive today because of the skills of Dr. William Guerin, who was present in the emergency room by chance that night. Dr. Guerin had rushed to Vale Memorial to be at the side of his son, Gregory Guerin, one of the boys injured in the tragic car accident that happened the same night. Dr. Guerin quickly evaluated the unconscious girl and rushed her into the operating room. There he spent eight hours working on the damage to her skull and brain. He stopped the bleeding, removed bone fragments, and sealed the fractures with titanium plates and screws.

During a second operation, performed days later in Manhattan, Dr. Guerin reduced the swelling in the comatose girl's brain by scraping away dead brain matter.

"Both operations were successful," said Dr. Guerin, "and the scars on her head will soon be covered by hair growth. What we do not know is when, or even if, the young lady will ever emerge from the coma she is in."

Dr. Guerin said that the victim may never remember the attack even if she does come out of her comatose state. "Usually the memories furthest from the time of the injury are the most completely preserved. It is highly unlikely that she would have much recall of her ordeal," the doctor explained.

Long-term coma victims are usually moved from the hospital to facilities that specialize in this sort of patient care. Patients who recover sufficiently to need therapeutic treatments are taken to facilities where their healing can be assisted by therapists in many specialties. A spokesperson for the Tri-State TBI Center, which treats traumatic brain injuries exclusively, said that recovering patients have many difficulties to overcome. Short-term memory can be limited to thirty seconds at the start and the brain needs to compensate and find alternate neural pathways to replace those that have been lost. Patients usually need speech therapy, work on writing as well as expressing thoughts, physical therapy that can even include learning to walk again, and psychotherapy to help them control emotions that are often out of control, particularly feelings of panic and anger.

He put aside the disturbing feature piece and concentrated on the case again. Several weeks had passed before Ronnie Rusket was finally charged, but he knew that the police would have been building their case. Rusket had to have been the focus of the investigation as soon as the rape was revealed. After all, the man had been found with Thea. He had a criminal record. Under pressure of questioning, Rusket admitted that he had gone to the area to commit arson and destroy the house. He also admitted driving down to the party before going to the house. Rusket's version of the night's events was of course not to be found, but would have come out during the trial. Unfortunately, the photocopied pages stopped before there was any trial coverage. Jack shuffled the pages back to the start and began yet another read-through, but then there was a noise and the door swung open.

"Thea!" He leapt from the chair as she stepped inside.

She froze, face white, eyes wide and shocked.

"Thea, it's me," he said, silently cursing himself for scaring her so badly.

She wheeled and ran. He bolted after her, catching her wrist midway down the hall. As soon as he'd stopped her he let go and held up both hands.

"Thea! It's Jack. I came to help you find David."

She sagged against the wall, hugging herself and sucking in deep breaths, counting with her eyes closed. He waited. The safe place. She was counting to her safe place. Taking herself to Carnegie Hall.

"I am so sorry, Thea. That was incredibly stupid of me."

She opened her eyes and looked up at him, tears rolling down her cheeks. He moved toward her but she flinched and drew back so he held up his hands again. "Let's talk about David," he said. "We can go sit in the restaurant. Let's talk about where David could be."

The suggestion transformed her. She jumped up, swinging her bag at him. It caught him sharply in the ribs before he could grab the strap.

"Don't you try any games on me! I know you came here with David!"

"What?"

"You've been hiding him and helping him! How could you?"

She tried to jerk the bag from his grip, either to hit him again or to run, but he held it tightly.

"Listen to me! I have not seen David since the afternoon I gave him a ride home from school," he said, giving the words a gravity and weight that he hoped would penetrate her fury.

She went very still, searching his face with eyes that went from skeptical to puzzled to frightened. Then the color drained from her face again. He reached for her, afraid she might collapse, but she flinched and pulled back.

"Then who is he with?" she asked in a voice that was barely audible.

The bright lights of the hotel's coffee shop made her face even paler and Jack was afraid that she might yet crumple. He ordered coffee and muffins for both of them.

"I don't understand," she said, speaking almost in a whisper. "How are you here if you didn't come with David?"

Speaking slowly and calmly, he told her how worried he had been and how he had worked to find them, keeping it vague, trying to explain without making it seem that he had been hunting her. He did not mention the Wynkoop Institute.

"I thought you were the one," she said finally. "I thought you'd brought him here."

"Believe me, Thea . . . I am your son's friend, and whoever is helping him do this is not his friend."

"But who is it? All this time . . . I've thought it was you. Now, I don't know if he's safe. Oh, God . . . Now I don't know who—"

"We'll figure it out. Together, we'll figure it out. And we'll find him. We will find him."

"How? What if he met this person who's helping him completely by chance and there's no way to ever identify him or—"

"No," Jack cut in firmly. "One of the rules I learned in my years of investigating crime is that you don't ever put anything down to chance or coincidence. Ninety-nine point ninety-nine percent of the time there are links. They might be vague or strange or inexplicable but they're there. You just have to uncover them."

"It's just . . . There are so many things you don't know." She lowered her eyes. "It's all so much more complicated than you think it is."

"Thea," he said as gently as possible. "I know the truth. You don't have to guard your secrets with me anymore. I know what happened that night fourteen years ago and I know who Ronnie Rusket is and where he's spending his time."

She lifted her eyes to his and something happened in his chest. A flip. Like his heart had been hooked and was trying to get free.

Then suddenly she was upset again and twisting her hands together. "There's something new," she said, "something I just learned." Her hands went still and she looked toward the ceiling as though seeking strength. "No one ever told me before. My mother never said anything. Maybe she didn't know because they never showed any pictures or gave a telling description and she wasn't a witness . . . she never went to the trial. She can't have known. . . ."

"What is it?"

"Ronnie Rusket . . . he's black. African-American. He can't be the one who . . . He can't be David's father."

Jack stared at her, absorbing the implications, thinking that there were always links, there were always connections. Even though sometimes it all appeared as pure chaos.

21

After she had told him everything, Jack stared down into his cup of coffee for some minutes, sorting all the puzzle pieces.

"Do you think Rusket had an accomplice?" she asked finally. "Or do you think he's innocent?"

Her voice was strained and Jack could tell that this question had been gnawing at her. He wanted to ask if she was certain she couldn't have been pregnant before the rape, but he decided against it. Given the length of time she had been living with this agony she had certainly asked herself that question and answered it.

"At this point, I don't know," he admitted.

On the table between them she had placed two thick stacks of bound pages. They were the first two volumes in the court transcript of Rusket's case. Rosalie had engineered their loan and the bulk of the volumes were in a box out in Thea's rental car. Jack thumbed open the transcript and read the defense's opening statement, then lapsed into thought again.

"Ronnie Rusket went on the stand in his own defense. Let's get the rest of the transcript and read his side of the story, shall we?"

There were two cardboard cartons in the trunk and Jack took the heavier one. They carried them into the hotel and up to their floor, then there was an awkward moment in the hallway and suddenly understanding dawned—she was afraid to be alone with him. She had always been afraid to be alone with him. And he realized that it was not just him; it was all men. She had engineered her life to be safe from men. And he thought how terrible it must be to live in constant fear of the other half of your species. And he felt both anger at her blanket condemnation of his gender and guilt for being part of a gender that was the source of so much violation and abuse. He felt a rush of pure murderous hatred for the man who had hurt her . . . for any man who attacked any woman. And finally he felt a deep sorrowful resignation because he could never make it right for her. He could not undo what had been done.

"Let's each take a box. I can read in my room and you can read in your room. We can leave our doors open and compare notes in the hall whenever we need to," he suggested.

She gratefully agreed and they retired to their separate rooms to scan the pages. As Jack flipped through he came across the testimony of the gynecologist who had examined Thea right after her surgery. The woman swore that a rape kit was done and that the victim had semen at every orifice. The defense questioned her over the loss of the evidence, but she was firm and convincing. It seemed to Jack that Rusket had an unenthusiastic defense lawyer. But then a young black man with no financial resources probably couldn't afford to purchase enthusiasm.

"Jack?" Thea called from the door. "I've got Rusket's testimony."

They sat on the carpeted floor of the hallway, leaning against opposite walls so that they faced each other. Anyone passing would think they were crazy.

"You want to read it, or you want me to?" he asked.

She passed the opened transcript to him. He thought about how hard it must be to read about your own brutalization in clinically detailed descriptions that you knew had been heard by everyone in open court.

"Okay . . ." He scanned the page. "It begins with his lawyer trying to build sympathy by asking about his wife and baby and his elderly mother. Then . . ." Jack turned pages, his eyes skimming the printed words. "Here we go. I'm going to skip reading any of the objections or legal duels.

"Rusket says, 'A dude called me and said he'd heard my rep. Said he had a old house that was causing a lot of trouble and he needed for it to have a accident.'

"His lawyer asks, 'What kind of accident, Ronnie?'

" 'He needed a total burn but not so's anyone would ask too many questions.'

" 'Did he tell you when he wanted you to do this?'

" 'That night. June 28. He said there was gonna be a party on the beach just a ways down from the house and he wanted it to look like kids from the party had started the fire by accident.'

" 'Did he tell you which house?'

" 'That big old one they called The Castle.'

" 'Did you agree to do this job?'

" 'I did and we talked money.'

" 'How were you to be paid?'

" 'Half up front and half after the job.'

" 'And was he going to pay you personally?'

" 'No. He had a whole drop deal worked where we was never eye to eye.'

" 'Why was that?'

" 'No identities, man.'

" 'But he knew who you were?'

" 'He had to call me.'

" 'But you did not have the opportunity to learn his identity?'

" 'No.'

" 'Did you get the first payment?'

" 'Sure did.'

" 'Did you feel any remorse about what you had agreed to do?'

" 'Why should I? It was just some dead rich person's house and nobody lived there for a long time.

It was strictly a job to me. Just like if he offered me money to load a truck or something.'

" 'If he had offered you money to hurt someone would you have considered that a job like loading a truck?'

" 'No way. I got my principles. I don't have nothin' to do with drugs and I don't hurt nobody. I never even owned a piece.'

" 'Did you go to do your job on June 28?'

" 'I did. He wanted it done at exactly three in the morning, but I was wanting to get it over with and get home to bed 'cause I had church bus duty the next morning.'

" 'Church bus duty?'

" 'My church has a van for the old people who've got no way to get to services and I drive it once a month.'

" 'Do you get paid for this?'

" 'Oh no.'

" 'So you wanted to get the job done earlier and go home.'

" 'That's right. I drove there a little after one and scoped things out. It all looked cool.'

" 'Could you explain that and detail your actions?'

" 'First I drove down to the beach and the party was going on just like he said.'

" 'Did anyone see you at the party?'

" 'Are you kiddin'? Even if I was dumb enough to want to show my face, that was not my kind, you know? They'da kicked the shit out of me.'

" 'For racial reasons?'

" 'What?'

" 'Was the party an all-white party?'

" 'It was a all-rich party.'

" 'And what did you do after you checked the party?'

" 'I drove back up almost to the house and found a place in the trees to hide my car. I got my stuff out of the trunk—the equipment I needed for the job. Then I walked to the house.'

" 'On the road?'

" 'No. Back through the trees and through all that big fancy garden around the house.'

" 'What did you find when you arrived at the house?'

" 'It was deserted, just like he said it would be.'

" 'Was it locked or barricaded in any way?'

" 'The covering was tore off one of the windows just like he said it would be so all's I had to do was break out the glass. Then I climbed inside and went to work.'

" 'What did your work consist of that night?'

" 'I was making it look like some kids had been partying in there and accidentally started a fire so I had this little hibachi thing and a bag of charcoal and a plastic jug of lighter fluid and I had a lot of regular cigarettes and some marijuana cigarettes and a couple rolls of paper towels and four cheap flashlights and a kerosene camping lantern and a glass jar of kerosene and three chair cushions and a plastic bag full of empty beer cans. And a package of hot dogs.'

" 'Could you tell us what you were doing with these things?'

" 'I climbed in with my stuff, which was hard you know 'cause the window was not all the way to the ground and there was all kind of big bushes. The room that took me into was kinda small.'

" 'Was it dark inside?'

" 'Pitch black, man. All the other windows was still covered over with these big plywood panels so no light was comin' in there. I had to use a flashlight and even with that, the place was big and easy to get lost in.'

" 'What did you do next?'

" 'I shined the flashlight around. There were three doors. I left my stuff by the window and went through the door on the right-hand wall to look for a good spot. I went till I found a room that was near the center of the house and with a wood floor and lots of old carved wood on the walls.'

" 'Why did you choose this room?'

" 'It was the right size for a party and it had all that old wood to burn.'

" 'Describe your actions then, please.'

" 'I fixed it all up with the cushions in a corner against the wood walls and the lantern and the kerosene and the hibachi and all that gathered up close. I spread out beer cans. I lit a bunch of cigarettes and stuck them on the cushions to smolder. Then I tipped over the bag of charcoal so it spilled out and I broke the jar of kerosene so it spread across the floor in a puddle that touched one cushion and the charcoal and I set the charcoal lighter right on top of the spilled charcoal.'

" 'What was the purpose of all this?'

" 'To make it look like the cushions accidentally caught fire and then people jumped up and spilled stuff and the fire spread—you know. I always tried to think of a little story in my mind about how the fires happened.'

" 'Then what did you do?'

" 'I was just waiting to make sure the cushions caught fire good enough. I went upstairs. The windows up there wasn't boarded over so I was gonna open one to make a good draft for the fire. I opened a window on the front of the house and that was when I heard the scream.'

" 'Can you describe the scream?'

" 'It was from a woman who sounded real scared.'

" 'What did you do then?'

" 'I looked out the window and I saw a guy kind of fighting with a girl, like he was trying to drag her and she wasn't likin' it none.'

" 'Could you identify either person?'

" 'It was too dark. I could tell they were both white and they both looked young.'

" 'What do you mean by that?'

" 'The way they moved and the way they was

dressed and all that. They looked around my age or younger. I thought they were from the party.'

" 'What happened next?'

" 'I was real worried and praying they'd go away but they just kept it up, him dragging her toward the house and her fighting him, but kinda like she wasn't all there. Like she was half passed out or something. Then he stopped and punched her to the ground and kicked her. Then he picked up something and hit her on her head.'

" 'Could you see what he picked up?'

" 'Looked like a rock.'

" 'And what happened then?'

" 'She didn't fight no more. He carried her to the house. I couldn't see after he got up close so I went real quiet to the top of the stairs and listened. I heard him come in through the window. Then I heard moving around for a few minutes and then it got all quiet. I went back to the window and I saw him walking away from the house by hisself.'

" 'Without the girl?'

" 'Yeah. Kind of hurrying away, except that he stopped to pick up the rock and take it with him.'

" 'What did you do then?'

" 'I ran downstairs to find the girl and get her out before the house went up.'

" 'Why didn't you just go stop the fire?'

" 'I didn't have no water or nothing and the way I set it up I was afraid to go back in that room because when it caught it was probably gonna explode.'

" 'Could you find her?'

" 'Man it was hard. That was a huge place and my sorry little flashlight didn't give much light. But then I heard moaning and that helped a lot.'

" 'Where did you find her?'

" 'In a closet.'

" 'What did you do?'

" 'I tried to talk to her but she was out of her head and bleeding all over. I picked her up like you see them firemen doing on TV. It was hard carrying her in the dark. I kept banging her into things and I was afraid I was hurting her.'

" 'Where were you taking her?'

" 'To the window I came in through. To get her out. But I never made it. The house went whoosh.'

" 'Are you saying there was an explosion?'

" 'Sort of. It's a air pressure thing that happens when the fire hits big and hard and really catches. I guess that old carved wood was just the ticket to burn.'

" 'What effect did this whoosh have on your efforts to leave?'

" 'It slammed me up against the wall and knocked me down. I dropped her. Then the fire was everywhere. I had to crawl and drag her along and I didn't know if I was going the right way anymore. I didn't think I'd ever find that window.'

" 'Did you find it?'

" 'Yeah. I found it. I was fadin' by then, from breathing so much smoke. I don't know how I got us both out. Next thing, I'm on the ground and a fireman is in my face and he asks if I carried the girl out and I musta says yes and he says good work— you're a hero.' "

Jack inhaled deeply and turned the page to continue into the cross-examination, but he could tell by Thea's expression that something had struck a chord with her.

"Something there?" he asked.

"His description of what he saw . . . the man dragging me and fighting with me, then punching me so that I fell to the ground . . . kicking me . . . and then picking up the rock. . . . That's one of my nightmares."

"Damn," Jack said, mostly because there was nothing else to say.

A soft pinging sound came from inside her room and she started, then jumped up. "I hooked up my laptop and left it connected to my service in case an e-mail came from David. That's the signal."

She glanced back at him as she went in the door, worried that he might follow. He stayed right where he was and waited. In just minutes she reappeared, frowning anxiously, with the laptop computer in hand. She passed it to him and he could feel that the battery was running.

"I don't have a printer with me but I've been making copies onto disc," she said, opening a screen so he could read.

VIOLATION

Dear mom,

  Why are you causing so much trouble? You are
not wanted here! Did you think I wouldn't find
out you were nosing around and trying to interfere
and stop me? Just because I am your son does
not mean you own me. I have done my part by
writing to you and letting you know I'm fine so
you don't worry, but you are not doing your part. If
you don't go back to California and let me do
what I have to do then very bad things could happen. And if they do you will be the one to blame!

                                                    David

22

Thea could not stop thinking about the e-mail.

"Those aren't his words," she said for the tenth time. It was completely out of context, but she saw in Jack's face that he knew exactly what she was talking about.

She was driving. Jack had wanted her to guide him around the area and had asked whether she'd rather be the passenger or the driver. She wanted to drive. Driving made her feel as though she had some control.

"Do you think that sounded like David?"

"No," Jack answered as he had every time she'd asked the question.

"The first ones sounded like him with just a few things thrown in from another person, but this one does not sound like him at all."

"Thea . . ."

"Don't you agree? I mean . . . I showed you all of them and you know David—"

"Thea . . ."

"You know how he talks and—"

"Thea!"

She startled and jerked the wheel slightly. "What?"

"We agree that it wasn't written by David. Now I want to go further and explore a theory. Try to keep an open mind, okay?"

She glanced over at him and nodded. To her surprise, she wasn't panicky about being confined in the car with him, even though he seemed so different . . . like a new improved Jack, nicely dressed and radiating energy.

"Is it possible," he began carefully, "that David met this person he's with on the computer?"

Immediately she knew that it was not only possible; it was the most logical explanation. "Yes. Of course. That has to be the answer. I would be aware if David had such a close friend living near us. He talks about Reg and Tommy . . . and you. The only way he could meet someone out of town would be on-line, which he does all the time. He likes to cruise through chat rooms and talk about astronomy with people. And he doesn't say much about that to me."

The idea of David's having met up with an on-line friend was much less frightening than any of the other possibilities she had been trying to avoid considering, so she eagerly embraced it. Even if the computer friend was older . . . that was okay. If they had met in a chat and bonded through their interests then age differences weren't important. She could imagine them, bent together over a monitor with a computer problem or taking turns at a telescope looking at the stars, so immersed in their own world that they didn't realize the seriousness of the situation they had created or the grief they were causing. It was probably just a game to them. Like one of those role-playing games that was popular on-line.

"Okay," Jack continued, "let's put that theory with the facts and with other probable theories. We're certain David is here on Long Island. It was a complicated and expensive trip, which suggests that the help he got was more than just advice and encouragement. Which means someone went to a lot of effort and possibly expense to get him here. That someone has a car and has engineered a safe place for him to stay. That someone has to be an adult, or at least an older teen—with resources. An adult he met on-line, sight unseen, possibly age unknown."

Jack hesitated as though deciding how to go on, or possibly how far he should go. "Now, we have to ask ourselves if David hatched this plan with his cyberpal and they met somewhere and then traveled here together or . . . if this 'friend' was already here— if the friend lives around here somewhere."

She didn't respond because she had an idea where he was heading with his theories and she knew the direction was plausible but she was terrified by it.

"And if we accept the premise up to that point, we then need to ask ourselves, did this friend meet David on-line by chance? Did he just stumble onto a troubled kid and innocently become involved in the kid's problems? Involved deeply enough that he would risk kidnapping charges to aid and abet a runaway scheme? And is it all just a giant cosmic coincidence that this on-line friend from out of the blue happens to live in the very area that you never would go back to and that you wanted to prevent your son from ever knowing about? Is it just a crazy fluke that someone has guided David right into ground zero?"

Her fingers clutched the steering wheel so tightly that her knuckles whitened. She wanted to shout *Stop!* but she had to hear. She glanced at him, and he was studying her.

"We have to face it, Thea. This man deliberately sought out David on-line, tracked him and befriended him and manipulated him, led him to question his paternity, and fed him just the right information to lure him here. Which brings us to why. And why will lead us to his identity."

"This is all guessing! None of these theories are based on anything!"

"Thea . . . remember what I said about chance and coincidence? In police work—"

"This isn't police work! This isn't a big criminal case. You're trying to make it all so sinister when it's not."

He sighed heavily, and silence fell between them.

Jack did not blame Thea for denying the connections—they opened up a minefield of frightening possibilities. And he hadn't even reached the part yet where he theorized about the man's identity. It was someone connected to the rape or the arson. He was positive. But he could tell that she was not ready to face that minefield at all. He was certain now that the key to David's whereabouts, possibly even the key to the boy's survival, lay within that minefield, and he had to walk right through to the beginning of it and examine every inch all over again, just as if he were investigating the case from the start.

He glanced over at her—face taut, eyes betraying an edge of panic, fingers clutching the steering wheel like a life raft—and he knew that he would have to keep his theories to himself for a while. He wished he could send her back to Humboldt County so he could solve this and rescue David without her being hurt or upset any further, without her being involved at all, without her knowing what he found out or what he had to do to bring her son back. But that was not going to happen. He wished she would at least agree to lock herself in her room and stay there while he conducted the investigation . . . but that wasn't going to happen either. He was stuck with her. But at least he'd be able to watch over her this way.

He looked out the window at the sights of inland Nassau County and cast about for a safe topic to ease the tension.

"Hard to believe this is all commuting distance

from Manhattan," he said. "It feels like a different world."

She pounced on the diversion, clearly relieved to get away from his theories. "Manhattan is the different world, not here," she said. "Take a look around. This is all of America—the very rich, the very poor, and the hardworking middle. All with cars. Robber baron mansions where the Native Americans used to have villages. Suburban housing tracts where farmers used to grow potatoes. Shopping malls and highways and expressways."

He grinned, pleased to have found a subject she could hide in.

"Where are we now?"

"The middle. But the upper part of the middle. Here's your basic upper-middle strip mall," she said as she turned into a parking area. "Anywhere USA, right?"

They got out of the car to go into the convenience shop/deli where David had been sighted. The woman who made the identification seemed competent and certain. She was positive it had been between seven and seven-thirty because that was the only time she'd been alone in the evening. He had wanted a sandwich and was surprised when she took meat out of the deli case and sliced it and made the sandwich from scratch. He'd said the stores didn't do that where he was from. He told her he was hungry because the food on the airplane sucked. She had not seen the vehicle David arrived in and did not think it could have been parked right outside the glass front of the shop. It must have been farther down the mall. He wasn't wearing a backpack or carrying anything.

Next they visited the ice cream shop. It was on a highly trafficked street that had no sidewalks or provisions for pedestrians. Again the sighter was a mature woman who struck Jack as reliable. She said she remembered the boy well because the shop was empty. She guessed it was around eight o'clock because she'd finished making up all the next day's cake orders but hadn't started cleanup for the nine o'clock closing yet. He had not had a backpack or the bag from the deli visit. He'd taken a lot of time reading all the flavors and said he wished he knew what his friend liked. While he was paying someone honked outside and he became very agitated about taking so long, but she hadn't seen the vehicle because it wasn't parked in front of the shop.

Jack and Thea got back into the car.

"Where now?" she asked him.

"Just drive," he said casually. "Let's look around here."

It was a pleasantly leafy neighborhood, a grid of streets lined with nice but not extravagant homes. He opened a map to get a better sense of location. The kid was hungry and complaining about the food on the airplane. . . . Suddenly he realized that they were just off a major highway that could easily have been used as a route from Kennedy Airport to the northern portion of Nassau County. The strip malls were both convenient to the highway exit.

He looked around. Either David and his friend's destination was in this general area or they were heading north and the driver swung off the highway here to find the hungry boy something quick to eat.

"Let's see," he said, turning the map this way and that. "Where are we exactly?"

They were on a residential street and she was driving slowly enough that she could look over and point at the map as she said, "We're here."

"And where's the county police building?"

She pointed to Mineola, which was south of their present location.

"I've only seen parts of southern and central Nassau. How about we go north. I haven't been north of here yet."

"North is where the rich people live," she said. "It's the real-life Gold Coast. *Great Gatsby* territory."

"Good. I like staring at the rich. They're different, you know."

One corner of her mouth twitched and he didn't have to wonder if she got the joke. Under different circumstances he might have even made her laugh with his literary reference.

She took him through Glen Head and then Locust Valley. The average cost of the vehicles on the road rose dramatically. It was impressive, though most of the major mansions were set back from the roads and hidden behind fences and trees.

"Are we close to the Vandeveer House?" he asked, knowing full well that they were approaching the vicinity.

"It burned," she said flatly.

"Can we drive by?"

She turned her head to look at him. "You don't have to treat me like a child, Jack. Just tell me you want to see where the rape happened. I don't have my head in the sand and I'm not in denial. And the fact is that I want you to find out more about the attack that night, because I want to know for certain that Ronnie Rusket was guilty and I want to know who else was there."

"Okay," he said, wondering if she realized that her rejection of his theories regarding David did indeed indicate a denial of reality.

Thea turned toward the Sound. She drove until she reached the northern shore, pulling the car over for a few minutes so Jack could look out at the view.

"Nice," he said. "Was the party near here?"

"Down that little lane. On a private estate with a beachfront."

"And where were the cars parked?"

"Rosalie's cousin's car was parked along the lane."

"The car you went to lie down in?"

She nodded in answer and pulled out, turning away from the water and the beachfront property to drive uphill toward the Vandeveer castle. Would there be anything left of the old mansion? Would the sight of the ruins trigger any memories? Or any panic attacks? She felt herself separate so that she was the curious observer looking down on the poor pathetic victim returning to the ruin, and she was grateful for the distance.

You could really make a fool of yourself here.

She could and very well might make a fool of herself but that didn't matter anymore. All that mattered was her son. Finding her son.

The area had changed. She backed up and turned around, then finally stopped at the lavish stone entrance to an upscale housing development. Copper letters weathered to an elegant verdigris were set into the stone: VANDEVEER VILLAGE.

"I'm afraid we might be looking at old Commodore Vandeveer's renowned mansion and gardens."

Beyond the stone entrance were curving streets with graceful trees and self-consciously unique minimansions.

"Who lives in these things?" Jack asked. "People who've inherited Daddy's money?"

"No. This is the territory of Wall Street warriors and bankers . . . the newly affluent. Looks like they won this round in the tug-of-war up here."

"Between the filthy rich and the moderately rich?"

"Between the old money and the new money."

He seemed preoccupied so she stopped talking. Did he have a plan? Could he really find her son?

"Let's drive to a pay phone," he said. "I've got an idea."

She headed for a commercial street and pulled up beside an outdoor phone. After only five minutes on the phone and fifteen minutes of driving, they arrived at a massive set of open gates.

The sign said:

FULLER HOUSE
An Historic American Home and Garden
Open 10 a.m. to 5 p.m. Wednesday-Sunday
SPONSORED BY THE ISLAND PRESERVATION FOUNDATION

She drove through the gates and up the long driveway to a stunning mansion with a parking area at the side.

"Who are we talking to again?" she asked, more than a little nervous.

"Mrs. Susan Maxwell. The leader of the fight to save the Vandeveer House. You don't have to go in."

"No, I want to. But should I give my real name?"

"No. I'll just introduce you as my associate."

"Okay." She inhaled deeply as she followed him to the door.

They were shown to Susan Maxwell's office on the top floor.

"Are you the man who called?" the woman asked, rising from behind an enormous antique desk that had a computer on one side and neatly arranged paperwork on the other. She was slim and athletic with short white hair against very tan skin. No jewelry other than a plain gold wedding ring. Her faded polo shirt and worn khaki pants looked as though they had been salvaged from a charity box.

"Francis Fitzgerald." He extended his hand across the desk. "And this is my associate."

Thea offered a tentative smile but the woman barely noticed her. Where had he come up with Francis Fitzgerald? But then she remembered that Francis was what the F. in F. Scott had stood for.

"Please sit down, Mr. Fitzgerald."

They sat. Thea marveled at the straightness of the woman's posture.

Jack began with, "As I told you on the phone, Ms. Maxwell, I'm looking into the arson at the Vandeveer House."

"There never was a determination of arson."

"Why is that, when Ronnie Rusket confessed to torching the place for money?"

Susan Maxwell sighed. "The feeling was that a man like that would lie about anything."

"But why tell such a detailed and plausible lie? Why tell *that* lie? It certainly didn't help his case to admit that he was there to commit arson."

"Personally I thought he told the truth about being hired. The girl's friend testified that the girl had felt ill and had gone to lie down in the car. I think he came across her while he was looking over the party, and forcefully took her up to the house with him to have a little sport before he lit the match. They say arson is often sexual."

"But then why did he risk his own life to get her out? Why bring her out at all?"

"Perhaps he planned to let her burn, then had a change of heart and went in after her. Who knows? Perhaps they were acquainted. A girl like that . . . well, she certainly had no business at that party, did she? Maybe she was there because she was in on the crime with him. But that is all in the past and the man is in prison where he belongs."

Jack gave Thea a sideways glance, and she knew he was worried about her reaction.

"Who do you think paid to have the house burned?" Thea asked quickly to reassure Jack.

"It would be unwise of me to make allegations," Susan Maxwell said, her lips pursed self-righteously. "But one must assume that the house was destroyed for financial reasons."

"So who built Vandeveer Village?" ·

"Harris Winslow's company."

"Who were you fighting over the preservation of Vandeveer House?"

"The North Shore 2000 Development Group."

"Was Harris Winslow active in that group?"

"He founded the group. One of these days they'll come after my house. It's been in our family four generations."

"To your knowledge did the police ever question Winslow about the arson story?"

"No." She smiled ruefully. "What is the point of all this? It's over. May God preserve me from another hellish night like that. Losing Vandeveer House. Losing Phillip Osburn. Deighten Freylen paralyzed. Dr. Guerin's son losing a foot. Chip White nearly dying. And my own son's face . . ." She shook her head. "I believe that it was arson and that the man who hired the arsonist went unpunished, but the pain of that night lives on in this community, Mr. Fitzgerald, and you will find no one who wants to open the old wounds."

"Your son?"

"Kenneth was in the car accident, and no amount of reconstructive surgery has been able to give him back a face that he can live with. He hides in his room most of the time. All five boys grew up together, went to Briden Academy together, played on a championship lacrosse team together. Theirs was the real tragedy that night—not the loss of the house. After that night they were never the same again . . . none of them."

"What a bitch, huh?" Jack asked as they walked to the parking area.

"Don't worry. She didn't bother me," Thea assured him.

But he was worried and he wanted to draw her out. "Could you tell whether she was old money, new money or no money?" he asked with sarcasm as they got into the car.

"She's got money so old it's moldy."

"She didn't look very prosperous."

"She did mention her four-generation house though. And you have to remember, new money is big jewelry, major hair, and impressive clothes. That woman was way beyond the need to impress. It takes generations of having everything to be so comfortable displaying nothing. There's also a subtle attitude thing. Old money is more reserved about their conceits."

"How did a peasant girl from the South Shore learn all this?"

"My music teacher was always putting together groups to play background at North Shore functions. All four years of high school I was a regular at their parties, dressed in my standard black dress, sitting in the back on a folding chair, playing my flute and watching."

"Why don't you play anymore?" he asked, forgetting to be careful.

She looked away. "You know about the head injury. That should explain it."

"Maybe that explains your not going on to try for a career as a professional musician, but it doesn't explain why you've given up music so completely. You don't even listen to anything interesting."

"Did you ever play an instrument?"

"I took sax lessons long enough to learn that I should give the world a break and stick to listening."

"But long enough that you're an expert on giving advice to others?"

"Touché."

He stayed silent until they were through the gates and off the estate.

"What did you think?"

She considered the question a moment. "I'm more convinced than ever that Ronnie Rusket was telling the truth about the fire."

"What else?"

"Harris Winslow either set up the arson himself or had one of his flunkies do it."

"Maybe we should pay Mr. Winslow a visit."

"I don't know, Jack. What good would that do? He'd probably get us arrested or something, and these people can't lead us to Rusket's accomplice. And what does that matter right now anyway? We have to find David!"

"You don't have to come."

"If you go, I'm going."

"Then we need another pay phone."

She waited in the car while he made the calls. He watched her. She was trying to hold herself together but the question of David's safety was wearing on her. He wished there were a faster and more direct way to investigate, but he was convinced that the route to David was twisted up in the arson and the rape, and the only way he could untwist the mess was to carefully pick it all apart.

He slammed the receiver down after being told

that Harris Winslow was out and unreachable till at least the next day.

"No luck," he told her as he got back in the car. "Maybe he'll be in tomorrow."

"Tomorrow. Oh God, Jack . . . another day almost gone and we don't know where David is. We don't know *anything*!"

"We know more than we did before," he said, hating himself for his helplessness in the face of her anguish.

Was he doing the right thing by respecting her wishes and tackling this himself? Should they go straight back to the police now and spill the whole story? It was her decision but he had a gut feeling that David was safer for it. A full-scale police effort and the resulting media might push David's friend right over the edge.

Thea was tired and discouraged as they ate dinner in the hotel restaurant. Michaels had not left any messages and she could not see that Jack's detective work had gotten them any closer to finding her son.

Jack checked his watch. "I want to read the rest of the transcript and the prin—and some other things I have."

They crossed the lobby and entered the hall that led to their rooms. She realized then that she had stopped looking over her shoulder and expecting an attacker to strike at any moment. Jack had made her feel safe. And suddenly she felt a rush of gratitude that was somehow coupled with skepticism. "Why are you here, Jack? Why are you doing all this for us?"

"Because David needs me. Maybe you need me a little too."

She nodded, though it was hard for her to accept that he had no other motive. Was he lying?

When they reached their rooms Jack watched over her as she unlocked her door. He checked her room for intruders, then stepped back out into the hallway and told her good night. As soon as she shut the door she went through the ritual of bolt, chain, and chair, then sat on the end of the bed, feeling empty and alone, tempted to boot her computer and go to a chat room for someone to talk to. But the fact that David had met his friend on-line kept her from going to the laptop. She turned on the television to make the stillness bearable, but there was nothing of interest to watch. As soon as her eyes got heavy she tried to sleep, hoping that she could make it through till morning. But she could not stop thinking about her son who was out there in the clutches of a stranger, and the rapist who was still free, and Rusket who could be innocent. It occurred to her that the rapist could be someone she'd already had contact with. For all she knew he could be Detective Michaels or Rosalie's husband or the hotel desk clerk. The only safe male on Long Island was Jack.

She went to sleep with the gun on the bedside table. When the nightmares came she woke screaming. Hands and eyes. Choking, gagging. The images were in the room with her and she fought to regain control. She huddled in the bed with the covers clutched to her breast, her heart slamming against her ribs and her breath a ragged pant. Even in the light of a lamp the images lingered. Within moments pounding started at her door.

"Thea! It's Jack. Are you all right?"

She nodded but could not make a sound to answer.

"Thea! Open up and talk to me."

She heard someone call "Quiet out there!" from down the hall.

"Thea, I'm going to wake up the entire hotel if you don't open this door and show me you're okay."

Trembling, she forced her body to move, jamming the gun under her pillow to hide it as she slid off the bed, eyes darting around the room, catching glimpses of the horrors that were seared into her vision. She had trouble unlocking the door.

Jack was standing there in hastily donned sweat clothes, his hair sticking up at odd angles.

"He was here," she whispered. "The other rapist . . . He caught me in the parking lot and he dragged me up the stairs and no one saw. No one heard. And then he . . . then he . . ."

And suddenly Jack was hugging her. A protective comforting hug. She stiffened, unable to accept the hug for what it was because the body that was hugging her was a man's body.

He released her.

"I'm sorry," she whispered. And then again, "I'm sorry."

"Don't be." He hesitated. "I could sit in the chair and watch over you while you go back to sleep. Or is that worse? Is being with me worse than being alone?"

She could feel his distress. He wanted badly to help. It was almost as though he needed so badly to help that denying him would be cruel and ungrateful. But the thought of being trapped with him in the room made her stomach go weak.

His shoulders sagged in defeat. "I guess there's nothing I can do." He turned to go back to his room.

"Wait." The panic threatened. It was lodged in her throat and clutching at her chest. But she fought it. "I'd like to try that . . . having you in the chair." She forced a smile. "My sentry."

He came into her space carefully, waiting for cues from her and asking which chair to sit in. She pointed to the one by the window; that way he would not be between her and the only exit. He sat down and averted his eyes as she got into bed, though the long heavy T-shirt she had on was less revealing than most street clothes.

"Sleep well," he said.

"Thank you."

She closed her eyes and took a deep breath. All the knots and kinks melted away and she was surprised at how sleepy she felt. She thought about Jack in the chair by the window. Jack watching over her like a knight guarding a princess. Jack who would go out and rescue her son.

The first thing Thea saw when she opened her eyes was the digital readout of the bedside clock, and she was stunned at having slept so long. Then she heard breathing and remembered that she was alone with a man in the room and she bolted upright.

He was asleep in the chair, looking slouched and uncomfortable, with his head falling forward onto his chest. She studied him. He appeared so . . . defenseless. She felt almost tender toward him, almost maternal. He was a sweet man—even though those two words together, "sweet man," seemed as oxymoronic to her as "jumbo shrimp" or "deafening silence." She'd grown up without a father or brother or even an uncle and had never known sweetness in an adult male. She had believed that little boys left all that behind when the change into manhood occurred. But now here was this man treating her with such gentle compassion, which was confusing because it went against everything she had thought was true. Yet it was heartening, because she had a son and she wanted to believe that such a man was possible. That her son could become such a man.

Then again . . . maybe this was an act, a subterfuge to make her let down her guard. Maybe there was something he wanted or something he was trying to keep her from finding out.

He startled awake, instantly alert. "Sorry," he said. "I must have drifted off."

"That's okay."

"Did you sleep?"

"Yes. Thank you."

"Well . . ." He stood. "I'll just . . ." He moved sideways toward the door. "I'll see you. . . . For breakfast, maybe?"

"Forty-five minutes? In the coffee shop?"

"Fine. Okay."

After he was gone she checked her e-mail. Nothing. But then there had been a pattern of the messages appearing midday.

She passed the long wall-mounted mirror and stopped, staring hard at the woman reflected there. Strangely, she saw a different woman from the one who'd left Eureka. A stronger woman. Not as strong or sure as the girl she was at seventeen, but better than she had been since.

The fear no longer possessed her . . . controlled her . . . *owned* her. Her son's plight had pulled her up out of the quicksand. Yet, she still felt the powerful tug of that sucking pit—that sheltered cowering life—and she knew that she could easily slip back into it. Did she want to? Would it be better to slip back than to go forward into an uncertain and unsafe future? What if the strength didn't hold? What if there was no longer a place for her out in the world? What if she was irrevocably tainted . . . forever unwanted?

"Who am I?" she whispered.

David's mother was the answer she expected, but instead her inner voice countered with another question.

"Who do I want to be?" And for the first time in her adult life she felt the flutter of possibility.

She closed her eyes and pressed her hands over the quickening in her belly—an awakening of self that was akin to rebirth. It shuddered in her bones, beat against her heart, pulsed through her veins. And suddenly she saw that there was danger in relying too heavily on Jack. Reliance could bring more helplessness and dependency. She had to do it herself—face her attacker, whoever he was and wherever he was. She had to deal with him herself. She had to get rid of him. And she had to do it without Jack because Jack might try to stop her.

She picked up her oversized leather bag and up-ended it on the bed. She wrapped the gun in a hand towel, then put it into the bottom of her bag and piled her other belongings on top of it. Jack would never see it or guess it was there. She had to free herself and her son from the nightmares. And there was only one way. Living so many years with her alleged attacker in prison had taught her that. Prison wasn't the answer. This man had to be wiped away. She had brought the gun because she was fearful. But now she could use it to end that fear forever.

23

"Now, David . . . that's not a very friendly look you're giving me."

"Why are you keeping me locked up? I'm like a prisoner!"

"It's for your own protection. There are bad men out there who might want to hurt you. And you've got plenty of activities to occupy yourself with. Look at all the wonderful things in this room."

"Oh, man. Forget it. I just want to call my mom and go home with her."

"Poor David. Well, I was going to wait to tell you but you're forcing me to do it now."

"What?"

"Your mom is gone. She's decided to give you up."

"What!"

"She wants to have a normal life now, and she can't do that as long as you're around. You are the source of all her troubles. You have nearly destroyed her."

"No!"

"I know it's upsetting, but she never wanted you. You were like a cancer to her. She would have aborted you if she'd had the chance."

"Shut up! Just shut up!"

"But you're a lucky boy, David. Your mother and I have come to an agreement. You're living with me from now on. You'll be my son."

"No! You're lying! And you can't keep me here. You can't—"

He grabbed the boy by the neck and squeezed until the shouting stopped.

24

Jack cleaned up at his room and then went to the hotel restaurant, where he drank coffee, read the local paper, and waited for Thea. The biggest story, of course, was the area's double murder. He avoided the story at first because he had had enough of murder, but eventually his curiosity got the best of him and he went back to it. The victims were a man named Carter White and his wife, Virginia.

"Hi," Thea said as she slid into the booth opposite him.

He couldn't help staring. There was something different about her but he didn't know exactly what it was. A change in body language. A change in attitude.

"Did I forget to comb my hair or something?"

"You just look rested, I guess. Did you check your e-mail?"

"Nothing. I should look again after lunch." She met his eyes for a moment, then quickly busied herself with the menu. "Have you ordered?"

"Not yet." He folded the paper out of the way. "Does the name Carter White mean anything to you?"

"Who's that?"

He picked up the paper, folded so that he could read the beginning of the murder story to her. "This morning's paper," he said. " 'Carter White and his wife, Virginia Tapper White, were found dead in their Locust Valley home yesterday morning by an arriving maid. The cause of death in both cases was gunshot wounds, and a police source reports that the shootings occurred shortly before the maid's arrival.'

" 'Mr. White was an executive with White Shipping Lines and a great-great-grandson of the founder. Mrs. White was . . .' and on and on." He put the paper down.

She had been reading the menu and he was not certain she'd listened but then she looked up and said, "Mrs. Maxwell mentioned a Chip White who was in the accident. Think they're related?"

"Hey, hey. Not bad." He grinned and looked straight into her eyes. "You can be on my team anytime."

Abruptly she slid out of the booth. "Can you please order me the bagel special? I'm trying Michaels again."

Jack watched her cross the room. Clearly he had done something to offend or upset her but he didn't know what. Was she so sensitive that she couldn't take a little teasing? But then maybe he hadn't been *just* teasing. Maybe he had been flirting a little too. It was such a natural and ingrained behavior that he hadn't even been aware he was doing it until he'd thought about it.

Damn! She was probably off thinking about what a jerk he was. What an insensitive lout. What a typical man.

By the time she returned, the food was on the table and his agitation was peaking.

"You didn't have to wait for me," she said as she sat down.

And suddenly he was furious.

"So I'm a jerk, right? A little chemistry is an evil thing, right? I can't respect you and like you at the same time, right?"

She looked at him with a puzzled, wounded expression.

"You're right." He slammed his fist down on the table. "I ought to be shot."

She blinked several times, and he saw tears in her eyes.

"Oh hell," he muttered, feeling ashamed. "What did Michaels say?"

She stared down at her bagel as though her appetite was gone. "He said there was nothing new at all. He questioned me again about possible relatives and friends in the area."

Something big filled his chest and closed his throat. He leaned toward her, feeling awkward and inadequate. Wishing he could wipe away all the terrible things that had happened to her, or maybe just make up for them. But he could think of nothing to say.

She sat very still, tears sliding down her cheeks.

"I guess I ruined breakfast, huh?" he said, pushing his plate away and then starting out of the booth.

"Don't go. Please. I don't know how to be friends with you, Jack. But I want to."

She had asked him to drive, but now she was pressed against the passenger door and seemed too nervous to carry on a conversation. He thought of the wounded crow he'd brought home as a boy. It had been shot in the breast and wing and he'd caught it and wrapped it in his jacket. Then he'd spent days nursing it, enduring attacks from beak and claws as he tried to change dressings and give it food and water.

His mother had finally exploded. "Your best jacket is stained with blood and bird poop, you've got gouges and bruises all over you, and the damn thing is dying anyway. When will you learn?"

"Where are we going first?" she asked.

"Since I haven't been successful making an appointment with Harris Winslow I thought we'd just pay him a surprise visit and see if we can shake anything loose about the fire."

"Okay," she said, sounding less than enthusiastic.

"Someone hired Rusket. Someone who stood to gain by the destruction of that mansion. That someone could know the identity of Rusket's accomplice.

And I think Harris Winslow is a good candidate for the 'someone' position."

The office building was a modern monstrosity of glass and stone, completely out of place in the quaint atmosphere of the street on which it was located. They went in past a poster-size photograph of a colorful hot air balloon floating in a blue sky. Across the balloon was the name WINSLOW in foot-high letters.

"Is Mr. Winslow in?" Jack asked the receptionist, whose desk sat in the middle of a large lobby with a ceiling that soared all the way up to a third-floor skylight.

"He's in a meeting away from the office," the receptionist said with a perfunctory smile. "Would you care to leave a message?"

"Will he be available today at all? I'm in from the West Coast and I'm not in the area long."

"You're from the West Coast?" The receptionist was more interested in them now.

"I can see you," a voice called from above, and Jack looked up to discover a man leaning over a railing on the second floor. "Send them up to my office, Angela."

The woman's eyes did a very subtle roll. Then, with a sigh, she said, "Go in and take the stairs to the right. He'll meet you at the top." Using just the pad of her fingertip so that her long yellow and orange nail was protected, she pressed a button and the ostentatious double doors to the inner sanctum swung open.

At the top of the stairs they were greeted by a short but well-built man in his late twenties or early thirties. He was wearing an expensive double-breasted suit and a white shirt with monogrammed French cuffs. Chunky gold cuff links set with little diamonds adorned the sleeves and there was a large diamond in the ring on the hand he extended to Jack.

"How are you? I'm Harris Winslow the Second. Heard you say you were in from the Coast? We've been waiting to hear back from you boys."

Jack felt like he'd put the winning coin in a slot machine. One mention of the West Coast and bells were ringing.

"I'm Ross Macdonald and this is my assistant."

Harris Winslow the Second flashed Thea a smile. Like Susan Maxwell he neither noticed nor cared that the assistant had no name. Jack suspected that he could have said *This is my dog* and Winslow would have flashed the same smile.

"Come on into my office. How are things out on the Coast?"

"Fine." Jack looked at Thea. "They're fine, right?" She nodded and when Winslow turned away she rolled her eyes in a perfect imitation of the secretary.

They were led into a room that had so many polished surfaces Jack wished he had his sunglasses. There were more pictures of hot air balloons and there were pictures of an older version of this man shaking hands with prominent Republicans. Winslow Senior no doubt. There was a black-and-white group shot of seven men in stylish hunting togs holding guns and dead birds. The date printed in the corner indicated it was taken twenty years ago and the men's faces said that the outing had been more business than pleasure. One of the men was a grim Winslow Senior and Jack suspected that the others were North Shore movers and shakers, leading him to think that the photo represented a coup of sorts or it would not have been kept so long and displayed so prominently. On a side bookshelf was a framed color photograph of Winslow Junior operating a piece of heavy wrecking machinery, or at least pretending to. He was grinning and looked very posed. In the background was a beautiful building that could have been Vandeveer House. In spite of the presence of Junior's photo the office clearly belonged to Daddy.

Jack took a seat across the desk from Winslow and Thea settled off to the side, next to a computer that looked like it was powerful enough to launch rockets.

"So . . ." Winslow tilted back in the impressive leather desk chair and rubbed his hands together. "Have you given any more thought to our proposal? Time is ticking away and the longer we wait the closer the preservation nuts get to landmarking the whole damn island."

"It's that bad, huh?"

"Worse! We like old things as much as anybody else, but they have to be in the right place. They can't stand in the way of progress." His smile was wide and his teeth were as straight and white as a tooth-paste pitchman's. His light brown hair was perfectly styled. Jack had an almost irresistible urge to mess something up.

"We took a swing past Vandeveer Village on our way here," Jack said.

The man's chest actually expanded. "That's what we intend to do all over this shore. Everywhere there's an estate. Everywhere there's a piece of undeveloped land."

"Anything special you have your eye on?"

The man glanced around as though afraid of eaves-droppers, then leaned across the desk toward Jack and said in a hushed tone, "This is strictly confidential. . . . I've got a little something that's starting to look available. It's an old run-down junk heap on sixty acres. Can you believe that . . . sixty acres! And a prime location."

"Will there be trouble again—like there was with the Vandeveer place?"

The man raised his eyebrows appreciatively. "You boys do your homework, don't you?"

Jack sat stony-faced.

"I assure you, there will be no trouble over this place. Like I said, it's very run-down. And the preservationists haven't been sniffing around it yet because it's still owned by the original family, or the descendant of the original family. The guy rattles around in that thing all alone." Winslow shrugged.

"He's actually a friend of mine from high school,

a terrific guy . . . we used to play sports together when we were kids . . . but he was in a car wreck sometime back and his legs are all gimped up. He's in a wheelchair now and almost as much a wreck as his house. Poor guy." He shook his head sadly. "It'll be no trouble at all to convince him how much better he'll be in a nice modern place that's been specially designed for a cripple."

"There won't be any fires, will there?"

The smile faltered but then returned to full wattage. "That is entirely out of our control. Some of those old places are real tinderboxes."

Jack rose, and Thea followed suit.

"Thank you, Mr. Winslow."

"Call me Win. Mr. Winslow is my father."

"You don't go by Junior, huh?" Jack asked with all the guile he could muster.

"No," Winslow retorted curtly. Then he remembered to smile again. "You'll be in town a few days?"

"Absolutely. And I expect to meet your father."

Winslow fished in the breast pocket of his jacket and came up with a gold card case. "There's no telling when he'll be back in the office, but there's no reason that the two of us can't take care of this." He handed Jack a card. "That's my direct office line."

Jack inspected the card. "How about your home number?"

"Oh . . . it's impossible to catch me at home. Impossible. But I'll give you my cell phone, too. Just in case."

He took the card back and scribbled a number on the reverse side. "Maybe we could do lunch or dinner?"

"Maybe," Jack said, thinking that Junior wanted badly to accomplish something on his own and impress his father, and wondering if the refusal to provide a home number meant that he still lived with his parents, no doubt in a modern manse with lots of shiny surfaces and expensive toys.

"Great!" Winslow rubbed his hands together, taking Jack's vague response as an acceptance. "Have your assistant call my girl in the morning and set it up."

"Did you get that?" he asked Thea. "Call his girl in the morning."

"Yes, sir," she answered.

As soon as they were out of the building she shot him a sarcastic look.

"Ross Macdonald? It's a good thing the man wasn't a mystery reader."

Jack shrugged. "Did I say that? Did I say Ross Macdonald?"

"Yes. And you demoted me from associate to assistant."

"Next time you'll be my valet."

She smacked him on the arm, pulled back as though she had startled herself, then deflated completely into the distraught mother of a runaway child.

"I need to stop at a pay phone and try Michaels

again. Why haven't they got something more? Isn't he looking for David at all?"

"We could go straight to his office," he offered.

"There's no point unless we know he's there."

As he watched Thea make the call on an outdoor pay phone he reminded himself that he could not be distracted by Thea's suffering. He had to be single-minded in his pursuit. He thought about "Junior" Winslow, the poster boy for new money. Junior was too young to have been the brains behind an arson scheme fourteen years ago. Winslow Senior was the man he wanted. But he hoped to reach Winslow Senior through the son.

She returned to the car looking glum. "They weren't in. But there was a message for me: No news." She was close to tears. "Do you think they're still looking?"

"I know they are. But that doesn't really matter because *we* are going to find him, Thea."

She buried her face in her hands and sobbed David's name over and over. It was very much like the keening he'd heard at funerals.

"We'll find him," he repeated, though this time he was speaking to himself.

25

Thea felt as though she were trapped on a speeding train, headed into the heart of the nightmare. She wanted off. She wanted her life to be back the way it was, safe and sheltered with her son and her butterflies, cloistered within the timeless serenity of the redwood forest. She watched the blur of the deciduous greenery of Long Island through the car window as Jack drove and she thought about the tall, cool trees she had left behind. So stately and tolerant, so towering and remote. Completely removed from the concerns of the human mind and body.

She had first experienced the redwood forest when her mother bundled them all in the car and announced a nature vacation. David had been six. She had been twenty-three. The forest was a revelation to her and it had been a wonderful trip. But she saw now that the dynamic of their threesome had been one mother and two children. Instead of supporting her and urging her into adulthood her mother had tried to keep her a perpetual child after the accident.

Maybe her mother believed that the brain injury had not only destroyed her chances as a professional musician, but had ruined her chances of ever becoming an independent adult.

It was hard to place blame. Her mother had endured so much and struggled so valiantly, never complaining except to God. Yet, she wondered now . . . if her mother had not been so determined to keep her a child . . . if her mother had encouraged her to—no—permitted her to take control of her life and her son's life, if her mother had allowed her to face the rape and get counseling for it . . . if her mother . . .

Oh grow up! You're on your own now and your mother is gone and you can't change the past so get on with it. Think about the future. Who's standing in the way now? Who's preventing that final leap into full-fledged normal adult womanhood now?

When she made that first trip to the forest it had called to her and she'd known she would live there one day. She'd wanted to hide amongst the trees, to lose herself in their aloof but gentle sanctuary, to take refuge there. The forest had not turned out to be quite the haven she'd imagined, but it still resonated within her, offering peace and solace in a world of chaos.

"I miss the forest," she said.

"Why?" Jack asked without taking his eyes from the road. "You don't hike or go out into it. You walk on that treadmill in your living room."

The comment made her angry, but it was fair. It was true. She was afraid to go out alone into the forest she loved because she might come across a man there.

"You're right. Pathetic, isn't it? I live like a rabbit, constantly on the alert for predators."

Jack had been focused on the narrow wooded roads because he was trying to follow Susan Maxwell's directions. He had called the woman and asked which of the old mansions had a solitary resident who was handicapped, and she'd immediately responded with Deighten Freylen's name and then had given him the directions—a series of rights and lefts on unmarked roads. But now, trying to focus on Thea, he could not keep track of the turns and had to pull onto the shoulder of the road and put the car in park. He turned in the seat to look at her.

"And rapists are the predators?"

"Men are the predators."

"All men?"

"Potentially. The problem is, you can't tell. What they are on the outside could just be camouflage."

"So any man could be a predator inside?"

"Maybe not a lion or tiger but certainly a jackal."

"A scavenger, you mean?"

"An opportunist. They don't actively stalk but if they happen across something helpless and alone they pounce. You were a policeman—you know the crime statistics. Most women are attacked simply because the men have the opportunity. The robber stumbles across the girl asleep in her bed or the carjacker realizes he has a female in his power or the frat boys find a coed who got separated from the party, or the star athlete—"

"Okay. Okay."

"It's a common occurrence, isn't it? And most rapes aren't even reported because the victim fears the system as much as she fears the attacker."

"But to label all men as potential predators . . . you're saying that every man has the capacity to rape and brutalize a woman if the right circumstances arise."

She hesitated. "Not all," she conceded. "But a lot. It's in their nature. Or it's in our culture."

"I'm definitely not capable of brutalizing a woman. My brothers and my father aren't. Except for the criminals I've chased I've never known a predatory man."

But even as he protested he acknowledged the truth of her central fact—rape was a uniquely male crime. And, like most human acts, the urge toward it could be imagined. He recalled a night after Eliane had left him. Anger and hurt had been eating him alive and he had driven to the house that had so recently been theirs together and he had watched, drinking straight from a bottle of scotch, as her lover kissed her good night at the door and went whistling off down the dark street. Her lover who was also his partner and fellow detective. And he had known she was alone, and he had had the urge to kick open that door and take her . . . take what used to be his . . . to show her . . . to punish her . . . and in some twisted way to reaffirm his worth, to reclaim his position in the world.

Of course, he had not acted on that urge. He would never have acted upon it. But it had taken him in its evil grip and shown him the dark abyss. It had shown him the twisted rationale behind a violent man's acts. Did that mean her bleak and damaged view of things had to be accepted?

"No one knows what another is capable of," she said. "Even with men who seem perfectly fine and who fit into society in other ways."

He recognized that as one of his own personal truths, formed through years of working murder cases . . . and through his partner's betrayal. Yet, it was a greater condemnation coming from her because it was aimed specifically at males. All males.

"How can you live with such an ugly view of half the human race? That's a perversion in itself."

"How can you criticize me when you have no idea what it's like to live as a woman? To be constantly afraid."

"I'm sorry," he said, reminding himself of what she had been through. "But don't you think that your circumstances are . . . extreme? You're speaking as a victim, not as a woman."

"Women *are* victims! Or potential victims. Men don't have to worry about leaving work late at night or parking their car in the back of the parking lot or getting into an elevator with a stranger. But for a woman . . . whether she's a corporate executive or a nun or a house spouse she has to be constantly aware, constantly on her guard. She has to organize her schedule and make her plans and conduct herself with personal safety always in the back of her mind. Always. And I'm not talking about seat belts and a low-cholesterol diet. I'm talking about men. Women have to constantly watch out for and protect themselves against *men*.

"Children too." She sank down into her seat as though losing steam. "Children have to beware of men, too." Then she looked around and frowned. "Why are we stopped here?"

He studied her for a moment, wishing he had a brilliant argument, something profound to say, something that would make her see the goodness in men so clearly that she never questioned it again. But he had no scathing comeback. How many times had he worried about his niece or Eliane or even another officer who was female? How many women had he walked to cars late at night or watched over while they unlocked doors and then locked themselves inside? He had not been protecting those women against asteroids or poisonous snakes; he'd been protecting them against his fellow males. And she was right in that he had never felt fear for his personal safety in the normal course of his life, whether jogging alone at three a.m. or stepping onto elevator cars with lone male occupants. Any fear he had experienced had been job-related. But he was angry nonetheless.

"So what's the answer? That all men are intrinsically evil? That the world would be so safe and perfect without men that maybe in our bright future they'll collect a supply of non-Y sperm and then ship all males to an atoll and nuke them to oblivion. And if those are the answers then what about David? He's one of us, you know."

She sighed, sounding utterly disheartened, and her voice was hoarse with emotion when she said, "I know. And it's so confusing. David . . . you . . . It's so confusing."

"And what about love? The way you see the world, love is impossible. Love can't exist. Men are too base and beastly to give love, and women would be fools to love their enemy."

"Romantic love is a fiction. A device used in songs and novels. It's a trick. There are other cultures that have no such thing."

"Oh, Thea . . . do you really believe that?"

She didn't answer.

He reached for her hand, then realized the touch might upset her so pulled back and raked his fingers through his hair in frustration. "I never hurt a female in my life. Unless you count Maggie in kindergarten, but I swear she pushed me down the slide first." He looked directly into her eyes. "I'd never hurt you, Thea. And I won't let anyone else hurt you either."

*   *   *

VIOLATION

Thea leaned forward to peer out the front windshield. The requisite stone entryway was deteriorating but there was a grace to its decay. Jack had stopped the car as if the gates were still in place.

"Roanoke," he said, reading the bronze plaque affixed to the stone. "Think that's the name of the original family who built it?"

"It's probably the name of the house." She rolled down the passenger window and leaned her head out to see the building just inside the entryway. "Most of these old mansions had names. Over the years Vandeveer House came to be called that because of the famous family, but the actual name was—"

"The Castle, right?"

"No. That was just a nickname. It was something like Windmere or Windleigh."

"Sounds like a budget housing tract around L.A."

"And that 'cottage' just inside the entrance is the gatehouse. The groundskeeper or some other retainer usually lived there with his wife, who would work in the house as a maid or cook."

"Why do you say 'cottage' with such sarcasm?"

"Because that's the way people always referred to them, saying it as though they were little thatched-roof hovels. When we played at parties on old estates Mr. Levy always had to stop the van and check in at the 'cottage.' And I used to compare those cottages to the crummy dump my mother and I lived in and wish I had a cottage."

"Wonder if anyone lives in this one now."

As if in answer a man came out the door and shielded his eyes to stare at them. He was young and muscular, with floppy blond-streaked hair that was dark at the roots. He padded out barefooted as Jack lowered his window and eased the car forward.

"We're here to see Deighten Freylen."

"Does he know you're coming?"

"Yes," Jack lied.

"Okay, I'll call the house for you." The man beamed a disarmingly guileless and boyish grin that Thea knew he had practiced. "Say . . . would you mind telling him that I'm running a little late today? I'll be up after lunch for his session."

"Will do," Jack said and started forward.

The drive curved through once formal plantings that had run wild. Immense lilacs crowded the narrow roadway, and overhead the arcing branches of trees formed a canopy. There was a sharper curve and suddenly everything opened to reveal an Italianate mansion. The approach was designed for drama.

"Ever seen this one before?" Jack asked.

"I think we played here for an outdoor party one night. If I'm right there's a big glass building in the back."

"A greenhouse, you mean?"

"Much more elaborate than that. More like a Victorian conservatory."

They parked next to a luxury sport utility vehicle, a designation which had always seemed absurdly contradictory to her, and walked up steps that had been fitted with a ramp to the side. Jack was just reaching for the bell beside the imposing front door when it was opened by a beefy Asian man in sweatpants and a white chef's jacket.

"Come in. Come in," the man ordered impatiently.

Thea exchanged a glance with Jack as they stepped inside. She was amazed at how often their thoughts were in sync and how easily they communicated.

"You're expected, huh? If you want lunch, tell me now," the white-coated man barked. "No add-ons later."

"I don't—" Jack started to say, but he was interrupted.

"Plan on their staying," a firm voice ordered from a shadowy doorway down the hall.

Thea exchanged another glance with Jack, then watched as the man came into view. He was in his thirties and handsome in an upper-crust outdoorsy sort of way, with sandy hair and a glow of tanned fitness. His V-necked white cotton sweater looked like sailing attire. But he was in a wheelchair and his legs dangled uselessly inside faded denim jeans. Thea had an immediate feeling of aversion which made her feel guilty: She had never been faced with a victim of paralysis.

"I'm Deighten Freylen."

"We really can't impose on you for lunch," Jack said.

"You 'say' that you were expected." One side of

Freylen's mouth tugged upward in sardonic amusement. "Then I 'say' you were expected for lunch."

She could sense Jack bristling so she cut in quickly with, "That's very kind of you, Mr. Freylen."

"Call me Deighten. Or Dey." He extended his hand.

Jack coolly returned the handshake. "I'm Gus Mahler, and this is my associate."

"How interesting to have such a musically historical name."

Jack stiffened, but immediately Freylen's sharp gaze shifted to Thea. "Do I call you 'Associate'?"

"Anna," Thea said without missing a beat. "You can call me Anna."

"We're insurance investigators," Jack told him. "Doing a follow-up on the Vandeveer fire."

"Of course." Freylen spun his chair sharply to face away from them. It was an old-fashioned push-it-yourself model, which surprised her because the man could obviously afford a Rolls-Royce of an electronic chair. "I'll give you a tour while we wait for chef's call," Freylen announced, rolling ahead of them briskly, propelling himself with hands that were protected by leather bicycling gloves.

As they went through the center hallway, past a small gated elevator tucked in an alcove and then a series of doors, he explained that nine tenths of the house had been sealed off. "I'm the last of my kind," he said with amused sarcasm. "Living here alone on my rock like the last seal in the herd."

"Oh . . . the fellow out at the gate said to tell you that he was running late and he'd be up after lunch for your session," Jack told him.

Freylen nodded. "He's my physical therapist and athletic trainer. A very good one too. But he's completely undependable. And my chef . . . he's temperamental and doesn't want to work full-time. Has visions of himself as a celebrity in the making. He wants to come in two days a week and leave me little packages to microwave for the other days. Cleaning women come and go, completely unconcerned with the quality of their work, and competent gardening help is nonexistent." Freylen's mouth twisted into an enigmatic smile. "Money doesn't buy what it used to." Then he led them out the back door and down a ramp.

"This is my crystal palace," he said, and they stopped to look upon a beautifully ornate greenhouse that was a lacework of Victorian curves inset with glass. The paint was flaking from the wood frames and the glass was filmed with grime in places, but that did not diminish the impact.

Thea nudged Jack with her elbow and he gave a subtle nod of understanding. This was indeed where she had played. She could still picture the rows of torches and the flicker of firelight repeated on pane after pane of glass. Glimpses of this fairy-tale life were what led her to the North Shore party that night. It was no longer fairyland here, though. Vines crept over the marble benches and weeds grew between the patio's carefully set stones. The greenhouse was decaying.

"This was an Ellen Biddle Shipman garden," Freylen told them with a sweep of his arm to indicate the tangled greenery beyond the patio. "I guess it still is." He chuckled. "Just what every cripple needs."

Though his wit continued to be deprecating he seemed proud of the greenhouse, telling them its history and the history of the family's amateur botanists, who had ventured out on collecting expeditions around the world and brought back exotic specimens to nurture.

"My great-great-grandfather brought back a plant that only blooms once every hundred years. At least I think that's the story. When it did bloom the flower was gigantic and stunk like rotten meat. Made the greenhouse intolerable for weeks."

Inside the glass house there were ramps and wooden walkways for wheelchair access. They were maintained but everything else was decaying. It was as though a real jungle had risen to claim the interior, with huge tropical plants crowding each other and big-leafed vines twining along the glass walls. Barely any sunlight penetrated the foliage that had grown upward to strain against the glass ceiling and she could not see very far into the shadowy center of the jungle. A strong aversion filled her but she inhaled the thick humid air and followed the men. The meandering wooden trail led them into a dark and steamy world that was completely foreign. Things brushed her—leaves and vines and trailing creepers, tattered remnants of webs that warned of huge spiders, and then a flutter of wings that made her duck and give an involuntary cry.

"Was that a bat?" Jack asked.

"Oh yes." Freylen turned his head to smile at them. "We have a fascinating ecosystem in here. Insects, arachnids, snakes, and bats."

They crossed a small bridge over a brackish stream that must have circulated mechanically at one time, and then finally came to a clearing near the back where there was a gathering of potting and display tables that were in various stages of rot.

"This was a wonderful place for hide-and-seek when I was a child," Freylen said.

Jack mopped his brow. "The old heating system in this thing really pumps it out."

Freylen laughed. "It's a beautiful system. They don't make them like this anymore. But I'm sure lunch is ready by now so I'll spare you a look at the boiler."

Thea was relieved to step back out into the open air. Jack fell into step beside Freylen and she followed, watching and listening. Their conversation touched on Carter White's murder. He was indeed the "Chip" White from the car accident. Thea could tell that Jack was closing in on questions about the Vandeveer fire. As they strolled back across the patio she looked up at the magnificently derelict house, struggling to maintain dignity in the face of complete neglect, and she felt a stab of regret. Decorative pieces had fallen from around the windows and there was a fungus creeping up one side. She tilted her head back to see better, shading her eyes against a flash of sun from the third-story terrace. The terrace was nearly overrun with ivy but it looked as though he was still using it. And she wondered at her own sense of loss over this dying building that represented the triumph of a despicable robber baron. Logic told her she should not care. Her conscience told her she should consider the obscene expenditure it would require to preserve this place when there were hungry children out in the world. Yet somehow she did care. Beauty was nourishing regardless of the source, and it would be sad to lose both the beauty and the history embodied in these walls.

Inside the house they were led to a small sunny room and a formally set table. The china matched but each piece depicted a different scene. The silver was weighty and had a mythological motif. She suspected that it was all very old and worth a fortune. Lunch consisted entirely of sautéed vegetables and rice.

"Do you remember seeing Rusket at the party that night?" Jack asked, and she realized she had missed some of their discussion.

"No. He definitely was not mingling."

"You're sure?"

"Of course. He was an outsider. He'd have gotten

the shit beat out of him instantly if he'd showed his face."

"But there were girls allowed who were outsiders."

"There were usually some outside girls invited." One side of Freylen's mouth curved upward. "They were always so grateful."

"Do you know Harris Winslow?" Jack asked brusquely.

Freylen chuckled. "Which one? Winowski Senior or Winowski Junior?"

"I thought it was Winslow."

"Harry Winowski changed his name to Harris Winslow after he made his first big killing in real estate. He pillages the island as Winslow but my father always called him Winowski."

"Your father was acquainted with Winowski Senior?"

"My father was forced to tolerate him. They even hunted together on occasion, though of course Winowski was never officially admitted to the hunting club. My father thought him a crude and boorish man."

Jack wondered if one of the joyless hunters preserved in black and white on Winslow's wall was Freylen's father.

"How about you? Do you know the son?"

"Since childhood. His father bought Win into everything we did. Even sent him to Briden Academy.

But Win always had the soul of a peasant barbarian. No amount of money could erase that."

"Was he at the party that night?"

"Probably. Everyone floated in and out."

"Do you recall him saying anything about the fire?"

"Perhaps I did hear him say, '*My dad's having the Vandeveer place torched tonight.*' Or maybe it was '*Come on, gang, let's all go watch the fire!*'"

Jack did not react to the sarcasm. "Do you remember noticing anything suspicious?"

"No."

"How about when you and your friends left the party?"

"We went the other direction, away from The Castle."

"So you didn't see Rusket in the parking area or—"

"Listen to me . . . *Gus.* I was drunk. I was celebrating my freedom from Briden and my acceptance to Yale. I was reveling in the presence of dozens of scantily dressed, eager girls. Then I was covered with blood and riding in the back of an ambulance. I do not remember seeing Rusket or smelling smoke or hearing the little fire dog bark. Is that clear?"

Thea held her breath while the men engaged in eye wrestling.

"You're Winslow's next target," Jack told him brusquely. "Your place is the site of his next housing development. He's already hatching the plan."

"That bastard," Freylen muttered, his face reddening with anger.

"Did you and your friends see something that night? Is that why you were speeding away in the opposite direction when the party wasn't even over yet?"

"Get out!" Freylen shouted. "Get out of my house. And if you're smart you'll get off the Island and mind your own business."

26

mom,

   What is wrong with you, you bitch. Don't you know that I am happy and have everything I want here. I have so many things that you would never get for me, space rocks and telescopes and computer software and everything else you can think of. Why would I want to go back home to your shitty little house and your boring screwed-up life?

   I know now that you never wanted me and I was an accident for you so consider yourself lucky to be rid of me and leave me alone. Stop this stupid hunt because you'll never ever find me and if you do we'll both be very sorry.

David

P.S. If you calm down and start acting reasonably maybe we'll come visit you one of these days. There's no reason we can't all get along.

P.P.S. It's good that you haven't told the police anything more. That was smart. When you go crying to the police you put us all in danger.

Thea looked stricken as she watched Jack read the e-mail. She had allowed him into her room to see the screen that was waiting when they got back to the hotel after their lunch with Freylen.

"David didn't write any of it," Thea said, pressing a hand against her heart.

Jack nodded agreement. "We're hearing directly from the 'friend.' He's angry about your trying to find him. That means he's aware of what we're doing." Jack thought a moment. "Go ahead and copy it to disc, then let's read all of them again."

He dragged the easy chair up beside the desk chair so they could sit together and look at the small screen.

"All this time . . . I've been angry, I've been frantic, I've been afraid that David would learn the truth . . . but I never allowed myself to believe he was in physical danger . . . until now." Deep, racking sobs shook her chest. "You don't think he'll hurt David, do you?"

"Can you take listening to theories?" he asked, searching her eyes for the answer. He had several possible scenarios in his mind now, but he didn't know if she was strong enough to face them.

Lifting her chin, she gave a firm nod.

"Who would lure David here?" he prompted.

She swallowed hard. "A pedophile?"

"We're beyond such a basic answer. And you know that."

She lowered her eyes.

"The person could have a fixation. He could want to be David's friend or he could want to hurt David. He could see David as a means to revenge or as a way to hurt or control someone else. He could see David as a threat. Or . . . David could simply be the bait to get you here. In which case he could want to hurt you or use you or hurt someone else through you."

He waited but she didn't respond.

"This could be something as offbeat as a crazed historic preservationist who's going to somehow use David to blackmail the young Dr. Guerin into buying the Freylen mansion before Winslow can demolish it."

She cocked her head, absorbing his wild premise in a tentative and almost hopeful way.

"You're saying we can't rule out anything."

"Right. There are connections but they might not be logical or obvious. We just have to keep digging and examining, looking for common elements. And we can't let our emotions get in the way or blind us."

"My emotions, you mean."

"Wouldn't it be better if you went back to Humboldt and let me do my job here?"

"It's not your job, Jack. And I'm not leaving."

He held up his hands to signal surrender.

She straightened in the chair, squaring her shoulders as she turned her attention to the computer screen. "Why would he say that about the police . . . that it puts us all in danger?"

"I don't know."

Crying to the police . . . As Jack read the phrase again, he had the neck-hair reaction. And he knew that he could not keep his other suspicion from her any longer. But in telling her he would reveal just how deeply he had invaded her privacy. Would that destroy the fragile trust he had built with her?

"I didn't want to show you this," he said, standing and heading for the door. "But I have to. I'll get it from my room."

When he returned she was by the window, finishing a glass of water. "I want my son back safely," she said. "Show me whatever you have. Don't worry . . . I can deal with anything as long as it helps get my son back."

That made him feel even worse. "Sit down." He motioned her toward one chair and pulled the other around so he was facing her but was not too close.

"What are those?" she asked, frowning at the papers he held.

He cradled his forehead in his hand for a moment, dreading her reaction, knowing that he was about to inflict more torture on her.

"After you took off so suddenly, I went into your house and looked around."

Her gaze was quizzical but steady.

"I was looking at your papers . . . and I turned on your computer . . . and I figured out your code. . . ."

Shocked disbelief flared in her eyes.

"You read my personal stuff!"

"Yeah."

"All of it?"

He hesitated. "All of it. The e-mails, the chats, Delian—everything."

Her cheeks went red and she covered her face with her hands.

"How could you do that?"

"I was desperate for clues so I'd know where David and you vanished to. I didn't mean to invade your privacy. No. That's not true. I did mean to, but now I'm sorry. Except . . . I can't be sorry because I learned some important things."

With her hands still over her face she shook her head. "I'm so ashamed."

"Oh, Thea, that guy was a master manipulator. You didn't stand a chance against him."

That made her cry.

"You were lonely. And in spite of all your fears and everything you try to tell yourself—you're normal. You opened yourself to an intimate relationship in the only way you knew how. That's nothing to be ashamed of."

She lowered her hands but did not meet his eyes.

He shrugged. "You just had bad taste in men."

Her mouth twisted into a rueful acknowledgment and he knew they had made it through the most difficult part.

"Okay . . . there's more. This is going to be hard."

"What can be worse? There was nothing else—"

"I think Delian was talking to David, too."

"That's impossible!"

"Is it?"

"Oh my God," she whispered, rocking herself slightly in the chair.

"If someone really wanted to track down a person on-line . . . in the chat rooms . . . and they had lots of patience and bits of biographical information . . . would it be impossible?"

"No. And why would he want to talk to David?"

"Why did he want to talk to you?"

"Is that an insult?"

"No! What I mean is—didn't you ever question the way he showed up in your chat group so suddenly and zeroed right in on you?"

She looked away but he could tell the question was working on her.

"I've read everything from the moment he appeared and believe me this guy was after you. He tailored everything to appeal to you. He flattered you and seduced you, all the while leading you to give him information about David."

"He wasn't interested in David."

"Look!" He flipped to passages he had marked with colored flags. "The guy spread it out and kept it very casual, but he asked you dozens of questions about David . . . what his interests were, what kind of kid he was . . ."

She read without comment.

"Now, consider this: He uses the name Delian with you. That's from Greek mythology and refers to someone from the island of Delos—Apollo's island. And in his Delian bio he said he likes rock climbing and Greek mythology.

"We don't know what name he used with David but look . . ." He handed her David's daydream essay. "David said he has a secret protector nobody knows about, a protector he's never seen but could see if he wanted to. He's strong enough to climb mountains—Delian told you he was a rock climber—and drive a chariot to the sun—Apollo drives the chariot of the sun in mythology. Apollo . . . Delos . . . Delian. He knows all the secrets of the universe and . . . 'I talk to him through my computer.' That is one hell of a lot of coincidences."

"Aren't you stretching things?"

"I'll admit it's circumstantial. But if you put it all together it has weight. And there's more."

He shuffled the pages and handed her three. They were from her private chats with Delian.

"Read this sentence," he told her, pointing.

She read it aloud. " 'You're just upset Thea because you don't have your mother to go crying to anymore.' " She looked up at Jack, puzzled.

"Now this one," he said, pointing to a sentence on the next page.

" 'You wouldn't like me if I was to come crying to you with all my problems.' "

"Now here." Jack pointed again.

" 'Did you go crying to your landlord, the mighty Jack?' "

She raised her eyes, understanding dawning.

"I took a course with this legendary documents expert, and he taught that phrases are even more telling than handwriting. The person uses them unconsciously and so never tries to alter or disguise them."

"Are there more examples?" she asked.

"Oh yeah. There are seven commonly used phrases in his writing and dozens of distinctive word combinations. But 'crying to' seems to be one of our boy's favorites." Jack crossed to the still booted computer. "Listen to the last sentence of the e-mail you just got from the person writing as David. 'When you go *crying to* the police you put us all in danger.' "

Jack turned back toward her. She looked numb.

"Delian went after you and then he used what he'd learned from you to go after David. Now he has David, and we have to figure out who he is and what he wants."

Jack was alone in his room. Thea had driven to the JAB to catch Michaels and Wilson. Since he did not want to have to lie about who he was, he had stayed behind. He worried that she was spilling the whole story to the detectives. But at this point there was no way to know which course was safer for David—silence or complete openness. His gut still called for silence. And Thea seemed to believe that too, but she was balanced on a thin edge and talking to the detectives could knock her right off. Jack tried to put it out of his mind. He had to focus. He had to make the connections.

Delian had David. But who was Delian and what were his motives? He lived in the area, and he had tracked Thea and David on-line. Or was it that he had only hunted Thea? What if the guy had gone after Thea without knowing she had a son and then in the course of his chats with her he learned about David and the boy became his target?

Rusket was locked away. Rusket's mother had died and his wife had moved to Detroit. Rosalie had no motive and was not the least bit suspicious. Who else might be interested in Thea and obsessed with David? The prime candidate was the so-called accomplice. The invisible party to the rape. But who the hell was that? And what if he hadn't been an accomplice at all but the sole rapist? What if Rusket was completely innocent?

He had not said anything to Thea, but if it was the rapist who had David, the man had every reason to kill the boy and hide the body forever. David's DNA was the noose that could hang the man.

He shook his head to clear his thoughts. This was a fourteen-year-old crime with no evidence, no witnesses, and no suspects other than the man in prison. He had to take himself back. He had to consider everything. How did Thea get from the parked car up to Vandeveer House? Did she accept a ride from someone and see something she shouldn't have seen? If Rusket was telling the truth then someone else had bashed Thea's head and dumped her in that house. Did that someone choose The Castle because it was convenient or did he put her in that house because he *knew* it was going to be burned that night?

Which brought him back to the fire.

Freylen was awfully touchy about the fire questions. But then the man had reason to be bitter and touchy about the events of that particular night—a night which had left him in a wheelchair. A "hellish night," Susan Maxwell had called it. So many disasters in one short time frame. And all of them were connected to one another through either the Vandeveer castle or the party on the beach. He felt certain that all of them were related in some ugly incestuous way. Maybe it would help to talk to another of the accident survivors.

He dialed the phone.

"Hello."

"This is Francis Fitzgerald calling for Mrs. Maxwell."

"Mrs. Maxwell isn't taking phone calls."

"Well, I'm actually trying to contact her son, Kenneth. I just wanted to ask her for the number."

There was a long silence.

"Kenneth would be at this number except . . . I'm sorry to have to tell you . . . Kenneth Maxwell drowned this afternoon."

Jack took the receiver from his ear and stared at it.

"Hello? Hello?"

"Sorry," he said, repositioning the phone. "I'm stunned. How did it happen?"

"No one is sure. He was at the shore and fell . . . hit his head . . . and . . . that's all we know right now."

"Please convey my sympathies to the family."

"Thank you."

Jack hung up the telephone.

"Damn!"

There had been four survivors of the car accident. Then suddenly one was shot to death and another hit his head and drowned the very next day? What were the odds against that happening?

A light tapping sounded at his door. "Jack? It's Thea. I'm back."

Quickly he opened the door and pulled her into the room.

"Did you see the detectives?"

"Yes."

Her eyes darted around and she remained standing. He was puzzled but then realized that she was uncomfortable being with him in his room rather than her own.

"They were nice and apologetic, and assured me that everyone is still looking for David, but I could tell they weren't as optimistic as before. And I think the entire police department is so wrapped up in that double murder that they don't have time for anything else."

"No new sightings?"

"Nothing."

"Did you tell them any more of the story?"

"I thought about it, but . . ." She looked at him as though torn by her decision. "Don't you think David is better off if we keep it as quiet as possible?"

"Yes."

"I keep asking myself if I'm preserving the secrets more for my benefit than for his."

"Too much attention could panic the person who's holding him."

"All right. I can tell that you've got something new on your mind so go ahead."

Her perception made him smile a little. Then he sobered.

"Kenneth Maxwell is dead."

"Susan Maxwell's son?"

"He hit his head and drowned this afternoon."

"Oh, that poor woman."

"Think about it, Thea. On one night in June there is a party, a rape, a fire, and a car accident with four survivors. Fourteen years later the rape victim's son is lured to the area. The victim herself begins snooping around the area. And within days, one of the accident survivors is murdered and another hits his head and drowns—a death which is either a suicide or a second murder."

"You think it's all connected?"

"If not it's a hell of a big coincidence, and—"

"There are no coincidences in police work," she finished for him.

"We have to talk to Dr. Guerin."

"The neurosurgeon who took care of me?"

"The young Dr. Guerin. His son. The one surviving survivor of the car accident who we haven't spoken to."

She cradled her forehead in her hand a moment,

then looked at him with pain-filled eyes. "It doesn't feel like we're any closer to David."

"I know, but that's the way investigations are. You look at everything. You explore the connections." He sighed. "You've checked into the on-line stuff and hit dead ends in finding out who Delian is or where the e-mails are coming from, right?"

She nodded.

"Winslow Senior isn't back to the office until day after tomorrow—and incidentally I called Wally Goon and started them on a full dig into the Winslow/Winowskis and their company."

"Good."

"You've done what you can with the detectives. You've called your friend Rosalie and found out that she knows nothing more about the fire." He held up his hands. "Where do you think we should go next if not to young Dr. Guerin?"

"We could talk to Ronnie Rusket."

"I called the prison. He's in trouble for something and his visiting hours have been suspended."

She thought a moment, then her expression hardened into determination.

"I'm going to send an e-mail to Delian."

"Saying what?"

"Come help me write it. We can be just as manipulative as he's been."

"We have to be very careful."

"We will be. And if we don't like what we write we can always decide not to send it."

27

Dear Del,

I am so afraid and so worried about my son. I still haven't found him. Jack has come and is forcing me to let him help though I can't see that he is doing any good. There are two detectives who I talk to but I haven't told them the real story at all—just that David ran away to Long Island—and so they're nice but not very interested.

The good news is that David has somehow landed with a friend who is taking very good care of him. You can't imagine how reassuring that is for me. I may have to accept that my son has chosen to live with some-one else. I hope not, but it may be true. In that case I will be alone. I have always dreamed that someday you and I would meet in person and that my son would be with us and we could have a great time to-gether, but it does not look like that will happen now.

Please write to me. I am so lonely for you and need your guidance and your support.

Thea

"I think we should do it," she said, and before he could either agree or disagree she clicked the send command.

He was surprised at her sudden combativeness. "You're right. That could soothe the bastard and get him complacent. Who knows—maybe he'll even invite you over after reading that."

She looked at him, and there was hope in her eyes. "Do you think I could convince him that we should all be together?"

"I doubt it," he said gently. "Not in just a few days anyway. Now we have to see Guerin."

"You know where he is?"

"I couldn't get a personal phone or address, but he runs a clinic in New York City and I've got the address and the hours. I called there and tried to set up a meeting. Either he was avoiding me or he has a very protective receptionist."

"And that makes you all the more determined to see him, right?"

"Right," Jack admitted. "We can take the train from Mineola station. His clinic is in a bad area according to my brother, but we'll take a cab from the train station straight to the door. I figure we can be there right about closing time and catch him. If it gets late, or if we have to go back and camp in his office the next morning, we can spend the night in Manhattan with my brother."

"You go," she said. "I can't leave the Island."

"We'll give Edmond's number to the detectives.

We'll take your laptop so you can check for e-mails. And even if we get stuck overnight, we'll be back here before lunch tomorrow. What are you going to miss by not being in this room tonight?"

She appeared unconvinced.

"I'm not leaving you here alone. I can't do that, Thea. Not with everything I know now . . ."

"And you think it's that important to see Guerin?"

"Yes." He watched her. "How about this. We'll take both our cars to the train station. That gives you the freedom to come back on your own anytime . . . even though I wouldn't want you to."

"If we have to stay, what kind of place will we be sleeping in?"

"Safe. Comfortable. You'll like Edmond. And I'll be right there with you."

Hours later they walked out of a storefront clinic in one of the most depressed and disturbing neighborhoods Thea had ever seen. Most of the faces were shades of brown and all of them wore a weary wariness. They skirted Thea and Jack on the sidewalk as though passing poisonous snakes. Guerin had managed to slip out of his office without seeing them, and Jack was more determined than ever to speak to the man so they were going to spend the night at his brother's. Thea was not happy about it.

But when she finally took a seat in the beautiful living room, surrounded by marble, the deep tones of carved wood, and the rich cadences of Edmond

Verrity's voice, Thea was not as panicky as she'd imagined she'd be. She accepted the glass of wine that Edmond offered and sat quietly, sipping and listening as the two men went over every detail of the case, picking it apart and examining possibilities that were increasingly far-fetched. Edmond was a fraction shorter than Jack but his hair and eyes were similar. His manner was more European and his clothes were straight off the designer's rack. But in spirit the man was very much like Jack. She could see that they were brothers. And she felt a twinge because she was without siblings and now she was raising a son who would have no one else close in the world after she was gone. And then she was stricken by thoughts of David alone now, David frightened and alone with a maniac.

"What about this," Edmond said. "Kenneth Maxwell was the accomplice. His friends picked him up after the deed and in speeding away from the scene they crashed. His mother found out and spent years tracing Thea, then stole the child who is actually her grandson. So Delian is actually Susan Maxwell! And when her son found out he threw himself off a cliff into the ocean."

"I think we've gone beyond productive reasoning," Jack said.

"Or! Rosalie's brother was Rusket's helper for the fire and he was skulking around looking at the party and he saw Thea go to the car and—"

"Edmond," Jack cautioned, glancing at Thea. "That's enough of the left-field stuff."

"Oh." Edmond cast her an apologetic look. "I'm sorry. I tend to get a bit carried away."

Jack stood. "We should turn in. I want to be at Guerin's door when he gets there in the morning."

"How was it over there? I've never ventured into that part of the city."

"It was grim," Jack told him. "Guerin can't be doing it for the money."

"Here's to altruists," Edmond said, finishing his wine.

Thea rose and took her glass to the kitchen. She felt incredibly awkward. Both men followed her into the tiny kitchen with their glasses.

"Good night, Thea," Edmond said, smiling a wonderfully warm and compassionate smile. "I'm certain that Jack will have your son back soon. You're in good hands."

"Thank you. Good night." The pleasantries sounded false coming out of her when she was so filled with turmoil. Listening to the puzzle of possibilities had set her mind racing and tied her stomach in knots.

Her laptop was set up beside the telephone. She had checked repeatedly for an e-mail reply from Delian and now she connected the phone cord once again and dialed into the service. There was nothing. What reaction would Delian have to the message she'd sent? Would he open himself to a trap?

Jack came to look over her shoulder. "Give the guy

time. You probably won't hear from him until tomorrow."

She nodded and shut down her computer, trying to mask her agitation.

"That's your bedroom," Jack said, pointing down the small hallway to where two doors faced each other. "You're across from Edmond, and you're shouting distance from where I'll be on the couch in the living room." He led her down the hall and pushed open her door. "I've already pulled all the drapes so the windows are covered. You're not at ground level and there are no terraces outside that room so those windows aren't a source of entry. The only way in is through the front of the apartment and past me on the couch."

"Thanks." She looked into his eyes and felt an intense physical reaction that almost frightened her.

" 'Night," he said.

Her heart was slamming against her ribs and she had the same hot, clammy, light-headed, but determined feeling she'd had before her very first concert as a child. "Wait . . . Could I . . . I mean could you . . . hold me for just a minute?"

His eyes were surprised and questioning. Then he gently put his arms around her, holding her close but not tightly, his chin resting on the top of her head.

At first she felt panic and the need to break free, but she forced herself to be still and gradually, ever so gradually, the panic melted away, leaving a sweet aching wonder that spread through her like the wine.

And suddenly she was crying. Not with sounds. Not so he would know. But tears were falling from her eyes, and they were not sad tears.

"Good night," she said, pulling free and turning to wipe away the tears before he saw them.

"Good night," he said, and his voice was like a caress.

She is sick and dizzy, lying in the backseat of a car. It is a hot night but the windows are up because they are electric windows and without the key she cannot open them. She can smell the upholstery and hear the distant sounds of the ongoing party, the nearer sounds of cicadas buzzing in the trees. She is angry at herself for misjudging her tolerance for the vodka they pushed on her. She wanted them to like her. She wanted to fit in. That didn't happen and it's not going to happen because she's a plain little South Shore girl and she sees that reflected in the eyes of every person at the party.

Her stomach dips and sways like the time she went ocean fishing with Rosalie's family. She sleeps a while. Something wakes her and she opens her eyes to see faces pressed against the dark glass of the car windows. Fuzzy, distorted faces. She squints, trying to bring them into focus.

"Hey, in there! Come out and party. The night is young."

She struggles to sit up, to smile, to gather her wits. Both back doors open.

"Have a drink with us."

Her stomach feels better, but the last thing she wants is another drink so she shakes her head. She smiles as she does it, though. Smiling because she wants them to like her.

"Come out and watch us drink, then! We need a scorekeeper."

Shyly, she slides out of the car seat, flattered by the attention. Figures surround her. Boys. The kind of boys she has always wished she could meet, and they are interested in her! They like her!

A hand takes her arm and the group starts to move.

"Aren't we going back to the party?" she asks timidly.

"That party's dull. We're going to start our own party."

Thea woke. It was two a.m. She was shaky and agitated. The dream had been so detailed that it was more primer than nightmare.

She sat up on the edge of the unfamiliar bed and rubbed her arms. Was that an accurate replaying of the events leading up to the rape or was it just her imagination at work? And why, with all that detail, why were the boys just figures with indistinct faces? Was she so afraid of remembering that her mind could not conjure up even an imagined face? Or was that a black hole in her brain: a place where damaged cells had been cut away during surgery? The site of a memory that did not transfer to storage because of trauma or because it had oozed out of her shattered skull?

There would be no more sleeping. She knew that

and so she pulled on her robe and tiptoed out into the hall. They had left small lights on for her. Edmond's door was partially open. She was certain that he'd done that out of concern for her.

Quietly she went to the kitchen and poured herself a glass of wine.

"Are you all right?" a voice whispered, and she jerked around to find Edmond hovering at the kitchen doorway.

"Yes. But I can't sleep."

He nodded and poured himself wine. Nothing about his appearance indicated that he had been asleep. He was neatly turned out in a flannel robe and his manner was sharp and alert.

"I'm a light sleeper myself." He gestured toward the small table and two chairs that occupied the kitchen's dining nook. "Will you sit with me a moment?"

She wanted to decline but couldn't with any grace so she took a seat. However, once she was across from Edmond it occurred to her that this was the perfect opportunity to satisfy her curiosity about Jack.

"You and Jack seem close," she said, hoping it wasn't too transparent a beginning.

"We always were close, but the last few years have been difficult. Jack hasn't wanted anyone close."

And she realized that this was what Edmond wanted too—a chance to speak with her alone about Jack.

"Why is that?"

"He hasn't told you what happened, has he?"

She shook her head.

"I'm not surprised. He's very . . . unforthcoming." Edmond paused. "You know he was a detective in L.A. . . . Well, he was also a husband. A very devoted husband. I actually introduced them. She was French, from Paris, and they had a long-distance relationship for more than a year before finally deciding that she would move to L.A. and they would marry. Jack was so happy. But I think she was more in love with moving to Los Angeles than she was with Jack, and eventually she had an affair, which he discovered. Then she asked for a divorce."

"That's terrible."

"It was worse than terrible. Her lover was Jack's partner so he was doubly betrayed. And the partner was female . . . which completely undid him.

"He was devastated, falling apart emotionally and drinking. And he was still paired with the partner—Trish. One night on the job he and Trish got caught in a situation where they were chasing an armed suspect in East L.A. They split up. Jack ran up a dimly lit stairwell and a male with a gun appeared at the top and Jack fired.

"It was a twelve-year-old with a squirt gun. The boy died in Jack's arms, talking to him, begging Jack to save him." Edmond finished his wine. "An investigation completely exonerated him, but he could not forgive himself. He believed that it wouldn't have happened if his mental state had been better. He visited the boy's family. He sold everything he could and gave them the money as an anonymous gift. Shortly thereafter a man pulled a gun on him and Jack didn't draw his own gun quickly enough. He was shot. I think he wanted to die. When he recovered, he left the force and headed north to the forest. We had spent lovely childhood holidays there with relatives . . . before our parents divorced. I think for him the forest is a refuge from reality."

She had stopped breathing and now she drew in a long slow breath. There was nothing to say. Everything was clear now.

"So you see," Edmond continued, "this is his chance to save another boy, perhaps to atone for the death of the first one. I suppose he was drawn to your son from the beginning, though I doubt he thought it out."

"Thank you, Edmond."

His eyes were filled with concern for his brother. "I don't know whether this is a good thing that is happening with Jack, but for my own selfish reasons I'm glad to have him wakened to life again."

Jack started the coffee and put bagels on to toast before tapping on Thea's door. To his surprise she appeared immediately, dressed and fully awake. Moments later Edmond came out to join them.

"You didn't have to get up, Edmond," Jack insisted. "Go back to bed."

"Nonsense. Do you think I'm a layabout?" Edmond peered out the window. "Uhh. A dreary, dreary day. I don't like spring storms."

Thea was quiet and pensive. Jack could almost hear the churning of her thoughts. Instead of following him to the kitchen she headed straight to the computer and attached it to the phone line. He took out orange juice and filled glasses, then heated milk for the coffee and put scallion cream cheese and butter on the table. Due to the pattern of previous e-mails he didn't expect that she would find anything yet, but he called "Anything from Delian?" when she did not immediately return.

"No!" she answered as though startled. "I'm just looking over the old e-mails."

"He'll probably answer you this afternoon," Jack assured her. "Now come in here. Breakfast is ready."

Jack ate standing while Thea and Edmond sat at the table. He couldn't stop looking at her. Was he falling in love with this woman? Or was he falling under the spell of her need? What a situation. Of all the women in the world to be attracted to . . .

"I'm going back," she said suddenly. "It's daytime. I'll be fine on my own."

He opened his mouth to protest but she cut him off.

"You can talk to Guerin without me. I need to be on the Island, Jack. It's daylight and I'll watch out for myself. I'll be fine."

"You're sure?"

"Yes."

He searched her face and was worried by what he saw there. She was almost too calm. But he could not force her to stay.

"We can meet for dinner at the hotel and compare notes."

"All right. Let me take you downstairs and put you in a cab. When you get to Penn Station—"

"I can handle it," she said. "Don't worry. I can handle it."

28

Jack made a polite nuisance of himself in Dr. Gregory Guerin's waiting room, questioning the receptionist repeatedly as to whether the doctor had found a few minutes in his busy schedule. Glaring, the woman explained each time that the doctor was sorry but the entire day was full, and each time Jack said that was fine, he'd just wait in case an opening arose. The waiting room was crowded with mothers and children. All the seats were taken by the adults. Some of the sickest children were cuddled on laps but most of them played on the carpeted floor with a variety of worn plastic toys.

Jack wanted to escape from the grimness and the collective hostility of the mothers and the gaze of one curious boy who kept watching him. He made a mental note to have some toys shipped to the place. That made him feel a little better, but not much. He tried to focus on his purpose. Guerin was important. He was certain of it.

Finally, after two hours, the receptionist angrily waved him into the inner sanctum.

"You watch that you don't take too much of the doctor's time," she ordered, dark eyes beaming death rays at him. "There's sick babies out there who need that man."

"I promise," Jack said, and she opened a door labeled OFFICE and gestured him inside.

It was a Spartan room containing only a scarred bargain-basement desk, cheap laminated bookshelves crammed with medical texts, and an assortment of hard wooden chairs. On the desk was a modest computer setup and a small reiku pot filled with pens and pencils. Behind the desk was a wall of diplomas, certifications, and awards. Dr. Guerin had graduated from Harvard Medical School with honors. Jack suspected that with those credentials the good doctor could have had any position he wanted and could have been raking in the cash or the prestige or both. What was he doing here?

The door opened and a gaunt man stepped inside. He wore a white physician's coat that was open over a casual shirt and faded jeans. A stethoscope hung around his neck. But it was his face that struck Jack— the drawn pale face of a long-term political prisoner. His shaggy brown hair was going prematurely gray, adding to the impression that the man was closer to fifty than thirty. Jack did a discreet check but could see no evidence of the artificial foot.

"Yes?" Guerin said, closing the door behind him.

"I'm . . . Jack Verrity," Jack said, unable to toss off a lie as his first words to the man. Some people couldn't be lied to. "I've already spoken to Susan Maxwell, Deighten Freylen, and Harris Winslow . . . the younger."

Guerin closed his eyes and drew a deep breath. Then he looked at Jack.

"Sit down."

The doctor moved around to the desk chair.

"When you told my receptionist it was about the fire . . . I hoped . . ." He shook his head as though disgusted with himself.

"You thought I didn't really know anything and would go away if you ignored me."

"Yes."

"Well, you were half right. I don't really know anything. But I won't let this go until I do. Chip White and his wife have been murdered and Kenneth Maxwell took a dive onto some rocks and drowned. Now a woman and child I care about are in danger."

The doctor recoiled in shock. "I didn't know about Chip or Kenneth. My God . . . I'm out of touch here."

"Your parents didn't tell you."

"We . . . ah . . . don't communicate."

"Everything is connected, isn't it?" Jack said. "The fire and the rape and the car accident . . . and now these deaths."

"Who are you?"

"I told you—I'm a friend of people who are being hurt by all this."

"A woman and child?"

"Yes. The woman was the rape victim."

Again the doctor appeared to be shocked. "The victim? But she was—"

"She didn't stay comatose. She's fine now."

"How much memory did she recover?"

"Almost all."

Guerin put his elbows on the desk and cradled his head in his hands.

"What are you atoning for with this clinic, Doctor?"

The man didn't respond.

"It was your father who got rid of the rape evidence, wasn't it?"

"Yes," Guerin answered without lifting his head.

"The woman suffered a lot. Her life was nearly destroyed. Now she has a child and someone here has taken that child."

"Oh God in heaven, will this never stop!"

"You can help me stop it."

The man lifted his eyes, and they were full of such torment that Jack hurt for him.

"How?"

"Tell me what happened that night."

Guerin pressed his fingers to his temples. His hands were shaking.

For some moments there was only the ticking of the large plastic wall clock.

"There were five of us," Guerin said finally. "Deighten Freylen, Kenneth Maxwell, Chip White,

Phillip Osburn, and myself." He drew a deep breath. "We were the sons of wealth and privilege, all sent to the same exclusive nursery school, and the same exclusive country day school, and then packed off together to the same exclusive boarding school when we reached high school age. The Freylens and the Maxwells and the Whites still lived in old family mansions. Phillip's and my families were only slightly different in that our opulent homes didn't qualify as historic and our fathers were outsiders. Mine was a noted doctor who married an heiress. Phillip's was a musical composer who married an heiress.

"We were . . . bonded . . . by more than privilege. I look back and I see that we were bonded out of need. It seems almost a blasphemy to say this when we're here in such a deprived area, but in spite of our positions in life we were neglected and needy. So we got it from each other.

"We were like a family. With individual roles just like a family has. I was the quiet, studious one. Kenneth was the clown. Phillip was sensitive and creative. Chip was boisterous and good-natured. And Deighten was the star—charming and bright and daring.

"We stuck together no matter what. We helped each other, defended each other . . ."

Guerin sighed.

"When we got home from Briden after graduation

it was dawning on us that we had one summer left together and then we would go our separate ways to different colleges. We got very clingy then. Doing everything as a group. Each of us had a nice car but we would choose one and all get into it.

"The party was actually Deighten's idea. There was an old waterfront mansion that had been made into a retreat. I don't recall the details but Dey found out it would be untended that weekend and put out the word. We went to the party together, of course. And we drank like there was no tomorrow. Kenneth brought a fifth of very expensive scotch that he'd taken from his parents' liquor cabinet and Chip brought tequila and there was a trunkload of beer from God knows where. But then that wasn't anything new for us. We'd never had any rules and we were never short of money so there'd always been a lot of carousing when we were home from school.

"That night was different though. We were all feeling a little . . . wild and reckless. A little like we were going off to separate wars soon.

"We were leaving the party for more beer when we walked past a parked car and somebody spotted the girl lying in the backseat. It was just silliness at first . . . making faces against the glass . . . trying to outdo each other.

"I was so drunk I was staggering, and everything was funny. Nothing seemed real. And I trusted those boys . . . I trusted that together we were good . . . even heroic.

"I don't know how it got so out of hand. I don't remember exactly who did what when. I know she tried to run and somebody tackled her. I know that when she screamed Chip took off his sock and stuck it in her mouth and everyone thought that was hilarious. And I know that we all got caught up in it as a game. God . . . we all felt *entitled* to treat that poor girl like a plaything—an object we'd found.

"I passed out and the next thing I remember is being in the hospital. And I lay there, trying to sort out what was real and what had actually happened. And that was when the enormity of it hit me. And I told my father just as they were wheeling me into surgery. He was incredulous. Thought I was delirious. I remember him saying, 'But Dey Freylen could have any girl he wants' . . . as though that made it impossible for Dey . . . or any of us . . . to have done such a thing.

"He never said exactly what he did. I know he spoke to at least one other father, if not more."

"Which father knew?"

"Dey's. Mr. Freylen made most of the financial arrangements to spirit the girl away. Between my dad and Freylen they made her completely disappear. And I always just assumed that she had remained comatose and eventually died."

"Who bashed her head in and dumped her in the house?"

"Rusket, of course. None of us would have intentionally hurt her." As soon as the words were out the doctor flinched. "I mean . . . not hurt her that way."

"How did Rusket get in on it?"

"She was left out in the yard of the house and Rusket found her there and panicked, thinking she was a witness to the fire."

"But you said you passed out?"

"Well . . . that's what I understood happened."

"Who told you that?"

The doctor frowned in confusion. "I'm not sure exactly. I saw Dey and Kenneth and Chip several times when we were all still hospitalized. The staff thought they were doing us a favor by wheeling us to see each other. But the friendship had been destroyed. We hated what we saw in each other's eyes. Nothing was ever the same after that. Not my feelings for my father. Not my feelings for my friends. And not my idea of myself."

"So who do you think would track down the rape victim and take her son?"

"It's beyond my imagining. But if Chip and Kenneth are dead . . ."

"That leaves Freylen and you. Or someone who's only peripherally connected."

"Or someone tied to Rusket?" the doctor said.

Jack looked at the man. His haunted soul was right there in his eyes. "Were any of your friends interested in Greek mythology?"

Guerin cocked his head in thought.

"I think Dey was. Yes . . . I'm certain. Dey called

his car a chariot and he was crazy for Apollo the way some people were crazy for the *Star Trek* characters."

"Deighten Freylen?"

"Yes."

Jack bolted for the door.

29

Thea looked out over the Sound. The water was churning beneath a pewter sky, and a salty wind whipped her clothes and cheeks. She had parked her car near the spot where the party took place. Near the beginning of her nightmare. She reached deep into her shoulder bag and pulled out the terry-wrapped gun. Carefully she examined it.

She booted her computer and put in the disc containing that morning's message from Delian—the message she had hidden from Jack. She felt bad about lying to him but it had been necessary. She had to do this alone. She couldn't take the chance that he would stop her.

The message appeared on the screen.

My dear Thea,
  You had your chance with me and you tossed it away to chase after that arrogant lying bastard—the mighty Jack. Don't tell me you're not enjoying his company—staying in that hotel together and

mincing around after him like a servant. Yes, I know
all about it. I know all the secrets of the universe.

If you want another chance with me you'll have
to dump him and prove where your loyalties fall.
Then maybe good things will start happening. You'll
find David and you'll get your wish of meeting
me and the three of us can watch the stars together
from our balcony and never be alone again.

Delian

She read it several times, then shut down the machine. There was no one around. No one on foot. No
cars passing. She draped the towel over the gun and
got out of the car. She pointed the gun down at the
deserted stretch of rocky shore, gripping it in both
hands, and she pulled the trigger. The noise and the
kick alarmed her. Quickly she scrambled back into
the car and drove away. The gun worked, and she
was certain now that she could use it. With the gun
she could erase the past. Erase the rapist. She could
take back hers and her son's lives.

The narrow back roads were confusing but she finally reached her destination. She did not drive
through the stone entryway of Roanoke, but instead
left her car at the side of the road. With her bag
on her shoulder, she headed out through the dense
vegetation on foot. David was here. She was certain
of it. Certain because of Delian's e-mail. Anyone
could have learned they were staying in a hotel but
referring to Jack as "that arrogant lying bastard"

made it sound as though Delian had had direct contact with Jack. Then there was "mincing around after him like a servant." Delian had to have seen them together to come up with that. He had to have seen Thea playing assistant. And when she'd read "the three of us can watch the stars together from our balcony" something had clicked for her because she knew then that the flash she'd seen when looking up at Freylen's terrace had been sunlight glinting off the barrels of telescopes. Not much for proof. Certainly not enough to get a search warrant. But with these slender connections she had become like Jack—she felt the certainty of it in her gut.

Branches scraped at her and barbed vines hooked in her clothing. The sky was so gray that she could not see very far ahead. When she reached the house she crept around to the back, barely daring to breathe. The glass house was empty. From the cover of trees she looked up at the terrace and could make out the ends of two telescopes pointing toward the sky. She could also see the top of a lighted window or glass door. It was one of the few lights visible in the house. Someone was in that room. Was it David?

Carefully she edged close to the house and peeked through a kitchen window. It was empty. The Asian chef was not there today. He wouldn't catch her sneaking in . . . but then he wouldn't be there to call for help either if she needed it.

She had come prepared to break a window, but when she tried the back door it was open. Heart knocking so loudly she was afraid it might give her away, she slipped inside. The staircase was at the very front of the hall near the entryway. She eased toward it, staying close to the wall. There were no lights on and with the storm it was more like dusk than afternoon.

She passed the small cage-style elevator and then reached the bottom of the staircase. One stair at a time, she crept upward. At the top she paused. A long hallway stretched out in both directions, bisected by other halls. She tried to picture the position of that balcony and how it might correspond to the floor plan she was seeing. None of the visible doors had a bar of light showing underneath.

She chose a direction, then turned at the bisecting hall and headed toward the back of the house. There was light visible under a door, and it seemed like the right position to be the balcony room. She pressed her ear to the wood and listened. From inside she heard the music of David's favorite band.

Heart hammering, she carefully tried the knob. It was locked. Was David alone inside? She waited, agonizing over what to do. Then she tapped lightly.

"You've got the key," David shouted belligerently. "What're you knocking for!"

Joy filled her and she leaned against the door, palms flat, cheek pressed to the wood.

"David," she called softly. "It's me. It's Mom."

The music stopped.

"David? Can you hear me?"

"Mommy?" His voice was just on the other side of the door. "Is that really you?"

She tugged at the door frantically. "How can I get you out, David?"

"He's got the key! Be careful, Mom. He's crazy! He wants to be my father and keep me prisoner here. He said you left me."

"I'm going to call the police, honey. We'll get you out. Just stay quiet."

A faint sound came to her. She froze, listening. It was the faint snik-snik of wheels on the wooden floor of a hallway.

"I've got to go, sweetheart. He's coming."

She ran along the hall, trying door after door in search of a place to hide. They were all locked. The wheels were coming closer and closer. She turned down a cross-hallway. It was short with a window and seat at the end and two doors opposite each other.

Snik. Snik. Snik.

She lunged for one of the doors and tugged frantically.

"Back so soon, Anna?"

She stopped tugging and turned to face Deighten Freylen.

"You know my name isn't Anna."

"Oh! Very good. Very quick." He smiled. "And you're supposed to be brain-damaged."

"Why are you doing this?"

"I get to ask questions first. Where's our leading man?"

"Jack is . . . on his way."

Freylen made a tsk-tsk sound. "I hate it when you lie. Jack doesn't even know you've come here, does he? Our hero would never let you come alone if he knew."

"Jack knows the truth."

"The truth? You say that as if there is one truth for all. You told me yourself once that humans are the only animals who deceive themselves."

"I thought we were friends. All that time on-line I thought we were . . ."

"Sweethearts?" He smiled cruelly. "What a pair we made in the electronic hotel suite. Delian and Butterfly. And then Jack ruined it all."

"I want my son back. I want you to unlock the door and let him out."

"Why, Thea, I'm surprised at your maternal devotion. I'd think you'd be glad to get free of the little bastard."

"Why are you doing this?"

"You haven't figured it out yet? I'm the one, Thea. I'm David's father. His real father."

"You? But that's . . . that's impossible." Not the man she had poured out her heart to on-line!

"Would I lie about that?"

"I don't believe you."

He nodded. "The five of us were leaving and we saw you in the backseat of the car and we teased you a little, just for fun. And you were groggy but smiling. You were glad to see us. So we were nice to you. But then you turned into a bad sport. You didn't want to get into Phillip's car with us and you started playing hard to get. Then you took off running.

"Well, that was an irresistible invitation to fun. We ran you down like we were on the playing field and your clothes got torn and there were your nipples all hard and Kenneth said, 'I'll bet her pussy is wet, too.'

"You wanted it, Thea. You were a dull, poor little nobody and you wanted a taste of what we had to offer, so we gave it to you."

She shook her head and whispered, "No."

"You don't like that? It gets even better. You were making an awful racket and Chip stuffed one of his socks in your mouth. It was hilarious.

"Phillip was turned on by your ass . . . not surprising since he was developing a fondness for all asses. Kenneth came on your breasts. Chip wanted to replace the sock and Guerin . . . he was nearly passed out and behaving like a baby . . . saying we should stop. We shamed him into an attempt at your breasts but he couldn't get it up. And I . . . well, we both know what I achieved. David looks like me, don't you think?"

She ignored the tears streaming down her face as she groped in her bag for the gun. But before she could pull it out, Freylen lowered his head as though bowed by his own words.

"What were we thinking? We weren't. We'd always been given what we wanted when we wanted it, and we'd always been the golden boys who were never punished for anything. Our fathers bought us out of every scrape. And there you were—a little South Shore slut . . . nobody whose family we knew. Nobody who mattered. A nothing. And you were hot for us. . . . You had to be because South Shore girls were always hot for us. All we had to do to get laid was drive our expensive cars south. And when you fought it turned into a game. Like cats playing with a mouse."

He raised his eyes to meet hers. "So many lives were destroyed that night. Look at me, Thea! This is what you were talking to all those late nights. This sexless half body."

"We could still be together," she said, trying to mask the desperation in her voice. "The three of us could be so happy, Deighten. Just, please, let David out."

"It won't work, Thea. Nothing is ever that easy, you know."

She jerked out the gun. Here was the source of all her terror, yet her hand was shaking so badly she could barely aim. Freylen raised his hand from his lap, and he also had a gun, and his hand was steady. Very steady.

"I think we have a standoff. I'll lower mine if you lower yours."

She dropped the gun to her side and he nodded knowingly, then lowered his back to his lap.

"I want my son, Deighten."

"He's mine, too. Your mother really pulled a fast one. She took my father's money and beat it as far away as possible without ever letting a hint of a baby get out. Dear old Dad would have been excited over a grandson."

"My mother took money from your father?"

"A kindly donation to take care of you and help her resettle you where the shame and heartbreak of the rape would be a secret. And then a continuing subsidy to help make ends meet."

"But I thought those were donations. My mother said they were donations and gifts from people who cared about what happened."

"That's true in a way, isn't it? You were paid by your rapist's father who cared about what happened."

"Your father knew the truth and covered it up?"

"You know how it is. . . . Fathers may not be around much but when something bad happens they stick with their sons. I'm sure there are men in my family who've had to buy their way out of worse scrapes."

"Did my mother know why he was giving her all this money?"

"She must have suspected, don't you think?"

"No. I don't."

"Suit yourself."

"Who else knew?"

"Guerin spilled his guts to his dad that night at

the hospital. That's why the good surgeon felt so obligated to save you."

"And he's the one who made sure the rape evidence disappeared, isn't he?"

Freylen smiled.

"How did you find out about David?"

"My father would never discuss what happened to you but after his death I was able to examine his finances. I found his cash expenditures and saw that payments had continued. I simply followed the money then. He had set your mother up with a financial management firm. That same firm manages the little nest egg you have left today. I hired a private detective to get more information on you and then I discovered your secret—David."

"He's not your son!"

The amusement vanished and his face darkened. "He's the only son I will ever have! Look at me! I am half a man! And it's all because of you!"

"Me?"

"Why do you think Phillip was speeding that night? Because you had us all nervous. Carrying on that way . . . sobbing and crying and making such a scene. You wanted it all along. You wanted boys like us to notice you and then when you got your wish you turned into such a baby. We knew you'd go crying to the police."

"So . . . the car accident was my fault?"

"Yes! And when I learned that you were doing fine, that you were healthy and working and had a child . . . I knew I had to do something. You owed

416

me something! Through my detective I learned about your little research business, so I had you do a few jobs for me."

"You were my client?"

"Several times. And we corresponded by e-mail and you mentioned your little chat group. You told me to drop in sometime. From there it was easy."

"You need help, Deighten."

"Oh, that's rich. Coming from a woman who couldn't leave her house after dark and had panic attacks if the slightest thing went wrong. A woman who's so afraid of living that she's wasting her entire life!"

"All right," she said, trying to humor him. "So you were mad at me. Why involve David?"

"Things changed. After a while I didn't want to punish you anymore because you were punishing yourself so well. And I started to think, What if? What if fate had always intended us to be together? I made plans for us. We seemed perfect for each other—you're afraid to fuck and I can't. But I thought we could be good together, that we could make each other whole and be parents to David. Then you wrote me about Jack and I knew I'd never be able to trust you. I should have known—a woman who comes on to five guys in the dark is not trustworthy."

"All I did was mention Jack's name!"

"That was when I knew . . . I'd been gathering information on David, getting to know him through you, and that was when I knew I had to find David on-line and find out where this journey was leading."

"Why did you persuade David to come here?"

"In the beginning I thought it was to get to you. But now I've seen the true purpose of all of this." He kept his right hand on the gun and used his left to make a sweeping motion. "Everything from the first moment I saw you in the back of that car. It was all leading me to David. To being the father that I never had."

"This is crazy, Deighten. I am not going to give you my son."

"Don't think of it that way. Think of it as finally getting rid of the product and reminder of that terrible night. Really, Thea . . . I told you all the gory sexual details. . . . How could you want the end result of such a disgusting experience? We can trade—the boy for lots of money. So much money that you can live in a mansion somewhere."

"David isn't for sale!"

He raised his gun again. "You're the mother of my son, Thea. I don't want to hurt you, but you have to accept what's best for David."

A shadow moved behind Freylen. Someone was approaching from around the corner in the main hallway. Jack! She'd known he would figure it out after speaking to Guerin. Now he had come in through the back and was sneaking up.

The form leapt into the hall, knocked Freylen's gun

aside, and put his own gun to Freylen's head. It was not Jack but Harris Winslow the Second.

"Thank God," she sobbed, dropping her gun and bag and rushing forward. "He's the rapist! And he has my son locked—"

"No!" Freylen cried, but Winslow whipped the gun across his mouth, replacing the teeth and lips with a bright fountain of red.

"What about a kid?" Winslow asked.

"I have a son and Deighten has him prisoner just down the hall. We have to call the police right away. He's a rapist. He and his friends raped me fourteen years ago. Now he's holding my child."

Winslow stared at her as though trying to understand, and she realized that he recognized her as Jack's assistant.

"Let me get this straight. . . . You're the girl who was raped and Dey has your kid locked up in the house."

"Yes."

Winslow threw back his head and laughed. He laughed so hard that he had to dab tears from his eyes. "This is too incredible."

"Yes," she said again, suddenly realizing that this man could have come to burn down the house and she could not trust him.

"The keys are probably on him," Winslow said. "See if you can find them."

She checked Freylen's pockets. He tried to speak to her and blood bubbled from his ruined mouth.

His eyes were pleading. She found a key ring and raced to David's door, with Winslow pushing Freylen's chair behind her.

As soon as the door was unlocked her son rushed into her arms. "Mommy," he said, sounding more three than thirteen. "He wouldn't let me out."

"Shhh. It's over now." She held him close, rocking slightly to soothe him.

"Okay. Both of you get over here," Winslow ordered, pointing the gun at them.

Thea was stunned. Her heart jumped into her throat and she turned to shield her child from the gun.

"Get over here. Now!"

"But I just came to get my son. I don't want any trouble. Whatever your fight is with each other—you can settle it without us."

"Move!"

"Please let us go. I don't care what you do to this house or even to that man. I'm glad to see him punished."

"Shut up!"

Winslow grabbed David's wrist and pulled him in close, jamming the gun against his head. "You push Gimpy. And if there's any trouble I'll shoot the kid."

He forced them out the back and into the glass house. The clouds were so thick that the sky was nearly black. No lights were on and she was surrounded by thousands of panes of dark glass. Yet all she could see was the gun against her son's head.

"I've been studying old greenhouses like this,"

Winslow said. "They're dangerous if you don't handle them right. They can blow up. Such a tragedy."

"This is all so you can develop the property?" Thea asked.

He didn't answer. His white shirt was plastered to his body with sweat and his movements were jerky. Intently he followed the walkways through the jungle, dragging David by the neck, the gun jammed into his temple. Thea had to struggle to push the wheelchair fast enough to keep up. Finally he stopped at the far end of the building in front of a pair of doors marked DANGER—NO ADMITTANCE.

At the doors he shifted David, clamping his gun arm around the boy's neck so that the gun was pointed down. Then he reached inside a door and began twisting knobs. There was a hissing sound.

Do something now! Now, while the gun is pointed away from David!

But then he was finished and the gun was back against her son's head. "Come on." He dragged David to a line of rotting plant shelves nearby and she followed, pushing Freylen. Suddenly he stopped and kicked the wheelchair off the walkway and onto its side. Freylen sprawled across the ground.

"I hadn't counted on the bonus of you two," Winslow said, looking around as though searching for something. "Saved me a lot of trouble."

"Please, let us go," she pleaded. "What will you gain by hurting us?"

Winslow continued to search. "There! Get that twine from over there."

Thea picked up a ball of green twine that someone had recently used in an effort to hold some drooping vines in place.

"Tie up the kid!"

With shaking hands she unwound the twine.

"We're not a part of this," she sobbed.

"Shut up! Why do you think I had to kill Chip and Kenneth? Think I wanted to do that? No! They were my friends. Buddies from high school. But they got word that 'the girl' was out of the coma and back in town, and they panicked. They were going to blow the whole thing sky-high. I tried to reason with Chip, but he was freaking. He demanded I come to his house in the middle of the night and I get there and the idiot had told his wife! What could I do? Then Kenneth goes off the deep end and I had to shut him up, too."

"What about Guerin?" she whispered.

"That's my next stop. Can't believe I have to drive all the way up to sleazeville to get him. The stupid jerk. Taking care of lowlifes practically for free."

"So you were there that night?" Thea asked, hoping he wouldn't notice how loosely she was tying her son.

"Not for the main event. I came along and there they were with you right by the side of the road, trying to shut you up and wondering what to do with you. Guys like that"—he gestured toward Freylen—"they're big shots on the playing field and at parties, but they can't take care of business when the pressure is on."

She saw that beneath his bluster Winslow was unraveling. "So you're the one who took me to the house?" she asked, buying time, scrambling for a plan.

"Always me! Everybody uses me to take care of problems! I'm not good enough for their little group but I'm supposed to solve the problems." He snorted disdainfully. "I told them I'd take care of it, told them I could give you a drug that would wipe out your memory and then I'd clean you up and dump you for your friends to find. They were as grateful as puppies. And it should have worked out perfectly. I knew the house was being torched at three so all I had to do was whack you on the head and hide you inside. No one would have ever figured it out. They might have even blamed you for the fire. But then that dickhead Rusket screwed it all up by dragging you out. And the assholes sped off and totaled their car.

"I'm the only one with any common sense! I'm the only one who could ever get anything done! Why can't anybody see that?"

Behind Winslow, Freylen was pulling himself along the ground. Thea quickly shifted her eyes so she wouldn't give him away. Too late, she understood that Freylen had been trying to warn her. In his perverted way he had wanted to protect David.

"You came here to shut Deighten up and fix it so that you'd get his property too," she said.

"It's my right! He owes me! They all owed me! Everything was ruined that night. It was supposed to be different! If they hadn't run into that tree I'd have finally been in the group. They'd have never been able to shut me out again because we were all in it together. We'd have run this county! But instead what did I get? Five fucked-up messes. Except for Chip. He was okay. And he helped me with some deals too.

"Because of them my father thinks I'm a loser, but he'll change his mind when I get this place to develop."

A flicker of panic crossed his eyes and be began to mutter to himself.

"Story . . . story . . . gotta have a story; that's the key. Dey tied them up to get rid of them and then set the boiler to explode, but then he couldn't get out fast enough. Yeah. Poor crazy Dey. He's been going nuts for years. Finally got psychotic."

"What about the others?" Thea prodded.

"The others? Dey killed them too. Killed everyone who was connected to the rape. Terrible thing. Guerin . . . Guerin . . . don't know what to do about Guerin. Dey will already be dead."

Suddenly Freylen lunged at Winslow's legs and locked his arms around them.

"Mommy!" David screamed as the gun jerked away from his temple.

Winslow fired into Freylen's back, then toppled sideways. She ripped the twine from her son's arms, shoved him behind some wooden potting shelves, then dove after him. Gunfire shrieked over their heads. A pane of glass shattered from its frame.

"Stay low and crawl!" she whispered, scurrying behind the shelves.

Winslow's feet came into view and she plunged into the jungle, dragging David by the arm.

"Thea! David! Where are you?"

"Jack!" He had come! He really had come. "We're here. He has a gun!"

Near her head a bullet splintered the trunk of an exotic tree. She grabbed David's collar and pulled him through the dense foliage in a crouching run, heading toward Jack's voice. Winslow crashed into the jungle behind them, but then the crashing stopped. Where was he? She saw Jack ahead, ducking low and moving toward them. She tapped David and pointed, holding her finger to her lips to signal stealth. Suddenly Winslow appeared, creeping silently toward Jack with his gun drawn. She grabbed a large clay pot and ran forward to smash it down on his head.

"He's done something to the heating system," she shouted. "I think it's going to blow up."

"Get David out of here," Jack ordered, bending to heft Winslow into a fireman's carry. She started to object but knew there would be no use.

"Hurry," she urged her clinging and stricken son.

When they came to Freylen's still and bloody body she held her son's face against her to shield him. But then she stopped. "Stay here!" she ordered, and went back to check for a pulse. The man was dead.

"He tried to save us, didn't he, Mom?" David said, and she looked up to see that there was grief mixed with the shock in her son's eyes. He didn't know what Deighten Freylen had done or why Freylen had wanted him there. All he knew was that his friend had locked him up. And that his friend was dead. Now he wanted reassurance that the world was still a good place. He wanted to believe his friend had been a hero.

"Yes, sweetheart. He tried to save us."

And then they ran. She didn't stop until they were safely inside the back door of the house. Holding her sobbing child, she watched Jack emerge, the weight of Winslow's inert form on his back. He was halfway to the house when the entire greenhouse exploded in brilliant cascades of glass. Jack was blown forward, and she jerked David back away from the window and the flying glass and the sight of another friend bloodied. When it was over she ran outside. Glass was everywhere. Jack lay facedown, covered with blood. Winslow was draped across his back, a sheet of glass buried so deeply in the blocky torso that he was nearly halved.

"Jack. Oh Jack." She struggled to pull Winslow off but couldn't. She fell to her knees in the blood and took Jack's face in her hands. "Please, Jack. Please don't leave me."

Then he groaned. He raised his head and squinted

at her. "What the hell?" With her help he rolled the body off him and struggled to his feet.

"Oh God, thank you," she sobbed, throwing her arms around him.

David ran from the house and nearly knocked them over to join the embrace.

"How did you know to come here?" she asked.

"Guerin spilled everything. The man was consumed by guilt. I called the hotel, then called Michaels, then panicked. It didn't take much detecting to figure out you'd come after him alone."

She tightened her arms, holding her son, holding the man who had saved her.

Later, after Jack was patched up at the hospital, and after hours of explaining to the police, they huddled together—a man, a woman, and a child, just as though they had always been a family.

"You know where we're going tomorrow?" Jack said.

"To see about getting Ronnie Rusket out of jail."

"Okay, then the day after tomorrow."

"Where?"

"We're going to Carnegie Hall. We're going to a concert in the safest place in the world."

Carnegie Hall. She laughed.

Was this love she was feeling? It was most assuredly trust. As strong and certain as any tree in the forest. And even a forest had to have a beginning.

Author's Note

This is a work of fiction that attempts to reflect painful realities. In my efforts to achieve this I relied heavily on the experience and knowledge of others, and I cannot thank them enough. I am grateful to the registered nurses and rape counselors who were so generous with their time and expertise. Though they all requested anonymity, I send a heartfelt thank you to each one individually. I am especially indebted to the survivors who trusted me with their too real stories—your strength amazes and awes me.

To P who fueled my need to write this book—wherever you are and whatever you're doing now, I hope you've found peace. I'm sorry I didn't know how to help more.

Thank you to all the nonfiction writers who have published so much valuable material. A sampling of titles follows for those readers wishing to learn more.

Once again thank you to Aaron and Audre—my AA team.

And thank you to my family, near and far, whose love anchors me.

Reading List

Catastrophe of Coma: A Way Back by Edward Alan Freeman.

Confronting Rape and Sexual Assault edited by Mary E. Odem and Jody Clay Warner.

The Female Fear: The Social Cost of Rape by Margaret T. Gordon and Stephanie Riger.

The Last Stand: The War Between Wall Street and Main Street over California's Ancient Redwoods by David Harris.

Men on Rape: What They Have to Say About Sexual Violence by Timothy Beneke.

Shattered Assumptions: Towards a New Psychology of Trauma by Ronnie Janoff-Bulman.

Transforming a Rape Culture edited by Emilie Buchwald, Pamela R. Fletcher, and Martha Roth.

And all the publications of the Save-the-Redwoods League, which is based in San Francisco, California.

For information or assistance contact R.A.I.N.N. (Rape, Abuse & Incest National Network) at 1-800-656-HOPE or www.rainn.org.

Dear Reader,

Thank you for purchasing *Violation* by Darian North. We hope you enjoyed it, but judging from the overwhelming reaction of readers so far, your response will be much more complex than the simple pleasure of reading an exciting and unusual suspense novel. In fact, the disturbing subject at the heart of the novel—violent rape—has provoked an extraordinary amount of passionate discussion, a degree of controversy that we seldom experience upon publishing even the most brutal serial killer novels or vicious true crime stories.

In a society that is constantly exposed to crime in all its variety and in the most graphic detail, what is it about rape that remains so mysterious, so deeply unsettling, and so difficult to talk about? Why is murder perhaps the most common element in commercial fiction, yet rape, considered the "second most serious crime," is almost never dealt with?

So many of us found ourselves still haunted by this powerful novel long after finishing it, we wanted to ask the author what prompted her to write it the way she did. We were so intrigued by her answer, we decided to include for you the following interview with Darian North. We hope that this glimpse into the author's thought process and creative choices will enrich your own reading experience, or provide an outline for a fascinating readers' group discussion.

Best regards,
The Editorial Staff
New American Library

VIOLATION
A Conversation with the Author

NEW AMERICAN LIBRARY: What prompted you to write *Violation*?

DARIAN NORTH: Every book I write tells a story exploring something that intrigues, puzzles, or disturbs me. The seed of *Violation* grew out of my having known a rape victim—a young college woman with a bright outlook and a promising future—whose life was profoundly altered when a stranger sadistically brutalized her in her own home. The person she was died that night. She dropped out of school, left town, and was lost to me. I don't know if she went on to rebuild herself. I will probably never know. And I can never truly understand what she went through. Though this is not at all her story, I suppose it's my attempt to understand, and to raise awareness.

NAL: Did your idea of the book change as you researched this crime?

DN: Most definitely. Even though I had a basic newspaper-reading knowledge of the crime, I was shocked by the actual statistics. According to the U.S. Department of Justice hundreds of thousands of women are raped and sexually assaulted every year. Given that many do not report the attack (Bureau of Justice estimates that only one in three victims report), that is a very troubling set of numbers. And, while crime is decreasing in general, the incidence of sexual assault is not going down and indeed seems to be increasing, though that is hard to quantify because of the problems with reporting. All this made me want to examine the broader social context.

NAL: In *Violation* there is a major crime in the past and the crime victim is one of your viewpoint characters. What led you to give the book such an unusual slant?

DN: I was concerned with our tendency to let victims fade into the background so I wanted to write a story that shifted the focus away from the crime, the criminal, and law enforcement, and brought our attention intensely on the victim. Above all I wanted to write a book that in no way glamorized the crime. It offends me that some truly depraved criminals have a sort of celebrity status in our culture today.

NAL: Rape is a difficult topic for most people to

discuss. Why do you think it is so much more difficult to address than murder?

DN: It is an unsettling topic because it leads beyond a discussion of violence to a host of tough questions about sex, power, and gender relations. Our attitudes and legal approach to rape are still undergoing a transformation from the old days of shaming or blaming the survivor, questioning what she wore and what her level of sexual experience was. Those attitudes rose from the idea of rape as a sexual act, which it is not. It is, according to experts in the field, an act of violence that uses sex, not a sexual act that uses violence.

Also, because we are a society that is striving for gender equality, we don't like to consider the implications of rape as a uniquely gender-based crime. We don't want to grapple with the stark reality of a crime that, in most cases, specifically targets females. And we don't want to face the horror of a crime that uses one of the most magical and mysterious of human acts, demeaning and defiling it, twisting it into a weapon that strikes not only at women but at our collective souls.

NAL: Thea and Jack have each withdrawn into isolated lives after being hurt, yet for all they have in common they see the world quite differently. What does their story show us?

DN: With Thea and Jack I wanted to explore issues of gender relations, but in a slightly different way. So much discussion of the sexes seems to focus on the ultimately unanswerable questions about the intrinsic natures of male and female. But we can't know our intrinsic natures because so much of what we are is determined by the society in which we live. It's the old nature/nurture question that we could ponder endlessly. What we can say about men and women, however, is that they experience the world in fundamentally different ways, starting with primal issues of safety and survival.

Both Thea and Jack are extreme examples, as fictional characters so often are, but they reflect the issues. Women, rather than men, are more vulnerable to sexual assault, and since we're up to a rape every six minutes in this country, fear of sexual assault is pervasive in our culture. This fear resides in the subconscious of every female and results in a constant caution that affects their experience of the world, and of course, the way they relate to males. This has little to do with whether a woman enjoys male company or has close relationships with men. Women who have always had completely positive relations with males still limit themselves without even thinking. They warily check elevators and avoid deserted stairwells and listen for footsteps behind them, and they hold their keys between their fingers as they cross parking lots. (One of every four rapes takes place in a public place like a parking lot or garage.) They have to be aware of men as potential threats. That is a sad fact. However, the reverse is not true. What man worries that a woman is walking behind him at night or fears getting on an elevator because there is a lone woman inside? With Jack and Thea I'm suggesting that men and women not only have very different experiences of the world but that they are often unaware of how drastically their perspectives differ. They have to go through the process of discovering the reality of the other, a process I hope readers go through in the course of my story.

NAL: What is your next book about?

DN: I've continued to explore the same area of violence, but from different perspectives. This time I'm looking at the world through the eyes of a very disturbed and disturbing psychopath who targets women—delving into his story in an effort to understand the why and how of such a monster. It's wrenching to be in his viewpoint, so I can only write from there for short periods of time. Fortunately, the book has a number of other focal characters who I like and admire. One is the obsessive female detective who's after him, and the other is a psychologist struggling against the forces that created him in the past and the force that he embodies in the present.